To Yvonne—
"Fair winds and following seas" on all your adventures!
Alo[illegible]
Beky
* Here [illegible] good old days!

FLYING

A Novel
by

PAULA HELFRICH AND REBECCA SPRECHER

To Al Topping, Pete Torralbas, our fellow Pan Am veterans, and all the other unsung heroes of the airline world:
"Fair winds and following seas."
With great respect to those murdered by political rage on Pan Am's Flight 103, *Clipper Maid of the Seas*, and on the ground in Lockerbie, Scotland; December 21, 1988.

Me kea aloha pumehana Laurien, Andrea and Greg

HAWEA PUBLISHING – int'l
575 Alawaena Street
Hilo, Hawaii, USA 96720
(808)258-5117

LONGFIELD MARSH
PUBLISHING – dom.
1715 Longfield Drive
Dataw, South Carolina USA 29920

For online orders and enquiries:
www.FLYING-a-novel.YOLASITE.com

Printed and distributed in USA by Lightning Source, Inc./Ingram Content
Group
www.lightningsource.com

First published by AuthorHouse, 2011

Republished:
ISBN 978-0-985-1667-0-0 (USsc) LONGFIELD MARSH PUBLISHING
ISBN 978-0-985-1667-1-7 (Intlsc) HAWEA PUBLISHING
ISBN 978-0-985-1667-2-4 (ebook) HAWEA/LONGFIELD MARSH
ISBN 978-0-985-1667-3-1 (UShc)
LONGFIELD MARSH PUBLISHING

Formatting: Devdan at Flippingimage, London, England

Library of Congress Control Number 2011914178

Cover artwork: NASA public domain image, Apollo 11, July 16, 1969
        US Postal Service (artist unknown) Transpacific Air Mail, 1936
Credits: Hector Venegas, lyrics "Where I live, there are rainbows", Jahred
Rehberg music&lyrics "Angels Standing By", Book/Song Titles – Burmese
Days/George Orwell; Moonlight Lady/Gabby Pahinui; Rubaiyat/Omar
Khayyam; Te Deum (traditional); Auld Lang Syne (traditional)

CHAPTERS

PROLOGUE

DECEMBER 21, 1988   OUTBOUND, LONDON-NEW YORK
PAN AM FLIGHT 103   CLIPPER MAID OF THE SEAS

Zoe Longfield dreamed she was cold, colder than death, and flying in the early evening light of the Northern Hemisphere. The sky was eerily reminiscent of the darkness of a Pacific night long ago, when she floated down a moonlit windward passage at sea between night-dark islands, clasped in the arms of her lover, held safe by a tandem harness and his strong, warm body, straining to the keening wind and the clatter of the sails on a starry night, the glint of phosphorescent sea creatures in the embracing waters, the thick, acrid smell of his rubber wet suit, their last night at sea. She had not been frightened then. She was not frightened now, but she knew her time had come.

She could see the lights of a town below quite clearly, could hear screaming voices. The wind? Her own cries? Something smashed into her; someone's squirming dervish body hit her a glancing blow, grabbing and screaming as it hurtled downwards, as they both plummeted separately, in the dusk of a late Scottish evening, screaming, screaming distantly, and without effect.

In her dream, she clearly remembered turning away from the Purser's station at the front of the plane just seconds before she felt the tremendous force, the hot thud of an explosion beneath her feet near the galley, deep in the aircraft. She sensed the explosive heat, rather than feeling it, just knowing that it had begun tearing the aircraft apart. She had reached for the telephone handset to warn…whom? Immediately, she knew it was useless, and drew her hand back. Will it hurt? Will it be mercifully quick? She looked out at the still-peaceful cabin, some passengers already asleep in the soft evening light, knowing.

And then chaos erupted as the blackness came with a cobra's roar from within a demon's soul, a hot scorching breath of evil done to harm, to murder, to destroy. The pressurized cabin air rushed out with explosive force, and swirling grey air sucked them all down.

She seemed to dream of massive sounds of tearing and shrieks of metal penetrating the blackness. For just that instant, she had remained, miraculously, standing at her post next to a jumpseat in the First Class cabin section of a mighty 775,000-pound aircraft 31,000 feet above the dark, rolling hills of the coast of Scotland below, in a windy, fitful sunset of light and rain. The sea glinted off the land, iron grey and immutable.

Then the nosecone ripped away from the fuselage in an apocalyptic fiery explosion, and was hurled at right angles into the right outboard engine, shearing away wing and engine in its urgent fiery descent to the still-silent, verdant lands below, homes and hearth-lights winking warm welcomes to unsuspecting occupants trudging home through the light sleet, anticipating tea and toast and a warm fire. Above the town, still high in the sky, the bulk of the fuselage groaned and bent and buckled, tearing Zoe's purse from its storage place beneath her seat, spewing forth most of its contents along with thousands of other mundane items of everyday life and workaday equipment: teddy bears and flight bags; crystal wine glasses with folded white linen napkins; a red high-heeled shoe; a tray of iced caviar; a birthday cake; an oxygen bottle. A section of the First Class cabin of four seats hurtled past, their occupants traveling openmouthed in soundless screams as the oxygen was ripped from their heaving lungs, downwards towards the earth, strapped in and utterly helpless, for the final ride of their lives. Falling fastest away towards earth was the nearly intact nosecone of the aircraft, with its inscription clearly visible: *Maid of the Seas*, writ large in flowing script.

As Zoe fell farther, she returned to consciousness; her mind cleared. She knew someone has done this terrible thing. How? Why? Was it the work of terrorists? But there were no more answers for her.

The cold was no longer biting any more, there was no anger left, no fear of pain or death. She arched her back in the cold twilight, an almost sexual surrender, her eyes on the stars. She breathed out, her heart and mind filled with all the colors and laughter of the years: her darling child Hawea; the inconstant love of Keoki; images of Sally and

Billy in the North Shore surf; Sao Johnny's eyes; the smiles of Khin Khin Su and Po Sein, as she whispered her last words.

"I'm flying…I really am flying away."

CHAPTER ONE

BURMESE DAYS
MAY 1, 1954   MOULMEIN, BURMA

Two children scampered in the golden dawn along the muddy Than Lwin River that the British had called "Salween". In the mists of early morning, Zoe Longfield breathed the rich musky smells along the river banks of the bustling port, while her friend Ma Khin Khin Su leaned from an abandoned dugout canoe in the mangrove trees overlooking the river, looking for fish and crocodiles. The comforting chime of the watch-keeper's hammer sounded on a rusting Japanese bomb shell, recycled to count the hours…ting-ting, ting-ting, ting-ting…6:00 a.m.

The early sun shone on Kyaik Thalan Pagoda, Kipling's "Moulmein Pagoda", and the wish-granting pagoda of Maha Myat Muni, perched on the spine of the dragon hills overlooking the town. Laughing brown children carried trays of flowers, their cheeks streaked with the sweet-smelling sandalwood paste of *thanaka*. They called out their wares: short garlands of jasmine; yellow and white ginger; joss sticks to decorate home altars, temples, side-car bicycles, horse-drawn buggies and lumbering teak buses; all for the glory of kindness and merit for the day.

Zoe was a Wednesday child, Su Saturday-born. To make their morning offering for merit in the Buddhist way, they knelt quietly in the shade of the old *bodhi* tree decorated with fading prayer flags in red and white, enjoying the soft warm breeze of the morning before the grim, sticky heat of the forenoon. In approaching the tree each day, they would stay just far enough from the roots and crevices to avoid the *nats*—the spirits—and the sinuous length of the *mweh,* the king cobra snake who shared the space. Sometimes Zoe fancied that its eyes glittered in the darkness, and felt the cobra smile.

Today she stood, silent and solemn, a nine-year old girl dressed in black coolie pants with an oversized bamboo hat covering her straggly blonde hair and serious grey-blue eyes, keeping an eye on Su in the boat below. She poured water on the tiny stone elephant figure, and placed a small banana on the makeshift altar. The daily offerings appeased the *nats* and fed the cobra because that was the order of all things.

She waited and felt again the rumbling exhalation, the caress of the old elephant's trunk behind her, coiling and uncoiling, the sparse stiff bristles grazing her legs and arms while the soft tip moved over her arm and hand, questing for the sweet miniature monkey banana she held hidden. She smiled, listening for the hup-hup-hup instruction to mount from the elephant's venerable mahout or *oozie*, her legs brushing against the cold iron of the elephant pick he carried as the elephant's trunk lifted her upwards. The two, elephant and man, had been born in the northern Burmese jungles many years before, and in the tradition of the elephant people, they were one. The two girls laughed as they scrambled up the elephant's rough trunk to its broad back, hoisted by the grunted commands of the *oozie*, Uncle Po Sein.

Zoe remembered these as her happiest times, when she and Su were a part of the chain of life for the elephant people, when she would rise to her flying perch high on the elephant's back each morning. She was part of the teak mill and the thousands of years of birth and rebirth that made up the ancient lands of the Great Rivers: the Bramaputra, the Irrawaddy, the Than Lwin and the Mekong, all born in the northern hills that new maps and old soldiers called the Golden Triangle, all born from the cold waters coursing down immense valleys and streams of the mighty, holy Himalayas.

Each morning, Zoe and Su would bring bananas to the river, offerings to the monks who walked barefoot and silent through the streets in the gleaming dawn, saving some for their private shrine in the *bodhi* tree, and especially for the old elephant, Shwe Sein, the "golden diamond". They knew the elephant's master and life companion, U Po Sein, would grumble, then smile and hoist them up for a ride across the mill yard before school began, the owner's blonde daughter and the mill doctor's dark-haired child. They called him *A Ba*, Uncle Po Sein, out of respect for his age and wisdom. His tattoos rippled blue in the morning sun, magic circles across his forearms and back, his thighs and forehead—circles which kept him safe from the *nats,* the spirits of the land.

This morning, Zoe and Khin Khin Su had explored the riverbank and the *bodhi* tree before Uncle Po Sein brought them to the long oiled teak house by the river. The first floor was the *godown,* the storage area filled to the rafters with stacks and stacks of polished teak wood for the furniture trade, since teak was all the rage in Europe and America in these early days of post-World War II Reconstruction. They loved treasure-hunting, rummaging through dusty old trunks with faded labels, and broken down boxes filled with yellowing papers and files labeled: "Office of Strategic Services, Detachment 101-X2". There were maps and photographs of Zoe's father and other soldiers in the jungle wars; there were even rusting old Samurai swords and long Shan blades that were great for pirate fights with her brother and sisters. The *godown* smelled of freshly cut timber planks, mildew and desiccated rats. The richly patterned gleaming coils of the guardian python rustled out of the shadows, extending to its full sinuous length in expectation of a meal. The girls ran, laughing and squealing, up the steep stairs to the living quarters of the cool, dark old colonial "shotgun" house, rooms stacked one after the other in a long row on either side of a 20-foot wide concourse of gleaming, hand-polished, foot-wide teak floorboards which smelled of wood oil and the delicate fresh ginger flowers already at the shrine.

They emerged on the landing next to the servants' rooms, breathless and panting. Zoe knew it was too early for her parents, sleeping off yet another gin-soaked evening at the club or a party. The cook, laundry-maid and sweeper were sitting by the breezeway to catch any movement of air on these hot, still days before the monsoons. The women bowed to Su, honoring her grandmother's exalted rank, upon which history had exacted a toll. They murmured and fussed over the girls, who fell on two steaming bowls of freshly prepared *mohinga*, rice noodles with fragrant fish soup, banana stalk, egg and coriander, crunchy with fried gourd. As they slurped, the servants chivvied them to dress for school, picking up their navy blue St. Joseph's Convent uniforms, snapping the freshly ironed white blouses, which smelled of sun and starch. The girls giggled, watching Ma Hla, the youngest servant, barely their age and Uncle Po Sein's daughter, wielding a heavy coal iron with its smoking load of red-hot gleaming coals and hearing the decisive *clunk* as the iron was returned to its heavy protective plate on top of the cool, smooth woven floor mats.

Finally dressed, the girls ran back down the stairs with school bags for one more trip across the mill-yard, again with a banana for the elephant in anticipation of their ride. As they entered the yard, the now-harsh sunlight was casting strange, sharp shadows across the ground, dispelling the early-morning mists of the river. Vast stacks of sawn logs were shaped into "sleepers", railroad ties bound for Iraq. The elephants' job that day was to heave the huge pallets onto rollers, which slanted down towards the river's edge and the loading jetty, where a rusting cargo ship lay high in the water. The workers in the mill yard were not yet at their stations, dawdling in the protective shade at the betel-nut stands and gossiping outside the gate. There was only, but wait…what were those piles of shapeless, formless rags strewn on the ground? The girls stepped forward, seeing Po Sein's familiar tattered cloth *paso longgyi* skirt on the muddy ground. There were dark stains in the mud. Sticks? Pieces of a crushed pot? No, not sticks or a pot; they were looking at…a foot, attached to part of a leg, an ear, wrinkled and bloody, attached to a piece of…Zoe saw these things, and she knew she saw Death.

"Oh no, Su! Run, run!" Zoe screamed. "Something really bad has happened to Uncle Po Sein!" She jumped instinctively up onto the ladder by a stack of logs, and stared mutely at the crushed skull of the mahout, not comprehending but knowing the finality, the turning of the wheel. His iron hook lay beside him, covered by bloody debris.

Startled by Zoe's anguished screams, Su dashed across the mill yard towards the workers assembled by the gate, as some were turning towards the sound of the screams. Zoe's last glimpse of Su was of her eyes, dark with fear, and her flying blue skirt beneath her blouse, so bright and pure it reflected the morning sunlight. From behind the stacks of railroad ties charged the huge, groaning grey bulk of the elephant, Shwe Sein, lumbering directly at the running figure of the child, catching her instantly and tossing her, doll-like, into the air. On either side of Shwe Sein's head a line of thick, yellow mucous flowed, a sure sign of *musth,* the uncontrollable madness that overcomes bull elephants in heat and turns them, without warning, into moving, murderous, mountains, striking out in random violence. The elephant bellowed in anguish and anger, the stream of mucous dripping, dripping.

In the scant seconds before the mill workers reacted—yelling, praying, swinging shut the huge heavy gate—the elephant's terrible deed was done. Zoe's childhood friend, Khin Khin Su—star-crossed descendent of queens—and the elephant's lifelong companion, Uncle Po Sein, lay crushed and broken in the mud of the sunny, silent yard, motes of dust drifting in and out of the harsh daylight and the dark shadows. Zoe looked across the now-enormous expanse of the mill yard separating her from the safety beyond the gate, the swaying bulk of the elephant by the stack of lumber, its passion spent. She began moaning, a chant of grief. "I killed her! I killed Su, like Shwe Sein killed Uncle Po Sein. I told her to run, and she did, and she died!" Hysterical sobs rose in her throat. She saw the doctor, Su's father, emerging from the clinic beside the mill office, moving past the elephant towards the small crushed and bloody form, the sparkling white blouse now ground into the sawdust, the blue uniform in shreds. His face was a mask of pain, borne through the karma that had come once again to his family's ancient bloodline, yet he walked with a calm dignity to his daughter's broken body.

The yard now erupted with activity, noise and clanging iron chains. Two wiry men with betel nut stained lips clad in faded *paso longyis,* grabbed Zoe from her perch on the railway ties and hustled her past the cutting blade and the sawdust heap, offering protection and reassurance. She could taste the sharp, resinous smell of blood and oil, and the gorge rose in her throat as she was carried, cold and shivering, through the cool, dim mill to safety. Ten heavily tattooed trainers approached Shwe Sein, carrying thick ropes and chains, and calling out chants. "Hup, hup, hup," they chanted, lassoing the elephant's legs together as the animal stood, swaying and grumbling, his trunk curling and uncurling. Ma Hla and her mother—the wife and child of the dead man—came through the gate, offering fragrant ginger flowers to the elephant in blessing and forgiveness, their loss enormous in its calm. Zoe ran to them to *shikoh*, to pay homage, while the crowd of mill workers and elephant people grew as word spread of the tragedy.

"Alas! The world is but illusion, transience and trouble, *Dokha, Dokha*," an old wrinkled crone intoned, using the ancient Buddhist words for misfortune.

Outside the mill gate, Zoe's father emerged from his battered station wagon, its engine still sputtering, found her with Po Sein's family, and tried to hug her close. She smelled the sharpness of his cologne over the mustiness of last night's gin, the exhaust and the sweat, as she buried her face, streaming with tears, into his nubby seersucker jacket. "I did it…it's my fault. I don't know how but I did it and Uncle Po Sein and Su are dead forever and I killed her. Oh I killed her, I killed her!" She struggled away from her father and sat keening with Su's family.

After the initial shock and grief and sadness had passed, Zoe's parents, Pat and George Longfield, tried to reach out to her, worried by reports from school and the doctor that their daughter's condition was not improving. She was constantly reminded of the accident by the sights and smells of the mill next door, the laughing hordes of her schoolmates in blue uniforms and crisp white blouses, even by the other elephants as they moved about their work at the mill. Her family, the servants, even the elderly retainers from Su's home, the crumbling mansion of Burma's last queen, all tried to help her deal with her sorrow. There was no concept of privacy or private grief—everyone shared pain and joy alike—but Zoe's depression grew deeper. Her nightmares led the servants to grave consultations with monks and seers and long sonorous chants of "Mettã Sutta" in the breezeway, redolent of ginger and linseed oil.

Zoe's teacher at St. Joseph's Convent, Mother Agnes, spoke to Pat Longfield of her daughter's listless performance at school, urging both parents to consider a change. "Perhaps," she suggested, "Zoe could benefit by transferring to a boarding school. There are many good ones in India, attended by the children of good families, and the nuns are accustomed to dealing with such deep grief, even in our children, because of the many tragedies the war has brought."

Pat and George, along with many other war veterans, were caught up in the heady atmosphere following the devastation of World War II, of hard-won independence and now the hectic social scene in newly independent nations all over Southeast Asia. They pulled away just long enough to decide that a change would indeed be good for Zoe, and enrolled her in Loreto Convent, located high in the Himalayan foothills in the tea-plantation hill station of Darjeeling in West Bengal. Known throughout India by its ancient Tibetan name, *Dorje Ling*, or thunderbolt, the location had been famed for a hundred years as the hot-season retreat of the British Raj, its first-flush tea, and a dozen prestigious Hill Schools.

Mother Agnes was persuasive. "Zoe will find peace at Loreto," she assured Zoe's parents. And so it was settled.

At the tennis club lounge, Pat nursed an early cocktail, confiding her worries to her partner, Daw Mya Than, who had four girls at boarding school in India for most of their school years. "It is hardly a cruel and unusual punishment to send her away," said Daw Mya Than, sipping from a cup of tea. "You Americans put so much store on keeping your children close to you, when most parents truly haven't the vaguest notion of how to make sure their children develop proper life skills." She eyed Pat's second gin.

Daw Mya Than and her husband had been involved in the 1941 Japanese invasion as part of the Burmese independence movement, Do Bama Asi Ayone, which later broke with its Japanese mentors and went over to the Allies. While her husband was fighting north of Rangoon, Daw Mya Than gathered up her meager belongings and her daughters, Ruby and Emerald, and walked out on the Burma Road into China. They traveled by night and hid in the jungles by day as Japanese air and ground patrols searched for Allied troops, sympathizers and refugees. The two little girls had died quietly of typhus on the Road, and Daw Mya Than, driven to distraction with grief, had buried them, alone and in silence, in the jungle. "I could not even cry, for fear of making noise that would alert the Japanese soldiers," she had told Pat during a long evening of getting to know one another. "After we returned to Rangoon in 1945, we supported the Independence movement. When our new daughters were born, we naturally named them Ruby and Emerald in honor of their first sisters. And then came two more girls, Pearl and Jade. They are our jewels." She sat gracefully, a beautiful, small-boned woman with almond eyes and delicate hands, a descendant of warriors. Daw Mya Than smiled. "You must not fear for Zoe. She has a soul of great courage, and because of this tragedy, she has two powerful spirits to guide her, just like my girls. Now come, we are here to play tennis and I must continue to work on my game." She stood and moved to the court in her full-length *thamein longgyi* skirt.

Scant weeks later, Zoe's parents had waved goodbye, as she sat wide-eyed and tearless, on the Pan American Clipper to Calcutta. Loreto nuns had met her at the Arrivals Lounge at Dum Dum Airport on the outskirts of the teeming city and transferred her to the peace and quiet of Entally Convent through noisy, smoky streets, passing ash-covered *sadhhus* and sacred cows in the median strips; the din of horns and hawkers and tinny high-pitched love-songs amplified at top volume; the thin beggars' arms thrust through the open car in stalled traffic. At the Convent, they had eaten *kedgeree* rice and sipped smoky sweet tea in the nuns' dining hall, its marble floors and white walls gleaming and cool. After an afternoon rest and tea, they proceeded to Howrah Station located on the banks of the Hooghly River, passing weddings with women clad in brightly decorated saris, as well as funerals, the dusty white-shrouded bodies being moved to the *ghats*, or burning platforms, by the river. They boarded the *Darjeeling Mail,* an ancient steam train headed for the hills.

That night, Zoe's 10th birthday, she lay on the floor of the train, breathing in the vapors of musty spices and decay as she listened to the drumming rain and harsh sounds outside. Zoe knew that monsoon rains have both a particular sound and odor. When the rains first break, the individual drops fall huge and heavy, creating a thunderous downpour, a humming on iron roofs and recently dusty windowpanes, that releases a smell of ozone and wetted earth. The rains are the annual ritual bath for the ancient dust-caked carriages of the Indian Railways. The coursing waters first find every particle of dust and mud and decayed matter and dirt, then turn them quickly to an ochre paste smeared across every surface, coating every smudged window, every cracked footplate, every venerable well-oiled steam engine. Every face is upturned to the sky, from 1st Class sleepers to 3rd Class windows, where occupants risk blindness from tiny fireflies of burning ash, and the running blast of the steam-whistle praises Lord Krishna for the rebirth of the land and the blessings of the waters.

But what Zoe did not know was that the coming of the rains in India also brought labor strikes, the *hartal*, to targets of opportunity—including the Indian Railway lines. Every year, the noise of angry mobs roared across India like a moving semaphore, a message throughout the land. "Listen and see," they said, their leaders screaming imprecations against some universal overlord, some eternal injustice. The mob leaders howled, secure in the knowledge that the rainfall would bring another crop in the villages, and they turned their attention to the settlement of other grievances, both real and imagined. The smoke of India's Partition fires was barely banked, the memories of epic violence along the artificial lines of West Pakistan, India and East Pakistan still raw and bloody, the memories of the Mahatma and his untimely death still harsh. The blood-thirst and angry mob-rule of those dark days continued, with hatred fueling wars and more bloodshed, not the peace that Gandhi and other humble men had pleaded for.

On this night, the strikers, the *hartalis*, wielded burning, smoking torches in the dark, hands and clubs and sticks drumming against the sides of slow-moving carriages of *The Darjeeling Mail*, echoing a bass-line to the music of the driving rain, the smell of burning wood and oil mixing with the rank smell of rage. Dozens of drenched dhoti-clad *hartalis* lay stretched across the rails in protest, flashlights and kerosene lamps catching the light of eyes and gleaming teeth, the torches reflecting in broken window panes and standing pools and ditches by station houses, the bull-horns of the constabulary adding yet more noise to this *Jehanum*, this hell of noise and flickering light and anger.

Zoe remained still and quiet on the floor of the railway cabin. The two nuns escorting her lay nearby, where they fearfully recited prayers to calm the disturbances outside. Curiously, she looked up and out at the swirling rain and the milling crowds. The kerosene torches lit the ancient station with leaping shadows and moving forms. The incessant drumming of the rain harmonized in some awful lullaby with the roar of the crowd and the pounding of the *lathis,* the thick staves of the strikers, hammering against the thin metal skin of the train. Zoe lay still, shielded by the dark and her fellow travelers. I guess I should be afraid, she reasoned, but really bad things don't happen when there's a lot of noise and rain. She remembered the silent pantomime of death in the quiet, sunny mill yard that seemed so long ago, so far away. Abruptly the thoughts of disquiet left her and she slept, lulled by the motion of the train, stirring now and again with the sounds of *pop-pop-pop* shots, screams and then darkness again as the train steamed whistling through the night. And still the lullaby of the rains sang, quelling the music of fear, cleansing the ochre mud and rusty bloodstains, along with the smell of danger, blood, rank bodies and despair.

She woke alone in the dim smoky light of an Indian dawn as the train swayed and chuffed towards another grey station in Bihar, where rows of bodies lay out on the platform, perhaps sleeping, perhaps never to awaken, surrounded by indistinct moving forms of men in uniforms, khaki, green, beige, as the *harijan* sweepers, the untouchables, hunched down to sluice the platform with buckets of water and skimpy hand brooms. And still the rains fell and the *hartalis* lay silent. She watched the tableau of tragedy and seasonal rebirth, not feeling the pain as the train hesitated in its motion, then resumed its steady pace. *Chuka-chuka-chuka,* sang the rails, rushing through the flooded fields towards the rendezvous point with the Darjeeling Hill Railway at Jalpaiguri Station in West Bengal on that Indian morning, in the midst of the largest strike since Independence Day 11 years earlier, when the killing had begun in earnest between Muslim and Hindu. It continued today in minor grievances and old grudges, with that night's death toll at 450 men, women and children sprawled along the lifelines of the railway.

Zoe rubbed her eyes, stretched, and jumped up, heading for the dining car next door to find her companions. They were young Goan-Portuguese novices, nuns of the Institute of the Blessed Virgin Mary, clad in black habits with white wimples, oversized rosary beads clasping their waists in a girdle. "Oh, sisters, did you hear the noise last night?" The nuns nodded assent and murmured words of prayer, helping Zoe to smooth her navy uniform and untidy braids. They broke open a package of biscuits and poured glasses of water from a nearby pitcher. The liquid filled the vessels, cloudy and tinged with the red dust of India, but slaking thirst nonetheless.

The train moved on, *chukka...chukka...chukka*, as light slowly spread across the cloud-laden sky.

Suddenly, the railway cabin door crashed open. A small woman advanced, her dark eyes flashing. She was clad in a nun's habit: a white sari with a blue border, a rough wooden crucifix on a leather thong tied around her neck. "No, no, no, sisters. This will not do. We cannot permit ourselves the luxury of this lounge car while people are suffering in the cabins in the back. Come, we must do God's work."

Without demur, the small party grabbed towels and refilled the pitcher. No stewards aided their passage across the unsteady plates to the 3rd Class cars, buffeted by the unceasing rains. They moved through the length of one car, which was empty of people but strewn with abandoned suitcases and clothes and discarded foodstuffs, all signals of distress and danger. As they maneuvered across the next clattering footplate, a crumpled child's body blocked the way.

"Oh, Mother, the child..." exclaimed one of the young nuns, looking quickly at Zoe, as if protecting her from the sights and sounds of the mute tableau before them, and the sorrows imagined in the cabin ahead.

The tiny nun leaned and picked up the broken toy-child with ineffable gentleness, murmuring prayers. She cradled the baby in death with a tenderness it had needed in life, murmuring, "Suffer the little children, sister, suffer *all* the little children." Then she turned to Zoe and looked directly into her eyes, "Come, my child, you must be very brave." Gently, she took her cold hand and led her forward.

When they entered the 3rd Class cabin, Zoe surveyed the scene of destruction that faced them. Bodies lay slumped in corners in pools of blood, flies buzzing over the darkening welts and glazed eyes. Injured men lay immobile, while silent women in saris cradled screaming children, some wounded, some hungry and thirsty. Two dazed stewards moved from row to row, carrying tattered towels and blankets. The shattered windows let in the light and the rain, soaking the dead, the injured and the healthy alike. Zoe gulped, remembering death. At least this time I can help, she thought, moving forward with the Loreto nuns, and the sari-clad leader of the new order known as the Sisters of Charity.

For hours, they worked to clear the car, transporting the children and their mothers to the empty cabins in front, and raiding the abandoned suitcases for dry, clean clothing. The stewards, responding to staccato orders from the older nun, jumped to provide clean water, *chapattis*, and meager rations, striving to restore order and comfort in the midst of chaos.

Zoe moved behind the nuns carrying supplies and giving aid as directed. It felt good to be able to help, and soon she was playing patty-cake with a solemn little girl with huge kohl-rimmed eyes and a bandaged leg as the train continued on its way filled with its cargo of carnage. *Chukka...chukka...chukka....*

By mid-morning they arrived, hours late, at the transfer station of Jalpaiguri where they were met by an army of uniformed railroad policemen, Red Cross trucks, local officials, red-turbaned porters, and cleaners with pails of water and brooms. The nuns helped officials supervise the disembarkation of the injured and the bustle of cleaning the carriages. Officials and porters carried their bags quickly to the connecting station where a tiny, narrow gauge railway train stood steaming at its gate. Nodding goodbye, they settled themselves for the remainder of the journey on the hard wooden slatted seats in the "Toy Train" of the Darjeeling Himalaya Railway. The miniature narrow-gauge railway was constructed in 1848 to carry the British Raj from the steaming cities of the plains in the hot season to the cooler realms of the Hill Stations. The breathtaking views of the steep ascent and cool breezes brought comfort to the travelers. After a huge "railway curry" tiffin lunch, the clicking rails and the fresh air lulled them into a well-deserved sleep. Zoe woke up when the train whistle sounded its arrival into the hill villages. She went in search of water to drink and wash. Finally, the tiny train pulled into the Darjeeling Station in early evening.

Whisked quickly to a dilapidated jeep taxi, the nuns and their charge arrived in the deepening dusk at an extended grove of tall, whispering pine trees flanking a long, narrow driveway ending in a wrought-iron gate, marked with a cross and the legend: *Loreto Convent*. Beyond, a graveled yard fronted a sandstone and concrete chapel, and a long, elegant three-storey gabled main building stood sheltered by pines and oleander hedges. Below the main building lay a sweeping lawn and garden set in the English style, with banks of flowers barely seen in the dusk, but giving up their heavenly scent. Far down the garden reach, a row of stately pines guarded the entry, although the twilight gave hints of the hills and valleys beyond. It was magnificent, peaceful, timeless.

Approaching the gate, two smiling nuns reached out in welcome to the tired travelers, greeting the religious and then turning warmly to their charge. In the shadows, Zoe saw only their smooth, resting hands and kind smiles. As though a huge weight was lifted from her shoulders, she stepped forward. The taller nun took her hand and said, "I am Mother Paul. Come, child, welcome to Loreto. Welcome home."

With her first step inside the gates, Zoe felt the pain lift out of her heart, and the sadness rise away. It would be safe here. It would be home.

CHAPTER TWO

SOUTHERN COMFORT
OCTOBER 27, 1958   LATHAM, KENTUCKY

Sally Wilder navigated her bicycle down the sidewalk of South Main Street to the Stone's Mill Overpass. She rode quickly, a slight, energetic child with watchful brown eyes, and hair pale and silky as an ear of Silver Queen corn. Drawing up to the foot of the embankment that led to the train tracks above, she jumped from her seat and looked upward in anticipation. In summer the embankment would be covered with honeysuckle, but now at the end of a colorful Kentucky fall, it was a tangle of brown stalks, a few dark green leaves scattered here and there. Holding her breath, she waited.

Presently, she could hear the singing of the rails in the distance, accompanied by the low thunder of a diesel engine. The wail of the engine's horn blared through the afternoon calm in mournful baritone notes as it roared into view, drawing a line of cars filled with cattle and grain, dozens of automobiles mounted on top of one another and giant tanks of fuel, all the stuff of agriculture and commerce. But to Sally, it was bound on an exotic voyage to a place where no one was ever sick, where evil caused no harm and danger did not frighten. As the train roared passed, it kicked up a plume of dust that cast a blurry image of the last car.

When the rumbling had faded away, she turned and began pedaling towards the Kendrick Tobacco Company's warehouse. Located several blocks away in downtown Latham, it was the second stop on her after-school bicycle route. This time of year, when the moon rose in the sky like a plump tangerine and the morning air held a nip, the precious tobacco was harvested, cured over smoldering fires in sharp-smelling, darkened barns and brought to auction at cavernous, echoing warehouses around town known as "loose floors".

Her grandfather, Earl Kendrick, held court in his office at the loose floor, where he and his friends would smoke cigars, chew tobacco and dip snuff, and get into lengthy discussions over tumblers of amber whiskey. Rearing back in their wooden chairs with their feet propped up on the desks they'd ramble on for hours, reminiscing about droughts and floods. Every so often, between the raucous laughter and the creaking of the wooden chairs, the men would pause, hawk, and spit streams of tobacco juice from their mouths into the polished brass spittoons that rested on the floor by each desk. The spittle landed hard, with a splat and a metallic echo, like the ringing of a bell. Sally would marvel that they never missed, but she was also wary of the sound of hawking in any direction, waiting for the inevitable stream of expectorant. She even tried practicing herself, her grandfather leaning over to show her the finer points of the art. Sally never told her mother about this acquired skill.

The office was utilitarian, but comfortable. The dingy walls were hung with calendars from the local feed companies and pictures of tobacco auctions in years past, and the desks were littered with samples of different blends of pipe tobacco, cans of snuff and "hands" of tobacco. Settling into a chair, Sally visited with everybody for what she figured was an acceptable amount of time. While she loved the bitter, earthy smell of tobacco, she had a hard time dealing with the smoke in the enclosed room, and watched it form into thin layers of clouds above her head. When she could stand it no longer, she tugged at her grandfather's sleeve. "Big Earl, I'm getting a headache. Can I go out on the loose floor?"

Earl Kendrick reached out to his granddaughter and gave her a hug. "Smoke getting to you? Of course you can, sugar plum. I think Sylvester is out there somewhere. He'll look after you." And then he turned back to his friends, scratching the back of his head with one hand and holding the cigar in the other, resuming his "bidness" talk.

Closing the door of the office, Sally contemplated the quiet, vast emptiness before her that was longer than a football field. There were no windows, and pendant lights cast dim pools of illumination on the floor at evenly spaced intervals. She buttoned up her coat, remembering that there's no place in this world colder than a tobacco warehouse, its brick walls trapping frigid winter air and holding it captive until spring. Shivering with excitement, she looked out at the expansive space. While the trains took her to imaginary far-away destinations, it was here that she conjured up the various characters that inhabited those enchanted places. It was her very own castle-keep, and it was while wandering alone here that she acted out grand tales of knights and ladies, brave soldiers and rescued maidens. Far in the distance, a cart piled high with tobacco rolling over creaking floorboards became the sound of horses' hooves on a castle's drawbridge. And the fawn-colored dust that coated everything in sight formed itself into little fairy spirits when whirled upward by a gust of air pouring in from a distant loading door. She would run forward, pirouetting and leaping, then dropping to a curtsy as part of an imaginary court dance.

It had all started—imagining the castles and the watching the trains—after Jimmy Earl died.

Her little brother had suffered from chronic asthma, and every attack brought a flurry of sneezing and wheezing, irritated eyes that overflowed with hot tears, and skin reddened from the itching of unknown rashes and eczema. And the bad things always happened late at night, for that is when asthmatics fight their battle between sleeping and breathing. On many a night, Sally had crept to the door of her room and looked down the hall to see the silhouettes of her parents outlined in the yellow light of the bedside lamp, her mother, seated on the bed and hovering over Jimmy Earl, checking to see if he was still breathing, her father standing beside her in his navy bathrobe, his hand resting on her mother's shoulder. It was then Sally learned to turn away from her feelings and climb quietly back into bed, listening for the quick footsteps in the hall, followed by the whirring and clicking of the telephone dial.

"Dr. Payton, Sugar Pie Wilder. I'm sorry to call you so late." Her mother spoke in muffled, but urgent tones. "Jimmy Earl can't breathe again. Yes, yes Jim and I will meet you at the hospital…an oxygen tent? I see. We'll be right there."

It was during these times that Sally needed her mother most, to explain it all to her and ease her fears. But there was no time. There never was; indeed, even with the most energetic and well-intentioned parents, healthy children suffer in their own way in a family where a sibling is chronically ill.

And then one summer evening a few years ago, Jimmy Earl's illness had taken a deadly turn. The family had driven out into the country to attend a fish fry, and Sally was playing a game of Red Rover in a field with the other children when her father scooped her up in his arms and ran back to the car. A crowd suddenly gathered around her mother as she held Jimmy Earl, his face swollen and red, his little arms flailing as he struggled desperately to get air. Nobody could have known that Jimmy Earl was allergic to fresh water fish; he'd never eaten it before. The desperation in the voices of the adults Sally knew and loved terrified her. In a state of panic, her parents hustled her into the back seat of the car, slammed the doors and roared off.

"We've got to get him to the hospital," cried her father, his voice cracking as he drove frantically along the twisting backcountry roads. A ribbon of light from the car's headlights unfurled in front of them as they raced past the silent corn and hay fields in the gathering darkness.

"Hurry, Jim! Hurry!" Her mother's normally calm voice was high-pitched and harsh. "*No*, don't take that turn—that road goes down to the lake."

At the next road, Jim slowed down. "This one?" A stranger to the county, he had lost his sense of direction in his panic.

"No, no…wait, I think it's the one by the church," Sugar Pie groaned. "Oh God, Jim I've driven these roads all my life and I…I can't think…wait, no….there! There it is. That road goes straight into town and right by the hospital." Then she began to scream again. "Jim, I don't think he's breathing. Oh God! Oh, Jimmy Earl, hang on, honey, hang on…."

Sally sat rigid in the back seat, hearing the screams, staring wide-eyed into the darkness as the air from the open windows blew in her face. It was filled with the scent of honeysuckle, fresh-cut hay and the deep odor of dried manure, just the way country air was supposed to be. What's going to happen, she wondered. Who will take care of me?

Then she let her seven year-old mind take over, blocking out the remainder of that terrifying night, the sounds of her parents' frantic cries and later, the sight of her baby brother fighting for his life in a room filled with strange equipment and breathing tubes, surrounded by doctors and nurses. At 4:00 a.m., her father woke her, his face ashen. He led her from her warm dark nest of blankets into the gleaming white cold of the hospital room to the bed and the clear tent, where her mother sat with Jimmy Earl, silent, on her lap. "You have to say goodbye, honey," he said gently, as she looked at her brother's pale face and pale hands, her mother's eyes red from weeping and exhaustion. She nodded, stroking her brother's fair hair, struck by how cold his cheek was when she kissed it. He's not there anymore, she thought. He's just…gone.

She had not cried in the days that followed.

After the funeral she began to retreat to a fantasy world whenever something upset her, like the sight of Jimmy Earl's red wagon in the back yard with its handle turned askew, waiting patiently for its master to return and play. As she pictured her little brother, so pitifully thin, his shoulders rounded and hunched forward from coughing and wheezing, guilt would overwhelm her. So she took refuge in envisioning great voyages to magical places that protected her, Jimmy Earl and her parents.

Jim Wilder, worried when he saw his daughter slipping into these other, distant places, and resolved to keep his sensitive child safe. A few weeks after the funeral, he went to the library and brought home a stack of books. "Sally, let's go out on the porch. I have a new book for you," he said, and for the rest of that summer, he would put her in his lap and read to her in slow, comforting tones. There, with the crickets chirping and the delicate calls of the whippoorwills to serenade them, they read *The Jungle Book* and *Kim,* by Rudyard Kipling. And when the nights became too cool, they went inside and sat by the fire in the living room, and read from a series of fairy tale books, each with a different color cover. Sally had reveled in the stories as her father puffed on his pipe, his arms safely around her, the smell of pipe tobacco part of the magic.

And now, as she danced at the loose floor, Sally wondered what would happen when she outgrew all of these fantasies; but at present those things need not be considered. Whirling and twirling, she pictured still more knights on white horses, dashing adventurers and handsome heroes—all bowing and smiling and vowing to keep her safe.

Jimmy Earl smiled too, his pale face the color of spirits.

Sally rode home as the late afternoon sun slanting through the trees began to turn a pinkish red and orange. Mindful that darkness would soon begin to settle over the town and her mother would be expecting her, she picked up the pace and pedaled furiously. She turned down Fraternity Avenue toward her family home, nicknamed the Alamo because of its yellow Spanish-style stucco walls and red tile roof. The light was already on over the Alamo's front door, and Sally announced her arrival by banging the door as she went inside, calling, "I'm home, Mother."

"Goodness, Sally. It's almost dark. I was getting worried," scolded her mother, as she scurried around the kitchen preparing dinner for her husband and daughter. "Go wash your hands and get your father. It'll be time to eat in a few minutes."

Elizabeth Kendrick Wilder, fondly known as Sugar Pie to her family and friends, was of medium height and blessed with an elegant, if not commanding presence. She was the Southern, apple pie, mint julep version of June Cleaver, Donna Reed and Harriet Nelson, all rolled into one and multiplied by a thousand. As was the custom in those days, she wore pearls at all hours of the day. If the doorbell rang and her thick, blonde hair was not freshly coiffed or her shirtwaist dress crisply ironed, she would not appear to answer it. Her round features and blue eyes, agreeable and pretty, served as the principal outlet for expressing her outgoing personality.

Pie had gone to the University of Alabama, a college that met with approval from Latham's gentry, pledged the right sorority and remained a die-hard fan of the school's football team, the Crimson Tide. On this night, like so many others, the obsession made itself known. When the family sat down to a proper dinner in the dining room, the table laid with china and silver, the candles flickering, they did not join hands to say grace like most families in town. Pie's blue eyes suddenly flashed as she emphatically waved an outstretched arm in front of her like a windshield wiper.

"Roll Tide!" she exclaimed, invoking Bama's battle cry.

Sally's glance found her father's at the other end of the table and together they smiled, rolling their eyes before dutifully picking up their forks. She saw nothing unusual about her family's table traditions; this was, after all, the South.

Despite the upheaval in Sally's young life, the harmonious flow of existence in Latham settled her and provided stability. Just as the crops had their seasons, so did the town's people have their rituals. Rigidly prescribed manners and gentility provided the mortar that held their way of life together. Every Sunday, they sat in the same pew at church and socialized with the same friends whose families had known each other for generations. People were born, grew up, married, raised their families, grew old and died, all within the velvet-steel rhythms of this well-oiled machine. It was a machine that had worked well for more than a century.

Sugar Pie was totally and completely enmeshed in the comfort of this system. Only occasionally during her life had she strayed from the fold, such as attending college in another state, or getting a job at nearby Ft. Campbell during the war and bringing home a North Carolinian for a husband. She had also bucked tradition when she and Jim Wilder purchased the Alamo, the house being in sharp contrast to the more traditional homes in town as well as the ranch styles out in the newer neighborhoods. But because she had been born into the gentry of old Latham, Pie got away with it. She knew the rules intimately, playing by the ones that were cast in concrete and bending the ones that were not. In 1960, she worked for the local campaign of John Fitzgerald Kennedy, a democrat, in his quest for the Presidency. "He's a gentleman," she'd say, "even if he's not a Southern Episcopalian." When Kennedy won against all odds, Pie was triumphant.

As the halcyon days of the 1950s drew to a close, the music, art and politics of the new decade was brought into the family's living room, courtesy of television. On the surface, life in Latham remained the same, the tobacco fields yielding their crops then lying fallow again. But in ways both large and small, the equilibrium of the small community was disrupted as the American South awoke, unwillingly, to the civil rights era. It would be the first of many issues and events that would come to divide Sally's and her parents' generation, isolating them from each other, and creating a gulf between them that would last a lifetime.

Sally was in junior high school when the first black students arrived. When she became friends with a girl named Esther in her English class, she asked her mother if she could invite her over to study. Pie was emphatic. "No," she replied firmly, "it might upset Miss Lucy," the elderly widow who lived across the street.

"How's Miss Lucy going to know?" Sally could not hide her amazement.

"She might see her come in the front door," said Pie, absent-mindedly sorting the day's mail.

"Mother, didn't you vote for Kennedy in the election? I mean, I don't understand. I thought you were for equal rights for everybody. Doesn't that count for my friends, too?"

"It just isn't...it just isn't done, Sally. Not in Latham." Pie's face turned to stone as she headed down the hall.

"What do you mean 'it just isn't done'?" Sally whirled around and stomped after her mother.

Pie gnashed her teeth, cursing all teenage daughters who were old enough to argue with their parents. "Well all right, Sally," she said, slamming the mail on the hall table and marching back to the sitting room. "But bring her in through the back by the garage."

Sally could not understand how a perfectly normal friendship with a classmate could flourish during school hours then end the minute she came home. She realized she could no more talk to her parents about civil rights, the savagery of Jim Crow laws or her friend Esther than fly to the moon. Secretly, she began meeting Esther downtown at the Grenada Theatre on Saturday afternoons for a movie, where they proceeded to the "White Only" seats downstairs and thumbed their noses at the sign next to the balcony steps that read:

"Colereds Upstairs".

And the mixed message about the racial situation was not the only thing that confused Sally. As Sally grew older, her parents had emphasized to her that higher education was an all-important credential. But implicitly, they sent a different message: while going to college was important, first and foremost, she was expected to find a suitable mate. Getting a degree fell second, a back up in the event of a catastrophe in her married life. Even at her young age, she was well aware that she had been brought up, carefully and lovingly, to be an accoutrement in an antique-filled living room, a sort of Southern-style Duchess, who entertained beautifully and mothered perfect children. Professions or careers for women were not often mentioned in Latham, either by her parents or those of her friends. For Pie and Jim's generation, the genteel South was as it had always been, with everything in its place.

In a family discussion one evening after supper, Sally made a feeble attempt to take a stand on her future education.

"Why don't you major in French?" Pie had suggested. "That would be lovely. Jackie Kennedy speaks French." The nation's First Lady had indeed inspired several generations of American women with her elegant, understated fashions and her bouffant hairdos.

"Mother, I know you don't think it's that important what my major is, but I really do think I can do a lot more for myself than study French." Searching in her mind, she desperately combed through a list of occupations that might be acceptable to both her and her parents' world. "Like music, or … like architecture. I've always loved to draw palaces and dream houses, and new spaces to live in. I could study, well, I could study French and architecture, and learn more about how all those incredible places were designed and built, and help create really beautiful new homes and schools and government spaces, just like…just like Charleston." She felt she'd hit all the right notes, but her mother and father just looked at her quizzically.

She pounded her pillow at night, crying silently. She didn't fit in with her old friends, her new friends, her school, her society, her dreams. It was like looking in a broken mirror: all the pieces were there, but they were splintered and uneven, with sharp edges and shadows in the wrong places. What is to become of me, she'd moan, where can I go?

One afternoon, at the height of the tobacco season in November of 1963, Jim Wilder's law partner Joe Tandy appeared at the doorstep of the Alamo. Pie, dressed in a blue sweater and grey flannel skirt, her blonde hair shining and curled, pearls encircling her throat, opened the door to let him in, but seeing Joe's rumpled tweed jacket and solemn face, let her hand drop limply from the knob. Whatever he had to tell her was going to be bad news.

"Now Pie...." Joe said gently, bending toward her, unable to utter the rest of the sentence.

Pie put her hands to her face. "Oh no. It's Jim, isn't it? Oh no!"

Sally ran from her bedroom just in time to see her mother crumple and fall to the floor, the pleats of her skirt spread about her. Sinking to the floor with her, Sally grabbed her shoulders, calling out, "Mother!"

Joe's face was pale as he repeated the sad news. Jim Wilder had keeled over at the office, dead of a massive heart attack. "There was nothing we could do," Joe said, his voice trailing off.

"Oh God," wailed Pie, "Oh God, Sally...." She reached out for her daughter and the two of them clung together, inconsolable at the loss of the bright, gentle man who had been the strong head of their household. Holding her mother in her arms, Sally felt a trifle awkward, as this kind of closeness had long ago disappeared between them. Mournfully, she looked up at Joe as he related the details of Jim's collapse. The stab of fear she had felt when Jimmy Earl died rose within her, and she let her mind once again lift her away from the terror of the current situation, gazing out the doorway at the leaves scuttling down the front walk in a sudden gust of wind.

She and Pie spent three surreal days in shock and grief, trying to cope with the funeral arrangements while handling the incessant calls of well-wishers both on the telephone and at the door, all asking why, when there was no answer. Then, amidst all the madness at home,

President Kennedy was assassinated in Dallas. At this point, Pie came positively undone. Sally was uncertain as to whether her mother was more upset about losing her husband, the President she had idolized, or her country losing its innocence. She remembered the arguments they'd had, knowing that Pie never truly shared the Kennedy political philosophy, and seemed to have no real grasp of the huge changes in progress across the nation.

That evening, they sat huddled together in Pie's cozy sitting room at the rear of the house, just off the master bedroom. The television was turned down low, with Walter Cronkite reporting the latest on the assassination. A jumble of sympathy cards, unopened mail, a bottle of bourbon and a half-filled glass littered the delicate Chippendale table in front of them. Pie picked up a framed picture of her husband when he was a young officer at nearby Ft. Campbell. She smiled at the image. "His unit was part of the mighty Screaming Eagles, the 101st Airborne Division that fought so bravely in World War II...."

Sally nodded, having heard the sentence a hundred times.

"We met at a dance at the Officers Club," Pie said tenderly, caressing the picture, polishing a tiny smudge on its frame.

"Yes, I know." Sally said, automatically, repeating the acknowledgement yet again.

Then Pie's face hardened as she looked at Sally. "See that bottle of sleeping pills?" she whispered, her voice tight with despair. "If I can't stand it any more, I'll just take them all."

This frightened Sally. Desperate to comfort her mother in some way, she went to the kitchen and brought back a pack of cigarettes she had purchased at Gordon's Market that afternoon, successfully convincing the cashier that they weren't for her but for Pie. She knew her mother once had a fondness for smoking, and had the devil of a time quitting. Approaching Pie, who lay on the sofa in the darkened room, she opened the pack and offered her one. "Mother, why don't you have a Winston, just for old time's sake? It'll relax you."

Pie, her face white in the flickering light of the television, pulled out a cigarette and lit it. She inhaled slowly, gratefully, and when she finally spoke, she was calm. "I'll be all right now, Sally. Thank you, sweetheart." She placed her hand on Sally's cheek and looked lovingly at her daughter's face. "Your father's brown eyes...." Her voice trailed off, and tears softened her eyes. "You know, he was so proud of you. He used to say, 'Our Sally is a true Southern lady in spite of these turbulent times.' He knew you'd have no use for these protesters and new ways, all this change, change, change for nothing."

After her mother's voice drifted away and her eyes closed, Sally fled back to the kitchen, the guilt and shame making her queasy as she thought of her mutinous uncertainties, the splintered pictures in the mirror of her life. She busied herself washing out casserole dishes, checking the list of food baskets and thoughtful gifts to make sure it was correct and up-to-date for the thank you notes that would have to be written. Several cards had already arrived in the mail and sat in a stack on the kitchen table. The section of the *Latham Gazette* containing Jim's obituary was folded in half and rested on top. Front-page headlines screamed of national mourning for President Kennedy and across the world, but time had stopped within the city limits of Latham, where the entire town would gather the next morning to bid farewell to one of its finest citizens.

To Sally, however, he was just "Daddy," and she mourned his loss. She sat at the kitchen table, tears clouding her vision, writing, "Dear Mrs. Bell, My mother and I are so touched by your kind remembrance and helpful words in our family's time of loss...Dear Dr. Payton, thank you so much for your words of support which are so important to my mother and me." She felt like a craven hypocrite, neither fish nor fowl, just a weak idealist. She longed for the magical safety of the days when she used to watch the trains crossing the overpass, and could visit her own personal Shangri-la at the loose floor. But the images reflected haphazardly as she slowly tried to pick up the pieces.

During the following months, Sally assumed a sober countenance beyond her years, setting aside her own grief and uncertainties brought on by the realization that life and death were indeed complicated affairs. Dutifully, she resolved to abandon her thoughts of studying architecture when she went to college and concentrate on French to please her mother. After she completed her education, she would teach at a school nearby so she could look after her.

As they sat together during Christmas Eve services at All Saints Episcopal that year, the lights of the church were dimmed and candles passed around to the congregation for the final hymn. As Pie lit Sally's candle during the singing of "Silent Night", they looked at one another, holding the wicks of their candles together, then separating them. In an old mirrored glass painting on the wall next to them, the reflections of their images ran together. Then, in the center of the image, Sally suddenly saw herself standing alone. Her candle flickered uncertainly at first then burst into flame, now glowing on its own.

Sally looked at the mirrored image of herself, standing assured now, alone and calm. "I have to find a way. I just have to hold on, and the way will come." She smiled at the image, her hair glinting in the candlelight surrounded by holiday wreaths.

CHAPTER THREE

DARJEELING MOON
MARCH 13, 1964   OUTBOUND LONDON-CHICAGO
                         PAN AM FLIGHT 59

Zoe sat quietly, numb from dozens of hours in the narrow seat of an aircraft travelling high over the Northern Hemisphere, now making its first dip towards descent to its destination. In the distance, ethereal lights and colors of the aurora borealis lit up the horizon. Her grey-blue eyes and flyaway golden brown hair were reflected in the winking windowpane at her seat. She looked at the flat cold white reaches below, mottled by stands of trees and grey lakes, and sighed.

She thought of another world now far away, of Sao Johnny, the misty hills of Darjeeling, the bright clangor of Calcutta, the green heat of Rangoon with the golden glint of Shwe Dagon at dawn. She remembered the raucous calls of crows in teak forests at sunrise, the rustle of green pigeons in flight, the open fields of paddy fields interspersed with hillocks crowned by gleaming white pagodas, the old wooden monasteries, the chanting monks.

She thought of the changes that had come to that part of the world, changes fueled by western pressures. New conflicts, newly aggressive nationalism, new prejudices forced old courtesies and relationships aside. Her parents and their colleagues had led seemingly charmed expatriate lives, but many were now increasingly sidelined and irrelevant to new alliances. They had lived in two worlds, enjoying close relationships with Burmese, British, Indian and Eurasian friends from the wartime years, enduring together the new hard-line socialism. Nothing worked, electricity flickered, trains were bombed, times were uncertain.

Zoe had returned from her last year of school in Darjeeling, and joined her family in a long vacation in a remote farming village in the

Shan States. These were not happy times, and she missed the serenity of the convent school. She and her brother and sisters covered their ears at night to shut out the sounds of their parents' booze-fueled quarreling that had become a nightly routine. Leopards had raided the chicken coop on the farm; her brother had hunted them with an ancient shotgun. They planted potatoes by hand with the villagers, who giggled at their crooked rows. She and her siblings laughed and chattered in the local dialect with their dark-haired playmates, culturally Burmese in every way except for their light hair and eyes. But Zoe was never close to her siblings; she stood apart, perhaps because of her faraway convent schooling, or possibly her teenage confusion. She'd barely seen them in the years since the tragedy in the Moulmein mill yard, and was a stranger.

Each night, while her parents drank with the village headman, they would listen to the battery-operated radio news on Burma Broadcasting Service, which reported outbreaks of violence by *dacoits*—highway robbers. During the heavy rains, they would trek out for hours on muddy paths to the village market, collect the mail, share a meal with a missionary family and get advice from trusted friends. This shining land was growing dim and fearful, and the children watched as their parents drank and fought, and drank again until they passed out.

Zoe withdrew further, increasing the distance.

In the midst of the turmoil, there had been a New Year's dance in the old British club in Kalaw, its greying teak floors newly swept and dusted with talcum powder, crepe-paper streamers hanging from the ceiling, the Ink Spots playing on a scratchy Victrola. Zoe had walked through the soft lights of the old ballroom, a striking young woman with light eyes and soft curves, clad in a shimmering blue silk *thamein* that hugged her body. She had fallen in love, instantly and completely, with a young Shan man, his lynx-like eyes upon her, his fine lean body against hers on the dance-floor. He was called Sao Johnny, the son of a Shan feudal lord and his Danish wife whom her parents had known for years. Both their fathers had fought in the OSS, the famed Kachin Rangers, the most-decorated fighting force in the China-Burma-India campaign of World War II.

Sao Johnny had quickly become a fixture on the old farmstead, much to her parent's chagrin. They joined a party of workmen at an old pagoda site nearby, where a restoration festival was in progress on the main shrine, perched on top of a steep, bare hill overlooking the whole Shwenyaung Valley. The red earth gave its name to the ancient pagoda, and to the old legends of ruby reliquaries hidden in the ruins—*Taung Ni*, the red mountain. Colonial civil servants had often desecrated sacred sites searching for treasure. And frequently, they found it—along with cobras and terrible curses which befell thieves. Sao Johnny spoke in whispers with one of the laborers, who soon produced a small, glinting piece of metal from a filthy worn pouch. It was a tiny perforated coin, with the image of a shell embossed on it, strung on a frayed string. He smiled as Zoe tied it around her neck—a talisman.

Zoe would sit with him during the night hours, mesmerized by his voice and hands. They listened to the old Shan retainers and the lethal Karen and Kachin soldiers, who had served with her father and his. They watched by the light of kerosene lamps and winking candles as the old men danced in an opium-induced haze, telling tales of stalking leopards in the dark, and of the silent, soundless executions of Japanese soldiers.

Zoe's parents expressed outrage at the intensity of emotion between Sao Johnny and their daughter, by the suddenness of the relationship, and Zoe's complete withdrawal from her family.

Pat Longfield entreated her, her words slurred by drink. "You don't realize what you're doing. Your behavior is ridiculous."

Zoe glared at her. "And what about your behavior? How does the booze make you smarter?" she jeered, throwing a half-empty bottle up against a house post and walking away from her mother's glazed, hurt expression.

George Longfield was openly angry. In spite of his long-held trust for the young man's father, he saw this romance as a dead end in the worst of economic and political times. During the preceding year, he had watched helplessly as long-time friends and business partners—Indians, Chinese, Eurasian—were abruptly deported, without any resources except their wives' gold jewelry and dowries of diamonds and rubies. And these were often taken in the Customs Hall, leaving families weeping and destitute for whatever journey lay ahead. The Burmese Way to Socialism was brutish, racist, rapacious and unkind.

Zoe had to escape from the fights, the nightlong drinking bouts, the endless conniving, and she needed to be closer to Sao Johnny. She pleaded an interest in a typing and shorthand course in Rangoon, and used the pretext to stay with family friends at their apartment in the Chinatown section of the city. She sat for days typing out practice exercises on ancient Remington typewriters, with English or Burmese characters, depending on what was available. She learned the swirls and dots and dashes of Pitman shorthand, not unlike Arabic calligraphy.

In the late afternoon, she'd sneak out to board a motorcycle driven by Sao Johnny, ostensibly at University reading economics. They would head for the privacy of remote benches at Inya Lake where passion overwhelmed them both, their bodies and emotions entwined. They decided to elope, discussing their plans often as weeks passed. They clung to each other, meeting surreptitiously at friends' apartments, in movie theatres, at private parties, dancing at the venerable Kokine Club, stolen moments alone.

Suddenly, one night, there was a visit to the Chinatown apartment by the Immigration Police. A deportation order had been issued for Zoe, as an "undesirable alien". She fled by overnight train to the Shan States, entreating her father to intercede, to allow them to marry. She threatened to elope, and he laughed, pointing out that no official would marry them with a deportation order pending.

He refused to help, banging the table as he drank down a shot of cheap country liquor. "No, Zoe, no. There's a whole world out there that you need to see, and you'll get nowhere with this new regime." Zoe howled with rage and sadness, then in the early morning, she kissed her nanny and her confused brother and sisters goodbye, and left quickly before her parents awoke from their usual stupor. Back on the train, she headed for Rangoon in a state of dry-eyed grief and helpless anger, and to the comfort of Sao Johnny's arms.

A few short weeks later, Zoe's father appeared at the Chinatown apartment to take her to Rangoon's Mingaladon Airport, vouching for her departure to the authorities. Sao Johnny waited by the airport restaurant, its walls covered with vivid murals painted by local artist U Ba Kyi, portraying Burmese life in happier times.

George Longfield shrugged derisively at Johnny. "He can't change anything, you know. You've got 10 minutes." He turned and headed for the bar.

Zoe sat speechless with Sao Johnny, clutching his hand, knowing that displays of public affection were frowned on. Then, she looked once more into his eyes, rose and walked towards the Immigration and Customs hall. "*Thwa-yah meh, naw*...I must go," she said, in the understated Burmese way. Sao Johnny did not move; he just looked after her.

Her father waited by the doorway. She stopped, stared at him, and said, "I will never forget this, and I will never, ever forgive you. My life is no longer your concern."

And she turned away, walking unseeing through the Immigration and Customs hall, surrendering her P-Form, D-Form and other paper requirements, all neatly stamped "DEPORTED", while Sao Johnny's lynx eyes watched her solemnly. Her father stood in the shadows, yards away, tears streaming down his face.

She walked across the steaming tarmac towards the shining Pan Am Constellation aircraft, moving from the ancient leisurely ways of her homeland and the love of Sao Johnny, to what her parents argued would be a "better life" in America, far from everything and everyone she knew and cared for. Her heart set into cold anger as the aircraft thundered aloft, and she saw the glinting lights of the golden Shwe Dagon pagoda receding, one last time.

She didn't count the cities, the countries, the descents and takeoffs, hours of sleepless contemplation until she arrived, coatless, in the cold mercies of a windy Chicago winter morning. She braved the first escalator she'd ever seen, and equally steely relatives waiting for her at the bottom. They held up a sign saying "Welcome, Zoe" and were kind but cool. Zoe imagined what they were thinking; she'd seen the letters and heard the stories. They viewed her parents as models of eccentricity rather than romance, the glow of post–World War II enthusiasms and altruism having faded. What were they thinking, running away to some god-forsaken crowded outpost of the Orient, with no supermarkets, highways, television or air-conditioning?

And they don't even know about the drinking and the fights and the new hardships in Burma, Zoe grimaced. Her heart hardened again, towards them all.

Her Uncle James stepped forward, smiling tightly, and offered a cool, dry peck on the cheek. Her Aunt Janet hugged her as Zoe stiffened slightly. They made small talk as they exited the terminal. She could see her breath as she exhaled during the walk to the parking lot, felt the tingle of cold in her nostrils and lungs. Her aunt pulled a blanket from the back seat of the station wagon, saying, "Here, at least take this to keep off the cold." Zoe wrapped herself tightly, smelling the dog odor, nodding her thanks. The cold, grey, flat vistas flashed past, the spidery branches of empty trees bordering the superhighways of Chicago. Her heart ached for Burma, for her smiling classmates in Darjeeling, for Sao Johnny's arms.

But she smiled gamely for her relatives, living with her uncle's family in a four-bedroom house on a corner lot in a town called a "suburb," surrounded by other dwellings. She enrolled in Northwestern University near her Uncle's home, a short train-ride away. President John F. Kennedy had been assassinated in Dallas, Texas, a few months before her arrival. Zoe attended lectures on the topic, and she watched several blonde, blue-eyed girls giggling with delight as they discussed some aspect of the tragedy. She wondered: the country's leader has been murdered and its citizens are gleeful? She remembered the assassinations of Mahatma Gandhi, Bogyoke Aung San, King Faisal and Ramon Magsaysay, thinking, this country is not so different from other places, in spite of all its power.

The weeks passed; she went to teas and sorority rushes, and met mothers and daughters dressed in identical suits or collared blouses and new fashions made from colorful "Mud-RASS" cloth. She received invitations: "Come over any time," they'd say, "we live five minutes away." So on a Saturday morning or Sunday afternoon, she would go, following on foot the directions to homes that were an hour's walk in the cold, quickly learning that people did not think in terms of walking times, but only of driving times. And when she rang the doorbell, surprised faces would arrange themselves into forced smiles. Thus she learned that they did not really mean "any time," they meant that one should call first and make sure that a visit was convenient. She yearned for the easy friendships of Burma, where people would drop by unannounced and stay for dinner—or for a month.

She wrote to Sao Johnny every day, never receiving a reply. She wrote to school friends from Darjeeling and Burma, describing her life:

...The houses look like magazines—shag carpeting everywhere, big soft couches. People all keep their shoes on, even walking on carpets. Furniture has legs, but it's for sitting in, not lying on. There is beautiful china stored in a cabinet called a "hutch" in dining rooms, but it's rarely used because it's delicate and difficult to clean. Every home has a television, and nobody talks during favorite shows like the "Ed Sullivan Show", or "Leave it to Beaver". And, there are no servants!

The most important thing Zoe learned was that, with no servants to help iron the shirts, bake the cookies, or clean the many rooms, the mother of the house was, in effect, a slave to the oven and the dishwasher and the vacuum cleaner and the tools of advanced living, and had no time for much else. She learned that servants were a luxury for the very wealthy, who did not include domestic help as part of the family.

She talked to her aunt about the new book, *The Feminine Mystique* by Betty Friedan. She said, "Auntie, all these American women say that they want more freedom; maybe they need to talk to the women of Asia. Burmese women have always kept their rights, their names, their property, and their roles as leaders, doctors, professors. They do it by running their households with a staff of servants, and there's always lots of laughter, noise and eating." Her aunt smiled, and said something about Americans valuing their privacy. To Zoe, it was meaningless.

She tried gamely to fit in both at school and at her relatives' home, learning to cook and baby-sit and go to football games and movies, but nothing ever quite jelled. Her clothes, her accent, her silence all served to set her apart. But the worst part of the adjustment, aside from the cold and the monochrome landscape, was the loneliness and emptiness left by her abrupt departure from Burma, and everything she knew. The silent anger crept around her heart. *Achit, achit* she would murmur, remembering Johnny's warmth and hardness. But she did not hear from him, although friends reported on his radical activities at the University. There were even rumors that he had fled the country, over the Thai border, into the Golden Triangle. In a bureau drawer, a growing stack of unopened letters grew, envelopes in her parents' handwriting.

Her status as a "foreign student" also served to set her apart at the university where, after endless wallflower evenings, Zoe joined a drama class, figuring that she could hide in acting roles and perhaps meet people with similar interests. In its mid-term production of a children's fantasy play, Zoe played the part of a princess in a mysterious land, where her accent was finally useful.

The producer, a 30-ish Englishman named Malcolm Sargeant, was worshipped by his students who found him wildly provocative. He had trained at Cambridge, dabbled in a few productions on the West End, and then came to Northwestern's fabled drama school via the Blackstone Theatre's revival of Agatha Christie's *The Mousetrap*.

Zoe stayed out of the social circle, but arrived on time, knowing her lines and showing a verve and sparkle onstage that came across the foot lights to the audience. One day, Malcolm stopped her after a matinee performance for inner-city school children.

"Zoe, that was a very nice bit you did, getting the kids in the audience to help you rub the lamp," he said.

She looked up and smiled, "Yes, sir. The children seemed to like it. Perhaps I could change the lines for the other shows?" she asked hesitantly.

"Zoe, of course you should. That's what the stage is for…the moment, the inspiration, the magic." He walked beside her, out into the spring air.

He looked into her grey-blue eyes, framed by light brown hair,

"You know, you really are very good. And you are so different from the rest of this noisy lot. I wonder what's going on in that quiet head? "

Embarrassed, she glanced away, looked down and said, "There are no secrets. I enjoy the acting because I don't have to pretend. I really am the Princess Zonda, and I really do have a pet elephant!" She laughed and her face lit up. "I don't know why I told you that." She lowered her eyes.

He took her arm and steered her towards the student café, saying, "Well, then, a cup of tea for the princess!"

Once seated, they ordered tea and he nodded approvingly that she took milk with her tea. "You know," said Malcolm, "I never get curious about my students' personal lives." He paused. "But tell me about yourself; where you're from, what you want to do."

Zoe said, " I grew up in Asia—in Burma, actually. I suppose I just got caught in the current political backwash, and was deported from Rangoon over a year ago. My parents did not object as they felt it was time for me to leave Asia and learn about America."

She swallowed. "And then I ended up here with some of my mother's family, and I'm grateful, but I'm just marking time. So much of my life has been spent in Asia that I don't understand American ways, and they don't understand me. All I want is to make enough money to go back to Burma."

She rose from her chair. "Thanks for the tea and sympathy," she nodded, moving to the door. He sat, nonplussed, taking in her words.

Then he got up and followed her, saying, "Look, would you consider a meal with a stodgy old professor? I might have some ideas, possibly about a job for you." He grinned, his dark hair worn slightly long in the English fashion.

Zoe said, "Yes, I think I would enjoy that." Malcolm's smile widened. "Great, then it's settled. What about Sunday after the final matinee, when you retire your princess role? And it's 'Malcolm', not 'sir', and not 'Professor Sargeant', or I really will feel like an old codger." They laughed and parted ways.

Zoe was astounded. Here he was, the romantic idol of the undergraduate girls, taking her to dinner. She was flattered, but deep down she knew that Malcolm could never be more than a friend.

After the final matinee performance and standing ovations from more happy children, the cast cleaned off their stage makeup and stored their costumes. They sat in the empty theatre with Malcolm, the prop men, the ticket clerks and several former students, laughing and telling backstage stories over several beers and soft drinks. Zoe wondered if he had forgotten their date. As she picked up her satchel and bags, and a small bouquet of roses from the children, he whispered, "Dinner at seven? I have a surprise! I'll pick you up at the Campus Center about 6:45?" She smiled assent.

They entered *The Tikka* restaurant with its entrancing smells of curry and incense. The proprietor seated them quickly. Playing on a small stage surrounded by votive candles, a sitar player and a young man on conga drums brought an otherworldly rhythm to the room— a fusion of the music of string and drum cultures. She was entranced with the mood, the music and the food, and touched by Malcolm's thoughtfulness. She sighed, inhaling, "Rice…real rice! You have no idea how I've dreamed about it."

After the set, Malcolm beckoned to the conga player. "This is my friend Luther Jefferson, who is a great jazz musician and the building manager at the INTRAV building in downtown Chicago." He went on to say that Luther was Trinidadian born-and-raised, and was also an ordained minister and deacon of a well-known Baptist church on the South Side of Chicago.

Zoe just thought he was beautiful. He smiled at her as he described various jobs at the International Travel Agency in the building he managed.

Malcolm said, "Zoe, Luther knows everyone in this agency, and there might be a great part time job for you, learning the travel industry from the ground up. Why don't you give it a try?" Zoe nodded, busy working her way through a third helping of chicken tikka, more rice, lentils and spinach with a generous dollop of lime pickle. They listened to the music and toasted the day's events.

With Malcolm's urging, Luther introduced her to INTRAV'S president, and she was soon working three days a week at the agency, in between her University classes.

She was happy to be working and learning new duties, and she would make time to sit with Luther, who was puzzled by her, trying to understand her quick mind, the quiet demeanor, and the cold rage that seemed to emerge whenever there was a discussion about family matters. Luther's "office" was a gathering spot for building employees seeking frank advice and spiritual counsel, and Zoe would listen in occasionally.

She tentatively entered more university courses in anthropology and archaeology, finding a fascination with ancient artifacts and cultural models. One of her professors identified Sao Johnny's silver coin, which she now wore on a thin chain—probably 4th or 5th century, he thought, inscribed with a srivatsa image of Shaivite and Buddhist iconography, an endless knot and a conch shell. It was possibly from South India, but more probably from Pyu regions in modern Burma. How had she come by such a piece?

She smiled, thrilled with the knowledge, and replied, "Oh, a friend gave it to me." But she kept the details to herself. Who would believe it? The misty hills, the old pagoda, the red earth.

She would join Malcolm or Luther on evening adventures, from South Side Chicago Jazz bars to quiet restaurants, to soup kitchens and gospel choirs on Sundays. Almost every week, she'd make time for the Chicago Art Institute or the Field Museum of Natural History, never tiring of their treasures. Malcolm tried to convince her to change her major to archaeology, but he admitted that even in the mid-1960s, the field was still a challenge for women.

The months went by, and another Christmas passed with snowstorms, holiday cheer and icy winds. Malcolm called her one evening, breathless, with the news of an exciting job offer back in England, and he urged her to meet him immediately. They sat in a warm café overlooking frozen Lake Michigan as he described the new position, a senior post at a highly regarded school of drama in Cambridge, where he knew the faculty and the strength of the institution. He'd already accepted the job, starting at the beginning of the next semester.

He said, "You know, Zoe, you've touched my heart in so many ways. I don't know what is to become of you, but I do know it won't be dull. You must plan to leave this place, though. It is too far from everything you love." Zoe hugged him, wishing things between them could be different.

A few weeks later, she trekked out to the airport with him, and he blew kisses to her as he disappeared up the escalator to the departure lounge for Pan Am's Flight 58 to London. She remembered her first trip down that very escalator not so long ago. She thought of the growing pile of unopened letters in a drawer, serving only to remind her of her exile and cold anger.

She continued to see Luther every morning in his office, a large room between the elevator shaft and the back door to Zoe's travel agency suite. Zoe still helped open, sort and date-stamp the mail for INTRAV and the dental clinic on the first floor. As her second year of employment with INTRAV began and her hours with the agency increased, she had switched to night classes at Northwestern, taking third-year history and anthropology courses. She was actually handling her own client roster, planning and booking extensive trips for wealthy elderly clients interested in offbeat excursions.

She had become close to the center of Luther's world of social activism, and they felt the beat increase in January of 1968 with the Tet New Year offensive in Vietnam, with its hundreds of military and civilian casualties and the shock that American soldiers could be so badly humiliated in the center of its immense buildup.

Zoe enjoyed the gospel services in South Side Chicago Baptist churches, storefronts with soup kitchens to one side and saloons on the other. It was a different world from the strict mission Catholicism of her youth. She was still puzzled by so much public display of emotion, the congregation's faith and feelings expressed through rich, incandescent music and song, and the sobbing ecstatic convulsions of the faithful praying for peace. So many had family and friends serving in Vietnam, so the recent events of the war were real and brutal to them.

Luther's parishioners and friends acknowledged her, although she was never sure what these proud young black people thought of her, working in the soup kitchens with the church ladies. Sensitive to the women, she made sure that she was always in their midst. She did not want any of the racial confrontations she had seen, and heeded

Luther's caution to "stay sisterly". Many of the men were young clerics who had gained fame as the Black Panthers—community organizers who had kept the peace on the South Side on the dreadful April night when the west side of Chicago erupted in a firestorm following the assassination of Martin Luther King.

Zoe walked in the Peace March soon after with a line of black women, singing of pain and redemption. And weeks later, they came out again following the assassination of Robert Kennedy. The nation was seized by a blackness of despair, lost hope, disbelief.

Zoe harbored the darkness in her own heart against her family. After these last few years, she thought, it really is a detachment from them, and it is not so painful for me to be alone. Even Sao Johnny's image faded, though she could still remember his eyes in the firelight with the old OSS Kachin warriors, and she fingered the Pyu coin around her neck at the memories.

Luther had encouraged them to join the determined throngs that summer protesting the war in Vietnam, and they were active participants in Democratic Party rallies, taking to the streets in thousands. At the forefront of the demonstrations was a group of New York "Yippies", who had been advocating unrest and protests during the upcoming Democratic Party Convention. Sure enough, the mighty Mayor Richard Daley and his infamous "shoot to kill" order stirred up the people's rage in August of 1968, with thousands in the streets for the Democratic National Convention at the Conrad Hilton Hotel spilling out across into Grant Park and uptown at Lincoln Park. Zoe and hundreds of others were caught in the street fighting with young National Guardsmen, arrested and jailed. Zoe called Luther from an echoing, tumultuous cellblock.

Yelling into the phone, she said, "Reverend, I need your help. I'm stuck up here in the Lincoln Park Detention Center, and we don't have any way to make bail for about 20 women. Can you help us?"

Luther arrived with four of his fellow ministers, bail money and sermons to heal souls. After they got to his church shelter, they huddled by flickering television sets that broadcast stories of mayhem across the city. They drank hot, nourishing soup, and worried about the chaos everywhere.

"*Dhokka, dhokka,*" Zoe remembered from her Burmese days, "the pain of trouble...."

Zoe sat with Luther in the days afterwards. It seemed to her that the best solution was to leave this city, and look for quieter, greener places. Luther consulted one of the managers, who had an immediate, welcome solution: a series of assignments as a tour-group leader for INTRAV's clients, shepherding groups from Mexico's Yucatan peninsula, to Rio de Janeiro's Carnival, hiking in the Chilean Lake District, and several tours in the Amazonian rainforest. The manager laughed at her eagerness. "Zoe, we're delighted you want to do this— we can never keep the senior guides on these jungle excursions."

Luther chuckled. "Well, girl, you do have to go to the jungles. These be American jungles, not Asian, but they're still full of creepin' biting things, eh?" She grinned happily.

Her uncle's family disapproved completely of what they termed her "gypsy lifestyle, just like your parents." Apparently, George Longfield had asked them for help in a reconciliation. Zoe had a short, terse conversation with her uncle, to ensure that he understood her gratitude, and that she was making her own decisions as an adult. "Maybe someday," she said, "I'll understand why my parents allowed this deportation to happen, but I'm not ready to now."

On her last day in the office, she sat companionably with Luther, and shyly asked for his blessing. He smiled, "Yes, Lord, I swear I have never met a white girl like you that don't know how to be white, and don't get to be brown."

She looked at him, his handsome face and shining eyes. She thought of the spirit of Sao Johnny, so far away and long ago, and imagined just for a moment that she could hope for happiness with a good man like Luther.

He looked at her, seeing the feeling in her eyes, and smiled. "You know, Zoe, I have fought the devil of desire for you a hundred times. But, you have so much anger in your soul, and until you can put that to rest for yourself, there'll be no peace and love for you or any man close to you." He leaned towards her and kissed her gently on the lips.

Zoe said, "Luther, I don't know how to let it go."

"That time will come, darlin', and you will know the moment. So, God speed." He rose and helped her to her feet, hugging her close.

That evening, the L-train finally rolled towards the Chicago and Northwestern Station, and she moved to the door, on her way to Winnetka for the last time. She stood still for a moment in the windy twilight.

She thought, I got past the loneliness and heartbreak, all the homesickness. I tried my best to fit in here, but I didn't, and now I'm ready to move on. It's not Burma, but somewhere out there, I'll find answers.

And maybe somehow I'll learn to let go of the anger.

CHAPTER FOUR

ROLL TIDE
JULY 17, 1969   LATHAM, KENTUCKY

"You simply may not wear that to Stanton's," Sugar Pie said flatly, glaring in disgust at the bell-bottom jeans and tie-dyed tee shirt that Sally had put on after she got home from her summer job at the local radio station. "I will not allow it."

Sally stood in the living room of the Alamo, cringing, as her mother's narrowing gaze looked her over from top to toe. Everywhere in the country, Jackie Kennedy's bouffant hairdo and elegant Chanel-style suits had given way to the 60s fashions of in-your-face hot pants, bell-bottom jeans and thigh-high mini-skirts—everywhere except Latham. Sally still hadn't lost the fifteen pounds she'd gained at college. Her mother thought it was too much beer, but unbeknownst to Pie, most of the fraternity and sorority parties were liquor-soaked events that featured late-night feasts of brownies laced with marijuana or hashish.

Her mother's gaze traveled down Sally's plump figure then back up again, stopping at her sun-streaked, sandy blonde hair. It was thick and wavy, just like Pie's, but her daughter wore her hair long and parted in the center, like most of her friends at school. "Whatever happened to those mid-length styles the girls wore in the Breck shampoo ads?" she wondered, referring to the dainty, virginal-looking young women whose wispy portraits appeared in the magazines down at Jeanette's Beauty Shop. "I simply don't understand why you girls go out of your way to look so dreadful. Don't you want to look like the young ladies that you are?"

"Honestly, Mother, what difference does it make? I'm just going for tea."

"You're not going just any place for tea; you're going to

Stanton's. And besides, what if somebody we know sees you walking over there with that on?" Pie looked at her daughter sternly, her eyebrows arched.

Sally started to say that nobody driving by on Main Street would give a hoot what she had on, but she stopped and looked at her mother. There were tiny lines around her eyes that hadn't been there before, and her mane of blonde hair was now streaked with grey at the temples. She's been through so much in the last years, why argue about clothes?

Back in her bedroom, Sally put on a yellow shirtwaist dress with tiny tucks down the front. At the base of the Peter Pan collar she affixed a gold monogrammed circle pin, and slipped her feet into her one and only pair of navy Pappagallo pumps with tiny, rounded toes. The gold hoop earrings she had on with her bellbottoms could stay, she decided, looking at herself in the full-length mirror and hating every pound of the freshman fifteen. There stood The Girl Next Door; in addition to her sun-streaked soft blonde hair and brown eyes, she possessed her father's sharp nose and jaw, which gave her face a finely boned appearance. Her mother's full lips always seemed to curve upwards in a little smile whether she felt like it or not. While not tall, she had slim legs, a small bosom, and strong shoulders from water skiing.

But, she thought ruefully, the whole damned package was encased in a soft layer of cozy fat just like a country ham. She stared into the mirror at length, trying to ascertain if there were qualities deep within her that had not yet surfaced. Surely there was the sophistication of an Audrey Hepburn in there somewhere.

"Sally!" Stanton Gardner exclaimed, opening the door and motioning her to come in. "Don't you look lovely." He held out his arms for a hug.

"Thank you, Uncle Stanton," said Sally, wondering what he would have thought of the bell-bottoms. He was so dear he probably would have said they looked like a Paris original or something equally flattering.

Leading the way into the drawing room, Stanton fretted briefly as he struggled to button the baby blue seersucker jacket that barely covered his own increasingly generous girth. The jacket matched his eyes, and the crisp, white Turnbull and Asser shirt with a dark blue silk tie he'd bought in London recently made him appear cool and collected, the look of a true Southern gentleman in the scalding heat of summer. His face and bald head glowed with the tan he'd acquired after a recent excursion on Kentucky Lake aboard a friend's houseboat. Settling himself into the plush cushions of the sofa, he motioned for Sally to join him.

"I put us in here today since it's so hot," he said, handing her a dainty cup and saucer and pouring tea from a silver pot. "Lemon, isn't it?"

Sally looked around the elegantly furnished room, admiring the quiet atmosphere of beauty and civility. "Yes, thank you." Stanton was the proprietor of the Stanton Gardner Shop, one of the most exquisite antique stores in the Southeast, occupying a stately building painted a subtle shade of grey-green that was just a few blocks away from where Sally worked downtown. A curved gallery on the side of the building was filled with lovely paintings, furniture and china in order to attract customers. When an important client arrived—say, a decorator for one of the country music stars in nearby Nashville—he would sweep from behind his desk in his back office and glide across the black-and-white tiled floor to give them his personal attention. They might wear costumes covered with glittering wagon wheels and cactuses while performing at the Grand Ole' Opry, but Stanton made sure they went home to calm, tastefully decorated homes.

Sally had known Stanton all her life. He and her mother had been devoted friends while she was growing up, and although people didn't talk about such things in those days, Sally had instinctively known that Stanton was not the marrying kind, finding fulfillment in life in other ways, while always accompanied by a charming male friend. Although running a store with a nationwide clientele and searching throughout Europe to find lovely things to fill it was great fun, it was his role as the arbiter of good taste in the town of his birth that he enjoyed most. An invitation to a dinner party at his home was the most coveted in town. His trademark Old Fashioned cocktails, prepared a full two weeks in advance, would be served beforehand in the upstairs drawing room amidst a collection of exquisite porcelain birds. When the guests were summoned to dinner downstairs, the table was laid with crisp white linens hand-embroidered with emerald green medallions matching those in his china pattern, and the finest English silver was tucked next to each plate.

After Jim Wilder's death, Stanton had become an even more important figure in Sally's life. Her grandparents had passed on too, and she needed older friends. Not having children of his own, Stanton enjoyed those of his friends, attending Sally's dance recitals and enduring the Neanderthal ritual of the football game when she was in the marching band, the latter made survivable by swilling bourbon from an antique silver flask tucked discreetly in his overcoat pocket. He also attended to the important milestones in Sally's life. When Sally graduated from high school and arrived at his shop to choose a silver pattern, he supervised her selection personally, mindful that in Latham, the choice of a young woman's silver pattern was practically a state occasion.

Stanton passed a little crystal bowl filled with flaky cheese straws, and told her stories of his latest coup—a pre-Civil War tea service. But soon, he got down to the business at hand. "Sally, have you thought about what you're going to do after college next year?" he asked.

"Well, I've been considering teaching French somewhere, maybe in Nashville," replied Sally. "I haven't thought too much about it yet, but I do know I have to have something lined up soon. Mother's been very clear about that."

"Ah yes, I remember now. Pie wanted you to be a French major because Jackie spoke French."

Sally nodded, recalling how she had originally toyed with other options. "But to tell you the truth, I don't know whether teaching is right for me or not, Uncle Stanton. I wanted to be an architect, but I wasn't sure if women did that. It's a bit late in the game for me to change majors."

Stanton regarded Sally carefully. Yes, he knew Sally possessed

Jim Wilder's good mind and Pie's innate good taste. But female architects were exceedingly rare, and there were certainly none in Latham. "Might the teaching in Nashville business have something to do with Lawton Richardson?" he asked casually, lifting an eyebrow ever so slightly. He knew the young man; Lawton was from a reputable family, and lived on a big farm outside of town.

Sally squirmed and smiled demurely. "Sort of. Well, yes. He starts medical school at Vanderbilt next year, and we thought it might be nice if I were nearby." Regardless of how enmeshed she and Pie were in each other's lives, Sally did not have these kinds of conversations about dating and the future with her mother; as carefully as Pie looked after Sally, she never really probed the depths of her daughter's feelings. Sally found herself wondering if there had ever been such a gulf between generations before, and why she felt more comfortable sharing her innermost thoughts with Stanton than with her one remaining parent. There seemed to be nothing in her mother's experience that would enable her to reach across the chasm from her predictable upbringing to the shaky new ground of the late 60s. But here with Stanton, she felt relaxed and spoke freely. "Lawton and I, well, I think we've been going out so long because neither one of us has anything else we'd rather be doing," she said, surprising herself with this moment of insight.

Stanton smiled and nodded as he retrieved a cigarette from a silver box on the coffee table and placed it in an ebony holder. He lit the cigarette and took a long drag. "You've done such a good job in school and taking care of your mother. You've worked every summer at the radio station to make extra money. And through it all, you've stayed sweet and done the right thing."

"Yes," Sally nodded ruefully, "I've really enjoyed working at the station, but I'm not sure writing copy about the price of hogs is my destiny. There's got to be more to life than that!"

Stanton rolled his eyes and chuckled. "I'll say. But you see, maybe that's part of the problem. You've been so busy being good that you sure haven't had much joy in your life."

Sally looked at him, speechless. "What do you mean, joy?"

He said, "Don't you ever want a little fun before you take on the responsibilities of a home and family?"

Sally nodded. "Well, yes, but...but ...you know my mother practically has my whole life completely planned out, right down to the wedding at All Saints Episcopal Church, and the names of the children." She looked away. "Not...not that she's ever asked me what I'd really like," she said, remembering her far-away dreams at the Stone's Mill train crossing.

"Sally, have you ever wanted to travel?" he asked.

"Oh yes," replied Sally, her eyes lighting up.

"Well, I've been thinking that you might enjoy being an airline stewardess. That way you would get paid to travel."

"An *airline* stewardess?" Sally was incredulous. This was not in the lexicon of accepted careers for most Southern ladies. They were supposed to choose something they could drop the minute the babies started coming. And being a stewardess certainly wasn't a career choice for her friends on campus, most of whom were getting married and going into teaching.

"As you know, I go to London several times a year and I always fly on Pan American, so I've come to know some of the stewardesses. Flight 100 leaves New York at about 10 o'clock in the morning. We have dinner and watch a movie, then take high tea with strawberries and scones with clotted cream before our late evening arrival. I take a taxi into town and stay at the Connaught Hotel, go to sleep and I'm ready for business the next day." Stanton tapped his cigarette methodically on the edge of a heavy crystal ashtray. "The crews really do seem to have a wonderful time; they go to all the important museums and palaces, shopping, nightclubs, the races...." He could sense that Sally was receptive to the idea, and he smiled with pleasure.

"Uncle Stanton, I...I never imagined that I could do anything like that." Sally sipped her tea carefully. "I've never even been on an airplane before."

"Pan Am hires attractive women who have had some sort of international experience and a college degree, and you must speak English and at least one other language fluently."

Sally laughed, "Maybe my degree in French would finally be worth something!"

Stanton nodded. "But, you will have to stop eating Pie's cornbread and fried chicken. Can you do that?"

Sally squirmed under Stanton's gaze, but realized she'd a lot rather hear this from him than from her mother.

When it was time to leave, Stanton accompanied Sally out to the porch. "What do you think of all of this, Sally? You can't be so afraid of life, you know. There's a big wide world out there, just waiting for you to go and see it." He extended his arm in a broad gesture across the horizon.

After years of confusion and uncertainty, Sally realized that Stanton was right. It *was* time for her to do something completely new, to try to find out just exactly who she was and where she belonged rather than waiting for others to define those things for her. She thought of her father's smile, the stories they had read together and the dreams that were spun from them. Maybe this is one way she could repay him—just by following these dreams. The idea of flying became comfortable to her and settled in. "Gosh, Uncle Stanton, I guess you're right. I never realized it, but this really is a way to see the whole world!"

"The whole world," echoed Stanton, gathering her into his arms and hugging her. "That's my girl," he said proudly as Sally stepped down to the ivy-bordered sidewalk. "Now don't tell Pie I put you up to this!" he called merrily as she made her way up the gentle rise of South Main and out of sight.

When she got home, Sally could smell the cooking of her favorite meal: a Southern vegetable supper of fried corn, green beans, squash and sliced tomatoes. Just as she walked in the door, Pie was removing from the oven a cast-iron skillet in which she had baked cornbread with bacon drippings. During supper at the kitchen table, they discussed their weekend plans. Pie mentioned that she'd been invited to play bridge at the country club after church on Sunday. "Lawton and I are going to the lake, skiing," Sally told her.

"All right," said Pie, "just don't stay too late. I worry about you out on that water when it's getting dark." They sat for a few minutes, lost in their own thoughts.

Sally took a bite out of her cornbread, and suddenly

remembering Stanton's admonition, put it on the side of her plate. Then she blurted out, "Mother, I'm thinking of applying to be an airline stewardess."

Pie was so startled she could hardly speak. "What? You mean I've paid all that money for your education and you're going to be an *airline* stewardess?" she spluttered. Sally might as well have told her she was going to join a traveling circus. "What on earth happened over at Stanton's? Young ladies from good families just don't do that sort of thing. He knows that."

"Stanton says they do now, Mother," said Sally. "And he says this isn't just any airline. It's Pan American. They fly only international routes, and the stewardesses stay at wonderful hotels and visit the theaters and museums, and serve exciting people on the way to Paris, or Rome, or London...."

"But that's precisely the point, Sally." Pie exploded. "What on earth would you say to people about...about being a...a *waitress* on an airplane going anywhere? And why on earth would you want go to Paris? Who do you know there? My God, what sort of people would you be meeting? No one you know anything about."

Pie got up and paced the floor, determined to dominate her daughter as she always had. "And why in heaven's name would you want to...to *serve* people on the way to Paris when we do a perfectly fine job of...well, there is a service industry that takes care of all that with...with the kind of people who are trained for that kind of thing. And you have Lawton to think of. Don't you care about your future?"

In her agitation, Pie turned to face Sally. The tirade went on and on, encompassing the usual themes of the glorious South, the family tradition, the right sort of behavior, the opinions of Latham. Sally was overwhelmed by this view of her mother as a petty, small-town tyrant, so she took refuge in common ground.

"Mother, you can't talk me out of this," Sally said with more defiance than she actually felt. "I'm 21 years old, I will be a college graduate soon and I will need a job. These Pan Am recruits have degrees, like me; they speak foreign languages, like me; and they are...are ladies of good breeding, just like you and me."

Pie looked at her daughter, startled by her outburst. Slightly mollified, or at least checked for the moment, she nodded abruptly. "We'll talk about this when I'm calmer and when you are thinking more clearly of your future," she said through tightly clenched teeth.

Sally grinned to herself, astounded by her courage. Oh, I can do this. I can definitely do this!

Late Sunday afternoon, Lawton pulled up in front of the Alamo in his Chevrolet sedan, towing the family motorboat behind on a trailer. They drove through the luxuriant green countryside to Kentucky Lake, skiing until sundown, when the surface of the lake smoothed itself into a giant piece of glass. The huge sky before them was streaked with coral and pink, as broad and unending as the horizon. She glided through her turns, the slalom ski slicing the surface and leaving a silver trail of glimmering s-shaped curves behind. This was freedom. It was like flying.

Taking the wheel, she pulled Lawton, admiring his strong, muscular body. Effortlessly, he jumped both wakes, a look of complete relaxation on his face. He was in better physical condition now than during his days as a running back for the Latham High School Cougars, the glory years when Coach Sonny Randolph had led the team all the way to the State AA championship two years in a row.

Strong and steady, that was Lawton. They had fallen in love during that fabulous football season, and dated regularly for the remainder of high school. Occasionally Pie suggested that they date other people, but Sally knew her mother permitted the relationship because, after all, Lawton *was* from the right kind of family. But her tolerance toward them did not mean that she didn't watch them carefully. When they drove up in front of the Alamo after a date and Lawton would lean over to kiss Sally good night, the light post by the sidewalk would mysteriously flicker on and off, courtesy of Pie, who crouched in her bathrobe behind a potted palm in the entry way.

Sally's physical relationship with Lawton had been more or less stunted during their high school years, as she had been haunted by

Pie's relentless admonitions about getting pregnant and that a young woman's virginity was crucial to finding a suitable husband. But that all changed once Sally reached college, when late-night conversations with her girlfriends in her dorm had set things straight for her. Discussions about the various new philosophies of sexual freedom found in the Kinsey Report and books by feminist writers, as well as the advantages of the new birth-control pill, were changing the entire social landscape on campus.

"My high-school boyfriend and I did things in installments, almost like we were on some kind of a schedule," said one girl. "I let him kiss me after a few weeks, French kiss after a few more, then a month later touch my left boob, then the right one after that, and so on. It took us almost year to work up to the back seat."

The girls giggled, sharing stories that were the reality of the dating scene in America, of the protocols of early withdrawal and "going half-way", of always bringing the show to a screeching halt before the main event.

"I think we *all* did that," said Sally. "Lawton and I could make out for hours, then I would say it was time to stop. Why on earth did we do it that way? I guess it was because my mother always told me that if I wasn't a virgin when I got married, I'd be damaged goods."

"And that's the big lie, sweetie," said another girl. "Just a few weeks after I got to college, my boyfriend and I went all the way, and I finally realized that it was really fun, and that he didn't care if I was a virgin or not. It was like discovering that there's no Santa Claus—it was no big deal."

Sally and Lawton had become lovers on an old mattress in the back of one of the farm's pick-up trucks. They had driven out into the blackness of one of the pastures, parking the truck near the banks of a stream and leaving the radio on, turned down low. She could just hear the guitar twang of her favorite country music performer, Merle Haggard. Hurriedly they climbed into the back, their lips and their bodies responding rapidly to the habits of familiarity. But this time, Sally began removing their clothes, and Lawton moaned as their naked bodies pressed together. As she lay beneath Lawton's broad shoulders, she felt him slowly pressure his way inside her.

"Are you okay?" he whispered. This was new territory for both of them.

And she had clutched him to her, this time not letting her feelings shut down or telling him to stop. Blessed by a warm summer breeze, an endless spread of stars overhead and the protection of The Pill, she allowed him all the way inside, feeling a new sense of urgency taking over that drove them forward until they both shuddered together.

Afterwards, they lay entwined, with Sally resting her head on Lawton's shoulder as he traced his fingers softly along her spine. She was supremely content, elated that she had found the courage to finally give herself to him, and she relished the heightened sensations of pleasure. But she would have to hold this newfound experience deep in her heart, for she had to make sure she did nothing in front of Pie that would cause suspicion. It was yet another facet of her double life, a daughter of the South and a child of the 60s.

When it got too dark to ski any longer, Sally helped Lawton maneuver the boat back on to its trailer at the boat ramp, taking one last look at the silvery blue water bordered by low hills that undulated along the shoreline like dark ribbons. In the car, she remained silent, contemplating her airline fantasy. They stopped at Pete Larson Springs, a tiny roadside restaurant with a single light over the front door, ordering fried catfish with hush puppies and coleslaw for dinner. There was no finer taste on a hot summer evening than the icy 7-Ups they drank from small, green bottles. When they returned to the Alamo that night, they found Pie on the sofa back in the sitting room, completely motionless with her hands folded in her lap, her eyes riveted on the television.

"They've just landed on the moon," she said, looking up at them in wonder.

Sally carried Stanton's words about Pan Am in the forefront of her mind when she returned to college that fall for her senior year, knowing that if she wanted to fly, she would have to go after the job in a big way. She swore off brownies and doughnuts, hit the books and began writing letters to the recruiting office. After several exchanges, she went to Washington, D.C. on a frozen March day for a formal interview and language testing, and was accepted for a training class in Miami after graduation in May. When the letter arrived officially inviting her to become one of 4000 trainees out of more than 40,000 applicants, she screamed her gratitude to Stanton on a drunken collect phone call. Her conversation with Pie was more decorous, but Stanton had worked his magic there too. While not enthusiastic, Pie was at least congratulatory, encouraging her only child to take time at home before her new adventure began.

The night before she left for training, she had a date with Lawton at the Skyway Drive-In. He had known about her successful application, but had not been congratulatory or helpful.

He lit a cigarette, slamming the lighter shut in irritation. "I don't understand why you want to go the hell off and fly around the world where you don't know anybody instead of getting a job in Nashville," he mourned. "I know med school will take a lot of my time, but we could try and find out if we're really right for each other."

Sally looked into those dark eyes that she had always found so irresistible, and took a sip of Budweiser from a six-pack they'd sneaked in. The speaker was attached to Lawton's window, but they had it turned it down so the movie, *2001: A Space Odyssey*, wouldn't intrude on their conversation. It was a moonlit spring evening, and a soft breeze blowing in from the farms held the scent of the country air that Sally so loved. She sat close to Lawton on the driver's side, his arm around her shoulder.

"Lawton, I don't entirely know why, I just have to do this," Sally said, looking up at the screen where a spacecraft floated effortlessly towards a gigantic space station. "Oh my God, look! That man is taking Pan Am on his flight to a space station!" The name "Pan American" was clearly emblazoned along the fuselage of the craft as it moved lazily towards its docking point, accompanied by a graceful Strauss waltz. She watched in amazement as the stewardess—the tiny Pan Am logo of a globe with wings affixed to her magnetized shoes—methodically walked up the walls and onto the ceiling of the aircraft in the weightless environment. "All I know is that I want to see Paris and London and Rome. I just have to. I want to go to exotic places, like Hong Kong and Singapore. And I wouldn't mind working that flight in space, either!"

"Paris, London and Rome," Lawton fumed. "Who needs them? And who gives a shit about Hong Kong and Singapore anyway? Jesus, Sally, I'm in love with you. What can you find in all those places that you can't have *right here?*" He hammered his palm against the steering wheel in frustration.

"Lawton, this way we'll find out for sure whether you and I have any future," Sally said, "and I will find out what I need to know about those places, and why Latham just does not fill my world." He'd taken her straight home after the movie, dropped her at the curb and pulled away with growling gears and screeching tires, the car expressing his frustration.

As Sally turned and made her way up the sidewalk, she saw her mother standing at the top of the steps, her arms folded, her face frozen as solid as a farm pond in the dead of winter.

"Well, Sally, I do hope you know what you are doing," snapped Pie.

Sally gazed up at the stars for a long moment, then walked inside.

Stanton drove Sally and Pie to the Nashville airport the next morning in his shiny black Cadillac. Pie didn't say much, seeming wistful, almost resigned. When they passed by the main gate at Ft. Campbell a short time later, Sally's eyes lingered on a giant eagle, its wings spread above the sign, "Home of the Screaming Eagles." The sight of the huge bird comforted her, reminding her of the days when she felt safe, when the country seemed so certain about things, before all of the madness of the last few years.

She checked in at Eastern Airlines, her hand shaking slightly as she presented her ticket to the agent. The truth was she was flat-out scared to death of her very first airplane ride. Pie dissolved in tears while Sally hugged Stanton and her mother one last time, and quickly boarded the plane. She herself didn't cry until she reached her seat and saw her mother standing inside the terminal, staring out at the plane. Stanton held her arm, supporting her. A lock of hair had fallen on Pie's forehead. Sally placed her fingers on the window in a futile attempt to reach out and brush it away. Her shoulders were heavy as she leaned back into the seat and clumsily buckled her seat belt, struggling through her tears. Then the engines began to roar and the aircraft sped down the tarmac, lifting them up into in sky and heading into the future. She could feel the silence and peace as they rose up into and above the clouds, bright light surrounding them.

Well, here I go, Sally told herself weakly, gritting her teeth with resignation. I don't know if this is right or not, but I'm in it now. In a small gesture, she waved her fist from right to left. Roll Tide, Roll!

CHAPTER FIVE

MIAMI BREEZE
MAY 25, 1970   MIAMI, FLORIDA

The noise and tension bounced off the walls of the Miami Airlines Motel as members of Class 18 prepared for their first day of training as flight attendants with Pan American World Airways. Along the worn corridors and rooms of the venerable motel, a pervasive smell of mold, old paint and Lysol clashed with perfume, deodorant and cigarette smoke. A few dozen young women thronged the hallways, dashing back and forth through open doors, inspecting their appearance, making last minute touches to make-up and hair, sobbing on long-distance telephone calls to boyfriends and parents, importuning for love or money or both, and generally adding to the din of excitement over their new careers. In a few moments, they would be heading across the street to the International Flight Training Academy to begin classes.

In Room 118, four of these young women waited quietly, dressed and ready but strangely subdued in the midst of the hubbub in the hallway. The sultry Miami breeze blew through the open door. They had arrived with their fellow trainees over the weekend one by one, meeting assigned roommates as they knocked on doors, forging new friendships as well as venturing out to meet other trainees in other rooms down the hall or at mealtimes.

Sally thought of the incredible changes in her life in just 24 hours: flying from Kentucky and the watchful eye of Sugar Pie to this huge, flat airport city of Miami, meeting so many new people. She sat with her roommates, two of whom had checked in late the night before and gone straight out without unpacking their suitcases. They had barely introduced themselves beyond their names—Daphne and Zoe—and a breezy, "Hello, see you later!"

Sally and the fourth girl had eaten dinner together the night before, and become acquainted. She was Pualani Kanawai from Hawai'i. With a gentle voice, caramel skin and almost hip-length black hair, she had travelled all over Asia with a hula dance troupe and spoke fluent Japanese. "The language, hey, it's the only reason they hired me," she'd said, as Sally had described her small-town life and they gawked at the glamorous girls at other tables.

Nervous and excited, they waited, watching the clock. Sally smoothed the skirt of her beige suit, checking her stockings and her honey-brown three-inch regulation heels. Her briefcase held her training manual, pens, her passport and copies of her papers.

On top of the bed next to hers, Zoe Longfield lay, clad in a navy-blue jumper, dark stockings, black heels and a silver medallion encircling her throat. She wore sunglasses and a pained expression as she rubbed her hands over her legs, mumbling about itchy bug-bites.

Pualani had unpacked the day before, and bought a huge supply of soda and chips, which she now offered to the girls, and munched contentedly. Dressed in a rose-colored shift and beige pumps that set off her golden skin, she cooed sympathetically at Zoe's plight, offering a medicinal cream from her store-box. Zoe tore down her hose and slathered her legs, which were covered with inflamed bites that reddened her skin. She adjusted her hose and sighed, "Ahh, better." Her roommates gaped. "Don't ask," she said nonchalantly. "They're from my last job as a tour guide in the jungles of South America. Later. I'll explain later."

The last occupant of the room groaned, her hand across her forehead, then stood up. Daphne Orrington-Black was a tall, glamorous woman with long wavy hair pulled into a tight bun, huge brown eyes and luxurious eyelashes, dramatic makeup and a model's stance. Her white linen dress was belted, her long, tanned legs glowing above strapped white high-heeled sandals.

"There is absolutely no point in going Over There," she said in a dramatic low voice, her English accent giving emphasis to her words. She looked at all of them over her huge sunglasses. "We did the unforgiveable; we went out for drinks and got caught. That bloody little man from Pan Am saw us, and he is sure to run us out on a rail. So sorry, darling, and you don't even drink." The last comment was addressed to Zoe, who had been persuaded to accompany Daphne for several illicit cocktails at the motel's seedy bar, forbidden to all trainees. "Actually, I wouldn't care except that it was such a grotty place and absolutely not worth the trouble. And my head is killing me." She walked to the bathroom to pop another aspirin.

Pualani giggled. "We can say that Sally and I didn't hear the doorbell, which is actually true. Daphne and Zoe were locked out of the room and had to wait in the bar until the front desk clerk came back to let them in." Sally nodded and smiled conspiratorially.

Daphne considered the idea. "Well, it might just work, so long as he decides not to remember our telling him about having dinner at the Versailles Club in Little Havana, and how we danced with his mate who owned the place."

They laughed, happy with the plan, and left the room. They struck off across the six lanes of heavy morning traffic on 36th Street. Zoe and Daphne approached the entrance, led by Pualani and Sally who headed purposefully toward the steps.

Manuel "Manny" Ortiz was at his station, welcoming the new students, checking his watch. The slight, dapper, grey-haired man in blue blazer and grey slacks stood on the steps of Pan Am's International Flight Training Academy, modeled after the United States Embassy in New Delhi, India.

Manny had been part of Pan Am's impressive international history for most of his life. Cuban born, Manny had joined Pan American's small operation in Havana straight out of a rakish nightclub in 1932, when the rum-running business to Florida was slacking off and the payoffs to some of the Havana waterfront thugs weren't working so well. He'd worked as a passenger boatman, then flight steward and eventually Purser, flying all over the world until his appointment at the training academy. He was Pan Am's trusted man in rough places, from the politicians and pundits of City Hall, to the Cuban underworld of Key Biscayne and the glittering high-life of Miami Beach.

The instructors at the Academy were busier than ever training the large numbers of eager young women for the new Boeing 747. Pan Am had inaugurated most of Boeing's new aircraft from pistons to the jet age, and the huge new model, they knew, would change aviation forever.

Manny surveyed the four women approaching him, sensing mischief.

"Oh, you must be Mr. Ortiz," said Sally in her most polite Southern drawl, her words flowing. "I just want to apologize so much for having caused a terrible problem for our roommates last night." She told their tale about not hearing the doorbell, while Pualani nodded seriously. Manny had heard all of these sorts of stories before, and knew exactly how high-spirited young women behaved. Besides, he said to himself, at least the girls had the class to go out and have their fun in a good Cuban establishment before visiting the sleazy motel bar.

The bar had been very busy the night before, filled to capacity, and Manny held court from his usual seat. He had spotted two good-looking young women who clearly needed a reminder that the bar was off-limits. Sighing, he had sauntered across the room to perform his duty.

Now those same young women stood before him, downcast and contrite, waiting to hear their fate as soon as their friend finished with her ridiculous explanation. "We are so sorry," said Zoe, "it will absolutely never happen again."

Manny surveyed them with a Cuban shrug and a big smile. "Ladies, ladies, I'm sorry, but I just don't know what you are talking about. I don't remember seeing you before this moment, and I look forward to working with you during the next weeks!"

The girls clapped in thanksgiving, and rushed into the large airy vestibule, decorated with an array of international flags. The walls held huge oil paintings and exotic posters from the 1930's showing the *Yankee Clipper* sailing ship with its airborne counterpart. Large photographs featured celebrities boarding Pan Am planes, smiling and jaunty. The 25 new trainees inspected the surroundings with interest, while Pualani pointed out a sepia-toned photograph of the famous *China Clipper* landing in Honolulu in 1935.

"We look like cookie-cutter Barbie dolls," Zoe whispered to her roommates. The circle of women was a matched set of pearly teeth, bouffant hairstyles, poster-girl makeup, smiles, lots of teeth and legs.

Daphne winked. "Don't worry, darlings. We're fine. We dodged one bullet—we're here to stay!"

The instructors took their places, and the room fell silent. A mature, well-groomed woman stepped to the front. "Ladies, good morning and welcome to Pan American World Airways," she began. "I am Susanna Jones, Director of the Academy. For the next six weeks, your instructors will introduce you to Pan Am's distinguished history, our regulations and procedures and our expectations for your careers with us. During this time, you will be provided with information and practical homework assignments, as well as essential documentation and visa requirements for many of you."

She shifted almost to attention and resumed. "Your status—and let me repeat, your very recognizable *status*—as Pan Am employees will permit unmatched access to a way of life, and a reputation for excellence. Any infraction of any rule, however trivial it may seem, will have consequences. You are subject to termination at any time, for any reason, during your training and probationary period, up to six months from today. This is a serious and important workplace, and we expect to receive your utmost effort and cooperation. Thank you for your attention. Now, let us begin." The room was utterly silent as the young women absorbed the import of the chilly announcement.

Another woman stepped forward. "Good morning, ladies. My name is Janet Weygood, and I'll be your lead instructor in policies, procedures and regulations. Manny Ortiz, here" she said, nodding to Manny who bobbed his head, "will provide technical instruction for in-flight services: bar and food preparation, announcements and protocols, especially in intercultural activities."

"At the back of the room, you'll see Frank Murphy, who will train you on emergency procedures. Later, you will meet our team of fitters and makeup experts to learn about Pan Am uniform and appearance standards."

She continued. "As you know, you'll be working with fellow flight attendants from 50 states and all over the world. Your Class 18 includes representatives from six nations and 12 states. Let's take a short break to get to know the person to your immediate right so you can tell us about her over a cup of coffee." Janet directed the class toward a buffet along the wall, heading toward it herself, shaking hands in welcome as she passed. The group followed, talking excitedly.

Sally joined Zoe and Daphne, eager to learn more and to introduce Zoe, who was talking to Daphne. "What on earth can I say about you that's believable? Standard DP stuff?"

Daphne shrugged. "Well, just tell them I was born in Cairo where my father was an airline executive, I was raised in several overseas locations, went to school in England and have done some fashion design and merchandising. Very dull, very normal sort of thing, you know."

"Right. Normal," said Zoe. "Okay, Sally, you can introduce me as the other DP."

"What's a deepee?" Sally wondered.

Zoe smiled. "It's capital D.P., short for 'displaced person,' essentially anyone who has been pulled out of their home environment and sent somewhere else. It can mean political refugees— like Eastern Europeans after World War II—or between India and Pakistan, but there are lots of other places in the world where people have been moved around in strange new environments, with no roots. In a way, that's what we'll be," she smiled, "only a lot more comfortable." She sketched out her background, while Sally took notes for the introduction.

Janet tapped a pen smartly on a glass, signaling resumption of the briefing. A student from Oregon cleared her throat nervously, welcoming a Swedish beauty that introduced a pretty black girl from Boston named Clarice James, holder of a master's degree in French literature from the Sorbonne. Several other Japanese, American and Swedish girls were acknowledged, including Pualani, and on it went around the circle until Sally was introduced as "a real southern lady from western Kentucky, who had never flown until her flight to Miami two days ago."

Sally stood, feeling like a country bumpkin and said, "I'd like for you to meet Zoe Longfield. She was raised in Burma, educated in Darjeeling, India and attended Northwestern University, studying archaeology. She's been a tour guide to places I've never even heard of in South America, and she speaks Burmese, French and a little Spanish, in addition to English." She smiled, and took her seat.

Zoe said, "Please meet Daphne Orrington-Black." Just intoning the name changed the tenor of the room, where most of the girls had led sheltered lives of suburban privilege.

"Daphne's father was an airline executive with British Overseas Airways Corporation," said Zoe. "She was born in Cairo, Egypt, and she's lived in Hong Kong, Nassau, Frankfurt and Johannesburg. She was schooled in England, worked as a model for Mary Quant in London and is looking forward to her career with Pan Am." God, she thought, how fatuous I sound.

Daphne sat relaxed and smiling faintly, perfectly groomed and poised. The Director leaned forward with interest. "Tell us, Daphne, with your father working for BOAC, how is it that you chose Pan Am instead?"

Daphne flashed a grin, "Well, I'd have to say the British are known to be a bit stuffy, and here you have lovely men like Manny to show us the ropes in the proper way." There was a coughing fit from Janet and Manny's corner, and giggle around the room, as the Director smiled and moved on to the next trainee.

After that, the biographies seemed to merge: blonde hair, check; long legs, check; flashing smiles; check, sweet voices, check. Zoe groaned inwardly, feeling inadequate and lumpish, her bites itching. Sally sat up straighter, wondering if she could really pass muster. All these girls were beautiful, and had interesting backgrounds. All spoke one or more languages in addition to English. And all of them seemed totally at ease, while she squirmed.

When the introductions were over, the trainees broke into smaller groups in different classrooms, where they were issued a formidable three-ring binder of charts, tables, menus and drink recipes. Taking their seats in a mockup of a First Class cabin complete with a tiny galley area, they waited nervously.

Manny swept into the front of the mock cabin and said: "I'm the Pope. How do you greet me?"

A trainee spoke up timidly, "Your Highness?"

Manny smiled, and whipped around. "You, Miss England? The

Pope just boarded your aircraft. How do you greet him?"

Daphne considered, "Well, I'm Protestant, so I'd just incline my head slightly, but I should think the Catholics would be groveling heavily." She acknowledged the titters of amusement.

Manny said, "Yes, but how do you address him? How do you address the Queen? Do you just say, 'Hi'? What do you say to welcome an ambassador, or a general? Or a child? Or a Buddhist monk? How do you know the difference? Where do you go for guidance?"

As he spoke, he tapped the book in his hand. "Here are your answers. Your *In-Flight Manual*. In this little blue book is all the protocol you could ever need in any situation, and you will be reading it, because it will matter a great deal in your future." Clarice already had her head buried in the index, looking through the lists of subjects to be covered.

Manny smiled. "There are two things you need to use—eye contact and your greeting. You get those wrong, you are a peasant."

Clarice looked up sharply, "Well, we are Americans. We got rid of all those kings and queens, and a few other things, too."

Manny gestured with the book, "Ah, but you must have good breeding and good manners, and that is what civilization is all about. And now, we give you a tool to tell you how to exercise that confidence in yourself. Let's get started. Turn to page four in the Protocol section."

Pages rustled as they read the lists of proper terms of address and the order of rank and precedence, charts of the peerage and military insignia, all incredibly complex and foreign to most of the girls.

Manny took them through the exercise. "You say, 'Your Holiness' and a bow of the head for the Pope and the Dalai Lama. To address a king or queen, 'Your Majesty', a nod on the first greeting, then 'Ma'am' or 'Sir' after that."

He went on. "Never speak unless spoken to, never appear to hear their conversation, never engage in casual conversation unless initiated by the distinguished person, never seem to hover, and absolutely never, ever ask for an autograph or to have a picture taken with them."

Quizzes followed, then more heavy manuals, which outlined

service requirements. One of the lists which intrigued Zoe was a roster of aircraft names and tail numbers ... all Pan Am aircraft were "Clippers", named after the fast and beautifully designed tea-trading ships that raced across the world's oceans in the 18th century. No other airline, stated the article, allowed an aircraft to be called by anything other than its corporate name.

After lunch, Manny delivered them to Janet Weygood for the more technical lessons on airline operations, ticketing, city codes and rules of carriage. It was a long day, and they groaned as the piles of books and manuals grew, and the homework assignments.

At the end of the day, they walked back across 36th Street with their bulging book bags to the accompanying whistles and whoops of the traffic cowboys. Zoe's stomach rumbled. A collection was taken to buy supplies for a poolside study session in half an hour.

Daphne and Zoe quickly located a Cuban liquor store in the next block, where they bought an Imperial quart of gin, two quarts of fresh orange juice and a bottle of soda water. Zoe grabbed cans of tonic water for herself, while Sally and Pua ordered up Cuban *tapas* snacks at a small snack bar. As she stood in line at the cashier's station, Sally listened idly to the news on the radio.

"...3:00 p.m. Eastern Standard Time today," whined the broadcaster's voice through a tinny receiver, "a 727 aircraft was hijacked from Chicago to Havana by a lone male passenger allegedly holding a weapon and two passengers as human shields. This is the fourth hijacking to Cuba this year. Authorities noted the record number of 33 hijackings in 1969, up from 15 in 1968." Sally shook her head, thinking of the dreadful statistics.

At the pool, the trainees sat exhausted from the day's lessons, settling on lounge chairs and cracking tiles under an old frangipani tree. Zoe went for ice while Daphne mixed cocktails and chivvied Pua and Sally to bring more glasses from the room, saying, "Like the Greeks—that's the first sacred rule: always bring your own drinking cup." They laughed and toasted each other, relieved and exhilarated, inhaling the warm evening air. Pua picked plumeria blossoms for each girl to tuck behind an ear, explaining the Polynesian custom.

On the other side of the pool, a group of young men eyed the new trainees, appraising them carefully. Zoe nodded, "Those must be the 'lounge lizards,' guys who hang around in hotel lobbies and swimming pools all over the world to ogle the flight attendants…uh, that's us!" She sipped her juice and waved a hand at the men, who smiled in acknowledgement.

"My God," said Sally, "How on earth do we absorb all this stuff? It's a boatload of information." She leaned back on a rusty chaise lounge, reviewing another list of airline city codes.

Clarice munched on the spicy peanuts. "No, it's more than the words in the books," she said. "It's an attitude. We'll be up there sharing the same space with lots of different kinds of people and it's up to us to find the common ground."

Daphne twirled her drink. "Spot on, darling. It is attitude—ours. No matter what happens, we must be simply unflappable. We are confident, we are gracious, and we make them laugh. And, of course, mum's the word. "

Sally looked around, frowning slightly and biting her lower lip, "Well, it may sound like a really dumb question, but I heard a report about a hijacking today from Chicago to Cuba. It said there were 33 hijackings last year, up from 15 the year before with four so far this year. What do you think of that? I mean, is this dangerous stuff we're getting into? Who protects *us*?"

The group murmured, then Daphne nodded. "Yes, it can be dangerous. It'll be constant change and movement, and well, adventure, which is sometimes scary but always exciting."

Pua said, "Yeah, it's pretty scary, but right now I'm going to go hijack me some dinner."

Amidst the laughter, Sally repeated her question. "Yes, but seriously, who protects us?" Her roommates started to move out of the pool area towards the buffet.

Zoe turned to her, "Why are you so worried about this, Sally?"

"It's just that there have been so many changes in the last years," Sally replied. "So much has happened. The 60s set off an explosion, and the pieces haven't fallen back to earth yet in a way I can understand. I think that's what makes me nervous. There's so much I don't know." She rattled the ice cubes in her empty glass. "I don't think anything scares you, does it?"

"Not anymore," replied Zoe emphatically. "After the way I grew up and lived, it's all about living on the edge and facing the fear."

"Really?" said Sally. "I thought with your background you'd be on your way to being a spy or an ambassador, or a professor of Asian history or something."

"You never know. There are lots of ways to play, just don't be afraid to try." Zoe winked and patted Sally's arm. "You just have to keep the balance, and look way out ahead. Now come on, let's join the others. I'm starving!"

Classes reconvened at 8 a.m. sharp, and Manny waded into the requirements of the Geneva Convention. He stated, "The original Convention in 1864 developed a code for the treatment of battlefield casualties. Then, after World War II, the protocols described specific treatment for prisoners of war, including civilians in a noncombat support role, and eventually civilian aircraft crewmembers." The trainees were surprised to learn that they were required to carry special-issue Geneva Cards as Second Lieutenants in the US Air Force if they were working flights that took them into war zones, such as Vietnam. Manny looked up. "What it really means, ladies, is that if you get captured in a war zone, your captors have to treat you with respect." He looked around at the laughing trainees. "But it is no joke, and it has never been tested, so don't go looking for trouble."

Sally raised her hand. "Manny, I just heard last night that there was another hijacking yesterday. Is…is this something we need to know about? Do these situations fall under the Geneva Convention rules?"

Manny sighed and nodded. "Yes, there was a hijacking yesterday, and you need to know about these things." He paced the room, looking thoughtful, then directed them to a chapter entitled, "Unusual In-Flight Conditions and Procedures." He pointed out the types of information needed for various disasters and emergencies, from hijackings, city evacuations and highly contagious communicable diseases, to drunks and stowaways. The students reviewed the lists and instructions with worried frowns.

Daphne joked, "Well this isn't quite what I had in mind for the glamour and excitement of travel."

Sally shook her head, thinking they had not bargained for these alarming conditions.

Manny said, "Don't worry. The first thing you have to know is that you have time here to ask your questions and get your answers, and all of the emergency procedures will be covered. These hijackings are not publicized, but nobody has ever been killed or injured, and so far, the policy of cooperation works. Obviously, if there is a growing trend in violent behavior, we'll need to do other things." He went on through the section, explaining the rationale behind every policy, the support system and backups in the air and on the ground.

He said, "This is a lot to throw at you on only your second day, but you asked about a serious new aspect of our business because of the hijacking yesterday, so I want to be sure you understand that Pan Am is a huge global corporation that takes all sorts of risks 24 hours a day, 365 days a year, in every country and in every time zone."

Zoe said, "I think it's about our attitude. Nothing will happen that we can't handle, right?" Manny nodded reassuringly, and the students relaxed.

That night, the conversation at the pool centered on the impacts of international conflicts, and of the great unknowns out in the world. But they knew little and cared even less, and talk quickly moved to their social plans, and a cadre of young military pilots across the pool.

The next weeks passed in a blur as they progressed through the intricacies of Pan Am's First Class service requirements, and learned their way around the equipment in tiny kitchens called "galleys". They learned to cook and carve a roast round of beef as well as other entrées, coddle eggs in an electric hot-water pot using a long martini stirrer and a splash of vinegar, and prepare "millionaire martinis" by shaking gin and vermouth over ice in a glass capped with a paper crew cup, then decanting the chilled silvery liquid.

Daphne bemoaned the lack of "proper" ingredients as she

practiced. Half-seriously, she complained, "We can't possibly know what we're mixing if we can't try a sip now and again. I mean, the champagne could have gone off, or the Bordeaux soured!"

Manny shook his hand in admonition. Drinking in uniform was never allowed, and meant instant dismissal with no recourse.

Manny described past glories of the flying boat days and the double-decker Stratocruisers of the 1950s, the elaborate eight-course meals cooked on board entirely from scratch by trained chefs, with menus developed by Maxim's of Paris. He educated them in elaborate service techniques for the finest Iranian caviar and condiments, the differences between gravlax and smoked salmon, Bordeaux and Burgundy, and how to identify the yeasty, toasty smell of good French champagne. A salad could be served before or after the entree, cheese or dessert courses could be interchangeable depending on the area and time of day. They learned formal "French Service" for plating and table settings, and practiced in teams as their skills progressed.

After a few weeks of interminable service and technical study, Janet Weygood greeted them at the door one sunny morning, and led them down hallways to another section of the Academy, a long room lined with curtains and mirrors.

She said, "Ladies, this is an important day. You have been given seniority numbers, which will be yours for your entire career with Pan Am. They were assigned by your date-of-hire and alphabetical order within the class, and will determine your flight assignment every month, for base assignments, for vacation, your working assignments on the aircraft, possible furloughs and even your retirement date in the dim, distant future." The numbers were called. Pua was #1 in the class, Zoe trailing at #22. They had lost three class members to visa problems or for other reasons. They never knew why; just one day the girls were gone.

Janet said, "Now, line up in the order of your seniority: Pua first, Zoe last, and try on your uniforms."

Seamstresses drew curtains to create a row of private, mirrored booths around the walls of the room, with rolling racks of new uniforms in various sizes. The uniform, designed by Evan Picone, featured a quasi-equestrian jacket, stock tie and bowler hat, with an option of skirt or jumper, in either beige or blue, and complementary honey-brown pumps and purses. The room buzzed as the fitters worked with excited students, choosing their sizes and tailoring as needed.

Daphne tried unsuccessfully to raise the hem of the blue skirt another four inches. Sally was entranced by the sophistication of the style, color and details. Pua surveyed the beige jumper, and clapped her hands with joy. They checked their images in the long mirrors, tipping the bowler hats this way or that.

In the afternoon sessions, each trainee had their make-up and hair done by professionals, the hair stylists following food safety regulations by gathering longer hair into the mandatory chignon, or a "George Washington" ponytail accented with a bow of grosgrain ribbon. Pua's eyes were misty as two feet of silky black hair was trimmed, and fell to the salon floor. Most of the trainees opted for longer hairstyles, which suited the uniform's image.

Special makeup and manicure workshops were held, and Daphne hosted one on how to apply false eyelashes, demonstrating a technique of clipping each eyelash into small segments and gluing each section on top of one's own lashes. Pualani, chomping on chips, went off into gales of laughter as the little lash-bits slipped from her lash-line into her eye. "Eh, I got cockroach legs crawling up my eyeball!" she exclaimed in island slang.

At the nightly pool gathering, they made plans for the upcoming weekend. Daphne was visiting a boyfriend in Nassau. Zoe said, "Clarice, Pua, Sally, why don't we go visit the original Pan Am terminal? It's now Miami's City Hall down in Dinner Key, and we can check out Coconut Grove?

Broke and innovative, they discussed bus schedules and pored over a city map. Across the pool, one of the regulars looked at them, measuring his odds. "Hey, ladies, I'm helping install a mural there. In fact, I'm planning a trip tomorrow morning. I could get you back by late afternoon if that works? I'm Ken, by the way...." He left the sentence hanging.

The young women looked at each other, gauging the opportunity to get to their destination without hassling with bus schedules. They nodded. "Okay, Ken," said Zoe, "you're on, but we're on a serious mission, not out to party."

Cruising down 36th Street in Ken's dilapidated Cadillac convertible, they savored freedom. "Our first day out of jail!" yelled Sally over the wind, as they gawked at the gracious boulevards lined with red-orange Royal Poinciana trees and art deco homes all the way down to South Miami near the Key Biscayne Causeway. With a flourish, Ken pulled into a large circular driveway in front of an imposing building. A large sign proclaimed: *City Hall, Miami, Florida—National Register for Historic Places—Gateway to the Americas.*

"I'll be back in a second," instructed Ken, leaving the car and ducking into the main building. He emerged in moments with a chubby young man whom he introduced as Jimbo.

Jimbo smiled, "Yeah, Kenny said you girls are new stews and want to see some of the old stuff." He waved his arm in a sweeping motion as they walked into the building. "Well, here it is!" The girls were astonished to see a huge mosaic mural being installed in the lobby, featuring the western hemisphere's map detail, compass roses, waves, winds and whimsical decoration.

Clarice approached the mural, tracing the early routes of Pan Am's Clippers throughout the Americas. "Why, this is magnificent," she said.

"Come this way," said Jimbo, motioning them towards a hallway that led to the large, dimly lit Council Chambers, and pointed up towards the ceiling. A work light picked out the glint of silver from another massive mural covering the walls and ceiling. "You see," Jimbo said, waving a flashlight that picked up the gleam of blue and silver far above their heads, "This was the old terminal hall, and the mural is an original design in art-deco style, of the signs of the zodiac and Pan Am routes." He moved the flashlight around the room, "Look, it matches the work on the beams."

Sally and Zoe walked slowly, craning their necks, and examining the old photographs that depicted the arrival and departure of the Pan Am flying boats at Dinner Key in the 1930's. There were pictures of celebrities, statesmen, and the serious faces of crewmembers and ground personnel in uniform, readying these latter-day Clipper ships of the airways to soar around the globe.

Emerging from the shadows of the former Pan Am terminal, they strolled with Ken and Jimbo through the quaint hippie section of nearby Coconut Grove, finding a ramshackle restaurant featuring stone crabs and conch soup. "You know, Ken," said Zoe, "we sure owe you an apology. We had you pegged for a lounge lizard, but you really are a good guy and so is Jimbo."

"The lunch is on us," said Clarice, lifting her glass and saluting the two men.

"I wouldn't have missed this for anything," said Sally, as they walked to the car.

Jimbo bowed and held the car door open, and they waved goodbye as they drove back out toward Key Biscayne Bay, past the dappled waters that had silently recorded so many adventures so long ago.

The weekend before their final week in training, the four roommates and Clarice boarded an early morning Greyhound Bus bound for Key West, to visit Pan Am's first departure site. They exclaimed at the beauty of the endless islands marking the Florida Keys, the miles of causeways across the shallow blue-green waters.

At Dog Key and Marathon Key, they stopped for breaks and read the tourist literature on the peeling walls of the little museum. Brochures spoke of huge storms, and treasure ships sunk in hurricanes of 1715 and 1733.

"Wow," Zoe said, checking the museum display cases, "it says here that the treasure hunters in these Keys are for real. One guy has been searching for a Spanish Galleon called *Nuestra Senora de Atocha*, and just look at the pictures of doubloons and silver pieces they've found right off this beach."

Pua examined the photos, "Hey, Zoe, it looks just like your silver coin, doesn't it?"

Zoe looked again; sure enough, it described a galleon found in the Philippines, with thousands of silver coins embedded in coral. They read the stories of voyages from Spain to Mexico, and thence to the Spanish possessions in the Philippines and the Spice Islands. There, stolen silver from Mexico paid for the exotic silks, cinnamon and peppercorns so highly prized in Spain. She said slyly, "That's my next ambition: treasure hunting in blue waters. With lots of handsome naked divers." They laughed, though Sally blushed at the implication.

After a long, thirsty day on the bus, they checked into a little inn next to the Ernest Hemingway house in Key West, and rounded up bottles of tequila, limejuice, and Zoe's tonic. They gathered on the shore to celebrate in the balmy twilight. As they worked their way through the bottle, they told stories of their native places, the meaning of friendship and love, their hopes for the future.

Pua described her huge extended family of Hawai'ian, Japanese, Chinese, Portuguese and Filipino relatives. She said, "The food just never quits at our parties and luaus; they bring every possible dish from their home country!"

Zoe raised her glass of tonic to the rest of them who were a little tipsy from the tequila. "It would be interesting to be like you folks—normal—with roots."

Daphne snickered, "Yes, and I'll take the country house and the Rolls-Royce, too, please."

Sally laughed and extended her hand, including them all in the gesture. "Are you kidding? I wanted to be all of you. You rode elephants before school, and grew up in exotic islands, and studied in Paris, and modeled. I just...am." She shrugged, thinking of what Pie would say if she saw her, slightly drunk on a public beach at sunset. The tequila in the bottle sank rapidly as they drank and talked and laughed. By early evening, the five were standing hip deep in the blue waters of the Caribbean while Zoe told pirate stories, arms around each other's shoulders.

Sally said, "Zoe, you never loose control, do you? Is that why you don't drink?"

Zoe hugged Sally, her eyes dark. "Like I said, Sally. There are all sorts of ways to play. I just happen to like being in control." She turned away, but Sally saw her eyes following a tall young black man, his eyes beckoning.

The sun, liquid and golden, sank slowly behind the palm trees. The shadows whispered.

The last week of training began with visits to health clinics, a series of essential inoculations required by the World Health Organization, and in some cases, TB scans. One student never reappeared for the next tests. Zoe was double-checked for malaria, which she'd had as a child. She joked, "That's why I drink so much tonic water." Sally groaned. Several trainees had been sent off for dental work or medical tests.

After classes, Zoe and Sally finally returned to their room, having noted the absence of Pua and Daphne all day. There, Pua sat quietly, looking up when they entered. "And just where have you been hiding, Miss Hawai'i?" said Sally.

Pua looked up gravely. "Well, actually, I had some...some important personal business that I had to take care of." Daphne came in, the room suddenly silent.

Zoe sensed something, her eyes narrowed. "And? Can your friends help you?"

Pua burst into tears. "It's done. I was afraid of this, and now it's over." Daphne held her shoulders. "Really, it's all fine now."

"Ah, shit," said Zoe. "What have you done?"

Pua looked at her sadly, her hand clutching her robe. "Well, it's the old story. Boy meets girl, girl gets hired by Pan Am, they party heavy on the beach...then...." Her voice faltered. "Girl gets caught, dammit." She sobbed. Daphne shushed her.

Zoe and Sally understood in an instant. Pua wiped her eyes. "Thank God for the Director and Manny, who arranged everything, and Daphne was with me to keep me steady." Pua hugged them close. "You know, I feel so stupid. The guy was a *haole* tourist, totally unacceptable to my family. But it's done, and I'm ready to fly."

Zoe nodded and said, "You did the right thing. I don't mean to sound cavalier about it, but it's best just to move on, and be smarter in the future." The women nodded, reluctantly. Sally cried with Pua, sisters, hugging each other.

At the end of the week, they prepared for the most important day of training, having completed their mandatory Federal Aviation Administration written examination in the morning. After lunch in the comfortable training academy, they boarded a terminal bus to the Pan Am Cargo section.

"Make no mistake," said Frank Murphy over the public address system, "you may think you're there to serve champagne and caviar, but the FAA wants you there to get people out of that airplane in an emergency and save lives. Your job is to get a planeload of people evacuated in 90 seconds."

The class looked blank. Zoe whispered to Pua, "Are you strong enough to do this?" Pua hugged her, "It's going to be just fine, it's okay now and I'll take it easy tonight."

Frank continued. "That's right. After 90 seconds, human beings are overwhelmed by toxic fumes that are the byproducts of burning fuel and other parts of the aircraft," said Murphy. "Who is going to instruct passengers how to inflate life rafts and activate the attached radio beacons in the event of a water ditching? That's right, you are. That's why you have to be strong and fit enough to lift and remove the aircraft doors over the wings. Everything that happens on that plane, every person who boards, should not escape your scrutiny. You must always be watching. Next to the pilots, who will be trying like hell to get that plane on the ground safely, *you* are the first line of defense in an emergency."

The bus braked noisily at the metal steps up to *Clipper Morning Light*, which had been specially positioned for this training exercise. Clustered together on the tarmac in the hot sun, they were awed by the huge bulk of the 747—the largest commercial aircraft ever flown—parked next to a Boeing 707 and two Boeing 727 freighter aircraft nearby.

They rushed up the metal steps and took seats in the second section as instructed. Frank said, "This particular event will be filmed for a training video, because we need to make sure we're preparing our crews properly." Murphy's eyes looked out over the top of his horn-rimmed glasses, gauging the reactions on each individual face.

Throughout the five cabins, white-shirted instructors, impassive FAA inspectors and Boeing Corporation personnel stood by to take notes on the equipment, the speed, and the skill and training level of the human element, the crew. Airline personnel and volunteers, hot and sweaty on this hazy afternoon in early June of 1970, began filing onto the plane and quietly filling the seats.

Sally stood poised at her station, the thought running through her head yet again, who takes care of us? The aircraft was silent, its occupants tense and nervous. This was it.

Then Frank boomed instructions. "Ladies and gentlemen, this is your Captain. Prepare to evacuate immediately!" Pua and Sally leaped into action, manning both sides of the second starboard door, commanding passengers. Sally shielded Pua, taking the lead position.

"This way! This way! Leave everything behind. Jump! Jump! Jump! Run away from the engines!" They yelled and yelled until they were hoarse.

At the front left-hand door, Zoe and Daphne attempted to shove open a recalcitrant door, returning it to a locked and reset position, then reopening it to the explosive sound of an inflating evacuation slide. The rapidly unfolding slide caused a chip from the lower edge of its cover to snap away and bounce off her right shin. "Ow!" Zoe yelped, as the passengers moved rapidly toward her exit door. Daphne blocked their way while Zoe checked the full deployment of the slide, then commenced the same command sequence. Noise filled the cabin, along with the heavy smell of JTD-9 fuel, and the cameras whirred.

After all of the passengers were safely out of the cabin, Zoe and Daphne kicked off their heels and jumped into the slide, zipping to the bottom in seconds. Down on the tarmac, they regrouped with their classmates around Frank, checking their time, hugging one another in excitement.

"That was an incredible rush!" Sally exulted.

The FAA crew chief blew a whistle and gave a high thumbs-up sign on the evacuation timing; the volunteer passengers, film crew and ramp staff clapped enthusiastically and the girls whooped in exultation. Zoe noticed with annoyance that her stockings were snagged and her right leg bleeding from the sharp plastic chip. She shrugged it off, applying spit to the wound.

At the "debriefing" party by the pool that night, the remaining trainees and instructors gathered. Manny embraced them all, congratulating them on their performance. Frank Murphy, newly freed of his onerous duty as FAA qualification watchdog, got almost ridiculously plastered and sang Frank Sinatra love songs to the two Japanese students.

Zoe stayed for a while, then made her excuses. Sally watched her disappearing with a man who looked like...someone they'd seen in Key West.

The next morning, their graduation day, the trainees assembled in dignified silence under the flags in the atrium, each one smartly outfitted in accordance with regulations. Director Jones congratulated each of them as she pinned a pair of gold-plated single wings onto their crisp new jackets. Dutifully, they posed for class pictures with Manny, Janet and Frank.

Zoe whispered to her roommates, "Oh, my God. Now we really *do* look like Barbie dolls!"

Daphne smiled at Zoe, "Nonsense. We are DPs: doubly perfect!"

Pualani nudged Clarice, "Eh, *haole* girls, there's some Brown Barbies in the room!"

Then, the reading of the Base Assignments began for the new stewardesses. Pualani and the Japanese girls were slated for Honolulu because of their language capabilities, while five, including Zoe and Daphne would remain in Miami. Sally, Clarice and the rest would be going to New York. The members of Class 18 hugged, laughed and cried at the reality of separation. But they all knew they were ready to fly.

That evening, they gathered at the Palm Bay Club for a graduation party. Manny brought along some fellow Cuban Pursers, and Ken and his friends showed up to help send them off. Manny took turns dancing with each one. As they moved to the music, they celebrated the starry skies, the wash of the waves, the happiness of the moment and the adventures ahead. In the distance, aircraft lights beckoned in the twilight, and contrails crossed the sunset sky.

And in the shadows of the mangrove swamps beyond the Club's manicured grounds, ancient alligators and whip-smooth cottonmouths floated, at peace, waiting their turn.

CHAPTER SIX

AFRICAN QUEENS
SEPTEMBER 6, 1970   ROME, ITALY

Struggling out of bed after four hours of sleep, Sally forced herself to shower and walk around the quiet neighborhood surrounding the hotel in the old Trastevere Quarter of Rome. She stopped to look at the display windows of shops and art galleries. Following her nose, she wandered through a small piazza, past a small, ornate marble fountain, to a tiny coffee bar and the scent of strong, rich coffee. "Doo-way espresso, please," she said, in fractured English and Italian, adding a biscotti. Surveying Rome through oversized sunglasses, she felt truly horrible and out of sorts, a kind of semi-conscious state that was the behind-the-scenes reality of flying: the constant challenges of fighting to stay awake or forcing the body to sleep outside its natural rhythms.

Hiding behind her sunglasses, Sally hoped that she might look mysterious and sophisticated to people walking past. She sat quietly while the second espresso worked its caffeine magic, crushing a few springs of rosemary growing in the window box and inhaling its sharp, full fragrance, reflecting on her upside-down lifestyle.

She and Clarice had found an apartment on 36th Street in Manhattan, just a few blocks from the East Side Terminal. The building was four stories of unrelieved shabbiness with most of the eight units occupied by flight attendants from various airlines, qualifying it as a "stew zoo." The tiny entryway never ceased to fascinate Sally every time she unlocked the outside door and negotiated the hallway. It was a misbegotten stage set: folding leather chairs from Beirut, a camel saddle, giant masks from Africa, stacked cases of Portuguese wine, sometimes a Saigon ceramic elephant purchased during a reroute through Asia—all waiting for their tired owners to recover enough to come back downstairs and retrieve them.

To Sally, Manhattan was all concrete and hard edges and noise. She felt like a fish out of water with no trees and birds to soften the landscape. In training, she had been too busy to get homesick; but now she found herself reading and rereading her mother's letters and missing her bedroom at the Alamo. Zoe wrote occasionally about her adventures in Miami, and Sally found that she missed her, too. In spite of their very different backgrounds, Sally had somehow felt connected with Zoe. They shared stories of childhood trauma, teenage alienation and a sense of not fitting in. Sally loved and hated her deep roots in the old South; Zoe disdained the American roots denied her by growing up in Asia. On many a night during training, their beds at right angles to one another, they had talked, long past the time when Daphne and Pualani were fast asleep on the other side of the room.

These women had all been brought together by a company that hired self-motivated and adventurous people, many of whom were quite eccentric. They came from far-flung places and trained together to work with friends or strangers, their flexibility providing the common ground that bound them to one another. They had accepted the separations after training, knowing it was part of the adventure. Sally had been tearful; Zoe had shrugged, and reminded her that reunions were a short, free plane ride away.

Sally tried to get the most out of living in Manhattan. She and Clarice were invited to a few parties on the Upper East Side thrown by their Pan Am friends, and a sprinkling of young men had actually braved the trek up all those flights of stairs to fetch them for dates. But they were never in town long enough for anything to develop. Lawton had come up for a long weekend but left early, declaring he was allergic to so much concrete. Since they were still on reserve every month during their probationary period, it was impossible to plan trips home. Clarice worried about her aging mother. Occasionally, being so unsettled made Sally a little gloomy.

But Clarice was quick to cheer her up, pointing out the advantages of being based in New York. "Even though we're stuck flying mostly Caribbean milk runs, you just never know what's going to happen on the next trip. We've got all the jewels in Pan Am's crown flying out of JFK—we just have to get lucky!"

"You're right. One of the new-hires on my last flight got called out on a two-week diplomatic corps charter out of Washington," Sally agreed. "Then some of the press guys on the charter got her on the UN assignment list, so she doesn't have to do San Juan turn-arounds anymore!" They laughed. The base was big, impersonal and difficult, and it was sure as hell the other side of the moon from their hometowns. Sally said, "I feel at loose ends right now, but I wouldn't have missed this adventure for anything."

Clarice nodded. "Every time I walk up Park Avenue towards Grand Central Station, and that big old Pan Am building up there, I just feel a thrill when I see that "PAN AM" sign way at the top. I listen to the roar of the traffic and hear the crowds, and I just feel so alive!"

The early months of flying out of New York had been like a combination of boot camp and finishing school to most new flight crewmembers. On every trip there were equipment and people challenges: coffee makers and lavatories that didn't work, obnoxious drunks, seating duplications, and angry passengers who had missed their connecting flights due to weather or air traffic delays. There were quirky stories too; Sally had been briefly enthralled by a famous movie actor on the two-hour flight from Montego Bay to New York who ate only toast points and Beluga caviar, tossing back shots of vodka and singing gypsy songs, before passing out and requiring a wheelchair to leave the aircraft. Engine blowouts had plagued the 747's Pratt & Whitney engines that summer, backfiring after take-off and belching huge streams of flames behind the aircraft, terrifying passengers and crew alike.

But, in spite of the ups and downs, here she was in Rome, the Eternal City. The jet lag was a small price to pay for the sweet-harsh espresso in her private cobblestoned piazza. She sat up straighter, feeling famous.

That evening, Sally joined the other crewmembers for dinner arranged by Gabriella Lindstrom, the senior Purser on the trip, who lead the way through the narrow streets of the ancient city's shadowed lanes.

Gabriella was tall, slender and very blonde, exuding a languid sensuality. The *maitre d'hôtel*, recognized her and strode forward to welcome them, his arms open wide. She chatted gaily with him in Italian as he greeted them, and showed them to tables outside with white tablecloths and red-checkered napkins, waiters serving glasses of wine and antipasti to start a beautiful Roman evening.

Gabriella moved Sally next to her. "She'll have the mussels," she instructed the waiter, "they are wonderful here."

Sally was hesitant. "Oh I don't know, Gabriella. I've never had them before."

Gabriella leaned toward her, smiling protectively. "Don't worry, Sally. You should learn to like mussels. I will show you many things!"

With that she won Sally's confidence, and when the steaming bowls arrived, they relished the aromas of garlic, white wine and the fresh, musky scent of the shellfish. Gabriella demonstrated mussel etiquette, scooping out the mussel from the other half and dipping the shell in the broth. They laughed as they sipped the juices, sopping them up with pieces of crusty bread. The group at the table glowed, the pilots and flight attendants animated—enjoying a simple but delicious meal in a city that had witnessed gatherings like this for over 2,000 years.

Sally looked across the narrow street to the ancient church and tumbledown buildings that flanked its side, now bathed in twentieth century spotlights, but with a watchful, age-old moon lingering above. How splendid, she thought, and how far from Latham.

By the end of the evening, Sally was infatuated with Gabriella as an ultimate sophisticate. As the group walked back to the hotel, Sally stayed close, a self-appointed acolyte, full of questions.

"So what's your favorite trip, Gabriella?" Sally asked, almost skipping behind the tall, gorgeous blonde on the narrow sidewalk as they navigated the swarm of taxis and scooters and hooting men.

Gabriella slowed for a moment, looking at Sally as though she were gauging her answer. "I suppose the Africa trips," she said, holding up her right wrist, circled with a gold bracelet in the shape of a "V." She smiled, "All the African Queens get these in Lagos."

"The African Queens? Who are *they*?" Sally was struck by the romantic title.

"Oh, it's just a nickname for a group of us who love to fly the Africa trips," she shrugged. "You fly down the western coast of Africa through Dakar, Robertsfield, Lagos, Kinshasa, Johannesburg, sometimes over to Nairobi, then back up again. There are several of us who fly them all the time. But, it's a pretty senior trip, so you'd have to get called out from the pool to get it."

"Why is it so senior?" asked Sally.

"Because it's...fun," replied Gabriella, smiling, a hint of a secret.

The Captain said, "The crew parties at Robertsfield in Liberia are the stuff of legend, Sally. The company finally hired some young pilots a few years ago, and they really know how to party. We call them 'Baby Gators', not just because of their, ah, predatory talents, but because they still have a ways to go before they're completely civilized." He smiled at Gabriella, who barely acknowledged him.

"What's at Robertsfield?" Sally asked Gabriella.

Gabriella said, "It's the major airport for Liberia, right next to the Firestone rubber plantation."

"It's basically a company town" said the Captain, "ex-pat doctors, engineers, schools, shops—all there to take care of the rubber plantations."

"Isn't it awfully lonely to be stuck in the jungle? Sounds like 'Heart of Darkness' to me," said Sally, remembering Joseph Conrad's novella about Africa.

Gabriella replied, "Some people get hooked on the ex-pat lifestyle and can't live any other way. They get pretty spoiled with the servants and the big houses, and they get to like being big fish in little ponds, far away from hometown responsibilities."

"And they all love their cocktails," said the Captain. "No excuse for a party is too small; there's even a sensational Halloween bash every year at the Robertsfield Hotel.

Sally noticed that Gabriella was gazing coolly at a handsome Italian man seated at a café along the narrow street, nodding acknowledgement of his toast to her beauty and presence. All this talk of expatriates and glamorous parties captivated Sally, and she was anxious to learn more about the Africa trips. But when they reached the hotel, the night manager was waiting for them with a message from Operations. Stepping to the lobby telephone, the Captain called Pan Ops and signaled the crews' attention. He returned carrying an evening paper with a grave look on his face.

"I have some pretty bad news," he said, motioning them all to a corner of the lobby. The crew gathered silently around as he scanned a copy of the September 7th issue of the *International Herald Tribune*. He read from the headline article; "A group called the Popular Front for the Liberation of Palestine has hijacked airplanes from several cities and flown them to Zerqa, or Dawson's Field, an old military airport in Jordan. Pan Am's flight 93, out of Brussels and Amsterdam to New York, was diverted to Beirut and then to Cairo," he said, looking up to glance around, "about the time we were having dinner tonight."

The crewmembers gasped as he read further. "These were gentlemen terrorists, dressed in expensive suits, carrying leather brief cases and traveling on First Class tickets. They were searched, but their weapons had apparently already been concealed on board." He snapped the paper shut. "Flight 93 was flown by Captain Jim Priddy, who many of you know. Operations here says that after take-off, the terrorists forced one of the Pursers at gunpoint to open the cockpit door, then demanded that the pilots fly to Beirut. They picked up colleagues and additional explosives, then made Jim and his crew fly on to Cairo. We don't know how this will end."

He looked at the crew. "I want you to think about what I'm saying very carefully," he said. "The show has to go on, and unfortunately, Pan Am is an international symbol of America. This may be the way of the future for all American carriers. Now, try to get some rest." He turned and went to the elevator, the door closing behind him.

Sally stood dumbfounded, remembering the hijackings in Miami. "Gabriella," she said, "this is crazy. Passengers all over the world just drive right up to airline terminals, get their tickets and go right to the gate. Nobody checks them for anything."

"I don't think that will be the case now," said Gabriella. "We are going to see a huge change. Airplanes full of people will now be pawns in international politics. It's a new kind of war."

The next morning, Sally listened in shock to the news that the *Clipper Fortune* had been blown up on the ground in Cairo just seconds after the last passengers and crew went down the slides. She packed her bag in tears, shaking. At Fiumicino Airport the tension was palpable, with new security measures already in place. Uniformed police and armed soldiers lined the halls and the check-in areas, while hastily improvised security checkpoints had been set up at all departure gates. Harassed ground agents searched through all hand luggage, and the crewmembers boarded the aircraft immediately to conduct a thorough sweep of the entire plane.

"I don't even know what to look for," Sally murmured to a fellow crewmember.

The stewardess shook her head, scared. "All I can think of is the crew and passengers out there in Cairo, with no water and a bunch of dangerous crazy people in charge."

The passengers came aboard, subdued and quiet, and soon they were airborne. Sally looked out over the city of Rome, its red roofs and leafy boulevards, the River Tiber and the massive walls of Castelgandalfo and Vatican City in the distance. Is this all about religious wars? And if so, whose religion? Whose rage? And she thought again, who takes care of us?

Weeks later, Sally and Clarice sat in the shabby living room of their Manhattan apartment. They held a bottle of champagne at the ready as they did the countdown: "5-4-3-2-1 …Hooray!!" Then they popped the cork and toasted the end of their probation.

Clarice yelled, "Here's to freedom."—they laughed, watching the champagne bubbles swirl.

They could now bid for a regular schedule. They no longer had to serve 24-hour standby duty, which required them to be ready for airport check-in within 90 minutes. They could plan their lives beyond a 20-minute relief period to get groceries and dry cleaning. And they could finally go home to see their families.

Suddenly, the telephone's urgent ring interrupted their

laughter. They looked at each other, hesitating, since they did not technically have to answer.

Sally sighed and grabbed the phone. "This is Sally Wilder, and it better be good!"

A husky voice came through the telephone. "Sally, this is Gabriella Lindstrom. Remember me from our Rome trip? I'm standing here in Scheduling and they are looking to fill a cancellation for the 156 to Robertsfield. I see you've just been taken off standby, but would you like to take it?"

Sally's whoops of delight completely drowned out Gabriella's description of the pattern to Johannesburg and back.

"Sally, I'm turning you over to the Scheduler and he will give you formal notification. I'll see you soon!"

"An Africa trip!" Sally screamed, hanging up the phone and running to hug Clarice. "What a way to go off probation!"

"Congratulations," said Clarice, a tinge of envy in her voice. "You won't be missing anything here except Halloween."

Halloween? Sally remembered walking through the streets of Rome with Gabriella as the Captain talked about the legendary costume parties. "That's right! Quick, Clarice, you have to help me put together a costume."

"You're kidding. Now?" said Clarice.

"I have to have one for Halloween at Robertsfield." Sally barreled back to the bedroom and began rifling through their closet. "I don't see anything that would work," she wailed.

"What about this?" Clarice pulled out a long green sweater and a red scarf from one of her drawers. "You could go as a...a," Clarice thought for a moment, "a...a stuffed olive." Sally looked at the sweater in Clarice's hand and burst out laughing.

"What? A stuffed olive? That's not very exciting, is it?" asked Sally.

"The sweater will come down to mid-thigh. That's the olive part." Clarice lifted the scarf in her other hand and instructed, "And you'll have this at the neck, poking out like the pimento." She began to giggle. "You can wear your red bathing suit underneath. And if you add dark hose and high heels...hey, that's the swizzle stick! You'll be kind of leggy and sexy."

"But we'll be in equatorial Africa. I'll melt!"

"The way I see it, you don't have a whole lot of choices."

"Well then, an olive I shall be. Would you mind if I borrowed this stuff? Are you sure you won't need it for the next 10 days?"

"Sally, I just want to hear the story about this when you get back," said Clarice.

"And I'll make sure there's one to tell!" Sally said, heading for the shower.

An hour later, Sally rushed into the airport briefing room, where Gabriella introduced her to the other members of the crew. Gabriella organized her briefing paperwork on the Purser's table, just as a handsome young man with sandy hair appeared at the door. "Lucien Martin?" said Gabriella, looking at her crew list.

"*Oui, Madame,*" he answered politely.

"*Bienvenue,* Lucien," said Gabriella warmly as he took a seat. "Good, you're our last crewmember. Let's begin. We have a light load tonight, just four in the front and about a hundred in the back. And the infamous Halloween party is tomorrow night. Pamela, did you bring your records?" she asked a red haired girl with a flawless complexion.

"Absolutely," said Pamela, her accent reminiscent of BBC English. "I've got the new Rolling Stones and Stevie Wonder albums, and several others, just in case."

"*Pardon,*" said Lucien, "but does this party require a costume or flight uniform?"

"A costume, Lucien. But don't worry," said Gabriella. "We will invent one for you."

After takeoff and a short snack service, the cabin's darkness created an atmosphere of comfort, inviting late-night crew discussions. Lucien was one of the first stewards hired since the 1950s, and he was careful to be up front about both his international background and his gay life style. Sally was fascinated.

"I grew up in a small, very conservative town in Brittany, but I had very big dreams," Lucien was telling Sally, as they sat together on the 707's double jumpseat opposite the rear galley. "When I graduated from school, I headed straight for Paris, because Brittany simply could not understand me. I was studying design, and wound up getting a job at the Clipper Club at Orly Airport because I spoke good English."

The Clipper Club was the premier international airline lounge operated at every Pan Am station, with bar service run by Pan Am for its First Class passengers and other important customers, who often used it for private meetings, even rumored assignations.

"What was that like?" asked Sally. She was able to picture him easily in such a setting. How elegant he had been when he was out in the cabin serving cocktails earlier, a white napkin folded over his arm, and a twinkle in the eye when presenting the snack service.

"We had quite a few adventures," said Lucien. He named a prominent French actress and Italian movie star. "When they were having their affair and had flights coming into Paris, we used to close the club for them so they could meet privately. Some say their daughter was conceived there!" Sally gasped, then jumped to answer a call button.

When she returned, Lucien continued chatting happily relating a story of another famous actress who presented the Clipper Club hostess with a $10,000 Givenchy gown, just because it suited her. He sighed, "That Miss Lorenzo, she is a lovely, generous woman."

The two spoke through the hours of darkness, the droning of the jet engines in the background of their conversation, until it was time for the breakfast service. In a short while, the *Clipper Nightwind* was on its descent path towards the African coast in the smoky dawn, and the crew readied for arrival and disembarkation. Sally and Lucien marveled at the smell of Africa, and the teeming rain, which greeted them as they ran for the hotel bus.

The Robertsfield Hotel was one of Pan Am's hallmarks, the template constructed in the long-ago flying boat days of the *China Clipper's*

routes across the Pacific, with basic structures built at Midway, Wake, and Guam on the way to Manila. Earlier Clippers had hop-scotched through the Caribbean and down the Atlantic Coast of South America, from Port of Spain, Guyana, Caracas, Belem and other locations, where overnight stopovers had to be accommodated. Pan Am simply replicated the same buildings for the Africa routes in the 1940s, shipped as hotel kits—plain single-storey frames constructed of cinderblock and wood. From a central lobby, two wings fanned out on the left and right, with communal showers in the center of each.

Rooms were comfortable, but basic, with simple bed frames spread with grey Pan Am blankets. A pitcher of off-color water and several glasses stood on the rickety chest in the sparsely furnished room that Sally and Pamela would share.

"The water's all right to drink," Pamela assured her, "but absolutely don't leave the windows open because crewmembers have found snakes curled up in the corners."

Sally shivered, checking the window frames suspiciously before looking out. The golf course glowed in the brilliant sunrise, its velvety green softness organized into fairways, so different from the wilderness of the surrounding jungle and a neighboring village where oil lamps still gleamed. She turned away from the window and closed the blackout curtains for much-needed sleep.

That night, crewmembers rushed up and down the halls comparing costumes. Sally donned the dark stockings, red bathing suit, the olive green sweater and the red scarf. She put on her uniform shoes and emerged from the bathroom, singing, "Ta-dah!" as she modeled her costume.

"What are you supposed to be?" Pamela wondered out loud.

"A stuffed olive?" replied Sally, her voice hesitant. "It's the best I could do on such short notice."

"A stuffed olive!" said Pamela, laughing. "Well at least you'll get points for creativity!" She adjusted a turquoise veil across her face, smoothed the folds of her harem girl's costume and opened the door. "Ready for Robertsfield?" she asked.

They joined the throng in the hallways, chattering excitedly as they headed for the garden. Lucien waited, and saluted them in the

Roman style, clad in a bed sheet fashioned into a toga. Pointing proudly to the garland of fresh green leaves round his head, he said, "Gabriella made this for me."

They joined a large crowd at the entrance of the hotel welcoming the costumed guests for the evening. The scene was like a Hollywood theatrical production that had been air dropped into equatorial Africa. Amidst waving palm fronds and banana leaves, an authentic Chinese rickshaw pulled up carrying an elderly, heavily rouged woman wearing a silk embroidered *cheongsam* and holding a fringed silk parasol over her head. Attired in black coolie pajamas and a conical hat, her sweating white-haired husband struggled to pull the rickshaw. They were followed by an extremely tall man clad in an authentic Roman gladiator's outfit, tooled leather breast plates and all, then by a bearded man dressed as Count Dracula in a heavy cape. Liberian bellmen and drivers scurried around their guests, bemused by the antics of these eccentric white people.

Sally leaned over to Lucien. "They've gone to so much trouble to look this good, but how will they survive the heat?"

Lucien laughed then shrugged. "Take it off, baby, take it all off!"

The crowd made its way through the gardens towards a large, brightly lit round hut with a high thatched roof, situated in front of the hotel on the banks of the river, set about with smoky fire-torches. The *rondavel* quickly filled with revelers who thronged the bar and hors d'oeuvres buffet, and soon the noise level and thumping music rose around them. Gabriella, who was standing in the back of the *rondavel* looking exquisite in a short white silk toga, a gold necklace in the Grecian style around her forehead, motioned a waiter to put Pamela's new Rolling Stones album on the record player. The first sassy song loosened up the crowd, and soon the dance floor inside and out was filled with swirling capes, veils, gowns, feather boas, glittering tiaras and tuxedo tails. From the dance floor, Sally saw Gabriella move gracefully towards the exit and she waved to her, curious as to where she was going. But caught up in the driving beat of the song, she found herself in the center of the crowd with Lucien, who was an excellent dancer—even to these new, wild rhythms reflecting freedom and social change, independence and arrogance. And the music itself reflected revolution; it was hard to envision dancing the Bop and the Swing of the 1950s to the raw, in-your-face sexuality of Mick Jagger's lyrics and harmonies.

Sally let herself go, thinking grand, unconnected thoughts fueled by several cocktails, scattered sleep and no dinner. As she whirled around the dance floor with Lucien, she felt the euphoria of Africa, this new life, these ancient rhythms. Inspiration struck them both at the same time; Lucien grasped her hand and raised her, laughing, to a tabletop, as the crowd broke into wild applause.

Looking down at Lucien, she was seized with a moment of panic. " Lucien! My mother would kill me if she saw this, but she might commit suicide first!"

"Now, now, *mon chou*," said Lucien warmly, "she is not here to stop you!"

Sally threw back her head, tentatively taking up the Stones' beat. Then her confidence and sense of rhythm took hold, and she gave herself over to the music, her body moving to the sexy, earthy lyrics for the revelers below.

The crowd closed in around her, clapping, undulating, singing along with the song, several of the young pilot "Baby Gators" gyrating at her feet, their eyes on her legs and thighs. "Go Sally, Go! Sally Wilder! Hey, Wild Sally!" The calls rose from below as she danced, sweat pouring down her back, and rivulets of moisture trickling down her face, her arms, her legs. She grabbed her thighs, encased in the dark hose, shiny with sweat, as she danced with abandon.

Then she stopped dead still. Laughing, she ripped off the green sweater and red scarf in one motion, tossing them away, her flying hair and her red bathing suit reflected in the mirror behind the bar. The crowd roared their approval, and the Liberian wait help and barmen, dancing at their stations, whooped tribal calls that brought the song to a rousing conclusion.

The crowd was screaming, delighted with this urgent, impromptu striptease. "Wild Sally, encore! More…more!" She was astounded at the power the music and these few sexy moves gave her—and she liked it.

Lucien waited to help her down. "Sally, does this mean you're now officially an African Queen?" Drinks were thrust at her, the crowd enchanted.

"I don't know," Sally laughed, throwing her arms around him. "But I do know this: you're *my* African Queen!"

The next few days' transits of West African cities were understandably low-key, the crew in recovery mode. The group revived upon their arrival in Lagos after an overnight in Johannesburg, and despite the stifling heat and rich odor of oil and sewage, managed to summon the energy to go gambling in the hotel's casino. In Dakar the next morning, Sally stood at the forward door of the aircraft with Gabriella, bidding farewell to the last passengers as they descended the stairs. The sky was heavy with clouds and oppressive heat.

"Excuse me, Sally, I have to go," said Gabriella, turning toward the lounge to get her totebag and purse. "A friend is meeting me."

Sally remembered how she had disappeared early from the Halloween party at Robertsfield. She had thought nothing of it at the time; many of the stewardesses had dates lined up when they arrived in various cities. Then she noticed a gleaming black Mercedes crawling slowly along the tarmac toward the plane. When it came to a stop, the driver got out, opened the trunk and picked up a suitcase with a fluttering yellow crew-tag that had been retrieved from the plane's cargo hold by a baggage handler. Obviously, Gabriella was expected, judging by the grins of the ramp crew. The windows of the car were tinted, so all Sally could see was the blurry silhouette of a broad-shouldered figure in the back seat. As Gabriella approached the car, the back door opened and she stepped inside. The car moved silently away.

"Doesn't she have to clear immigration and customs?" Sally asked.

"Not with him she doesn't," said Pamela, who had come up the aisle from the aft section of the aircraft and stood beside her, regarding the progress of the limousine.

"And just who in the hell is *he*?"

"Sally, Gabriella is a beautiful woman who enjoys a wide circle of…shall we say…friends, all over the world," Pamela replied matter-of-factly. "And I'll leave it at that."

Sally looked at her fellow attendant, then at the disappearing limousine, and then back at Pamela again, comprehension slowly spreading across her face. "Oh my God," she said simply.

"Where do you suppose she gets all the Hermès scarves, the jewelry, the Gucci bags, the Charles Jourdan shoes?" Pamela asked pointedly.

Sally said. "That's not fair. Plenty of the flight attendants have nice scarves and shoes and jewelry and…."

"*Not* like Gabriella," interrupted Pamela, turning to get her purse.

"But…but, they're just gifts, aren't they?"

"Does it matter? She's an African Queen." Pamela stared at Sally, her tone mocking.

Sally was aghast. "So what does that make you and me and the rest of the crewmembers who fly this trip?"

Pamela smiled wryly, "Amateurs, Sally. Just … amateurs."

Sally was tired and deflated from the trip, the humidity in Dakar, and crushed by the revelations that her heroine had feet of clay. The rest of the crew had opted to spend the afternoon by the pool, so she decided to strike out on her own and visit nearby Gorée Island, a somber fort built to house African slaves from the interior before they were shipped to the plantations of the Caribbean and the Americas. The bellman summoned a taxi, an aging Citröen with a bulbous nose, which steamed up in front of the hotel, its engine clattering.

At the harbor, she joined a small group of African-American tourists from New Orleans, who were boarding the next ferry to Gorée. They wore colorful dashikis and bead necklaces from the Kermel Market, reveling in returning to their ancestral homeland. The English-speaking guide had not shown up for the afternoon tour, so they strained to understand the substitute guide's garbled attempts at the language. After a few more unintelligible attempts, the guide shrugged and switched to speaking French entirely.

The tiny island was a fishing village now, less than a mile off the coast, a weekend retreat and artist's haven rife with grand old moldering Portuguese-built houses on bougainvillea-shaded alleys and cobblestone streets. As the group gathered in front of the somber grey stones of Slave House, the last African place for those long-gone souls, Sally hung back, allowing the group to be closer to the guide.

"I wish I could understand what he's saying," said one man to the others around him. Several nodded, their expressions showing their frustration.

Sally gulped, raised her hand, and said to the guide in French, "If you don't mind, I can perhaps help with translation." The group leader shook her hand in great relief, and beckoned her forward. Mindful of the glances of the group, and taking care to look at the guide, Sally began to translate from French into English. They regarded her with grateful surprise as she began to tell the apocalyptic story of their ancestors in her soft Southern drawl, so similar to their own accents. She told of the prisoners, who were brought here to be held until they were loaded on boats at the beach about 200 yards away. The voyages they endured were the most arduous of what was called the Triangular Trade, sealing the fate of 12 million human beings.

Moving through the hallway, they reached The Door of No Return, the symbolic passageway of a slave's last contact with his native Africa. Its lintel was worn and low. Gazing at the sea beyond, Sally could see that these people remembered in their bones the aching past, feeling the winds cooling their faces as it had cooled their ancestors, blowing from the Americas. There was no sound but the waves crashing on the rocks below and the screaming, wheeling gulls.

The guide stopped and looked at Sally, shaking his head as he whispered to her, "I cannot say this, for I have never said it for African brothers and sisters returning to their place."

"No," said Sally, patting his arm reassuringly, "we'll say it together for all of us."

While the guide spoke in French, she translated carefully. "Your guide says he has never done this for black Americans before. He says that this is hard for him, because this is where your ancestors left their culture, their language, their blood, their homelands and their own histories behind. They surely knew that when they walked through this door, they would never see their homes and their families again."

She waited for the guide's next words. "But you have come back to honor them, and Africa welcomes you."

And these descendants of slaves faced her—speechless—touching the lintel in the gentle breeze. Sally whispered to herself, "And I never really knew...."

They all stood together, contemplating the watery expanse and the unseen lands of the Americas and the Caribbean plantations far beyond the horizon, before walking slowly from the Slave House to board the ferry.

Sally trailed uncertainly behind until two men in the group walked back towards her.

"Thank you for your help," said one. "Of course we know the history, but to hear the stories translated and see the place, to feel it," he paused, looking about, "it's a journey we all needed to make, and we thank you for making it your journey, too."

He took her hand and held it tightly, smiling into her eyes, his own gleaming with tears.

On the last leg of the trip into New York, Sally deliberately avoided Gabriella. After her visit to Gorée, the Robertsfield experience and decadent parties seemed tawdry, not to mention the moral issues of paid dates with mysterious men in limousines who gave elaborate gifts. But she had a problem; she'd accepted an invitation from Gabriella several days before, while still in the throes of admiration for her.

Gabriella had put her hand on Sally's arm, stroking slightly. "There's a big conference going on at the United Nations the week we get back. Lots of important and attractive men from all over the world will be there. I think you would enjoy them, and I know they would enjoy you. They *love* pretty American girls, particularly ones with Southern charm." She'd agreed to meet Gabriella with a group of the delegates the following night at La Fleur, one of Manhattan's most beautiful and sophisticated restaurants. Sally had heard the flight attendants rave about it, and she had always wanted to go.

Now, on the way home, squeezed into a crowded, rattling bus that bumped its way into Manhattan, Sally was grateful to be surrounded by regular people in varying stages of dishevelment, the odors of long-distance travelers mingling with diesel fumes. So much for the rarefied world of the African Queens, she thought.

Nevertheless, she appeared at La Fleur the next drizzly evening at the appointed time in her Little Black Dress and pearls, and was introduced by Gabriella to the U.N. luminaries. Their calculating gazes unnerved her further. In spite of the luxurious ambiance and the legendary flower arrangements, she felt herself growing more and more squeamish, especially when the delegate seated next to her, having pawed her leg and accidently brushed her breast twice, leaned over, his lips wet, his hand on her knee, and toasted "to our evening ahead." His hand moved up her thigh, deliberately. Sally gritted her teeth, giving the man's hand a hard shove. He looked startled, "Hey, bitch, goddammit, I paid for this." And he grabbed her thigh again, squeezing roughly this time, his fingers probing higher.

She rose quickly, feeling the gorge rise in her throat, thinking, what have I done? I'm no better than Gabriella. She smiled falsely at the group, claiming faintness, nausea, fatigue and apologies, as she moved quickly away from the table, her thigh smarting.

Gabriella rushed after her, her eyes solicitous but hard as they stood in the small entryway. "You can't just walk out on these people," she said. "They have...they have expectations."

"Let me stop you right there, Gabriella." Sally did not try to hide the anger in her voice. "I'm disgusted by your friends. You've been generous and kind to me, but this...this arrangement with this type of people...uh...just isn't my thing."

Gabriella lips parted in a crocodile's smile, taking it all in stride. "Okay, Sally. But let me know if you're ever interested." She turned and glided gracefully away.

Interested? Sally fumed silently. You can bet your Gucci scarves I'll never be interested! And she stormed towards the taxi stand, knowing she had just enough money for the fare and tip. The rain felt good, and clean.

CHAPTER SEVEN

TWO GARDENIAS
JANUARY 9, 1971   INBOUND, NASSAU TO MIAMI

Zoe kicked the heavy doors of the tiny 727 galley, struggling to get them back in place in preparation for landing. The latches of this particular door were thick with grime and she grimaced with the effort. Francisco, the diminutive Cuban Purser who had led the day's four turn-arounds to Nassau and Rock Sound, stood in the doorway and offered suggestions without moving to help.

"Come on, you turkeys," she said, as much to the Purser as to the uncooperative galley doors. The worn interior of the galleys matched the workhouse appearance of the cabin: 129 grey-blue economy seats flown four times a day back and forth to Nassau at full pop of $29 each way.

That morning, they had made the first run from Miami to Rock Sound on the windward Bahamian island of Eleuthera, one of 700 coral and sand spits slipping southeast off the coast of Florida. Eleuthera sounded grand but had no distinction other than the legendary treasures of Spanish Galleons and pirate treasure ships sunk in past hurricanes in the gin-clear waters, and the fact that it was the retirement home of Juan Terry Trippe—the equally legendary founder of Pan Am. Upon arrival on the flat, windswept island, Francisco shoved a folded *Wall Street Journal* and a flat briefcase into Zoe's hands, saying, "Here, you go and kiss up to the Great Man. He'll be at the gate."

Trippe had retired three years before, but still shuttled back and forth to New York on Pan Am business. His eminence was still evident in this daily dispatch case and newspapers specially delivered to his nearly private island. Just half a dozen passengers disembarked, the rest bound for Nassau.

Across the runway, the brilliant aquamarine seas and shallow waters glinted, palms, mesquite scrub brush and orderly bougainvillea swayed in the breeze, and the piped-in music of the Caribbean's ubiquitous steel drums drifted through the small, solid coral-block, tin-roofed arrival hall. By the open gate stood a white-haired man in a floppy golf hat and open shirt, speaking to the Pan Am agent, who nodded deferentially. That's got to be him, thought Zoe, fixing her best Pan Am smile and stepping smartly.

"Mr. Trippe, sir," she said, "your morning paper!" God, what a stupid line, she thought.

The man looked up and smiled, briefly, then eyed the headlines. He folded the paper and said, "And where are you from, young lady?"

Zoe blurted out, "I'm from Burma, and I used to fly Pan Am Flight One and Two when I went to boarding school in India."

He considered her answer and nodded, "Now there's an answer I don't hear every day. Yes, Burma. Beautiful place. Amelia Earhart and Fred Noonan even spent two days there on their way to Lae, right before they disappeared in 1937; did you know that? Now Burma is almost as much of a mess as our company, wouldn't you say?"

Zoe gave a start. "You've been there? Yes, it is beautiful and you might think it is messed up, but I love it anyway. And I love being with this wonderful company you started."

He patted her hand, smiling. "We'll all keep working to keep the Clippers flying, and you, young lady, you hang on to your dreams." He turned and walked slowly and steadily towards a waiting jeep, his steps crunching on the coral driveway, the palm trees swaying in the light sea breeze, the sweet smell of frangipani in the air.

The rest of the day they flew sunburned tourists out of the islands and shuttled pale new arrivals back between Nassau, Freeport and Miami. While Francisco supervised, the three crewmembers moved at a frantic pace: boarding passengers; performing routine emergency demonstrations; serving iced rum-punch to a full cabin in 20 minutes; securing the cabin for landing; bidding farewells consisting of robotic thank you-thank-you-'bye-now-thank-you's; then repeating the process all over again. They worked non-stop and without lunch, grumbling when they found that the crew lunches had been accidentally off-loaded.

Hot, tired, sweaty and out of sorts, the stewardesses looked at each other and grabbed the cool rum punches. Even Zoe. It couldn't hurt, they thought.

Two hours later, after a mechanical delay and fortified by another rum punch or two, they made their last run of the day back to Miami. Sailing off of the aircraft, Zoe joined her crewmembers in a spirited conga line down Miami's E Concourse, arms clasped around waists, singing and laughing.

Bemused passengers and airline workers stopped to stare, wondering out loud if *they* could travel on *that* flight. Francisco, lugging the crew bags down the concourse, laughed and said, "Show's over folks! Come back tomorrow, same time, same place." They made it through the arrival hall to their respective rides, waiting curbside.

Zoe saw Manny right outside the Southern Air Transport counters, which were always deserted. He was fresh from the Training Academy in his blue blazer and grey slacks, every silver hair on his head in place, his eyes shining. God, don't let him smell the rum, she thought.

"Hey, Zoe, you were supposed to call me after training. Come on, I'll take you home," he said.

They chatted comfortably on the way through the tree-lined boulevards to Brickell Avenue, where Zoe shared a breezy apartment in a new three-story building with another stewardess. She recounted the adventures of the last few months.

"Manny, I thought I would die the first time in Rio when we walked across the Avenida Copacabana to the beach, and I saw all the sewage in the water and the worms wiggling in the sand," said Zoe. "It was the most disappointing, disgusting thing, and I just went back to the room and cried."

Manny laughed, "Yeah, but the music! It's like Cuba, it's like my home. Everything goes wrong, but it is still incredible." As they drew up to her apartment, he chucked her on the chin. "Okay, tomorrow is Saturday. I will collect you at 6 p.m. for dinner at my friend's house on Key Biscayne, where you will meet interesting people and forget your worries, eh?" He leaned back in the seat and regarded her carefully. "And stay away from the Nassau rum-punch; that *bastardo* Francisco has been pickled in it for years, but you don't need that stuff! Pan Am will fire you, and there will be nothing I can do to help you. *Finito.*"

Zoe groaned, disconcerted, "Oh, busted—I should have known. And I don't even drink."

Manny laughed and waved at her as he drove away, "*Hasta mañana*, Zoe!"

The next evening, Zoe answered the doorbell promptly at six, and bowed for Manny's inspection. She wore a white crushed linen and lace Mexican country dress with an elasticized flounce at the bust, and an enormous flared skirt. The simplicity of the dress complimented her deep tan, sun-streaked hair, her silver pendant together with the rough-polished ruby at her throat.

"My God," said Manny reverently, his eyes traveling up and down her body, "how will I protect you from the animals?"

"Oh, dear," said Zoe, "I'll change. I didn't know what to wear."

"No, no," Manny laughed, "you are perfect. I can never get over the difference between you ladies in and out of uniform. You are sensational. Let's go."

They proceeded down Brickell Avenue, past the lush gardens and over the Rickenbacker Causeway to Key Biscayne, while Manny told stories of rum running and horse-trading. At this hour on the island, the frantic rush subsided, and the residents of the Key walked or drove slowly, waving and calling to friends and neighbors.

"These people still like each other," she observed to Manny.

"Yes, this is still the old Florida here, but maybe not for long," he said. "This has been a wild place with a peaceful face for a long, long time, and tonight's party is part of it."

"There are two special friends—old hometown boys you might say—who are just returning to Miami, so we are welcoming them. Our host is a very, very famous man, but he protects his privacy and his family events. And above all, he protects his friends. He used to fly for Pan Am, way back in the old days with me, and since we have known each other for so many years, we are family. My special guests become his family too. His name is Carlito Ramirez.

"Ramirez?" Zoe knew the name sounded familiar. Oh, *that* Carlito Ramirez? President's Nixon's friend? This is *his* house?" Zoe shifted in her seat uncomfortably, remembering the tumultuous 1968 Democratic Convention in Chicago, and the election of Nixon that followed in November.

"Just relax and enjoy, and I'll explain everything as we go." He smiled conspiratorially as he drove up a crushed coral driveway with a flourish, greeted by a team of beautiful young men with sparkling eyes and smiles.

Out on a wide terrace facing the sea, a full Cuban orchestra played romantic melodies while the guests promenaded, exchanging warm Latin greetings…touching, touching. Zoe met a dozen handsome men together with their female companions or wives, and in every case she noted that she was carefully vetted. Feeling the inspection, she accepted Manny's introduction to a striking woman named Livia, who was on her way to visit the ladies' powder room. They sauntered slowly across the terrace, speaking of life in the heat and her role as Manny's student at Pan Am.

"Then you know Francisco and Jorge at Pan Am also? No, maybe you're too young, and they are such dreadful Cuban playboys." Livia laghed and introduced several of the ladies seated at the mirrors.

Maria Esteban-Rodrigues stood. "What is that amazing necklace you are wearing? It is so powerful, so deep." She fingered the silver and ruby pendant at Zoe's throat.

"This is a ruby from my country, and an ancient silver coin," said Zoe.

"And where is this country, since America does not have such rubies?"

"I was born in Burma, where these stones are mined," Zoe replied, then added, "The country became unstable in 1963, and when I left, I brought these with me as a remembrance of my home and loved ones." She thought of Sao Johnny, so long ago now.

Maria, who had escaped a death-squad in Haiti and had married one of the most powerful Cubans in Miami, himself a cousin of the former dictator, startled Zoe by embracing her. "Then we know your pain. And many of us do not have such lovely remembrances."

Zoe continued chatting comfortably, and returned to the terrace arm-in-arm with Livia, followed by several other women.

Manny approached her. "My God, princess, you have managed to capture the evening. The men are always easy, but our women are almost impossible."

Zoe rolled her eyes and held out her hands. "Manny, dance with me!" He raised his arms, leading her to the dance floor. He danced with the instinctive sense of rhythm so natural to the Latin world. A light breeze was filled with the scents of evening, the sky glowing and a newly risen moon hanging above the horizon. She felt a gentle hand on her arm and heard a voice near her ear addressing Manny.

"*Amigo, diga me*, do you think you can keep her all to yourself this evening, this flower?" said the man.

Manny turned, bowing deeply, "Carlito, this is my child, my treasure, my love. Guard her with your life! Zoe, this is our host, Carlito Ramirez." Manny gave her hand to the handsome man facing them, slightly shorter than Manny, but exquisitely dressed in a white dinner jacket and creased black trousers, with hair greying at the temples, heavy eyebrows, generous lips and a quiet smile.

Zoe stiffened at the prospect of dancing with one of Nixon's henchmen, but soon he swept her up in the new melody, singing the Spanish lyrics softly in a pleasant baritone. "Do you know the music, my dear?"

Zoe replied, "I know the song and the feeling, but I don't know the Spanish translation, only that it is famous all over the world as a Cuban love song."

He smiled, nodding as the song came to an end. "Yes, and about betrayal, also."

The audience applauded, and Zoe saw that they had been dancing alone, her white dress and his white dinner jacket contrasting with the terrace and the deepening night, soft lights and flowers. She bowed slightly and took his arm as he returned her to Manny.

"Yes, Manny, she is very special," he said. "Now tell me, young lady, are they treating new flight crews any differently or any better than in our day?"

Zoe smiled, "Well, maybe not better, but differently, for sure. I did eight flights yesterday and again today, from Miami to Nassau and back, and I don't think I went anywhere the whole 12 hours." As they laughed, a tall curly-haired man in a brilliant white shirt, open at the neck, approached them leisurely, holding a champagne glass and a cigarette, his eyes on Zoe.

"*Ola, viejos,* I must claim the pleasure of my first dance in Miami with this beautiful woman. My sister is talking of nothing else but you," he smiled, indicating Livia on the corner of the dance floor, waving.

Zoe glanced at Manny, who nodded his approval, "Yes, Lorenzo, this is my honorary niece Zoe Longfield. Zoe, this is Lorenzo Perillo-Compostela, one of our guests of honor. He is a graduate of West Point and the new director of Southern Air Transport, so he should know how to be an officer and a gentleman." Manny bowed in mock seriousness and Lorenzo led her to the floor.

Zoe laughed inwardly, noting the music, a steamy cha-cha she'd heard at the Blue Fox nightclub in Calcutta on her way from the Hill Schools back to Rangoon. She kept her expression serene and noncommittal, following Lorenzo's lead, but not the urgent message in his eyes. This is one very attractive and very dangerous man, she thought. I am just fine so long as Manny and Lorenzo's sister Livia are around.

The music ended with a flourish and Lorenzo raised his hand to blow her a kiss. "Again, very soon again," he murmured, gazing intently at her as he backed away and returned her to Manny's arm.

"You know, they are all watching you handle him, and that was just right," said Manny. "Most women would be terrified or brazen it out, but you kept your cool. It was your move all the way, and his sister is sure to remind him of that."

Someone appeared at Manny's side and whispered to him. Nodding, he guided Zoe through the group to introduce her to an excitable cigar-shaped man with pale skin and angry eyes, who turned from conversing with a tall red-headed American man and another shorter, good-looking *gringo* with a patrician bearing and the longish hair favored by Ivy League academics. "Octavio, may I present Zoe

Longfield, my protégé at Pan Am? Zoe, this is Doctor Octavio Buenavista, who has just returned from an extended absence."

Zoe smiled and shook his hand, noting a few chortles at Manny's description of Octavio's absence. Where was he, she wondered. In jail? In the jungle? In trouble? Who *are* all these people?

Octavio smiled, "It is a pleasure to meet you, my dear. Don't mind these foolish men with very tiny minds. I think you are beautiful, and any friend of Manny's is always a friend of mine. Now stay away from that Lorenzo. I can tell you he is nothing but trouble. But my wife and children and I welcome you to visit." He concluded their brief meeting and turned away. The younger, dark-haired American man surveyed her with a brief smile and nod, his eyes questioning.

As they walked away, Zoe said, "Manny, I need to get some air, and I want you to explain all these characters. This is like an onion— peeling, peeling, peeling—and I don't know what's in the middle." She smiled at him and he nodded, leading her away from the music across the terrace to the walkway bordering the sea. They stepped down a few stairs to the water, where several boats rocked in their moorings.

Manny looked out to sea, now glimmering in the light of the fully risen moon. "Zoe, here you become part of an amazing chain of people and events you can't begin to understand, except with time."

Zoe said, "Manny, why are there so many mysteries? Why are you such a puzzle?"

Manny shifted in his seat. "It's a long story, and I will tell it in the parts I know you'll understand," said Manny, lighting a small Cuban cigar and savoring its pungent aroma. He described the turbulent 1950s when thousands of Cubans aligned either with Bautista or Castro in a time of revolution. Then came the inevitable break in the Cuban community in Miami, with those Cuban families scattered around the country, torn between ideology and the stark necessities of making a living in America.

"Many came, many believed, many still think they must go on fighting for a cause that is perhaps lost," Manny told her. "I try, as many of us do, to take care of my family members and keep them from going to extremes. My wife, though, is very close to the extremists and although we share a special love, it's hard for us to be together, even now." He looked at her, but his eyes were far away.

He recounted an extraordinary history of the men whom Zoe had just met, classmates of Fidel Castro's at the University of Havana in the 1940s. He mentioned a shadowy man named Howard Hunt, known as a CIA operative in Cuba and Miami.

Manny said, "There was also a closed, secret operation called JMWave, headquartered in an ordinary office building on the University of Miami campus." He went on to describe a complex organization, which housed a training and weapons delivery system employing a large number of CIA staffers, Cuban exiles and "trainees" in the run-up to the Bay of Pigs operation.

Manny shook his head. "You see, there was a lot at stake, with hundreds of front corporations like Southern Air Transport that hired thousands more. A lot of Cubans depended on this system."

Zoe nodded, his stories so similar to the ones her father and many of his friends told. It just went on and on, all around the world, this endless cycle of money, power, and control.

"These activities acted like a magnet for dissatisfied exiles, angry men and desperate refugees who flocked to the cause," continued Manny. "When JMWave closed in 1968, thousands were left without work or hope, so they went into gun-running, the mercenary business, even organized crime and drugs—a lot of bad stuff. Lorenzo Perillo-Compostella and Santiago, whom you just met, are leaders in this underground, and it continues with this Southern Air Transport, and supply to the Contra forces in Central America. Many know that it is CIA, but not many know how or why."

Zoe shook her head, "Manny, I barely understand. But what about the danger to you?"

He puffed on his cigar, looking off in the distance. He sighed. "I can only say they are family, they are blood, they are brothers, and we have all been through many, many years together, as well as with my wife. Perhaps they do what I cannot. Perhaps I do what they could have done, if times had been different. We don't always know what awaits us on this journey."

He paused for a long moment, then said, "All Cubans benefit from the association between Carlito Ramirez and his powerful friends, especially President Nixon, if only from the pride that we Cubans, whether refugees or humble immigrants, can feel in the association. We've survived this far, so anything is possible, eh?"

Zoe looked pensive. "You know, politics everywhere is all the same. It all starts with good intentions and it all ends badly, here and everywhere else where there are too many secrets." Manny put his arm around her shoulder, and they strolled back towards the house.

Weeks later, Zoe was flying to Sao Paulo, Brazil, by way of Caracas and Belem. The creaking 707 was an old "straight-pipe" model, outlawed in most metropolitan airports because of noise level restrictions and its lack of pollution controls. She struggled up and down the aisle in the full cabin, the air over the meandering Amazon River becoming increasingly bumpy. The cabin crew of four was attempting to serve a dinner of *coq au vin*, rice, salad and fruit tarts to 178 economy passengers. Out to the left of the aircraft, ominous thunderheads loomed beyond the aircraft's 31,000-foot altitude, and lightning storms lit up the sky along the horizon.

Suddenly, there was a blinding crack of lightning accompanied by an instantaneous clap of thunder, followed by a slamming drop of the aircraft. Passengers screamed as a flaming fireball appeared at the front of the cabin, and hurtled down the aisle towards Zoe, who dropped a loaded tray of cocktails, grabbing the seatbacks. The tumbleweed-like chimera seemed to pass straight through her body, though she felt nothing. At the same time, the aircraft gave another tremendous lurch and dropped sideways into a steep, yawing descent. Trays and food items seemed to be spinning towards the ceiling. She grabbed the armrest of the seat next to her and tried to keep her feet on the floor, wedging her left leg and foot in the struts of the seat, passengers hanging onto both of her arms. As she looked down their incline of descent she gasped in fear, thinking, God help me, I can't hold on.

An elderly woman in the next row tried to stand, crying out. Other passengers sat transfixed, holding each other or the heaving seatbacks in front of them. Zoe reached her hand towards the woman, intending to keep her seated and reassure her, thinking, there…there madam, we're going to crash and it won't hurt a bit. Then with another lurch, the aircraft righted itself and soared back up towards the stratosphere.

With a sickening wrench, Zoe felt her wedged leg twist and break, the hot pain flooding her body. She inhaled sharply, grabbed the woman and pushed her back into her seat, her calf twisted at an odd angle while the pain pounded. The cabin was full of flying debris: magazines, glasses, trays and personal items. Seats and people were soaked, trays and meals from the galley toppled and crashed on the floor, sluicing platters of *coq au vin* down the aisles. The salads appeared to levitate before spilling, shredding into hair and faces and clothes, while bread rolls bounced almost comically down the aisle from the galley.

Finally the Captain's voice came over the public address system, his tone nonchalant. "Ah, sorry, ladies and gentlemen, that bump was more than just crossing the equator. We hit a tough squall and an unreported high-altitude CAT cell—that's clear air turbulence. We think we've found a safe altitude now, so it should be all right to move about the cabin. But keep those seatbelts fastened when you're in your seats, just in case there are any more bumps out there."

Two crewmembers struggled through the mess towards her as she tried to stand, looking around the cabin, which was strewn everywhere with salad, rice, pieces of chicken, cutlery and plastic coffee cups. The passengers looked at her for further instructions. "Okay," she laughed and clapped in between spasms of pain, "that means all drinks are on the house since it looks like we're all wearing your dinner!" The passengers cheered, glad to be alive and recovering from the fear of moments before.

The crew helped her to the forward jumpseat, where they strapped ice bags to her rapidly swelling ankle and lower leg. A veterinarian from the First Class section used a racehorse splint and butyl painkillers in his medical bag, and she lay wrapped in blankets on the tiny lounge seat for landing in Sao Paulo. She was embarrassed by all the attention from the ambulance crew carrying her stretcher, not to mention the smiles of gratitude from the old lady she'd pushed unceremoniously back into her seat. The ambulance wailed to the hospital.

On the flight home the next day, she sat propped with her cast in the First Class lounge. The crew spoiled her, making a great fuss over her and joking about the broken leg being a convincing way to get off reserve. The medical officer pronounced a fracture in three places, and at least three months in a cast.

Manny was sympathetic, and practical. "There is not much you can do for the leg," he said, "but you can do a lot for your mind if you volunteer with our archivists in the Pan Am Dinner Key offices. There are huge archives of materials that have been collected from all over the world, and the stuff is being catalogued for storage. There's almost 50 years of history in those boxes—and that probably means 50 years of palmetto bugs in some of 'em, too." Zoe accepted the assignment, her interest piqued, remembering her visit to Dinner Key during training, the old photographs and twinkling stars on the ceiling of the old Terminal.

Awkward on crutches, Zoe reported to the Dinner Key complex the following week. The large, airy hangars with white painted floors contained racks and racks of storage boxes, which seemed to stretch forever. Several historians from the University of Miami were working on the project, as well as student volunteers and retired Pan Am employees. It was a cheerful group in spite of its diversity in age, education and rank. The academics were hardly dour; they reveled in the aviation archaeology before them, and their eyes danced as they flipped through documents and recorded the amazing first-hand stories of the retirees, whose "early days" adventures were the beginning of airline history. Zoe felt the familiar pull of ancient knowledge, and looked through the master catalogue at the areas of the collection, at the early Latin and Caribbean routes prior to World War II, and the reams of documents labeled "*China Clipper*".

The archivist introduced her to the team leader. "Zoe, this is Dr. Harrison. He's an eminent Asia scholar and really needs help with the Pacific area files here."

Zoe leaned on one crutch to shake hands with the diminutive

scholar. "I'm sorry I'm not very mobile," she said, "but I can be pretty useful in sorting through the boxes."

Dr. Harrison nodded. "Zoe, it's a great pleasure. I was just a young college student in San Francisco in May of 1935 when the test flight of the *China Clipper* took place. I'll never forget it, as well as many historic flights after that. I actually kept a diary of the departures from Treasure Island, out over the Golden Gate Bridge towards Asia."

Zoe loved the dry musty smell of old papers and India ink. Documents were stacked helter-skelter. Dr. Harrison gave her a smaller box labeled: Box 714: *Pan American Base, Treasure Island*, 11-22-35. "It's probably easier if you have an idea of what we are trying to accomplish. Everything in this room relates somehow to the event described right here," he said, tapping the box. "Enjoy!" He smiled and rushed away to another dusty corner.

In the box were just three thick folders and a slender manila envelope: one was stamped *Pan American World Airways: Publicity Department* and the other two were ledger files; copies of a handwritten flight log, a compilation of several mimeographed lists of aircraft numbers and names.

She pushed the files and folders aside as she opened the first folder, which contained articles that described the take-off of the *China Clipper* from Treasure Island in San Francisco on November 22, 1935, an event that was broadcast throughout the world. She read the original record of the first trans-Pacific radio roll call from Honolulu, Midway, Wake, Guam and Manila, as well as the ocean station aboard the US Coast Guard cutter *Itasca*.

Captain Edwin Musik's log was detailed. When he and his crew of six airmen received their orders to commence the historic journey, they made the take-off run in the fuel-heavy aircraft through heaving seas, making "a magnificent unplanned pass through the fortunately incomplete span of the great Golden Gate Bridge." Remarkable, thought Zoe. The Clipper carried the mail, a sewing machine and a dentist's chair, as well as all the fixings for big Thanksgiving dinners for the folks on Midway and Wake Islands, along with some Chinese cooks to carry them out.

Zoe read of the triumphant arrival in Manila Bay just a few days later on November 29th, entranced with the narration that described huge throngs of cheering people gathered to watch the landing of the flying boat, celebrating the historic feat of completing an 8,000-mile journey in less than 60 hours. The fastest ship's surface time of the day would have taken 21 days.

She found herself yearning for that part of the world, wishing that she could go home to Asia again.

In the back of the boxes of *China Clipper* history, there was a large catalogue of files from a ship called the *SS Newhaven*, personal correspondence with Bill Mullahey, the man who'd put the logistics of the *China Clipper's* Pacific flight together, and a plain folder entitled "U.S. Navy/Dept. of the Interior—*Hui Panala'au*—Howland, Jarvis, Baker." She noted another file with the words "Earhart—Howland and Nikumararo". She put them aside for further study.

That night, she sat entranced as she read of the inspirational voyages of several dozen young Hawai'ian men who'd been sent to the flat, equatorial guano atolls of Howland, Jarvis and Baker from March, 1935 until January, 1942. They were volunteers from Kamehameha Schools in Hawai'i who were recruited to settle the atolls. The history of colonization was interwoven with the early years of Pacific aviation.

She was suddenly surprised to see a familiar name. "George Kanawai returned to Honolulu on September 25, 1935 aboard the USCGC *Itasca*, which served as a spotter radio ship for the voyage of the *China Clipper* shortly thereafter." Zoe paused, wondering if he could possibly be related to Pua.

She put the records in chronological order in archival folders, yellowing piles of letters and radio logs for the Department of the Interior, the Navy, the Department of Commerce, diaries and what looked like lists of supplies. There were photographs of strapping young men on islands and boats, and again the name, George Kanawai.

The smaller folder contained copies of radio traffic reports from Amelia Earhart's ill-fated aircraft, purportedly lost off Howland Atoll along with Pan Am navigator Fred Noonan. She smoothed the faded print dated July 3, 1935, and thought of destiny.

The last items were two files on Nikumaroro Atoll and the 1929 sinking of a British freighter *SS Norwich City*, investigated in the

1940s, possibly during a later search for Earhart's aircraft. A handwritten, undated note was affixed to the file: "Unconfirmed—marine salvage notice," it read, "possible earlier wreckage rumored, three-masted whaler or Tea Clipper ca. 1790. Shallow water—large unmarked metal fragments resembling pre-WWII wing assemblage." Zoe fingered the page, wondering what it could mean.

The weeks passed quickly. Dr. Harrison and the staff were bemused by Zoe's passion for these fading papers, but they appreciated her slavish dedication. She stayed on after hours, even going through the World War II era files and the folders marked "1944: Kunming, China-Burma-India Theater," remembering her own formative years in Asia. Inspired by these *China Clipper* records, she felt an increasingly urgent need to return to the Pacific.

And then, out of the blue, news from former school friends. She read and reread a classmate's letter regarding young guerrillas involved in border conflicts between the Chinese Kuomintang troops and the Shan and Kachin tribes of northern Burma in unmapped jungle areas in the remote Chinese/Thai/Laotian border region. The letter contained a rumor, just a speculation really, that Sao Johnny was one of the leaders of the Burmese resistance movement that financed its operations by smuggling antiquities and gemstones out and guns back in. She swallowed hard, remembering. It was possible, she admitted, but we are still so young. These things should not be happening. She sat re-reading the letter yet again, while looking out over the sparkling waters of Biscayne Bay, a world away.

One evening, she broached the subject of these intrigues with Manny, the possibility of returning to Burma and looking for those she had loved. She even mentioned another career, perhaps further study in archaeology.

Manny laughed, "You ladies have it so good flying around the world, living the high-life. Why would you even think of swapping the glamour for all that hardship?"

Zoe looked out over the water, her face serious. "Manny, you said it yourself. You do what you must to help where you can, and in my way, I have to do the same thing, and for the same reasons. I didn't ask for this new awareness in my life, but I may need your help to get a transfer to Honolulu. I won't do anything stupid, but I have to at least think of the options. Would you do that for me?"

Manny took a long look at her, then patted her arm, nodding, "You know, I keep hoping that all wars everywhere will end. I hate to see you do it, but I know your heart is in other places, and that you're torn—just as I have been. And I must help you just as others helped me. We'll get the paperwork started."

That night, as he dropped her off at the apartment, she drew him in at the door, and Manny held her close all night, again and again. They knew it was not forever, but it was good for the time they had. Zoe, her eyes steady, thought of fires in distant places.

Zoe's cast was chipped off, and the doctor determined that she was fit to return to the flight line. On her last day at the old hangar, she returned her files and findings, and the researchers gathered to wish her farewell. Dr. Harrison smiled as he handed her a new leather-bound ledger, stamped in relief: "LOG OF THE *China Clipper*: 11-22-35 to 12-08-36."

"It's just a copy, Zoe, but I've watched you read it over and over," he nodded, smiling. "I thought you might like to have one as a keepsake."

Zoe took the ledger, running her hand over the smooth leather. Reading it in the original had made the historic voyage come alive for her. Not only had the *China Clipper* connected the shores of America with the Asian continent, but it provided a link to her past. The Pacific was home; so much lay ahead, most of it unknown.

"Thank you, Dr. Harrison," said Zoe, her eyes moist. "I will treasure this for the rest of my life." Slowly leafing through the pages, she stopped at Musik's conclusion after the *China Clipper*'s voyage: "…The entire mission was accomplished without incident of any kind."

The following month, Zoe and Pualani sat behind their newly rented house on the North Shore of Oahu, the beach washed in the pastel colors of a gentle tropical evening, the sand between their toes, the sun sinking low over the long Pacific swells. Zoe had recounted her adventures in Miami and Key Biscayne, the Cuban underworld and the CIA, the strange story of Sao Johnny's intrigues, and her determination to return to the Pacific.

Zoe was thoughtful. "I'm still a displaced person, no matter where I go. Sometimes it can overwhelm me, Pua, when I read about the stupid political decisions that hurt us all. I just get so incredibly angry. Maybe being back out here, I can do some things that can help. I don't know yet what or where, but I just need to be closer to Asia."

Pua nodded. "It's all in the history. You'll find the way."

Zoe remembered her question from the archives. "Pua, I came across some files about a group of young Hawaiians who went out onto some remote islands in the Pacific to colonize them for the United States to establish air bases. One of them, George Kanawai, was stationed on Howland Atoll, and on the Coast Guard Cutter Itasca that monitored the *China Clipper*. Does that ring a bell? Is he a relative of yours?"

Pualani was staring at her open-mouthed. "You never cease to amaze me, *haole* girl. Yeah, you could say it rings a bell. That was my uncle. He died right after the Korean War, but he was such a hero to all of us. Wait till you meet my cousin, Keoki; he's the one who knows all the family legends, so long as he's in the right frame of mind to tell them. Hey, girl, welcome back to the Pacific!"

They saluted the horizon, towards the west, towards Asia and whatever lay ahead.

Pua said, "We have one more job today. We have to call Sally and get her to transfer out here right away."

Zoe laughed, and they went inside to grab the telephone.

CHAPTER EIGHT

NORTH SHORE DAYS
JANUARY 21, 1972   HONOLULU, HAWAI'I

Sally sat waiting for the *Clipper Jewel of the Ocean's* doors to be opened after landing. Her legs were stiff from 12 hours of flying, and her head was pounding with a hangover from the previous night's farewell in Manhattan with Clarice and Lucien. But as she stepped out on the ramp of the 707 and into the late afternoon light, the island breezes lifted away the aches and pains. Walking down the metal stairs, she felt the softness of the air that swirled around her like a silk scarf, despite the hot smoky vapors of jet-fuel.

And suddenly there they were, Zoe and Pualani waving from the baggage claim area, carrying leis of purple and yellow orchids, fluffy white plumeria and fragrant tuberose studded with pink carnations, which they placed around her neck with hugs and laughter.

Pualani grabbed her. "Oh, you pretty *haole* girl. Wait until the local boys see you!" Piling her luggage and moving boxes onto a groaning baggage cart, they maneuvered out to the street.

"We haven't bought a car yet, but we've borrowed the perfect transportation from our neighbors!" said Zoe, proudly pointing to an enormous hearse sitting at the curb painted a brilliant, iridescent orange with spectacular fins jutting out from the rear.

"Holy shit!" exclaimed Sally. "A *hearse*?"

"This is the Big Orange," said Zoe as they approached it. "But it's a free ride, and it's the perfect airport car—there's lots of, uh, room." They proceeded to throw boxes and suitcases into the casket section. Sally gawked at the sight.

"Come on, Sally. Let's get you home!" said Zoe. "I can't wait to show you the house that Pualani found, which we rented for a song."

They squeezed into the front compartment, with Pua driving, and Zoe and Sally perched on jumpseats.

"I'm leaving the windows down, if it's all right with you," said Pua. "The air conditioning isn't working all that great and besides, we're headed for the country. We certainly won't need it out there." They turned onto the highway, heading towards the western part of the island.

"We aren't going to be living near Waikiki or Diamond Head?" Sally asked.

"Heavens no! That's too 'town,'" replied Zoe.

"That's right," said Pualani, "we've vowed never to live in a town or a city again. It's the North Shore, kind of the hippie section of Oahu for surfers, farmers, military personnel and *more* surfers—if you catch the drift." She looked at Sally pointedly and smiled.

"And there are also employees of the pineapple or sugar companies, artists, drifters or just people like us flight attendants who don't have a daily commute," added Zoe. She rummaged around and found a simple map, handing it to Sally. "We're heading up this old road towards the mountains over there," she gestured. "Between the Koolaus and the Waianae Range down below are beautiful white sand beaches, and some of the best surf in the world."

"It's serious business out here," said Pualani. "The Hawaiians invented surfing a thousand years ago; it was a sport for the ruling chiefs. We may get some big waves tomorrow, big enough to break at Waimea Bay. And when Waimea breaks, it's big—20 feet and up."

"Can people really survive that?" asked Sally.

"Sometimes they don't," said Pua. "Ask some of my family. You have to be one hell of an athlete and in perfect condition, both physically and mentally, to take on Waimea."

"This is a big weekend, Sally," said Zoe. "Not only will the waves be up, but we're having a huge party tomorrow night to welcome you. Some of Pualani's cousins have a band, and they're going to play. We're going to have the works, including a pig!"

"I've never been known to turn down a party!" cried Sally. "This sounds wonderful."

After they passed through the little town of Haleiwa, Pua slowed the Big Orange and eased the hearse into a sandy driveway shaded by long-needled pines and old plumeria trees, fragrant with flowers and salt air. Two houses stood in the open yards, constructed of single-wall board and batten, with double-hung windows and shake roofs. At the house Zoe and Pualani had rented, red and white flowered trader-cotton curtains flapped gaily from unscreened windows, and a big hand-lettered sign across the door proclaimed, "Aloha 'Wild Sally' Wilder!"

"Welcome home!" Zoe and Pualani hugged her, dragging Sally indoors and grabbing boxes and suitcases on the way.

"Oh, Zoe…Pualani, how lovely," Sally said as they walked into the small living room. A set of "pretzel" sofa and chairs were arranged on woven mats, and leant an old-fashioned air to the simple island décor. Just off the covered lanai out back lay an expansive, pristine beach. They showed Sally to her bedroom, where she sat down on the bed, feeling the soft breeze, taking in the strong colors of the sea and sky. This was so different from anything she had ever known, and yet she felt comfortable.

The three women walked out on the beach. Sally sank her toes into the cool sand, still trying to absorb the changes in her life and location. To salute the sunset, Pualani brought out cold beers, and Zoe her inevitable tonic water, and they toasted each other, sighing contentedly as they sat on the sand and talked through the adventures of the year. Soon, night fell and the stars lit the sky one by one in the deepening twilight. Although weary from her journey, Sally gloried in the whole aura of Hawai'i as the ocean rumbled and crashed.

"We call the ocean the *moana kai*, the deep blue waters of Kane, of infinity," said Pualani.

"*Moana kai*," repeated Sally. Even the language was soft and beautiful. She hugged herself as she sifted the sand through her fingers.

The next morning at seven o'clock, Zoe and Pualani headed out for a morning beach run, while Sally remained asleep. They waved cheerfully across the yard at a man standing on the lanai. Pua called to him in the local pidgin dialect, "Eh, Moke! Looking rough, brother!"

The man grinned sheepishly, sipping a cup of hot coffee. "We sang too long at the Eagle's Nest last night. It's a new bar in the Pan Am building downtown," he said.

He surveyed the surf carefully. "We gonna see some waves today, big time." The swell that had been forecast by the radio stations was now arriving, and he was preparing for a day in the water.

"So, ladies, what's the deal next door?" asked a tall, tanned man, slamming the screen door as he scratched his short sandy hair. He nodded to the house across the empty lot.

Zoe and Pua laughed. "Now Walker, that's our new roommate trying to sleep in, and we'll thank you not to disturb her." They shook their heads and started moving out towards the beach, breaking into a run.

The door slammed again, and a third man, burly and redheaded, joined them on the lanai. "So Zoe told me the scoop. This one is Wild Sally Wilder, and she has a title." He sipped his coffee, while Walker and Moke pondered.

"Diz, you're not making sense. A what?" asked Walker.

"A title," repeated Diz, "as in royalty. She was in training with Pua and Zoe, and she's an African Queen, although I'm not entirely sure I understand what that means. I think it's time we awaken Her Majesty, don't you?"

He led them across the yard and positioned them under the back bedroom windows with closed curtains, where they commenced an uneven, raucous chorus of "Anchors Aweigh".

Sally snapped open the curtains, yelling, "You can take your anchors and shove 'em up...just what do you think you're doing?" She knelt on her bed, wrapped in a quilt, her mind a fog of jet-lagged confusion. She surveyed the unshaven faces, and said, "Okay, which one of you early-bird assholes is the Lion, the Scarecrow and the Tin Woodman?"

"Lt. Walker Sheppard, Barbers Point NAS, and this is Moke Cabral," said Walker politely, smoothing his sandy hair. "We just came over to offer some hospitality."

"And I'm Lt. Diz Langford, sole representative of the United States Army Reserve," added the redhead. "You came home from the airport in my Big Orange yesterday." Sally nodded in hazy recollection.

"What's going on in here?" said Zoe, marching into Sally's room followed closely by Pualani, their skin glowing from the run, Pua's dark eyes glaring at Walker Sheppard, who stared back at her in rapt appreciation.

Seeing the three faces in the window, Pua put her hands on her hips and clucked, "Don't you slobs have any manners? This is a hell of a way to introduce yourselves." Suitably chastened, Walker grinned, and Pualani looked into his eyes with a small smile. "Well, you folks go on about your business. We have work to do cleaning up this place for the party tonight." She waved and left them.

"And Diz," Zoe said, "you're supposed to make a run up to Schofield this morning to pick up liquor and food for the luau tonight. You've got stuff to do, now get on it!" She shooed them away.

"Right away, ladies," said Diz, saluting, "but why don't we take Her Majesty Wild Sally with us. Give her a little orientation tour, you might say. We can take a run over to Waimea on the way so she can see the big waves before all the crowds get there. It's supposed to break at 30 feet by noon. Sally, we're kidnapping you for the morning." She groaned and rolled out of bed.

When they piled into The Big Orange a few minutes later, and started off down the road toward Waimea, the air was almost white, infused with the salt spray spewed by the enormous waves. A few hundred yards before they reached the bay, cars were lined on both sides of the road with dozens of people walking quickly towards the water, listening to the ominous roar of the waves in the distance. As they rounded the curve, the roar hit Sally's ears with a force, like the rumbling power of jet engines. She could see the bay below them, a u-shaped body of water crowned by a broad sandy beach.

"There's the lighthouse," said Diz, pointing to the outcropping of rocks across the bay at Waimea Point. The sets were breaking at the Point, forming gigantic walls of water. Foaming and roiling after this first break, the water rushed for the shore in long stretches before gathering for one final blast of energy and heaving forward in a second break, or shore break, about five feet high, hissing and foaming on the sand.

"There's a *heiau* up there," said Moke, pointing to the rocky reddish brown cliff rising straight up above them from the opposite side of the road, "the ruins of a Hawai'ian temple. There's also supposed to be a burial ground there and it's considered a very sacred site."

"Moke, are you from the islands?" asked Sally.

"My family is Portuguese Hawai'ian," replied Moke. "My Dad's side worked the sugar plantations on Maui. But on my mother's side, I'm descended from the *kanaka maoli*, the ancient Hawaiians. I'm in law school at the University of Hawai'i."

"How did you run into these two characters?" Sally nodded toward Diz and Walker.

"The water," Moke shrugged, nodding at the crashing waves. "People from all walks of life love to surf. That ocean is the great unifier."

They climbed onto the Big Orange's hood, leaning back against the windshield. "Here," said Diz, handing Sally a pair of binoculars. "Take a look through these."

She saw a group of surfers sitting on their boards in the water, clustered together, waiting. When a wave came along, a few would peel away and paddle rapidly, piercing the crest, then with the agility and grace of trapeze artists in a circus, launch themselves down its face like they were—Sally could find no other word for it—*flying*. Their skill and bravery in the face of such danger overwhelmed her.

"Wonder if Billy Righteous is out there this morning," said Walker.

"Who's Billy Righteous?" asked Sally.

"Probably the finest surfer in Hawai'i," replied Moke. "He's a legend on the North Shore, a Marine who lives in a Quonset hut at the Pipeline, right near here."

"Is that his real name?" asked Sally.

"Nah," said Moke, "it's his surfing handle, but it should be his real name. He's rescued people from drowning lots of times, and he's a real leader in the surfing community up here. They're not always the most stable lot, and they can get into all kinds of trouble. Many of them give up everything—their women, their educations and careers—just to surf these waves. Some get jobs in construction, while others just collect welfare. Some of them start dealing drugs to make money, particularly cocaine, and get hooked on it themselves. Billy lets them stay at his house while they detox and can get it together again."

"Can you see him? Is he out there now?" asked Sally.

"Check the glasses. He usually wears black trunks and a black wetsuit top," said Moke. "*Haole* fellow. Big guy."

Sally scanned the group of surfers and watched for a while as several caught waves. Then she saw a deeply tanned man in black trunks and sleeveless rubber tank top, his muscled arms gripping the sides of his board. Quickly hoisting his legs, he straightened, unfolding like a seabird. Then he turned his body to an angle, his arms spreading as he dropped down the face of the wave, slicing through the water, perfectly balanced. When he reached the bottom, his legs flexed, and he turned his board into the curl of the 30-foot wave hanging over him. Outrunning the wall of water bursting down behind him, he crouched then straightened, turning back up the face of the wave, staying high, then zipping down again, squeezing every inch out of the ride he could all the way along the curl, until at last he stood down and began to paddle back out. The crowd on the beach burst into spontaneous applause, yelling, "Go Billy!"

"I think I see him," said Sally, breathless, the image imprinted on her mind.

After the commissary run, Sally lay down for a short nap. Suddenly Zoe was shaking her arm, "Hey, sleepyhead! The party's starting! You've been napping for hours; time to rise!"

Sally raced through a shower, hoping the jet lag didn't show in the late afternoon, as the yard began to fill with people. She joined Pua and Sally welcoming guests; many were Pualani's family and friends from neighboring Wahiawa, Waialua and even further out from Waianae on the leeward coast. Five muscular men had stripped down to their shorts with towels wrapped around their heads. They had dug a hole in the middle of the lot, lined it with chicken wire and filled it with smoldering charcoals and stones. They set a trussed pig in the ground and covered it with damp banana leaves and wetted-down burlap bags. Now, the smoky, roasting fat filled the air with a pungent aroma.

Next to the cooking area, two large Hawai'ian men, their skin and clothing redolent of the *imu* cooking fire, were helping Diz pick up a large drum-shaped container with a wax seal. Pualani beckoned Sally and Zoe over, explaining, "That is my cousin, Keoki Kanawai, showing Diz the ropes. Keoki is the world's most dangerous Swipe manufacturer."

Keoki hefted the drum aloft, smiling, his dark eyes accentuating his bronzed face and body, right out of a Hawai'ian etching. He wiped his forehead on his faded tie-dyed tee shirt, emblazoned with "Haleiwa Poi", his hair tied back with a bandana. "I learned this in the Cook Islands. They swear by these old coconut stumps." He went on to describe the *tumunu*, a hollowed-out coconut stump that was filled with oranges, pineapples, limes—even yams or mangoes—along with sugar and water. "Then we put a cork in it, in this case a big wooden disc covered with wet rawhide and sealed with wax."

"It sounds like the Pacific's version of an Old Fashioned," Sally said.

Keoki grinned at Sally, his dark eyes mischievous, his chest heaving with the effort of holding up the heavy log. "Okay now. Stand back. When she blows out the cork, she's ready to go!"

Zoe laughed, and Keoki nodded. "Yes, ounce for ounce it's one of the most potent alcoholic mixtures anywhere. But that *pake* Pualani got it all from her grandma's yard and then forced me to make the Swipe." He smiled as he teased his cousin about her thrifty habits.

"This stuff is like gold," said Keoki, "it sells for big money at the baby luaus. So here goes!" He raised the *tumunu* log, held it above his head, then threw it back on the sand, upright. Within seconds, a shrill fizzing sounded, and the foot-wide disk blew off the top. The crowd cheered. Grabbing a small coconut bowl, he dipped it in the mixture.

"Here's some for *ka'aina*, the land," he said, reverently pouring a measure on the earth, "and here's for our *makua*, our ancestors." He offered another measure to the land. "And here's for our *malihini*, our newcomers." He handed the bowl first to Zoe, then to Sally.

They tasted the sweet, harsh liquor. Zoe inhaled the fumes, remembering old Shan campfires and smiling her thanks to Keoki, while Sally sputtered and howled at the potency. Zoe took the bowl and dipped it again.

"Like this?" Zoe asked, pouring a drop on the earth and proffering it to Keoki, who accepted it with a smile in his dark eyes.

"Eh, a quick learner…good," said Keoki. He went on serving the crowd that had now surrounded him.

In addition to Pualani's family, Zoe had invited their Pan Am friends, and the men next door had invited many of theirs. The girls stood on the lanai to greet their guests as the waves broke on the rocks, illuminated by the setting sun. Sally received colorful lei from new friends, who greeted her like a long-lost family member. "It's the island way," said Pualani, her dark eyes flashing, a delicate white stephanotis blossom at her ear.

Pua beckoned Zoe to come sit with her and Keoki, sorting through the tapes and records of the island music they wanted to hear, some of which Keoki had brought from Tahiti and the Cook Islands. Pua spoke enthusiastically about their similar interests in historical research projects, and teased Keoki about Tahitian women.

Keoki smiled, glancing at Zoe. "Nah, she knows, she knows. It's all about the history."

Zoe saw the appraisal and the questions in his eyes. What are you, who are you? She found herself intrigued with this quiet man, feeling a spark that had so long been dormant.

Diz and Moke had hauled their stereo system out onto the lanai and were putting the finishing touches on hooking up enormous speakers that were the size of washing machines. On the record changer, they stacked records from Santana and War, as well as Keoki's new albums of Hawai'ian music: Peter Moon and the Sunday Manoa and Gabby Pahinui. They stacked the records high, as the guests moved and swayed to the rhythm of the music.

When the mouth-watering smells almost overwhelmed them, the men unpacked the *imu*, passing generous portions of fresh roasted pork; *lau-lau* bundles of taro, pork and butterfish; fresh yams and roast chickens. The food was passed hand over hand to the tables, already loaded with rice, lomi salmon, 'opihi and shellfish, poi, island fruits and haupia cake. Then the diners joined hands in a circle, while the elders sang a Hawai'ian Congregational hymn and blessing. The laughter and camaraderie continued through the evening as some of the guests moved to the sand to rest, content after their meal. One Auntie said, "Oh, we eat till tired," as others laughed and the air cooled with the evening breeze.

After dinner, a fresh fire crackled in the *imu* pit, and Moke joined Pualani's cousins as they began to play Hawai'ian music. Aunties and friends danced hula, the old raucous party hulas with double entendre meanings and naughty words. Young and old, they sang songs of the land, of the smell of flowers, all words of comfort and history in the fire's glow.

Pualani suddenly rose and began to dance, hearing the strains of a familiar song coming from Keoki's 12-string guitar and his lilting tenor voice singing a friend's composition: "Where I live, there are rainbows…With the laughter of morning…And starry nights…."[1]

It was song of love and loss, the gentleness of the islands and its golden children. Pua dipped and swayed, bringing the music up through the *na'ao*, the center, up through her soul to embrace all who were gathered around the fire. She was a graceful, fluid dancer, and Walker Sheppard sat at her feet, entranced, now profoundly in love. She returned the feeling with her eyes, dancing only for him, embracing him with a lei as the song ended.

Then Keoki started a more forceful, pounding rhythm, a demanding cadence, while the elders slapped their ukuleles in percussion. "Go on Pualani, dance the story," he said. "Dance 'The Stone Eating Song'."

A group of the young cousins joined her, men and women, dancing now in a different form, a determined, upright, urgent voice, their faces solemn and composed. Several sang along, calling the words in a cadence. An elder spoke the English words: "*Kaulana na pua a'o Hawai'i*…famous the children of Hawai'i, loyal to the land."

The dancers mimed the refusal of the Hawaiians to accept the islands' annexation to the United States, calling on the people: "'*A'ole a'e kau i ka pulima*…no one will sign the paper of the enemy."

Pualani and her cousins joined in the chant: "We will eat stones, the food of the land; we will support our Queen."

Sally stood with Zoe and Walker, taking in the powerful performance, watching the movements of the dancers as their shadows flickered on the ground, the sharp words of the chant cutting through the night air. Like captured peoples everywhere, these islanders used song and dance to express their loss and pain, and most importantly, to remember. At the end of the song, the whole group rose to kiss the singers and the chanters, and Sally embraced Pualani.

"You have given us a gift," Sally said to her friend.

"It's the history," said Pualani, simply. Then stepping forward, she smiled at Walker. "We know you cannot all understand this song, but it was written in 1893, by a beloved friend of our Queen, Lili'uokulani. Many Hawaiians are learning their history again for the first time. We hope you'll learn with us."

Walker nodded, looking into her eyes. "Yes, we have much to learn together."

Then Keoki stood, leaning his guitar gently against the stones. "You all say you want to learn, but so many newcomers and so many military are ignorant, or won't change their minds, and there are so few of us Hawaiians left." He nodded and turned to leave, quietly.

Zoe, standing by the lanai as he passed, reached out her hand to him. "Keoki, I do, I want to learn."

He looked at her, his eyes masked. "Yes, I know. And you *will* learn. That makes you dangerous." He looked at her again, deep into her eyes, and moved away into the night.

The party broke up slowly, the guests discussing the powerful moments of the dances and the concept of Hawai'ian sovereignty. Moke was concerned over constitutional questions of statehood. Diz and Walker brought up the standing of U.S. military personnel. Zoe thought about the conduct of the war in Vietnam, and a similar ignorance of culture throughout Asia. Shaking her head, she said nothing. All recognized the need for more knowledge. The talk was earnest and real, relaxed and idealistic, even hopeful.

Zoe sighed, thinking of the fighting of that other, larger war far across the ocean, and imagining the smaller battles by distant campfires in her homeland. The moon rose. Night deepened.

Late the next morning, Sally was out in the yard hanging up her laundry, fighting with the stiff on-shore breeze that snatched at her clothes. She looked briefly at the choppy waves outside, remembering the amazing figure of the man called Billy Righteous out there in the surf at Waimea. A day ago, she had never seen Paradise, and now here she was, living some sort of a Pacific dream. When she went back inside she was reminded of the events of the previous night, as she caught the sweet scent of dozens of last night's fragrant leis that were spread about the living room, and draped over the windows and doors. The shrill ringing of the telephone interrupted her reverie and she moved to answer it, speculating as to whether or not it could be Scheduling.

"Aloha, Sally. It's Polly and I'm the crew scheduler on duty. I know you just arrived the other day, but we have an emergency assignment for you this evening. Do you think you can handle a trip this soon? Are your cholera shots up to date?"

Sally groaned inwardly, but said, "Polly, I'll be a basket case, but it's okay. I'm sure the other crewmembers will sort me out."

"Great," said Polly, "Ready for some black air flying?"

"Some what?"

"Black air flying. Honolulu crews have very few daytime flights—Tokyo, San Francisco and Los Angeles; all of the other report and arrival times are late at night or before dawn, so…black air! But at least you'll get one hell of a blood-red South Pacific sunrise. So, sweetie, your report time is 2200 hours, and you'll be taking a 10-day trip to Guam, Manila, Saigon and back. Come early so you can get your picture taken for your Geneva Card. It won't take but a few minutes, but you've got to have it along with your passport and shot card."

"My Geneva Card?" asked Sally. Polly's maternal tone made her feel comfortable, unlike the impersonal schedulers in New York. "Is this a MAC charter by chance?" Sally asked, thinking of the Military

Air Command, which chartered flights on commercial airlines for R&R's in and out of Vietnam, as well as moving other military personnel from base to base around the globe.

"Well, it's not all MAC charters." Polly shuffled through her papers. "Let's see, the first part is a standard 841 pattern from Guam to Manila to Saigon, but it looks like you are on an extra-section MAC coming home after that. Stay tuned. We'll see you tonight. Bye."

Sally looked out the window at her laundry flapping in the breeze. Fortunately everything would dry quickly. She went to her bedroom to pack.

That night, as the diminishing waves broke gently against the seawall and the breeze swirled in the coconut trees, she dressed for her first Pacific trip and headed out to the Big Orange, where Zoe and Diz already had her bags loaded, ready for the airport run.

As the hearse pulled out of the driveway, Pua yelled, "Aloha, Sally! Watch out for black air!"

Notes:

1   From "Hawai'ian Lullaby", lyrics by Hector Venegas. Used by permission.

CHAPTER NINE

SAIGON RUSH
JANUARY 30, 1972   SAIGON, VIETNAM

Sally had immediately been drawn to the sights and sounds of Saigon, and meandered down the gracious boulevards, taking in the peeling yellow colonial buildings, the brash neon and market atmosphere, the thump of rock-and-roll music, the smells of this Asian city. Slender women in conical hats, flesh-colored arm-length gloves and simple white *ao dhai* sat primly on mopeds and rickshaws, navigating their way through streets clogged with bicycles, cars, buses and pedestrians. Whole families of five crowded onto one moped. Street vendors sold lottery tickets and street-food as smells of star anise and ginger wafted out from *phở* noodle shops. Funeral shops built coffins and grave decorations right on the street. Incense shops sold bundles in five hundred varieties. Children walked in convent uniforms by street corners, carrying their homework, while urchins frolicked in the ponds of water and rotting vegetables, street sweepings and flowers. Soulful Vietnamese music filled with love and longing echoed through tinny speakers.

In another section of the same street, there was a different, more urgent beat. The colonial buildings had long since deteriorated into gummy, multi-storied apartment buildings, bars and clubs blasting disco music, pink-lit massage parlors and tacky souvenir shops. Although the scene was novel for her, she watched the faces and body language of dozens of beautiful young Asian women lined up outside the bars and cheap hotels, dressed in tawdry mini-skirts and rhinestones, chatting with each other, smoking, reading—always with an eye out for fresh clients. The street life had an urgency, a life-or-death rawness, a smell of cheap perfume and sewage. She had walked along, aware of the glares of the bar hostesses, and the hungry glances of young American men with short haircuts and compressed lips. The men's bright tropical shirts belied the darkness in their eyes and their empty smiles. Some mimed manic camaraderie with one another, others wound themselves around bar girls, still others slumped by themselves on stools at the bar. One soldier sat on the curb, his face hidden, his shoulders convulsed. Sally had stopped, uncertain.

"Are you okay?" she asked, reaching a hand to his shoulder, but he slapped it away, glaring. A buddy came forward to restrain him, "Sorry ma'am. Jim's lost his manners today—he's not drowning his sorrows real well."

After a few more blocks, she had stopped into a coffee bar and ordered a Vietnamese-style coffee. It came with a strainer atop a small glass of condensed milk over ice. As she watched the caramel liquid swirl into the glass, she heard snatches of conversation between two men seated behind a screen of ragged palms. The older, scruffier man smoked a strong, noxious French cigarette.

"Shit, everybody knew that Vang Pao was the opium lord of Laos," the man was saying. "He had his pick of Air America flights until late last year, just like Khun Sa out of Burma."

Sally heard the second taller man mumble, "Did you guys know what you were carrying?"

"Mostly we didn't care. We hauled everything from pissing pigs to rice-bags and hard rice—boxes of ammunition and weapons. Whatever the customer wants, we fly."

"And the customer's always the Company?"

"I dunno, but they probably don't call Laos and the Golden Triangle 'Spook Heaven' for nothing."

Sally could not understand the reply, but she heard "Golden Triangle" and "Burma" in the sentence, and stored it away to tell Zoe. The conversation had a surrealistic quality.

"So how did the heroin start coming into Saigon?" asked the taller man.

"It's all double-cross central. Apparently a few years ago they brought in some master chemists from Hong Kong who turned the shit into high-grade heroin. Things were going along fine—those piss-ant Chinese and Burmese warlords were making money and buying guns, but now it's backfiring. The stuff has wound up on the streets of

Saigon, in the veins of our GI's, and all the way back to the U.S.A. But it ain't nothing we can change with this job, so we'd better get over there now." They'd scuffed their chairs back, ready to leave, and Sally quickly turned attention to the dregs of her coffee and rummaged in her purse as they walked away. She headed for the hotel and the privacy of her room, her sleep confused and uneasy.

Later that evening, she sipped a drink with her roommate Ruby Santiago in the rooftop bar of the Caravelle Hotel, an infamous watering hole in the city. The hotel served as the nerve center for wartime Saigon, its blocky architecture and comfortable art deco style welcoming foreign journalists, soldiers, aid workers, diplomats, spies, contractors—even missionaries and airline crews. The bar was busy, with additional clientele from the nearby Continental Palace and Majestic Hotels drifting in for cocktails. A bored bartender flipped a channel on the bulky TV screen overhead, where a crew cut American broadcaster reported, "In 10 days, President Nixon will arrive in China for an historic visit."

"I'd give just about anything to fly the press charter to China," Sally said.

"All this attention on China, I hope there won't be changes out here." Ruby's face darkened. "It would be a disaster for my social life."

"Oh for God's sake, Ruby," said Sally, "You can't be serious. I don't think *anything* is going to hurt your social life. Not after seeing you operate in Manila last night."

Hailing from a tough background in the Panama Canal Zone, Ruby grew up learning the languages of the customers who frequented her mother's small restaurant and casino. She had strong shoulders and a generous bosom, long legs, a glowing cocoa skin, and ebullient Latina confidence. Her heavy, unmanageable black hair was wound up in a chignon, more comfortable in Saigon's thick afternoon humidity. Her dark eyes and her teeth flashed in an ever-ready smile that lit up rooms. The previous evening, she had marched straight into the middle of the dance floor at a Manila nightclub and taken the place by storm. Sally had trailed behind, awestruck, while Ruby electrified bystanders as she danced to the latest song from Earth, Wind and Fire, performed by a Filipino band that sounded just like the real thing. They never had to buy a drink, and they rarely sat down.

"Yes, but you have to admit that it wouldn't have been any fun at all to come home early," Ruby pointed out. "All the action happened between midnight and 5 a.m."

Sally yawned, "But dancing all night, then getting back to the hotel for a shower and pick-up at seven this morning was no drill." She grimaced, "Hey, I didn't think I'd survive the flight to Saigon, but I went for a walk and now I've got my second wind."

"*Ay, que bueno, chica!*" Ruby said. "You have it just right!"

Ruby was completely unlike anyone Sally had ever met, and she went completely against type at Pan Am. But after the initial shock wore off, Sally decided that she liked her full throttle approach to life, especially in the war zones, and the incredible impact she had on every man in every situation. Ruby knew she had to make her mark before the lights went out and her beauty faded—and she didn't do it for scarves and jewelry, like Gabriella. No, for Ruby it was the sheer gusto of living that fueled her sparkle.

As if to prove the point, two attractive men sauntered up to their table, wearing worn bush jackets, one bulky with long-lensed cameras.

"Oh Stan," Ruby cooed, "I'm so glad you made it. You remember my friend Sally from the flight this morning?" The men smiled, though Sally didn't have any recollection of seeing them. The Caravelle was the perfect environment for Ruby, and she had worked fast. "Stan's a photographer from the BBC and Peter's a journalist from one of the news services. I met them again in the coffee shop this afternoon while you were napping." Ruby blinked her dark eyes at Stan.

Sally did not miss the gesture and smiled. Ruby's magnetic personality was already at work, and Stan was clearly smitten.

"Why don't you join us?" suggested Stan.

Exhausted from the revels of the night before and feeling punchy in spite of her nap, Sally yawned again. "You all go on ahead.

I'm just on my first nights in the Pacific, and I haven't quite gotten the hang of this black air thing."

Peter said, "I'll stay here and keep Sally company for a while if she can stand it. I've just got to run downstairs to file this deadline report first." He turned to Sally and tapped her arm. "Don't go anywhere. I'll be right back."

When he returned and they'd ordered fresh drinks, Sally told him about the sinister coffee-bar conversation she'd overheard on Tu Doh Street.

"Peter, what were they talking about?" she asked. "The war is here in Vietnam, isn't it? These guys sounded as though there's stuff going on all over the place."

Peter turned away thoughtfully, his face grave. "You know, Sally, you really shouldn't discuss what you heard with just anybody. We don't know what it all means, but there's a lot more going on than appears. First of all, the Paris Peace Talks are a matter of time. Fairly soon, they'll sign some sort of bullshit accord, declare peace and demand a U.S. withdrawal. I'm willing to bet it'll be within the next year, no later than, say, June of 1973." He paused, shaking his head ruefully. "Secondly, there are just too many strange, uncorroborated stories floating around, and we aren't allowed to pursue them. We've all heard about a bandit airline of the CIA called Air America, or Air Asia, or some other names. Supposedly their pilots are total war junkies, eccentrics and adventurers, not to mention hotshot pilots of the first order. Thirdly, the minority groups and hill tribes throughout the Golden Triangle have been fighting each other and the Communists and everybody else, just so somebody would take out their dope and keep that whole economic cycle going. But we don't have verification about any of this for sure, and it's just too damned dangerous to go asking questions."

Peter drained his glass. "It's pretty crazy out here, just like the bloody Opium Wars all over again, and the West just won't learn that Asia always wins. Their leaders sure don't want any of us white folks around telling them what to do; they've had just about enough colonialist claptrap, thank you." He looked around the room. "Of course, their real secret weapons are these gorgeous, beautiful, submissive women. They've already won without a shot being fired."

Sally pondered these words for a moment. Then she stifled a yawn, the cocktails and the lack of sleep taking their toll. Rising from her chair, she gave Peter's shoulder a pat. "Hey, I'm sorry but I'm really dragging. I enjoyed our chat, and I know I'll see you on other deadlines. Thanks so much for the drink."

She turned and threaded her way among several tables of middle-aged westerners accompanied by gorgeous sloe-eyed Vietnamese girls. Sally lifted her head and smiled slightly to the women in greeting: here's to you, sister. Here's to all women of the world who survive as best they can. And by God, here's to Ruby.

Stepping in the elevator, she pressed the button for her floor. Peter leaned out to look after her, raising his hand in a mock salute as the doors slid shut.

Just before boarding at Tan Son Nhut the next morning, Sally assumed her duty position at the bottom of the stairs to greet the passengers. Clad in her blue bowler hat and white cotton gloves, she felt a little conspicuous. The airfield was busy with a myriad of aircraft scattered about the tarmac, from Air Force C5-A's, to assorted helicopters, fighter jets and a World Airways 727. Dozens of unmarked smaller propeller aircraft moved around a nearby Air Asia hangar. She remembered the conversations of the day before.

Ground crews were busy loading the 747 with all manner of baggage, strollers, suitcases, trunks and boxes onto the conveyor belts up to the cargo holds.

As she watched, a line of vehicles pulled up with a different kind of cargo: glinting metal coffins, draped with American flags, which began their short sad journeys up to the hold, the ramp workers lifting them into the dark interior. Sally felt her stomach lurch as she walked toward the belt. She placed her hand on one of the coffins and patted it briefly in a gesture of comfort to the silent, still occupant. It was a futile gesture that depressed her; the soft cotton flag and the cold coffin her first tangible contact with the razor-sharp edges of war.

She sighed, remembering the same helplessness she'd felt at Gorée Island's Slave House. She returned to the metal stairs, not daring to look back at the lonely journey of the coffins. Tears stung her eyes in the hot morning air, and the whine of the 747's auxiliary engine rang in her ears.

There are too many of you dying, Sally thought, too many.

Moments later, the ticket agent opened the door of the departure lounge and waved. Passengers were walking toward Sally, including a large group of soldiers in fatigues carrying duffle bags. Surely these young men would be happy to be going home, she thought.

But they were withdrawn, silent. She smiled as each one reached the steps, but it did not take her long to read their faces— twisted, individual diaries of pain. Her smile felt forced when she tried to make eye contact as the heavy boots clanked up the metal stairs. She thought of the line of metal coffins behind her, shaded by the aircraft cargo door, and redoubled her grim effort. Something must cheer them up, she thought. When a young man with red hair about her age paused and looked at her hesitantly, she touched her hand to his arm.

"Welcome home, soldier," she said softly. He looked at her blankly. The boarding continued in complete silence.

After takeoff, dinner was served rapidly. As she picked up the dinner trays, she noticed that the redheaded young man to whom she had spoken on the tarmac had not eaten anything. His forehead was covered with beads of sweat, although the cabin was cool.

"What can I get for you?" asked Sally, thinking, he doesn't look right.

"I don't feel well," said the young man, grasping the seatback in front, his eyes staring head.

Sally brought a leftover cold towel from the galley. She sat next to him and wiped his brow. "Have you got malaria or something?"

Some of his seatmates took an interest, chortling, "Yeah, he's got something, all right!"

"No," he said flatly. Then after a moment said, "I...I think I'm going to be sick."

Sally dug into the seat pocket and whipped out an airsick bag.

She held the man's head as he vomited, retching over and over, as if he were purging himself of more than just the contents of his stomach. Feeling queasy herself, she rolled up the ends of the bag and secured it with the little tabs on the end. But she felt too sorry for the man to let nausea overcome her. After being in such a sweat, he leaned back and began to shiver, and Sally put a blanket over him. As she placed his arms under the blanket, she stopped cold. There were ugly red marks forming little tracks in his forearms. At that moment, she recalled the conversation with Peter about the high-grade heroin that was circulating on the streets of Saigon.

"What's your name?" asked Sally quietly.

"Larry," said the young man, his face ashen, now covered with sweat.

"Where are you from, Larry?"

"West Virginia, a little place up in the mountains, right next to the Pennsylvania line. Nothin' you've ever heard of." Larry shivered and pulled the blanket up to his chin.

Sally patted his arm, "Soldier, I'm from Latham, Kentucky, and I can guarantee you that nobody's heard of that either."

He almost smiled, nodding sheepishly. "I'm sorry, ma'am. I didn't mean to be any trouble. It's just that…"

"Now Larry," Sally comforted him, "don't worry. Lots of passengers get sick. Here's another bag in case you feel sick again. I'll be right back."

Returning to the galley, she disposed of the airsick bag and asked Ruby for some more towels. "I've got a sick soldier here," said Sally, explaining the situation.

Ruby rolled her eyes. "You can't see what's going on, Saleee?" asked Ruby, her voice impatient. "He's going through withdrawal from heroin, is what. They think they can shoot up one last time at Tan Son Nhut and that will be it. I'll call the cockpit and tell them to have a doctor meet us when we get to Guam. Until then, there's nothing else we can do for him here except keep him calm and feed him fluids. Talk to him and reassure him. He's going to have a rough night, I'm afraid. Sorry, that one ain't my war, honey. He's all yours."

Sally returned to the now-shivering soldier and leaning toward him, spoke in a low voice. "Larry, you've been doing heroin, haven't you? How long?"

"About six months," Larry replied, his teeth rattling. He was beginning to writhe in pain with stomach cramps. He retched again and moaned.

"What in hell did you do this to yourself for?" asked Sally, adjusting his blankets and handing him more airsick bags. "It's hard enough to stay alive in combat without adding this stuff on top of it."

"I dunno," mumbled Larry. "It just sort of happened. Lots of guys were doing it. It helped with the dysentery. Made us forget the bad things, like being afraid, like being mixed up in all this shit. I thought I could take one last hit and quit."

"Listen to me, Larry," instructed Sally. "We'll be sure that a doctor meets the plane when we land in Guam. You're going to have to lick this, starting right now. You don't want your parents to see you in this shape, now do you?"

Larry began to sob. "I don't know if I *can* lick it."

Sally put her arms around him and cradled his head in her shoulder. "Shhh, now. You did the right thing over there, but you just got sick along the way. We'll get you well again. We're going home now, we're going home." And she held him like this through the remainder of the flight, as the young man's chemical demons came out in full force in his twisted mind, as he cried and shook and sweated again and again. At last, the landing gear of the *Clipper Polynesian Trader* rumbled down for final approach to Agaña Airport on Guam. Sally returned to her jumpseat just in time for touchdown.

She hugged him good-bye as the medical team moved him gently to a waiting ambulance. The doctor patted her arm. "Thank you. You brought him through the worst. We'll have him on his way home in a week. There are so many, so damned young...."

Less than 24 hours later, Sally's inbound military charter from Guam landed in Honolulu at four-thirty in the morning, with 400 sleeping soldiers headed for the Hickam side of Honolulu International

Airport. Dragging through customs, she and her crew headed back to the Pan Am offices.

Just as Sally collapsed on an aging, overstuffed sofa, Zoe sailed into the room. She was fresh after a good night's sleep and had a purple orchid lei on her arm to celebrate Sally's first arrival home. In uniform, she was ready for her early eight o'clock report for a Los Angeles turn-around.

Placing the lei around Sally's neck and giving her a kiss on the cheek, Zoe said, "I've left the Big Orange outside in the parking lot to get you home." She reported on the full-fledged romance now underway between Pualani and Walker Sheppard during the last week. Sally smiled for Pualani, then groaned, lying back, groggy and numb from eight hours of flying.

Shift Supervisor Doug Correa was just getting off the graveyard shift in Crew Scheduling. "Welcome to the Honolulu Base, Sally," he said. "You look like you could use a beer." Zoe chortled and shook her head.

Removing her stock tie and unbuttoning the top button of her blouse, Sally looked at Zoe in amazement. "You guys, I'm in uniform and it's barely five o'clock in the morning."

"Not to us it isn't," grinned Doug. "For me and the guys, it's quittin' time!" He took her arm and led her down the hall. "Come on, we'll show you something special. Zoe, follow me in your car? You know where to go."

"Where are we doing?" asked Sally.

Zoe was no help and just smiled as she led the way out to the Big Orange. "You'll see. I did it last month and it is pretty incredible. But that's all I'm saying!"

They followed Doug's faded-green Chevrolet Impala as he drove out of the parking lot ahead of them and along Nimitz Highway, turning left along the fenced-in airfield of Honolulu International, and passing by a collection of battered old Quonset huts and a three-story tower. They roared up in a cloud of dust, parking the hearse next to a collection of similarly battered vehicles facing the airfield. They could hear the whine of jet engines above and behind them. Doug got out of the car, gesturing for Sally and Zoe to follow him through a hole in the rusty fence. Several men and a couple of women sat in the pre-dawn gloom of the peeling Quonset hut, some in unbuttoned blue shirts of Pan Am ground service uniforms signifying their status as "ramp rats." Doug gestured to their dusty surroundings.

"Aloha, welcome to the *real* world! Way back, this was the original Pan Am terminal, and the bosses still use it as a cargo hangar whenever there's stuff coming through that nobody's supposed to know about. But here, let me introduce you ladies. Folks, this is Sally and Zoe. Ladies, these guys are the best mechanics in the universe, bruddah. No can read the manual but they can fix 17 generations of aircraft from DC3s to these honkin' 747 suckers!"

The men laughed and they all hugged, island-style. Zoe introduced Sally to the two women from catering whom she'd met on recent late-night forays to Pan Am's impressive in-flight kitchens.

"So, what, we gonna rock and roll?" asked Francine, who held up a doobie of marijuana to share.

Sally accepted with a smile, shaking her head. "Now I *really* know this isn't JFK," she said. Hanging out with the caterers and ground service people would be unheard of in New York; but out here, it was all about *ohana*, about being a part of a family. Waves lapped in Ke'ehi Lagoon on one side of the run down building; on the other lay old fishing huts and abandoned boats, Pacific trawlers and party houses.

"Okay folks, so what's happening here?" Sally announced as she looked around in the pre-dawn light.

Suddenly a receiver squawked in one of the mechanic's hands. "Clipper 812...Outer Marker in sight."

Francine laughed. "So, what, ladies, you gonna come party or stay back here?"

Doug smiled, "Eh, they cool, they comin'." He walked Sally and Zoe outside the Quonset hut into the cool early morning air, the sky still washed with stars. "Okay, here's the routine. See over there at the end of the runway, the blue arrow markers?" He gestured towards the marker beacons: three rows of blinking lights on speed bumps in an arrow formation that pointed toward the runway. "That's the Outer Marker. The 812 from Fiji is out over Pearl Harbor on final, and the pilots are lining up right now with these arrows. They're still on autopilot, but they're going to switch to manual pretty quick. They line up here, and then their landing point is about two or 300 feet down the runway."

Sally and Zoe followed the group as they hurried towards the marker. In the east, they could see a glow of early dawn in the distance behind Diamond Head, the sun still below the horizon. Heading west into the darkness, they walked rapidly toward the arrows. The men moved ahead, keeping an eye out for police or airport patrol, their arms filled with heavy cargo tie-down straps.

Sally looked out into the night at the approaching aircraft. "So, what's the big deal?" she asked. "The plane is coming in over the marker. They know where they're headed, so what?"

Doug and two of the ramp workers laughed. "Hey, sister, come." He pointed to the arrows. "Remember that we're right underneath it as it lands. It'll be so low that you'd be able to see the treads on the tires if it were daylight. And if it sucks you into the jet stream, you get bounced along the runway like a rag doll." He waited for her reaction. "Want to come along for the ride?" He smiled wickedly.

Zoe leaned towards Sally. "Sally, you lie down here in the middle of these Outer Marker lines, and the guys tie us all down with the cargo straps to these old steel rebar posts. The pilots can't see you. But you lie there, invisible from above, hanging on to the beacon and the marker post, and you pray like hell that a whole 747 loaded with passengers and cargo doesn't miss the marker and land short or bounce you into the bad stuff generated by the air whirling back off the wings. But believe it or not, it is absolutely the most incredible rush! You'll never regret it!"

Sally, a little giddy from the marijuana, said, "Hey, what a way to say Aloha!"

Grabbing their arms, Doug rushed them towards the blinking blue lights, which were arranged in three concentric rows pointing towards the landing runway. They wrapped themselves in old grey Pan Am blankets to ensure invisibility, the blue lights of the Marker casting an eerie glow on their faces. He settled them into position, and the ramp men tied them to each other and to the closest rebar pole. Then he ran for the adjacent rebar, grabbing his own tie-down straps just as the headlights of the inbound aircraft suddenly illuminated the runway. Although they couldn't hear the radio communications as the huge airliner approached, they could see the wheels of the landing gear swerving as they settled towards their points of touchdown. The plane, still held by the winds, headed for earth. The engines screamed and whined as the aircraft drew closer.

"Oh my God...oh shit...oh my God!" screamed Sally, clutching Zoe's arm, now fully aware of the danger in which they had placed themselves. But suddenly she stopped in wonder, feeling the thrill of engines roaring at peak power, the clash of metal, the groaning hydraulics, the keening of wind and thrusters. It was a magnificent sight. Then the enormity of what was about to happen now finally hit her, and her eyes grew wide as the fuselage of the colossal airliner, now visible in the first pink rays of sunlight, thundered down towards them, its wings feathering as the pilots kept the craft on course for landing. Then she heard herself screaming again in terror as hundreds of thousands of pounds of metal hurtled over her head almost within touching distance, bringing with it a blast of toxic wind: a draft of jet fuel and burning ozone fumes. As the Clipper passed overhead, she could see the intricate landing gear mechanisms as the engines were powered down just before touchdown. Then a 50 mile-an-hour hot gust of afterburner wind blasted them, and the huge jet settled down for landing several hundred feet down the runway.

Sally lay blinking at the sky, exhilarated, breathing hard. All about her was the calm beauty of a new day, a soft morning light now settling over Ke'ehi Lagoon and the leeward coast of the island. They could hear the sound of reverse thrusters bringing the Clipper to a stop far down the runway, and soon the noise faded away. In the moment or two of silence that followed, it occurred to Sally that in a strange way, she was one of the luckiest people on earth to be part of such insanity.

Her fellow adventurers erupted, hooting and laughing. As they stood up, Zoe hugged her, rocking her triumphantly in the early morning light. "That's it," she crowed. "You're a true member of the Honolulu base, but you can't tell a soul." They laughed and hugged the ground crew, then headed quickly back towards the Quonset hut and the beer cooler, away from possible censure and airport police patrols.

"Doug, thank you," said Sally shaking her head. "I wouldn't have missed this for anything. But let me assure you, I will never, never, *ever* do it again."

Zoe laughed, "And I will do it again, every chance I get, if you'll let me!"

"I never get tired of watching these birds land," said Doug wistfully as another giant 747 went roaring by, the pilot flaring the nose up slightly just before touchdown. Linking arms, Zoe and Sally walked back toward the cars, waving good-bye to the others.

Zoe grinned, as she opened the door of the Big Orange. "Madame, your chariot awaits!"

Sally slid into the front seat of the vehicle, chuckling that she'd never driven a hearse before, much less at dawn after having been up all night, pulling a couple of tokes off a joint and drinking a beer. In uniform. And being overflown by a 747. She must be on another planet.

Navigating the hearse carefully back to the Pan Am building, she dropped Zoe off for her briefing and turned out onto the Nimitz Highway. Gunning the engine, she headed towards the North Shore.

She awoke that evening to fragrant smells coming from the kitchen. Pualani had prepared a delicious Hawai'ian stew and rice, with her *tutu* grandmother's mango chutney and slices of fresh pineapple. "Eat, eat," she said to Sally, fussing over her in a maternal sort of way. "Then I want a rundown on the trip. Zoe called from Los Angeles a few minutes ago and said you have one helluva story."

Sally ate hungrily. Other than the two beers with Doug, she hadn't eaten anything all day except a croissant grabbed hurriedly from a foil bag during final approach over Pearl Harbor. After dinner, Pualani pulled a long-necked bottle of Gallo Hearty Burgundy from the refrigerator and poured a glass for each of them. "Come on, Miss Magnolia, let's head outside and sit on the beach. I have a surprise."

Sally looked carefully at Pualani. "You know, that's exactly what Zoe said at five o'clock this morning. I don't know if I can *take* another surprise. You people are scary." They walked out through the grass and sank down on the sand. It was quiet, with little waves gurgling before them in the darkness. The lights were out next door. Perhaps Diz and his roommates had gone into town for the evening. As Pualani's good food settled in her stomach, Sally relaxed as if she'd been hit over the head. When Pualani presented her with a small, thinly rolled joint, she declined. "I will go immediately to sleep," she said.

"No, no, no. You won't go to sleep because this is PC 106," said Pualani. "I have no idea what that's stands for, but it's grown on the Big Island and it's terrific stuff. Guaranteed to lift your spirits, which I believe, just by the look of you, is in order. It was a present from a friend. Now go for it."

As they passed the marijuana back and forth, Sally shared her adventures, from the Outer Marker story and dancing all night in Manila with Ruby, to Larry's withdrawal from heroin. She also related the clandestine conversation she'd overheard in the coffee bar on Tu Doh Street and her chat with the journalist on the rooftop of the Caravelle Hotel.

Pualani nodded. "Sally, you have to remember that opium is what they do, just as it was common here in old Hawai'i. It serves many purposes, from killing pain to providing a sort of fantasy nursing home for people whose useful lives have come to an end. That is why you see so many old people in Asia sitting in peaceful silence."

"But the GI's...."

"Yes, and that is tragic," said Pualani. "I don't agree with using any of that heavy shit. But these cultures are thousands of years old, and a lot of government folks think you can take them into the twentieth century overnight, whether or not they even want to go there. Like Walker said at the party, we all need to learn from each other."

Sally grabbed her arm, "Speaking of learning, Pua...I don't get Zoe's fascination with strange, kind of anonymous, amorous adventures. She did it in training, and now I've seen her grab guys off the beach here a few times. Is that something we should talk to her about?

Pua laughed, shaking her head. "No, no, Sally. That'd be judgmental and Zoe knows what she's doing. That's her drug of choice, so to speak. She doesn't drink or smoke pot, so this is her way. She'll find her own man, when it's time."

Sally nodded. "And what's this I hear about a heavy romance with Walker Sheppard? I've only been gone eight days. What happened?"

Pualani laughed. "Hey, it's just pandemonium. When I was dancing that night at the party, he was looking at me, and it just...happened. Keoki is pissed at me for dating a *haole*; my Mom is worried that it is too quick. Walker's Mom is afraid I've got a bone through my nose, like some heathen. *I'm* afraid he's going back to Vietnam. *He's* afraid to let me out of his sight. It's so completely far out, and maybe someday when everybody calms down, it'll work out to be a good thing."

They laughed together. Above them, thousands of stars shimmered in the dusty-looking mass of the Milky Way. The galaxy spread from one end of the sky to the other like a giant veil embroidered with sparkly sequins. This far from town, no city lights dimmed the magnificence. The stars shone brightly in an inky blue-black firmament full of magic and promise.

"Pua," said Sally, "when I see this great Pacific sky and vast ocean, I think of all the stories waiting to be discovered about them." Sally spread her arms and looked out toward the horizon.

"You remember the singing and dancing at the luau," said Pualani, "you saw that this is how our people learn their history—through chant and dance. And a great deal of that history involves all those stars up there."

"Is it true that the ancient Polynesians used them for navigation?"

"I've been doing some reading on it," said Pualani. "All the ancient chants speak of it, of sailing from the southern islands, of long blue-water voyages from one tiny island to other tiny islands. Keoki has been working with the *kupunas*, the elders, and he's learning celestial navigation."

They were quiet for a few minutes, gazing upward and contemplating these heroes of old.

"They all had such courage," said Sally.

"The ancient Polynesians?" asked Pualani.

"Yes, them too...but Larry and his fellow GI's, and all those Vietnamese folks who are trying just to survive," said Sally. "Pualani, I don't know if I have that kind of courage."

"Yes you do," replied Pualani. "We all do. You just haven't had to use yours yet.

CHAPTER TEN

TAHITI NUI
JULY 12, 1973   PAPE'ETE, TAHITI

Zoe sat hunched over a pile of manuscripts and books stacked on the long, polished table of the Archives Room at the Musée du Tahiti. Outside the graceful arched windows, the island of Moorea shimmered across the blues and greens of the channel through the reef. She rubbed her eyes, recovering from last night's flight from Honolulu and Pago Pago. The ceiling fans turned placidly overhead, the quiet of the Archives Room inviting her to nap, but she was too excited to sleep.

After several months of MAC charter flying and an unusual trip to the British/American naval protectorate of Diego Garcia in the Indian Ocean, she needed a change of pace. She'd seen an announcement posted in the flight service office, asking for volunteers to work on what was described as an "active archaeological dig" on Huahine, Tahiti. The organizers were a team of scientists from Hawai'i's Bishop Museum, and the mission involved working on an archaeological site, a *marae,* a temple, uncovered near a planned resort hotel. Work included digging for artifacts, cataloging, preservation efforts and the organization of records and daily project reports in exchange for food and accommodations. Zoe's schedule showed 10 days off between trips, and her application to the Museum was accepted.

Riding a spare jumpseat from Honolulu to Pago Pago and Tahiti, Zoe volunteered to help the working crew. The economy section of the aircraft was a lively scene of beautiful men and women, many heavily tattooed and bedecked with shell and flower leis, strumming all manner of guitars and ukulele, banging beer cans together or tapping spoons, rattling seat-backs and singing like angels as they danced wild *tamure,* or dances, in the aisles. It was a more sedate scene in the back galley, where the Archbishop of Samoa stood sipping a light Scotch, taking confessions from his parishioners who had strayed in the fleshpots of Honolulu.

After landing in Pago Pago in the dead of night, the passengers had disembarked into an equatorial squall, where they were given an enthusiastic welcome on the tarmac by what seemed to be the population of the entire island, complete with dancing girls and shouting drummers. Zoe stayed behind to listen to the members of the Bishop Museum group, who were in deep conversation with the pilots about celestial navigation capabilities.

Zoe spoke up. "I just flew with a very senior aviation navigator charting a flight plan in the Indian Ocean from Colombo to Diego Garcia," she said. "They were using original calculations from Amelia Earhart's trip in 1937." The navigator had also told her about ancient star-charts and celestial navigation along the old trade routes of blue-water mariners.

"That's exactly the kind of navigation we are going to check out on Huahine," said the most senior of the group, an eminent and renowned Pacific scholar. "All of it relates back to navigation capabilities from Africa through the Indian Ocean and Pacific over 1500 years or so, and we are always looking for more clues."

The team leader briefed them about the next day's plan. "It's just a short hop from Papeete to Huahine, so it will be a long day collecting supplies. Zoe, we'll pick you up at about 2 p.m. tomorrow at the Museum, so that you have time to review some of the project files there. You should be warned about this dig, though; it's hot, the no-no bugs are nasty, the mosquitoes are fiercer, you'll be sleeping in tents, sifting through mud and braving the swamps."

"It sounds just perfect," Zoe had said, "And I'll bet the stars are brighter right over the excavation site." They nodded, laughing.

She'd spent the morning reviewing the files. The dig was an elaborate undertaking, and had been underway for three years. The proposal outlined a significant discovery: the team had uncovered the massive Te Ana complex on Mata'ire', a hill on Huahine, with its villages and chiefly home sites. There was a sense of urgency associated with the project, as the development of a major hotel and airport nearby threatened the site, and local cultural experts had called in the Bishop Museum. Zoe read that some of the artifacts might be a few remnants of the 3500 year-old Lapita culture, originating all the way from Malaysia. That's getting very close to home, she thought excitedly.

She read of epic voyages that were recorded in ancient place names, and preserved through oral history and chants by the seafaring Polynesians. These mariners eventually established a unique "canoe culture" of double-hulled and single-hulled canoes with outlying pontoons and claw-shaped sails which sailed throughout the region, with regular migrations from the islands of Tahiti and the Marquesas to the islands of the north, to Hawai'iki...Hawai'i. These people grew taro for food, fished, ate pigs and dogs, practiced intricate tattoo arts and danced to the urgent music of drums. They worshipped the stars, the mountains and waters.

Zoe knew the tragedy of colonial explorations and the Pacific Islands saga, starting with James Cook and then the whaling ships, which brought disease, death and catastrophic depopulation to the islands. The exploitation continued with the arrival of the Catholic or Congregationalist missionaries, followed by more idealization of these "noble savages", all the while grabbing land in the name of the Lord or colonial trading ventures around the world. In response to the changes caused by losing their lands and their language, native peoples of these idyllic places turned their faces to the wall in silent despair, surrendering their hope and their lives. While Western civilization spread throughout the Pacific, the ancient cultures disintegrated, or hid in sheltered swamps like Huahine.

The 20th century had brought a new kind of exploitation through Pacific aviation, Zoe learned, when the chain of archipelagos and atolls crisscrossing the middle of this great ocean was suddenly recognized as strategically significant for landing fields and radio transmission. The race was on to colonize uncharted islands around the entire Pacific basin as colonial powers sought to exercise "Manifest Destiny". For the United States, it was the Philippines and the

Marianas; the British grabbed the strategic islands and whole countries in Asia; the French occupied Indo-China, Polynesia and Melanesia. Western storytellers captivated audiences with exotic tales of adventure, treasure, heroism and idyllic islands, but it was really all about maintaining control for their respective nations.

After World War II, aviation's new reach spawned further development throughout the Pacific in the form of tourism. The pace had increased dramatically since the new 747 had taken to the skies. Now, more than ever, there was a critical need to identify important archaeological sites and excavate them before they were lost to history.

Zoe read the concluding statement: "We believe there is a connection between the voyaging canoes of the Lapita from Indonesia, the chants of ancient navigators, and possible links between the islands of the Pacific that will restore the traditions of these ancient voyagers to their rightful place in history."

Zoe thought, this could be my direction, too. She stared at the charts and figures in the following pages, an outline for the National Science Foundation grant that had brought these scientists to this place. Something was beginning here.

Zoe heard a discreet cough at her elbow and smiled up at two young women.

"Hi, I'm Maia Buntin," said a tall dark-haired woman, clad in a pink flowered *pareau* and slippers, "and this is Heifara. We're collecting the working team to head for the airport."

Zoe acknowledged them, gathering up the books into a large pouch. Heifara was stocky and strong, and hefted the pouch and Zoe's overnight bag. They headed for the sunny entrance to the Museum, with its large pleasant garden set with pandanus trees and fragrant bushes of tiare Tahiti; she grabbed a half-open blossom and tucked it behind her ear. They walked towards a beaten-up van loaded with supplies and idling at the curb, where Maia directed Zoe to the front seat.

Zoe opened the door, and her eyes widened in surprise. The driver was Keoki Kanawai, Pua's cousin. She remembered their last meeting, his eyes dark as he had walked away from the beach party.

But now he smiled briefly, his face lighting up, his eyes open and welcoming. "Aloha, Zoe! Welcome to the labor camp." He reached for her book-bag and stowed it in the well of the gearshift along with coils of rope and wire. She tried, without success, to hoist herself up into the high front seat.

Maia hesitated, looking back and forth between them. "Oh, so you two know each other?"

Zoe nodded. "Yes, well, sort of. Keoki's cousin, Pualani, is my roommate in Hawai'i. I sure didn't expect to run into him here." Turning to Keoki, she smiled and reached out a hand. He grasped it and pulled her up into the high wooden seat, covered with gaily printed trader cotton, and reached over the piles of supplies to kiss her on both cheeks in the Tahitian way. His warmth and the fragrance of the tiare flower tucked behind his ear left a lingering tingle up her spine.

On the trip to the airport, Maia quickly went over the itinerary and supply requirements. Keoki was the project foreman, taking instructions from Maia and the two archaeologists ensuring the logistics of the project.

"It's pretty wild," he said. "It's hot, dirty and wet." He maneuvered expertly through the breakneck traffic, veering around vehicles blaring loud Tahitian music and wooden flatbed trucks laden with large fish, zipping along the road leading to Faaa Airport. After making a quick stop to buy baguettes and beer, they pulled up to the airport entrance. It was thronged with exuberant passengers and well-wishers carrying fish in coolers of ice; rolls of fabrics in bright floral patterns; an engine block and several assorted woven baskets of personal goods. They stacked their supplies beside the mix of goods awaiting transport, while Tahitian guitar music blared from loudspeakers as friends greeted each other with languid kisses on each cheek, eyes flashing and brown limbs gesturing, pointing, touching.

Zoe joined the group, carrying supplies towards the Air Polynesie counter. A gorgeous young man smiled a greeting, cooing in accented English, providing a boarding pass and giggling with his cohorts as they weighed baggage and stout passengers. Keoki seemed very much at home in the crowd, pulling together a large assortment of material and supplies at the counter, arranging passengers. He spoke a mixture of broken French, Tahitian, Hawaiian pidgin and English, with gestures punctuated by smiles and laughter at the progress of business for a typical Tahitian inter-island flight. Finally loaded on board, the taciturn French pilot surveyed the mix of scientists, fish coolers, laborers, panniers and equipment that bulged out of every space. "*Ça va,*" he nodded brusquely—it'll go, it'll go.

The turbo-prop engines sputtered, turned over and they were on their way, the close air in the aircraft heavy with the odor of bodies, fish, tiare and engine oil. Within seconds, they were out over the channel to Moorea, engines thrumming, lifting higher away from the fairy-tale mountains and valleys of Tahiti.

Keoki was seated in the front, next to the pilot. He turned to Zoe. "So how's my cuz? I've hardly seen her at any of the family events for the last year since that guy Walker Sheppard showed up."

Zoe nodded. "Well, they sure are an item. I know they've been over at the family house a lot, and I think your uncle has already had a chat with him about their future. I definitely know she's happy!"

Keoki nodded, "She's been my best buddy since we were kids in school. I taught her how to surf way back before any of the other girls even thought about it." He paused briefly, as the pilot received instructions from the tower to make the turn out toward Huahine. "It just seems strange not to see her as much, but then again, I've been here a lot and sailing. Hey, that means you've survived your first year in the Pacific. How's it been?"

Zoe sat up. "Busy. Busy and too many night flights. Pua's got Walker, and Sally's seeing guys in every port, but nothing serious yet. Everybody's happy." Zoe paused as she marveled at the greens and blues of the changing sea below, the currents of waves and wind forming distinct patterns, then spoke again. "I got bored with all the MAC charters, so I've been looking at other things, too, spending more time at museums and libraries."

Keoki raised his eyebrows. "So you want to be a scholar?"

She laughed, and waved off the comment. "Who knows? I've been studying for years, so maybe it's the next step in my life."

Zoe was yelling above the engine's insistent humming, and Keoki leaned closer to hear her. "Keoki, that's why I'm so excited to be here. I don't know much about the project, but I do want to learn and do something useful, if I can." Pulling back, she looked him straight in the eye and added a plea, "You'll have to help me see if it's right for me."

Keoki nodded, his eyes smiling as he gestured out at the sea around them, the craggy peaks of Moorea now receding in the distance. "We're all learning together, Zoe," he said. "A whole lot of what we've found has been due to accidental excavation around the new hotel complex." He went on to tell her that there had been a recent discovery of huge whalebones in the swamp, as well as hundreds of ancient artifacts throughout the area. He described the finds, his voice was animated, his face and eyes focused, intent. Zoe thought he was the most beautiful man she had ever seen. She wondered how it might feel to just reach out and touch his bare shoulder, so close and warm.

He continued, "This site is even more important than we first thought; it's an archaeological treasure trove. There are dozens of theories about why the ancient sailing traditions died, but there's a group of us who are determined to bring it back. We're putting together a plan to build a large double-hulled sailing canoe, a replica of the old blue-water canoes, to learn just exactly how our Tahitian ancestors got to Hawai'i. It's all there in the ancient chants and legends. We can prove that canoe cultures did indeed exist, that they were masters at celestial navigation. Anything we find on Huahine is valuable in telling us what went before and who we are."

He pointed out their route as the aircraft droned over the dark blue seas, the skies reflecting clouds and distant islands; waterless Taha'a; the fairy-tale atoll of Bora Bora, ringed by its reef and scattered little islands called *motus*, distant Raiatea; and finally on the horizon, Huahine. As the aircraft descended, Zoe saw the clear lagoons and flat sandy plains dotted with rows and rows of coconut trees, with other lower plantings running in long mounds by the sea.

Keoki pointed to the green rows on the shore. "Watermelons!" he yelled incongruously, over the noise of the thrumming engines. She nodded, watching the sandy shores and blue waters rush up towards the plane, which bounced twice on the sandy tarmac and motored towards a small Quonset hut, where a French flag fluttered in the breeze next to a worn windsock. A lovely Tahitian girl in an impossibly short uniform skirt and high heels walked toward them in welcome, a generous smile on her face, cloudy green eyes, and an orange hibiscus in her long, wind-blown hair. No wonder Gauguin came all the way out here to paint these incredibly beautiful people, Zoe thought.

Within half an hour, they had been transported by two rusty open vans through the small village of Fare, to a series of tents and a long framed building. A crooked, hand-painted signpost proclaimed "Vaito'otia" in peeling, faded paint. Maia introduced Zoe to the expedition leader, who smiled gently in greeting her.

"Doctor Nishimoto, I will be happy to do anything you need to help with the project," said Zoe. "This is incredible!"

He bowed courteously, saying, "Oh, there is always work for good hands, you can count on that. Just follow Maia and she'll keep you busy."

After dropping her gear in a small open tent near the water's edge, Zoe busied herself with Maia and several other team members in the open building, which served as a gathering place at one end and a cookhouse at the other. Looking out over the site, she saw Keoki and a work-crew out over a series of staked-out ponds, gesturing and talking with Dr. Nishimoto. The men had shed their shirts in the strong heat of the afternoon, their bare, bronze skin presenting a contrast to the small, spare frame of the scientist, clad in sun-hat, bush-jacket, clip-board clasped. Even at this distance, Zoe's eyes lingered on every muscle of Keoki's brown back, his arms crossed. She looked away quickly, almost guilty at enjoying the sight.

The afternoon sun beat down. The air was hot and breathless, no breeze stirring although the sound of shallow surf was gentle and constant. It felt like a long, welcome nap, she thought. Unbidden, she imagined lying by Keoki's side, stroking his brown skin, her hand tracing the ridges of his spine. She could almost feel her fingertips tingle—then Maia and Heifara called to her, breaking her reverie, to explain the daily routine. Maia handed her a huge ledger recording supplies and expenses for the project, and a sheaf of new receipts and notices for entries. She bent to her assigned chore, thinking of the flowers waving outside as a shore breeze sprang up.

In the early evening, Keoki whistled, signaling the end of the workday and dismissed the workmen, wiping his face as he entered the cooler shade of the cookhouse, leaning against a stout pole for a moment's rest. He poured himself a glass of cold water, drank it down and poured another before sitting down at the table, appraising her before he spoke.

"So, what do you think?" he said, smiling at her neatly printed ledger. "Seems like we finally found someone who can actually handle the paperwork. We all hate it."

She said, "Well, it's a start on a real project. I've always been fascinated with ruins, old pagodas and legends, following maps in deserts and jungles, and the real fun was always the research to find out what had been there. I did a few years of archaeology in college, too, then I got lucky when I was based in Miami, and spent a lot of time helping organize Pan Am's archives. The best was to work with the records from the early days of the *China Clipper* and all the stories of aviation in the Pacific."

Keoki nodded, "Yes, there's a lot of history, and most of it is in those old books you are carrying around. It's good to read about the early days. My family got involved way back—don't know what they were doing for the first thousand years, but in the last 50, my Dad was involved in the explorations of the Line Islands."

"The Line Islands?" Zoe remembered her conversation with Pualani months before. "Keoki, I knew there was something Pua told me to ask you about. When I was working on the *China Clipper* logs, there were some contemporary accounts about the Line Island atolls in the Pacific, and how they were settled almost at the same time. Pualani told me you would remember something called the *Hui*...." She paused. "Now let me get it right, the *Hui Panala'au*? There was a man with your last name on some of those expeditions."

Keoki nodded, "That was my father, George Kanawai. He left with a group to colonize Howland, Baker and Jarvis Islands just after they had graduated from the Kamehameha School for Boys in 1935. It was all very hushed up, and the family didn't know anything much about it. They sailed down there on a Coast Guard Cutter, the *Itasca*, with lots of Navy brass and Department of the Interior folks." He rummaged through his books and pulled out a battered volume entitled, *Hui Panala'au Memoirs*, by E. L. Bryan. "This was our Bible growing up."

Zoe exclaimed, "That's it! *Hui Panala'au*. Pua told me that your father was part of an important expedition, and the dates match right up with Pan Am's early Pacific flights."

Keoki smiled, watching her.

"They were pioneers—*panala'au*", said Keoki. "My Dad said they were just to live on the islands and keep a log of the daily occurrences. They made weather reports, kept track of the wind, barometric pressure, the cloud formations, wind velocity, any contacts with passing ships, any changes in the fishing—things like that. They had to build their own huts, cook, fish, and even build a landing field in useable condition."

At that moment, several workmen entered the cookhouse, asking Keoki's advice on offloading some newly arrived equipment and supplies. Excusing himself, he left her, promising to return and finish the account at dinner.

The women had disappeared to their tents and showers down by the water, while Zoe picked up the story in Keoki's worn book in the cool evening breeze. She sat cross-legged on one of the rough benches, leaning up against the open windows of the cookhouse, looking out at the limpid bay and the rustling coconut palms, the rubble of the coconut trees, and the smell of the high, salty breeze as she read the yellowed pages.

She looked out at Huahine's salty marsh, green vegetation, and the blue lagoon stretching out to the line of surf at the reef. She compared it to the hot, windless atolls of the book, imagining the smell and feel of several thousand years of bird droppings—a hot, powdery base of desiccated guano—entering the lungs, eyes and mouth, stinging and burning. And she could only wonder how these young men must have felt when the *Itasca* sailed away and left them behind in the emptiness of that lonely place, the sun burning down from a cloudless sky. There was nothing to see or hear for thousands of miles, their only companion the endless sea and sky of their Pacific Ocean.

But the boys loved it. In spite of the hardships, these young Hawaiians became exuberant explorers of these deserted islands. They learned to observe the tides through the angle of ocean currents, they became expert fishermen, they sang old songs and chants; and gazing at the infinity of stars in the night sky above them, they knew their ancestors could read them like a map. It was on the tiny islands of Howland, Baker and Jarvis that they rediscovered their own forgotten Hawai'ian blue-water histories. They'd even worked on the rescue efforts for Amelia Earhart and Fred Noonan in 1937. She leafed through lists of project participants noted in the 1930s, the dates of the voyages, and their sudden end right after the Japanese invasion of Pearl Harbor, and the subsequent attack on Howland Island that killed one of the boys.

She sighed as she closed the book, startled to see Keoki sitting out on the grass, leaning up against a coconut tree, gazing at her. She got up, stretching her back and arms.

"Keoki, I can't believe this is all real." She looked about her, shaking her arms and shoulders, working out the kinks.

"Got to you, didn't it? Yeah, we'd sit with Dad for hours listening to his stories. And the uncles, the other guys in the *hui*, they stuck together pretty close all their lives, and that's probably why we all got the bug about our history." He tossed a stone towards the marsh. "Lots of work ahead. Lots of work and lots of study." He stood up and held out his hand, "Come on, you can't spend the next three days reading history in the cookhouse. Let's get you out to the lagoon, then you can shower and we'll talk some more at dinner."

They walked along a broad, deserted beach, companionable in the soft evening air. They passed four languorous young women, their slender bodies wrapped in brightly colored *pareaux,* their skin golden, their eyes indifferent, lips pouting, their long silky hair caught in the light breeze, posing for all the world like a Gauguin painting. Zoe smiled at them, and they turned like flowers to smile and wave. She felt lumpish and spotty in the presence of such exotic beauty.

"In my next life, I'm coming back as a 16-year-old Chinese-Tahitian girl with no brain and no worries," she grumbled, as Keoki laughed.

As if to echo the thought, the girls waved at Keoki, calling his name seductively in Tahitian, "*Iorana*, M'sieur Tihoti, *ça va?*"

Keoki grinned from ear to ear, smiling at the girls as they passed. "Just natural charm, Zoe, just natural charm."

Unthinking, Zoe threw a small wad of beach debris at him, and they raced to the end of the beach, laughing and out of breath, out of sight of the figures far behind. He paused by the blue shallows, gesturing at the ocean booming distantly beyond the reef, his arms stretched wide.

"Zoe, soon, that's where we'll be sailing. We're going to sail from Hawai'i to Tahiti in the ancient way, and I'm going to be there."

His eyes deepened in the evening light as he beckoned her out past the shallow tide pool, and they swam slowly back towards the bungalows, floating as they talked, their bodies moving side by side in the rhythm of the tide. She ached to reach out and touch him, feel his warmth. She thought, this is so different from my usual anonymous encounters; this feels *real*. They both seemed caught in these golden moments.

After a congenial dinner by the light of kerosene lamps, the group faded away to early bedtimes. No television or radio static interfered with the quiet sound of the waves. A full moon rose above the water and spread its light softly on the beach, turning the dark waves and rustling coconut leaves to liquid silver, highlighting the floral patterns of the window curtains fluttering in the night air. Zoe, sleepless, her body restless, left her bed and walked out onto the dark beach, where the water beckoned and glimmered. As she walked, she thought of floating again in the tide-pools with Keoki, of laughing with a man so full of life, but at the same time so connected to the other worlds of the stars and the ocean. A million stars flickered overhead.

Up in the shadows of the coconut palms, she saw the glow of a lit cigarette, the harsh perfume of a Gauloise punching through the mellow scents of tiare and salt spray. He moved towards her out of the shadows and she inhaled the scent of him. He reached for her, and they melted wordlessly together in an urgent kiss. His arms embraced her, sheltered her, and she moved her face to rest in the warmth of his shoulder, tasting the salt on his skin. They stood together, cradled in the moonlight, until a cracking branch broke the spell and they stepped apart.

"Goodnight...goodnight," they whispered to one another hurriedly, as they moved away.

Zoe thought her heart would pound right out of her chest as she watched Keoki walk back into the coconut grove toward the tents beyond. We are alike, both of us almost prisoners of our history, she realized. But he is on a voyage inside himself. No matter what, I will always watch him walk away.

At dawn the next morning, the crew was roused for an early breakfast, and a briefing on the day's work. They sipped strong, acrid French coffee, dipping lengths of fresh baguettes slathered with butter into the coffee. As usual, they would try to do as much as possible in the early morning before the sun took over and sapped their energy, their enthusiasm and clear thinking. Zoe looked hopefully for Keoki, but he was not there; a generator pump had broken in the night, and he had been dispatched to find a replacement at the small general store.

Maia looked at her, appraising her wordless query. "You never know with him; he comes, he goes."

The crew moved out to the digging site and commenced the back-breaking work of moving large piles of sand and loamy mud from the carefully flagged sections around the dig site.

The excitement had begun some months before in excavation of a pit for a hotel tennis court, when several stone artifacts and bone implements had surfaced. The local crew, superstitious and surly, refused to dig further until the village chiefs were called in. They in turn called the scientists to tell them the histories in the swampy lands, the accidents and misfortunes if things were not done in the proper way.

All morning, Zoe sat in front of a makeshift screen, pouring loads of sand and jetsam, brushing through the piles in hopes of finding ancient sharks' teeth, implements or ornaments. Meanwhile, the pile of sieved sand and rubbish grew at her feet, and the workmen came, sweating and dirty, to shovel away the piles. She was surprised that some of the men were smiling at her, teasing gently, one even calling her "Madame Tihoti" without explanation, but they just laughed and gestured.

Clearly there are no secrets in these islands, she pondered idly while her hands moved over the sand. So who squealed? Did someone see us on the beach? Or swimming? Did they just make it up? Did Maia see something? Or do they just know? She could only shrug it off, glancing idly at the sun's progress, noting that the generator was still silent, and that Keoki had not reappeared. As the heat climbed in the late morning, Maia called them into the longhouse for a rest break, her eyes distant. Oh Lord, groaned Zoe, I think I've made a misstep.

After lunch, she returned to the files, and spent the afternoon going over boxes of receipts and order forms in an effort to organize the project reports. The files had withstood two years of cockroaches and silverfish infestations. Two other volunteers helped her to sort the material, and they spent the afternoon completing the logs, comparing the cost of air tickets, petrol, new boots, the baguettes and beer, which fueled the workforce. They checked the condition of the artifact inventory records, dusting away dead insects and termite wings from the documents, which would survive if laminated.

Late in the afternoon, the men gathered in a swampy area of the dig to feel around with their bare hands for artifacts in the primordial soup of the lagoon's borders. These murky, odiferous waters had not only given up huge scavenged whalebones, but other secrets as well: dozens of stone chisels, shell scrapers, graters, fishhooks, wooden clubs, spears, hand awls and hundreds of adzes. The nearby rubbish dump had also revealed thousands of pig, whale, turtle and fish bones, as well as cast off *vana* shells and other leftovers of past lives. Zoe turned to see Keoki walking towards the group, and breathed a small sigh of relief at the sight of him.

He waded into the pond, feeling his way towards the deepest part. A few months before, Dr. Nishimoto had astounded the archaeological world by diving into these waters to bring up a whalebone *patu,* a carved whalebone hand weapon, never seen outside of New Zealand, which provided the first definite link between islands of Tahiti and A'otearoa, the Maori word for New Zealand. Now Keoki stood in the pond beside him, towering over him as the men surrounded them on the banks of the pond, gesturing towards the edges and motioning Keoki to dig.

He dug around delicately, pulling up a length of whalebone, feeling his way through the stones and muck of the bottom. As he passed his find to the men on shore, he tripped and fell, floundering in the shallow murk of the pond, and grimacing as he dislodged a waterlogged artifact from the depths. Reaching down, he pulled a large, roughly cylindrical object to the surface.

The director peered at it. "Could be house post? No, it looks like it's hollow."

Keoki felt the rough wooden edges and openings on the sides, "No, it's not long enough. It…it's almost like a coconut stump…and the holes and ridges here…could it be a drum?"

The scientist mused, reverently touching the rough carvings, even an embedded tooth. "Yes, it could be." He grunted with satisfaction. "This treasure we must keep underwater and send to Papeete quickly, tomorrow even." The deterioration of waterlogged wood was a danger in these climates, and immediate preservation was everything.

Zoe met Keoki's knowing look. "It could be an ancient *tumunu* stump," he joked, referring to their first meeting. But clearly he was excited at the possible importance of the find. He clapped the director on the shoulder, saying, "Someday, maybe we'll even discover the bones of a sailing canoe that will be the foundation of the new Pacific." But this waterlogged object, if it in fact was confirmed as a drum, was probably the first of its kind to be discovered, and the crew gathered around Keoki, offering their congratulations.

The evening was spent hammering at a large plywood crate, carefully insulated to carry the ancient object on the journey to Papeete's Museum. Keoki broke away from the discussions and approached her. "I think it might be best if you came back with me to Papeete tomorrow. The Museum here may not be able to do anything with this, and if we have to, we'll ship it out to Honolulu on the next Pan Am flight. That way, maybe you can lean on some of the crew to get it safely to the Bishop Museum." His face was serious, the artifact obviously very special to him. She nodded and moved back to her work with the project files, hoping to get the bulk of it sorted before she left.

"Drums have a sacred place in Hawai'i's ancient history," Keoki explained on the short flight back to Papeete the next morning, as the plane skimmed over the emerald and blue waters below. "The most famous were the two massive drums brought from Tahiti by the chief La'amaikahiki. One was named in his honor, the other 'Hawea', a name that has come down through my family line. They were made of huge coconut stumps, stretched with sharkskin and studded with human teeth, and they were used to announce the Polynesians' arrival in Hawai'i from Tahiti in the 11th century, where they reverberated all along the shorelines of the islands. They were the voice of power all over the Pacific."

"Do they still exist?" asked Zoe.

"Unfortunately, no. They disappeared in 1820 with the death of Kamehameha I and the overthrow of the 'ai kapu, or taboo system, by his favorite queen, Ka'ahumanu. These drums have huge mana—spiritual power, which has to be respected. They say that is why they disappeared." Keoki's eyes clouded at the telling of the story, and although he sat close to her, there was a chill as the plane descended into Papeete.

Already, he has walked away, Zoe thought, remembering the moonlight and their embrace.

They worked at the Museum for a few hours to ensure the stabilization of the artifact they were now calling "Hawea", in honor of Keoki's family, and the legend of the drum. The conservator shook his head. No, it should go immediately to Bishop Museum. They called Pan Am's cargo section for cargo requirements, exit permits for the artifact and the appropriate, endless paperwork which they were told would be ready à demain, tomorrow.

That evening, Zoe and Keoki, along with several of the Pan Am ground staff, made their way down to Papeete's waterfront for the last days of the Bastille Day celebrations that were famous around the world. The Tahitian Fête version was spectacular, and extended well beyond the traditional July 14th of each year. Hundreds of dancing and drumming troupes lined the harbor for an intense three-day competition, while the crowds ate, drank copiously, danced wildly in the streets. They enjoyed the dozens of carnival games; some dangerous looking rides in decrepit condition; an ancient merry-go-round; and the *roulettes*, or food carts, offering dozens of entrees and desserts, candies and savory sandwiches.

At the Royal Papeete Hotel, music blared from La Cave, an infamous nightclub that had become even more frantic after a recent fire had closed the legendary Quinn's Bar on the ramshackle waterfront down the street. Dozens of gorgeous women danced the unique Tahitian waltzes and *aparimas,* clad in the latest Western sundresses and crowned in wreaths of fragrant tiare Tahiti blossoms. The incongruous black lights of La Cave's décor lit up white surfaces, a sort of bizarre 1960s touch that had somehow made its way all the way down here. Teeth, shirts, underwear, and tiare garlands glowed. Enthusiastic patrons, fueled by the dances and liquor, moved passionately to the beat of the *tamure* drums. Caught up in the moment, Zoe and Keoki danced with arms entwined, facing each other, their eyes intent.

Later, they walked along the promenade around the harbor, breathing in the fresh scent of the sea that mingled with the fragrance of flowers, harbor odors, and pungent raw fish mixed with seaweed in coconut milk from the food carts. The strains of music still echoed from La Cave, along with the nearby guitar strumming and harmony of a group of harbor workers and their women, sitting around a brasserie of coals, roasting chicken strips and dozens of empty Hinano beer bottles.

Strolling hand-in-hand along the streets, they gazed at the neighboring island of Moorea's lights beyond the reef, as the sounds of merriment faded in the distance. They walked quietly, savoring each moment in silence. The tiare bushes in the hotel garden had now blossomed fully, their white stars reaching for the moon, their perfume filling the air. She plucked a flower, offering it to Keoki as he bent to kiss her lightly on each cheek. She held him closer, imprisoning the flower between their bodies, trying to capture the moment in the perfume.

They kissed again and again, and moved into the darkened hotel room in a rush to touch each other, the warmth of their secret places, the insistent need to fill each other's bodies and souls. There was no need for words, just the sighs sensing each other's desires. They spoke with their lips, their arms, their hands and tongues, the strength of a man and a woman seeking love, and that brief moment of stormy climax. Over the hours the moon moved through its course, and they reached for each other, touching, whispering, then slept until the dawn found them, exhausted and content, to begin the day again.

Clasping hands, Keoki and Zoe entered the Permit office of the Musée du Tahiti the next day just before noon to pick up the various approval forms that would accompany the artifact on its journey to Hawai'i. The crate was already at the Pan Am cargo office in readiness for its departure that evening. After a leisurely lunch at Acajou's Restaurant Tiare, they returned to the hotel again so Zoe could check with the crewmembers to find a suitable escort to the Museum.

She read the crew list and details of the flight that night. The crew of the *Clipper Winged Racer*, Flight 816, was scheduled to leave the hotel at 7:30 for Faaa Airport, in time for an 8:30 briefing and a 10 p.m. departure for Honolulu. She jotted a note to a friend on the crew, explaining the circumstances and the need to ensure that the crate was handed off to the Bishop Museum representative, who had been alerted by telex. They made one more trip to the airport for a careful discussion with the operations manager, which satisfied Keoki that all transportation conditions were met, and that the crate would be safely handled in Honolulu for transfer to the museum. There was nothing more they could do, but Keoki stood protectively over the crate in the darkness of the cargo hangar, smoothing the wooden frame as if to comfort the occupant. He said, "I know I shouldn't assume, but to me, this is a treasure; this is the drum Hawea, nothing less." His voice dropped to a whisper. "I feel that I and my family are chosen, again, to care for it."

Zoe sensed his commitment, his passion. She covered his hand, resting on the crate. "Yes, Keoki, I think you are right; it is Hawea, and someday we will know how this all happened. I'll visit the museum the day I get home, even before the crate is unpacked. It'll be fine." She was grateful that Hawea would be her physical connection to him, since he was not expecting to come back to Hawai'i for another month. But nonetheless, she felt a chill.

Turning to Keoki, she smiled wickedly. "Well, I guess our work is done. You and I will have to suffer through another evening together, unless, of course, you want to take the last flight back to Huahine."

He regarded her with a lazy smile. "No, no. No flights tonight." He drove quickly back to the hotel, where they lay together again, at first urgent, and then again slowly, slowly.

Later that night, they sauntered by the *roulettes,* drawn by tantalizing smells of fresh seafood and noodles as they walked towards the pier to end their last evening with a few dances at La Cave. The pier and waterfront were crowded with people celebrating the last evening of the festival. Music blared from every *roulette* and game-site, families chattered happily. Just after ten o'clock, the gaiety at the pier was drowned out by the distant, harsh revving of aircraft engines at full take-off throttle.

Zoe pointed. "Look, there she goes! Hawea is on its way to Honolulu." The Pan Am 707 aircraft was fully visible across the harbor, the blue globe on its tail illuminated for the night-time take-off as it banked and turned out towards the reef, its engines whining harshly at the strain of the ascent, banking, turning, turning away from the island.

All of a sudden there was darkness and silence. Again, Zoe felt a chill, and knew instantly that something was terribly wrong.

"Wait a second. Listen, listen…can you hear the engines? Keoki, can you see anything?"

The crowds on the pier had fallen silent, straining to hear the normal, accustomed interference of jet take-offs over Papeete Harbor, looking out over the dark waters. Nothing.

There was a rush for the airport, and Keoki and Zoe joined the confusion of screaming relatives, officials, airline personnel, a babble of sound and fear, incongruous against the cheerfully-lit ticket counters and the broadcast music of strumming guitars. Some saw a flash, others heard an explosion. There were no answers. Sobbing families consoled each other. Zoe sat with Keoki in the upstairs lounge as they mourned this incomprehensible loss of the plane, the passengers and crew…of the crate.

His eyes were anguished, his voice whispered. "Zoe, we may never know what happened. There are terrible ways to die, but the sea is kind. She just takes you in, and you become part of it. These people now live in both worlds, and they can't ever be hurt again."

Out beyond the reef, in the deepest part of the dark, cold waters, lay a broken aluminum tube, where 78 men, women and children along with 12 crewmembers floated in puzzled, silent death, their lives extinguished in an instant. And in the cargo hold, the drum Hawea lay, once again consigned to the Pacific waters that had protected its history for a thousand years.

CHAPTER ELEVEN

DOWNLINE DON'T COUNT
NOVEMBER 9, 1973   SYDNEY, AUSTRALIA

Sally awoke to a lovely summer afternoon in Sydney. After a quick shower, she dressed and boarded a bus in front of the hotel and headed for the new Opera House, intent on a discounted ticket for that evening's performance. Disembarking a few stops early, she walked quickly through the Royal Botanical Gardens, figuring the exercise would help her wake up after the brutal 12-hour flight down through Fiji. As she came into a clearing, the spectacular Opera House lay below, jutting out into the harbor. An artist hovered over a sketchpad nearby. She stepped closer, "Why, Captain Dave McFarland. A hidden talent!"

She had worked First Class galley on the way down, stopping by the cockpit often to tell jokes to the pilots and make sure they were all awake. McFarland had struck her as an attractive man, with strong features and a shock of salt and pepper hair. While not handsome, he was interesting looking. And with his trim physique, he looked younger than his age.

"That's great! You've caught the whole skyline and the birds over the Opera House," she said. "Nicely done."

McFarland turned, startled. "Oh, hello…Sally, isn't it? What are you doing here?"

"I'm headed down to the Opera House to get a ticket for tonight's performance of *Tosca*. Would you like me to pick up another one for you?" Such invitations were not unusual among the crews; the serendipitous nature of layovers allowed for the sudden formation of groups from two to twenty, for everything from sightseeing to tennis matches.

"I hate opera," he said, grinning. "Too many fat ladies."

Sally said, "Maybe you should give it another try. You're doing great work with your sketchbook. It's all related: art, music, dance—even fat ladies and opera."

He smiled at the cheekiness of her response.

She could sense that he was on the verge of accepting. "I've got my flea-market black dress...."

"And I've got a jacket. Yes, yes... all right," he shrugged, standing up, smiling sheepishly.

"Great. Now, I hate to rush, but we need to hurry so we can get back before the curtain."

As they walked up the long staircase to their seats in the upper balcony, they surveyed Sydney Harbor Bridge and the lights of the city.

Dave said, "This is an incredible setting, but why opera for you?"

"It's always bigger than life...drama, music, romance... *Tosca* is about love and glory and honor. My favorite part is in the third act, when the poor hero Caravadossi, gets himself put in front of a firing squad. He looks up at the sky and sings this aria called '*E lucevan le stelle*,' the light of the stars. It's about how the stars are shining, and he's remembering holding Tosca in his arms in a perfumed garden, and how he can never have her. The dream of their love will die with his death. He grieves for that, and for the fact that he has never before loved life so much. The drama is sad, but the music just grabs you, and it's so real, so timeless, so important for all of us."

Dave nodded as the curtain rose. "I'll try to listen for it, " he said.

During intermission, he bought them glasses of champagne in the soaring atrium. "I must admit I've never enjoyed an opera this way," said Dave. "How did you get to be such an expert?"

"I grew up in Kentucky's tobacco country, in a place you never heard of called Latham," explained Sally. "I used to listen to our ironing lady sing when I was a child, and she sang the church music of the South. It was from her that I learned the power of the human voice in telling stories. Then I took courses when I was in college and listened to the best recordings. And when I flew out of New York, I got tickets to see the real thing, the real stars, wherever I could: Rome, Buenos Aires, London, Paris, the Met." Sally looked up at the stars twinkling lazily in the summer evening through the huge skylights. "You've just got to believe in the stars, and the music, and the power of love." He laughed, enjoying her intensity.

The next night, Sally and Dave took the remaining seats at the end of the table when the crew gathered for dinner at a Greek restaurant in the Paddington section of the city. Wine flowed and the talk was cheerful.

Dave looked at Sally thoughtfully. "May I tell you something? I think you have an understanding of yourself and the world that is unusual for someone your age."

"Thank you." Sally flushed slightly at the compliment. "It has been a rollercoaster. I came from an enormously conservative society right into these wild times. And Vietnam has been hard on all of us," she said, shaking her head. "Your generation had so much more certainty about your war. But we weren't so sure about ours." She shrugged. "You know, I grew up believing that our government always knew best. I believed everything I read. But I've lost my trust. Nothing is what it seems any more."

Dave let these remarks settle in for a bit. "You're a throwback, too, you know that?" he said, swirling the wine in his glass.

"A what?" Sally was unsure what to make of this comment.

"A throwback. Most of these gals out in the Pacific walk around in blue jeans and tee shirts, and you put on a black dress and pearls to go to the opera. It's like you're stuck with one foot in the elegance of the past and the other in the rebelliousness of your generation. In spite of that, you've held back. You haven't gone totally crazy."

"Don't bet on it, Dave. Leaving my mother and everything I knew was the ultimate act of rebellion, leaving Latham, leaving my high school sweetheart, taking my first plane ride to Miami for training…that was pretty crazy, for me anyway."

Dave chuckled. "Oh, I don't know about that. Pan Am people have been flying a lot of airplanes to a lot of places for a long time. Crazy things are always happening."

He looked around for a waiter to bring the check, and the crew split the bill in the time-honored tradition of multiple currencies and denominations.

On the way back to the hotel Sally and Dave walked side-by-side, lagging behind the group, talking; no subject seemed to be uncomfortable or out of range for their age difference. But when they reached the hotel lobby, Sally scattered, along with the rest of the crew; she had avoided the pilots since her African Queen experience.

But this man was different.

Back in Haleiwa, all three roommates were home, and in the house at the same time. Pua laughingly declared a curfew; the house was off-limits to Walker, to her cousin Keoki, and to all of Sally's sundry friends, neighbors and acquaintances. Nobody was invited.

"That's it, guys," she said. "Auntie Pua is cooking, Sistah Zoe is taking the notes, Sistah Sally is cleaning, and we're gonna have us a Ladies Night In. It's the only way to make sure you folks aren't making even more mischief." And she chased Moke Cabral away with a spoon, stirring a huge pot of fragrant beef stew, a pot of rice bubbling on the side.

Pua had embraced Zoe's relationship with Keoki. "You two fit, you just do," she smiled happily. "I can't believe you guys had to come from all over the world to meet here, and then…ah, romance!" She hugged her, and they'd all spent hours together at family events. But Zoe was still uncertain, not only because Keoki's eyes were far away across the Pacific, but because she was still searching for her own way.

Since Pua's relationship with Walker was deepening with every passing month, they were comfortable in talking about the ups and downs for mixed-race couples, especially given Keoki's penchant for distant horizons and blue water. Pua shook her head. "I guess Polynesian men are no better and no worse than these guys like Walker that fly around in airplanes. We just gotta let 'em go, and sooner or later, if they have the smarts, they'll find a way to get back where they belong."

Sally said, "Or maybe they choose something else."

Zoe laughed out loud, seeing the matriarch emerging in Pua's beautiful face and trim figure. Walker would need to toe the line, she thought. But still, as much as she loved Hawai'i and Keoki, she looked back towards Asia with longing.

After dinner, they went outside and built a fire on the beach. Sally listened to the stories, unusually silent, watching the flames. She turned to them, hesitantly. "I met someone," she said, "someone really special. And I know you are going to disapprove. He's a pilot, a 747 Captain. He's wonderful, but he's 20 years older than I am, and of course, he's married."

Pua and Zoe were silent for an instant, then groaned loudly in unison. "Oh, Sally," cried Pua, "that is such a stewardess dream, the Sky God sweeping us off our feet. You just *can't*. Lie down, honey, and rest until the feeling passes."

They all chortled, although Sally looked embarrassed. "I can't help it. I can't help thinking about him, even though I know it's absolutely *not* appropriate."

Zoe looked at her, her eyes hard. "Sally, just don't go there. You've had a tough time, learning to deal with this 365-day, 24-hour world. But there are hundreds of good guys out there that would fit the bill and be your slave. Just don't do anything stupid."

Sally's eyes flashed, "I only want the same kind of love you both have. Is that unnatural?"

Zoe looked at her. "Pua may have a good thing with Walker. I say 'may', even though he's a military jock pilot. Keoki and I, well, the jury is out, so I can't advise you. But I can say that you don't need to be an old married man's darling. Just slow down, take your time."

Sally turned stubbornly, ignoring them both, and stared at the fire. Soon the music of a guitar drifted over from next door, growing louder as three figures moved toward the beach from the shadows. Walker and Moke waited until they were invited to sit down, but Diz quickly offered to clean the bottom of the stew pot in exchange for leftovers. Keoki called. Moke strummed his guitar and sang of a beautiful island lady with a voice like a rushing stream. The night wore on, and Sally sat looking at the stars and feeling lonely.

Two weeks later, Sally walked into the cockpit before a morning departure from Honolulu for a long, 10-day Delhi trip.

"Morning, gentlemen. My name is Sally Wilder," she said, pouring on the Southern treacle a little heavy, "and I'll be looking after you today to make sure you don't get bored staring at all those pretty little red and yellow lights."

And there was Dave sitting in the left seat. Gulping, she smiled in her most professional manner. The pilots introduced themselves and Sally took their orders for coffee or tea.

Dave was going through the pre-flight checklist when Sally returned a few minutes later with their coffee and a quip.

"*E lucevan le stelle*, Captain," Sally murmured, bending forward and handing him his cup.

"Thanks," said Dave, glowing, touching her fingers lightly as he took the cup.

They arrived at Tokyo's Haneda Airport in late afternoon. Fog and mist obscured the sun and most of the city for the long drive to the Keio Plaza InterContinental in the Shinjuku district of town. Dave offered his hotel room for the customary crew "debriefing" that evening. He propped his door open, welcoming people as they straggled in at various times, some of them comfortable in the blue and white striped cotton *yukatas* provided by the hotel. All carried the water glass from their bathrooms as essential equipment for the bar. They also came bearing the customary supplies for crew parties in Asia: packages of Japanese crackers in all shapes and sizes, and leftovers from the opened bottles of wines in First Class.

Sally looked at the people crowded into the room. Six or seven had perched around the edges of the bed, two were seated on chairs, and the rest sat cross-legged on the floor. Most were in their twenties and thirties, and they ran the gamut of every race, creed, color and nationality. Rather than feeling isolated by these cultural differences, she was thrilled. She felt part of it all; she belonged. She could not imagine ever going back to Latham, where everything—and everyone—was either black or white, and did not mix.

When someone left the seat open next to her, Dave sat down.

"So how've you been?" he said.

"Fine, fine, thanks," Sally replied. His eyes lingered on her and she was flattered, though somehow shy. "I've been flying a lot of overtime to make some money to buy Christmas presents on this trip. How about you?"

"Just got through with my checks in the flight simulator in San Francisco."

"What's the best part of the job?" asked Sally.

Dave did not hesitate for a moment. "Flying is total freedom," he replied. "Ask any pilot. When you're flying, you feel like you can go anywhere, do anything. It's a world of infinite possibilities."

Sally nodded, "I guess it is the same for us, even though we aren't doing the actual flying. So what's your favorite airport to fly into?"

"Oh, I think that would have to be Kai Tak in Hong Kong. The 'Laundry Line' approach," he answered.

He shook his head. "It's the toughest flying there is. And the crazy thing is, you get to play voyeur on the last several hundred feet. Apartment buildings line both sides of the glide slope, and just before landing the plane is actually at a lower altitude than the top floors of the buildings. You can literally see laundry strung out on lines, folks out on their verandahs, kids waving. Ever sat in the cockpit for it?"

"Not yet, but I've heard people talk about it," said Sally. She was laughing to herself, remembering her Outer Marker escapade last year, with about a zillion pounds of airplane landing practically on top of her. She didn't dare mention it to this serious, attractive man with his sad eyes.

One by one, the crewmembers headed for bed. Sally smiled long into Dave's eyes at the door, thinking just how strange this was getting.

They landed in Bangkok in the wee hours of the morning, where golden temples glimmered, enshrouded by smoky, incense-laden air. The lobby of the Siam InterContinental Hotel was deserted on their arrival, and a yawning front desk clerk carried out the crew check-in. Sally found herself watching Dave as he walked towards his room, his hat cocked jauntily on the back of his head, a thick wedge of salt and pepper hair poking out beneath. She turned aside towards her own room, her heels clicking on the marble floor, imagining walking the other way, following him. Then she cursed herself for these inappropriate desires.

After a few hours' sleep, she joined a few crewmembers for an early shopping excursion, hoping to distract herself from her growing attachment. When she returned to the hotel, she saw Dave lounging in a chair in the lobby, reading a copy of the *Herald Tribune*. Summoning all the self-discipline she could muster, she walked briskly through, pretending he wasn't there. But he saw her and called out in greeting, waving and smiling. She felt sticky and grimy, hoping her hair was neat.

"What time's our wake-up tomorrow?" she said cheerily.

"You've got enough time for a nap and a snack, not necessarily in that order," he said. "Care to join me?"

Sally pondered for an instant, then shrugged, "Oh I'd love to, but I just have this down-line routine I stick to. Rain check?"

He smiled, "You got it. I'll save you a seat on the bus."

"See you then." Sally felt his eyes following her as she walked away. Was he trying to sound nonchalant, or did she detect a note of regret that he couldn't spend more time with her? She thought of Pua and Zoe's disapproval. Every alarm bell she had ever possessed inside her head was ringing madly as she entertained these notions. She knew all about long trips and the seductions they could entail, and she felt foolish about her feelings. She remembered the old crew adage: "Down line don't count."

But it did. Oh, it counted.

In New Delhi the next day, Sally went downstairs in the early evening to have a drink in the Ashoka Hotel's spacious, English-style garden. When the waiter approached, she ordered tea, inhaling the scent of the roses, and thought more of Dave. There were so few days on this trip, so many missed opportunities; she'd never know if he shared her feelings. Nervously, she considered asking him to join her for a drink here in the garden, but decided against it. She'd tried, without success, to push these fantasies away. The man was married, she told herself with more firmness than she felt. You can't date a married man. He's a husband. With children. The tea arrived, the little pot clad in a colorful Kashmiri tea cozy. Sipping slowly, she longed for the shot of gin that might calm her nerves and assuage her guilt.

Sally thought of the pilots she had met, who always seemed to stand apart from their fellow Pan Am employees. The only real difference was that they just happened to be responsible for the safety of hundreds of lives and a multi-million dollar aircraft every time they went to work. All maintained an air of command and, as Dave said, they loved more than anything to fly.

Their home lives were often tempestuous. Some led one life at home and another when they were out on trips. The temptations worked the other way as well. It was hard for flight attendants to resist some of these attractive, sophisticated men, but many, like Zoe, simply refused to have anything to do with them.

All this weighed on Sally's mind as she sat in the garden. She hated what she was feeling, and yet the attraction to Dave was there, like it or not. There was a big age difference and she knew the psychologists would say that she was attempting to replace her dead father. She looked around at the crowds of roses, gladioli and marigolds. There were no answers.

Suddenly she heard a familiar voice behind her, warm and serious. "I was thinking of going to the *son et lumière*, the sound and light show, at the Red Fort in Old Delhi. Care to join me?" There stood Dave, his face aglow in the twilight.

Sally jumped, embarrassed, as if he'd been reading her lascivious thoughts. "I'd love to," she replied, without hesitation.

"We'll need to stop by my room so I can pick up a blanket. It'll be cold later on," said Dave, gently leading her from the garden into the hotel.

In short order, the taxi dropped them off at the entrance to the great fort, which was situated on the banks of the river, surrounded by a tumultuous arcade of shops and lights and beggars.

Reaching a large courtyard they found seats under the stars, and with the blanket for cover, let themselves be caught up in the magical story of the rise and fall of the Mogul Empire. The announcer boomed the story to the crowd, describing the emperor's installation of the gem-studded canopied Peacock Throne in his private audience hall. Inscribed in several places around the chamber was the Persian couplet:

> *If there be paradise on earth*
> *It is this, it is this, it is this....*

At the end of the show, Dave and Sally remained in their seats, drawing the blanket around them for warmth, like teenagers on a first date at a drive-in movie. He tentatively reached over and took Sally's hand in his.

Nervously, she murmured a pleasantry and they stood up, moving slowly back through the bazaar to their waiting taxi.

The next day, Sally carefully closed the cockpit door, having been informed by the Purser that she was invited to the cockpit for the Hong Kong landing.

Dave keyed his mike. "Clipper Two, Kai Tak, good day. Out of 10,000 for 8,000, change to approach frequency 119.1, Clipper Two." After receiving the weather details, he advised the tower that his Clipper was "heavy with gravel", or carrying a full passenger complement and running low on fuel.

She settled into one of the extra cockpit jumpseats behind him that was normally used for check-rides and deadheading pilots. As he focused on the window display before him, she fumbled with the earphones, the Flight Engineer helping her with the audio.

"Clipper Two, right turn 30 degrees, descend to 6000 feet," instructed the tower.

"Roger, Kai Tak. Clipper Two, right turn 30 degrees, 6000, Clipper Two."

"Good day, Cathay Pacific 53, descend to 6000 feet. Be advised you're following a heavy," the tower cautioned, referring to the air disturbance in the wake of Pan Am's wide body jet.

"Cathay Pacific 53, out of 8000 for 6000. Roger on the heavy aircraft; we have you in visual, Clipper," answered the Cathay pilot.

The 747 began its slow descent, hydraulics and mighty engines vibrating as it moved ponderously into descent mode. On their starboard side Victoria Peak seemed to be within touching distance off of their wingtip. Below lay the might of British Asian commerce: the grey-blue harbor, the misty slopes of the mountains, the repeater lights on every peak. The mountains of Kowloon rose up ahead, the beacon blinking a bright red. Then as they turned, the airfield stretched dead ahead, looking impossibly small.

"Clipper Two, do you have the field in sight?" asked the tower.

"Clipper Two, we have the field in sight, Clipper Two."

The Flight Engineer turned his chair from his desk to face the field, and Sally heard the metallic scraping sound as he brought his seat on a track close enough so he was right behind the two pilots, locking it into position. He took a laminated card from his flight manual and began to read the prescribed ritual for the landing checklist. She held her breath as the countdown started.

As they continued the checklist, the tower issued further instructions. "Clipper Two, you have clearance to land, runway 13."

"Clipper Two, roger that. Cleared to land, runway 13, Clipper Two." Dave guided the plane according to the monitors of the automatic pilot system in front of them to the glide slope, watching his altitude carefully even though it was a clear day and he could see the hill at the end of the runway. As they came closer, he lowered his speed and brought the nose up, flaring the giant craft into the airman's art of control.

"500, 300, 200," counted off the First Officer, looking out the right window at the ground, gauging the distance, matching the autopilot's system. The giant aircraft squeezed into a flight-path that was smack down the middle of a heavily populated corridor of busy roads and high-rise buildings, hovering just above the line of buildings to their right.

Sally swallowed hard, her eyes wide. Although it was occasionally allowed for crewmembers to sit in the cockpit, it was generally forbidden, certainly for a dangerous operation like the "Laundry Line". She could see cars whizzing by on the road below, and sure enough, she glimpsed a field of fluttering pennants of colorful clothes snapping in the wind, strung out on lines from roof-top to roof-top and in-between. A group of teenagers played a ball game on the rooftop just yards away from their approach. As the giant aircraft thundered by the streets, it was just another everyday occurrence, and the ball team did not even raise their eyes. A child in a red shirt waved from the safety of his mother's arms.

They felt the wheels grab the runway in the depths of the airplane far in back of them, then the nose gear, as Dave placed the throttles into reverse thrust position. The thousands of pounds of metal, engines, fuel, people, luggage and cargo slowed to a stop, just shy of the end of the runway. White caps from the harbor battered the rock revetments of the runway's end in front of them. Sally took a deep breath.

"Clipper Two, welcome to Hong Kong. Switch to ground 121.9. Good day," said their calm guide from the tower.

"Clipper Two, ground 121.9. Good day."

As they cleared the runway, Sally removed her headphones and rose somewhat shakily from her seat. "Thanks, Captain. I enjoyed that. Looked like someone's idea of Paradise on earth," she said, closing the cockpit door behind her as she went back to her duties downstairs.

That night, Dave took Sally to a Laundry Line celebratory dinner in the second floor restaurant at the Peninsula Hotel near their layover hotel in Kowloon. She loved everything about the old colonial hotels. The front part of the dining room was bordered entirely by tall windows that framed a sweeping view of the harbor and Hong Kong's Victoria Island.

On this night, the harbor was busy with barges, traditional Chinese junks and all kinds of motor craft rushing back and forth. Across the water, layer upon layer of lights climbing up toward Victoria peak provided a shimmering backdrop. Dave ordered a bottle of Pouilly Fuisse and fresh grouper for two.

"This is a treat for me, you have to know," she smiled, looking out at the harbor. "I've only been here for orange pancake breakfasts, and never realized how beautiful it is at night."

The attentive staff hovered, smiling. They'd seen this before.

Dave had made it clear on the phone that this was an invitation to dinner. With him. She had accepted. Neither of them attempted to recruit anyone else to come along. Still, she wasn't sure what exactly she was doing or why; all she knew was that when she looked into Dave's eyes, she felt happy.

"So what did you think of the landing today?" he asked, reaching for his wine.

"Oh my goodness." Sally lifted her glass to toast him. "It was exciting and a little—no, a lot—scary. I've sat in the cockpit before, but I've never seen anything like the Laundry Line. That runway looks *awfully* small when you're coming in so fast in the middle of all those buildings and people and washing." She touched his glass in appreciation, giving him a special smile.

"You know, you're quite removed from everything up there," she continued. "It's almost like the cockpit has no relationship to the rest of the airplane, rather than being its center of control. It feels like you're a small metal tube with the wind rushing by. Downstairs, we've got engines and spoilers roaring, flaps coming in and out of the wings, the rumbling of the gear as the plane descends, hundreds of passengers wiggling and talking. It's all very quiet and antiseptic up where you are. You only see the beginning and the end, not the journey."

Dave smiled. "That is an interesting observation…the end, not the journey."

He reached for her hand. "I'm glad you were there," he said. Then he raised his glass again towards hers in a toast. "To your first Laundry Line landing, Sally. May you have many more such adventures."

The attentive staff smiled discreetly. Things were going well. There would be a good tip.

Sally smiled proudly. "Thank you." She glanced at the ring on his finger. "So, tell me about your family." She chose her words carefully to encourage his story.

"My wife's name is Louise. She was a flight attendant and we met on a trip out of Miami." Dave told her their story, the recitation familiar, and tonight, somewhat flat. They had married quickly, and their two sons arrived soon after. They had moved to Pan Am's Berlin base in the 1960s and lived a good life: concerts at the Philharmonic, dinners at fine restaurants, and invitations to important society functions within the expatriate community.

"That sounds glamorous, but what brought you back?" Sally asked.

"I wanted the 747." Dave had wanted to fly that airplane, and he wanted it more than anything in the world—not to mention the fact that a 747 captain was the highest paid pilot in the industry, and the aircraft the most technically proficient ever built.

But as much as he enjoyed flying and the ego boost of the left seat, he never seemed to be at home when things went wrong. "I think my children would be better people today if I'd been there full-time while they were growing up," he said ruefully, looking out at the harbor. "What about you? Is there a man in your life?"

"Not really," said Sally. "I'm gone so much, and it's hard to meet the kind of men I'm interested in." She paused to sip her drink. "Most of them are military guys who have been in and out of Vietnam or rotating back to the mainland, and the ones who were raised in the islands have to go to the mainland because of the lack of good jobs and high cost of living. I meet lots of men—lots of them. But…"

"But what?"

"Sometimes they just don't understand our lives. It can be intimidating when we have to turn them down for a date because we have to go to Singapore." He laughed.

After dinner, Sally had an inspiration and led him towards the Star Ferry Terminal. "Let me show you something," she said, bypassing the ticket window for First Class passengers.

"Where are we going? First Class only costs three Hong Kong dollars," Dave wondered. It was the equivalent of about 50 cents. The Star Ferry was one of the few places the flight attendants could afford to go First Class, so usually they took advantage of it.

"You'll see." Sally purchased two tickets at the Second Class window at the bargain price of less than a quarter for the two of them. There were two separate entrances for each class. First Class passengers were seated on the upper deck of the ferry, the sides encased in glass to keep out the chill or the heat, depending on the weather. Second

Class passengers walked down a dingy gangplank, signs posted everywhere advising an alert for pickpockets. There were no seats, and they shouldered through a standing-room-only crowd, the deck open to the wind and the salt-spray, the noise and fumes of the harbor.

Sally led Dave to the railing and as people crowded in, they found themselves looking suspiciously around. He put one arm around Sally's shoulder and the other hand over his wallet in his pocket. As the ferry departed, they began to hear the sound of the waves lapping against the boat and the engines groaning. Then suddenly the salty sea breeze blew in their faces. The tremulous lights of Central danced on the waves like golden treasures. Above Central's towering office buildings shimmered the layer of luxury apartment buildings known as Mid-Levels, and crowning the whole backdrop were the regal jewels of the mansions atop Victoria Peak.

"Thank you," murmured Dave in Sally's ear. "I would never have thought of doing this."

When they reached the other side, Sally took his hand. "That was so much fun, I have another treat." Leading him over to the taxi stand, she instructed the driver, "The Peak Tram, please."

Dave had taken the tram to Victoria Peak before, but always in the daytime. They climbed aboard a car crowded with tourists, tired businessmen who had stayed late toiling in their offices down at Central, and domestics who were headed for work in the apartments and houses up above, the odor of garlic on their breath.

The tram began its climb up the steep ascent surrounded by the darkness of underbrush. Then slowly, the lights of the great city began to emerge from the trees and rooftops, the dark slash of the harbor dividing Victoria and Kowloon. When they reached a stop just shy of the peak, Sally grabbed his arm.

"Why are we getting off now?" he wondered. "We're not there yet."

"I'll show you," she murmured, leading them down the steps of the tramcar to the small waiting area. The stop was made of concrete that jutted out from the side of the cliff topped by a corrugated metal roof overhead and its sides open to the air. It was deserted. A few crickets chirped in the brush, occasionally breaking the silence. The smell of grease on the tracks mingled with damp leaves that had fallen from the trees on the ground below. They stood side-by-side, resting their arms on the railing.

"See," she said, "you get the view without all the people."

Dave looked out at the lights. "My God. This is magnificent. It may even be better than the view from the Laundry Line approach." They were quiet for a few moments, taking in the incandescent grandeur of Hong Kong at night.

"Sally," Dave said after a while, "what's happening here?" She was quite close to him and she could feel her breath on his face. The only light at the tram stop was right next to the tracks, and they stood in the semi-darkness just out of the yellow pool of its glow. They looked at each other silently for a long moment, then he took her in his arms and kissed her. It was a long kiss, intimate and full of passion.

Sally felt exhilarated, intoxicated. They stood there together for a long while, holding each other close. Then Dave said, "Sally, what's your view of this thing—or whatever it is—that seems to be going on between us?"

"I think I'm surprised at myself," she replied, "and I'm embarrassed that you are married, and that there are a couple of decades between us in age, but it seems like only a couple of months. And I'm appalled that I let you kiss me, although I *liked* it. I know that when we go home, I won't be able to stand not being with you. But I know above all that you have to…you have to try and work this out with Louise because that is your obligation. Otherwise, it's no good." She broke away from him.

"I must be crazy," she said, looking out into the mass of glowing city lights.

Dave reached into his pocket for a handkerchief to brush the tears brimming in her eyes. "No, Sally, I think you're the sanest, most decent *lady* I've ever met," he said, placing it in her hand and curling her fingers around it.

They took a taxi back to the Star Ferry and headed back across the harbor towards the hotel. Just before they reached the front entrance, Dave began to lag back, so they wouldn't walk in at the same time.

"Sally, one more thing," he said. "If you change your mind, please, let me know."

She nodded and turned away, walking up the steps quickly. Marching straight through the crowded lobby back to the elevators, she looked at her reflection in the polished doors. Alone again. Empty. She looked down at the white handkerchief, aching.

CHAPTER TWELVE

WHERE I LIVE, THERE ARE RAINBOWS
JANUARY 30, 1974   HONOLULU, HAWAI'I

Sally tripped up the steps of the Kuhio Hotel at 9:00 p.m., noting that Walker Sheppard's battered blue Corvette was nosed up right behind the Big Orange near the valet stand. It was a cool night in the islands, the winter tradewinds seeking out channels in between the tall buildings, whipping around corners and causing her floral print dress to cling to her body. Pulling her shawl around her shoulders, she crossed the open-air lobby to the entrance of Nick's, a favorite nightspot in Waikiki for the single crowd. Once inside, she turned left, heading for familiar territory on the far side of the rectangular bar, a cozy lair from which one could view the piano and watch people come and go.

Sally spied an empty seat next to Walker, and gave him a hug. Sally was grateful for her friendship with him; in addition to his relationship with Pua, he was just always so dependable.

"So, did you meet Lucien?" asked Walker.

"I did, right around the corner at Hula's." Hula's Bar and Lei Stand was a well-known establishment that catered to the gay community, holding mail at the bar for the newly arrived and providing job locator services in addition to a vibrant nightlife for the island's demimonde. "I'm so glad I finally persuaded him to transfer out here from New York. And the reason I'm early is that after dinner, I introduced him to a super guy named Kaleo Price, who owns the manicure salon on Keeaumoku Street. I left the two of them at a table under the banyan tree, staring into each other's eyes. Isn't love grand?"

She climbed on to the barstool. "I owe you, dear friend, for letting Pualani swap trips with me so I could be here to welcome Lucien in proper style."

"Don't give it another thought, Sally," said Walker. "You know

I would do anything for you Pan Am people. You're like family to each other, and I understand that. And it meant a lot to Pualani for you to be able to do this."

"Walker, you are a true gentleman, even if you are nuts enough to fly A-4 fighters. So how was your day?"

"Well, nothing new and different," Walker smiled. "Same old jet-jockey kind of day. But let me tell you why I wanted you to meet me here. There's something I need to talk over with you." He retrieved a small box from his pocket, which he placed on the bar in front of her. She opened it, and nestled in the folds of velvet was a diamond ring.

"Oh, Walker," Sally breathed, "how beautiful!"

"It was my grandmother's," said Walker awkwardly. "What I want to know is... do you think she will say yes?" His eyes peered anxiously into Sally's. "You know that we come from very different worlds, and I need to think about that carefully, and so does she. She's an island girl, and I don't know if she could ever leave this beautiful place for long. And there's another thing: I'm just not certain of what I'm going to do with my life yet. This crazy war has me torn between the loyalties of the naval tradition in my family, and the fact that this... this stuff in Southeast Asia has torn our country apart, along with my whole generation—both military and civilian. We can't even talk to each other any more. Even though all of the ground troops are out, it's still a mess."

He signaled for another round of drinks. "Like most military brats, I grew up with the confidence and optimism of my father's generation, their victory in World War II, their almost blind loyalty to authority, their faith in America." He moved his chair around. "I knew I'd be drafted myself after graduation, so I figured I'd make everybody happy by attending Officers Candidate School. It seemed to mollify my dad, so after OCS, I asked him—and perhaps it was the only thing I'd ever asked of him—to pull some strings so I could be assigned out here."

Walker smiled. "And, as you know, that was when I met Pua, that incredible woman. I'd never seen anyone like her, dancing in the moonlight at your luau. There's nothing quite as special as watching a beautiful girl spontaneously stand up and dance hula in a pair of shorts and a tee shirt."

Sally said, "Pua taught us all a lot that night. I began to understand how chant and dance had been part of Hawai'ian culture and history for thousands of years. I can't imagine how they must feel about the missionary *haoles* who tried to stamp it out during the Monarchy period."

"I don't know," replied Walker quietly. "There are so many things I don't know about those days and why our country and the other colonial powers were so arrogant and cruel. All I know is that I will never love anyone like her, ever, ever."

Walker told her stories about meeting her family in Wahiawa, so many events since then, how he had discovered warmth and hospitality of local families that was so special to mainland *haoles* like himself, and so unlike the stilted, formal manner of his own family events, cold, distant and serious.

He loved the food and the laughter and camaraderie. "Maybe this is getting too personal," he said, "but after those dinners, I'd just bury my face in that silky black hair, to find the little stephanotis blossom that she wore behind her ear. For the rest of my life that flower will always remind me of her. I just want to know, am I asking too much?"

"Walker," Sally said, "I know this is serious business and I don't want to try and influence you one way or another. But this just is not our parents' world. Look at how many of our friends are dating people all across the rainbow. The seeds of something very important are being sown here in Hawai'i. It's not going to be perfect over night, but it's happening. As for Pualani being a Navy wife, you're not asking some little hayseed to marry you; she's been all over the world, and with her warmth and charm, she will be an asset to you." Sally paused for a moment as she watched Walker digest what she had said. "And besides, I know she will say yes."

Startled, Walker turned to look at her. "How do you know that?"

"We talked last month at home, and we were having a rather philosophical conversation about whether or not there is a life after flying. And she said something quite profound. She shrugged her shoulders and said, 'I love. The rest will take care of itself.'"

Sally leaned forward. "Walker, we can't always have everything mapped out in our lives. There are no guarantees. But I don't believe Pua would have spent the last two years with you, knowing full well that you might possibly make the Navy your career, if she weren't willing to be at your side no matter what." Sally placed her hand gently on his arm. "Take your jet-jockey blinders off, Walker. Could it really be any other way?"

"Thanks, Sally. I needed to hear that." He thought for a moment then set his glass down firmly on the bar. "Okay, Sally, this is it. Tomorrow. Tomorrow when I meet Pualani at the airport, I will ask her to marry me right outside of the frigging Customs Arrival area, down on my knees, and that's that. I will do this one right, and not waste another minute." Sally laughed and hugged him. Walker gestured to the bartender to bring another round. Suddenly, he spotted a familiar husky figure walking toward him.

"Hey, brah," said the man, greeting him in the local style.

"Jack Wright!" exclaimed Walker. "As I live and breathe. Meet my next-door neighbor, Sally Wilder. She flies for Pan Am."

Jack looked at Sally for a long moment before extending his hand. "I've met Zoe and Pualani, but I think every time I've come up to the country to go surfing with Walker and Moke, you've always been on a trip. Pleased to meet you, Sally." Then he turned to Walker, "I haven't seen this many good-looking women together in one place since I left Saigon."

Sally nodded toward the crowd. "Jack, that's because half of Pan Am's Honolulu base is here tonight. Nice to meet you, too, by the way."

"Jack and I have been friends since 'small kid time,'" said Walker. "Our families became close during my father's first tour at Pearl, and we were in elementary school together. We've stayed in touch all these years, so as soon as I got to Barber's Point, he was the first person I called."

"Oh, so you're from the islands?" asked Sally.

"Born and raised right here in Honolulu," Jack replied. "Some of my ancestors were bad old missionaries, who came to do good and did well."

Sally smiled at the old joke, appraising him. His eyes were startlingly blue. It was a pleasant face, with a ready smile, a clever sense of humor and even a hint of wickedness. He had broad shoulders and a husky physique, with a steadiness in his bearing, and his thick brown hair had begun to curl around his ears. "Well you're obviously not in the military, are you?" she said, reaching towards a lock of hair.

"Ex-Marine. Just got out a few months ago." Jack gazed admiringly at Sally.

"And you're a pilot."

"Helicopters. And how did you know?"

"I've been around pilots long enough to know 'em when I see 'em," she said, arching an eyebrow at Walker good-naturedly. "You boys just have that *look*...."

"What *look*?" Jack and Walker responded in unison.

Sally considered them carefully for a moment. "Like 'stay out of my airspace baby'."

"And I'll bet nobody better get in yours, either," quipped Jack. They laughed.

Walker lifted his glass to Jack's. "So here's to you, pal. How does it feel to be a free man? Are you going to stay here in town?"

Jack shook his head thoughtfully. "Well, you know me. I'm still decompressing, but I've got a few ideas. This place is so much a part of me I can't imagine not spending my life here. I must know almost all the eccentric people and how things tick, most of the back roads and hiking trails in the islands; the surfing spots; the trees, the flowers, the fish, and the legends and the superstitions." Jack suddenly became thoughtful. "But still...."

Sally said, "Well, it sure isn't Latham, Kentucky, but I know all about small town life—good and bad." They nodded in mutual understanding.

"I'm struggling, too," admitted Walker. "I've got to commit to the Navy one way or another pretty soon now. You know the traditions in my family. I never could have conceived of questioning a military career. He looked around and lowered his voice. "But, I have to say to you both that this war has left a bad taste in my mouth." He chewed his lip for a moment, recalling his conversation with Sally earlier that evening. "Who knows, hey, maybe I'll stay in just for the flying."

A group by the piano bar hailed Sally and dragged her away. "Will you all excuse me? Some friends I never get to see just got back from Timbuktu. I've got to catch up!"

"You people," said Jack, shaking his head. "Is there any place on the globe you don't know about?" Jack watched her move away through the crowd then turned to Walker. "Are they all like that?"

"If you'd ever hang around long enough, you might find out," said Walker dryly. "You've just been out of the service a short time, so you need to branch out, meet some people around here. I'm sure Sally and her crowd could take good care of you."

"Walker, I need to tell you something."

"Okay...."

"It's about what comes next. God help me, but I haven't had enough of Asia yet. I don't know if it's the danger I'm addicted to or the adventure. In spite of all I went through out there, I still want to help. I'm just not through flying. Maybe I'm crazy, but I'm gonna do some flying someplace where they don't do things by the book. That's all I can tell you about it."

"Sounds, uh, fascinating," observed Walker, suspecting what his friend had in mind. "When do you leave?"

"In a few weeks," said Jack, handing him a card. "Here's my card. It'll tell you how to find me. Look me up if you get out there."

Walker looked at the card Jack had handed him. It listed his address as a P.O. Box in San Francisco. That was all. Walker shook his head. Spook stuff. Air America for sure, the crazy jock.

Tapping Jack's card on the bar, Walker's thoughts returned to Pualani's arrival the next morning. He drained his glass, looked at his watch and clapped his friend on the shoulder. "I've got a big day tomorrow, so I'd better get going. Tell Sally I'll see her tomorrow, will you? And let's have dinner before you leave. "

Moments later, Sally emerged from the group and sat next to

Jack, who gave her Walker's farewell message. She said, "What a guy…you know he's in love with my roommate Pua, and he's picking her up tomorrow with a big surprise!" She ordered another drink and turned back to him. "So what's your next adventure after the service?"

Jack nodded, his face becoming serious. "It's different now, being out of the Marines," he said. "In Saigon, there were so many people trying real hard to make that situation work. But you know how frustrating it was trying to accomplish our objectives when the South Vietnamese military guys weren't as committed as we were. Those folks from the North, the Viet Cong and the NVA, now there's a very different story: total determination against huge odds. But I was amazed at the bravery of our American soldiers in the face of such a challenge. No, I take that back. Not amazed, overwhelmed." He took a long pull from his beer and continued. "When I came home after the drawdown last year, it was painfully obvious that the South wasn't going to be able to sustain their sovereignty. All that Paris stuff was just rearranging the deck chairs on the *Titanic*. I've done my time and I could go to law school, I guess, but I'm not quite ready. I think I may be heading back to Asia for a time." He looked away.

Sally nodded, her face serious as she thought about his words, his commitment, his courage. She started to tell him about the soldier going into withdrawal from heroin on her flight out of Tan Son Nhut, but decided against it. There was much that was unsaid here, and she sensed that now was not the time to inquire about it. "When will you leave?"

"Soon." Jack rose, and signaled the bartender for his tab.

"Jack, I know what you mean about trying to plan your life," said Sally. Their eyes met for a moment, not in instant passion, but in a deeper way that was borne of shared feelings and experiences. "Good luck to you. I'm sorry I won't know you better."

"Maybe some day," he said. "Aloha, Sally."

She watched as he melted into the crowd and disappeared.

Early the next morning in the false dawn, Sally was awakened by the persistent jangling of the telephone. She picked up the receiver, just feeling her mind beginning to function.

"Hello," she croaked, her voice still ragged from the cocktails and cigarette smoke at Nick's.

"Sally, wake up, wake up. It's me," said Zoe, her voice anxious.

"I'm awake," Sally said. "At least I think I am. Where are you?"

"I'm in L.A., and I'm due to fly up to Fairbanks in a little while. Sally…."

"Zoe, are you still there?" said Sally, thinking the line had gone dead, but then Zoe spoke again.

"Sally, there is really, really bad news. The 806 went down last night at about 11:30 in Pago Pago, the *Clipper Radiant*. They hit about a mile short of the runway in a bad squall. They had a full, long-haul load of fuel for the next leg up to Honolulu. There was a huge fire."

"Oh Jesus," whispered Sally, her heart sinking, the grim reality dawning on her. "Oh, God! That was my flight—that was my trip! I could have been there. Were there any casualties? Everyone got out okay, right? Right, Zoe, right? I mean, everyone is okay, everyone survived, didn't they?" Then an ominous thought hit her. "Oh, Jesus, Zoe—Pualani. Oh, no…." Sally felt her voice rise as the tears and emotion closed her throat.

"No, Sally, they didn't make it. There were only four survivors," said Zoe. "They got out over the wings. It appears that the other 97 died. The crew report here says they all died of…asphyxiation." Zoe's voice sounded contracted and small, and Sally could hear her sigh heavily.

Sally felt her heart pounding from the huge rush of adrenalin in her body. "Oh, God, Zoe, I swapped that trip with Pualani. She was due in this morning. Walker's going to the airport to meet her! She has to be okay, she has to be." She felt the fear tear at her mind.

"Sally, I'm sorry. None of the crew survived," said Zoe gently. "And Pualani *was* on board. All the flight attendants were Honolulu-based. I just confirmed it with Operations here in L.A. There will be a huge investigation, so lots of information will be in the newspapers later today."

"Walker is supposed to pick Pualani up at the airport in a few hours," whispered Sally, looking outside at the frothy white caps on the water that were just beginning to lighten as sunrise approached. "I have to go next door and tell him before he leaves for the airport. Oh, heaven help me! I swapped the trip with Pualani. It should have been me, not her." Her cries deepened to a moan of despair.

Then she dropped the phone, went into the bathroom and threw up.

In the near darkness, Sally stumbled across the yard to the house next door. When she reached the lanai, she began scratching on the window to what she knew was Moke Cabral's room. Soon there was a shadow on the door and he harrumphed his way out. "Something wrong, Sally?"

Sally clutched his arm. "Yes, really wrong, and you and Diz have to stand by to help Walker. Now listen to me. This is real. Pua's plane went down in Pago Pago. Zoe just called me. There were no survivors. There was a huge fire. Oh, God, Moke," Sally's voice broke, "she's gone." Moke groaned and hugged her quickly, then left the room to find Diz. Within minutes, they were whispering on the lanai.

Hearing voices, Walker had stumbled out through the living room, looking for them. "Hey, who's out there? What's up? Everything okay?" He caught sight of Sally.

"Sally! Are you all right?" said Walker, looking her over for any sign of injury. "You didn't have a break-in over there, did you?"

"No, no, nothing like that," Sally whispered harshly, her face in her hands. "But it's not okay, Walker. I don't know how to tell you this, but the 806 went down late last night in Pago Pago and Pualani was definitely on it."

Walker absorbed the hammer blows of the news. "Is she all right?"

Sally hesitated. "Walker, a few passengers survived, but...oh God...none of the crewmembers." Sally dissolved in tears and Diz soothed her, while Moke clasped Walker's shoulders and they stood together.

Walker's eyes lifted to the Pacific's ocean swells beyond, on out to the limitless blue horizon where sea and sky merged, the same sea of Samoa. Then she thought of the velvet case containing the ring that he'd shown her the night before.

Diz coughed respectfully, giving him time. "Walker, we're all here for you, and it's better to hear it from Sally than hearing it on the radio on the way to the airport." His voice faded.

"Sally, thank you. I guess there's no other way you could tell me," said Walker, his voice rough with emotion, his teeth clenching, his big hands reaching up to rub his face, shield his eyes.

There was silence, except for the swishing of the ocean.

"You all right, brah?" inquired Moke, placing his arm around Walker's shoulders.

"Yeah, I'll be okay…okay. Well, I have to think, have to take it all in." Walker's voice was thick. He sat down heavily, with his head in his hands, his eyes empty. "She's gone, they're all gone," he said slowly, pausing to gather his thoughts.

Then he rose and went to the phone inside, rifling through the pages of the phonebook to find the listing for Pua's father, Moses Kanawai.

Days later, Sally and Zoe sat in a grass and bamboo *fale* by the pool at the Rainmaker Hotel in Pago Pago together with fellow steward, Tom Ryan, and Russell Cray, a junior Flight Engineer from San Francisco who was a member of the crash inspection team. The bar across the deck was rowdy at the end of the day, with construction workers mingling with local residents and a smattering of tourists. A policeman presided at the front door in the event that things got out of hand—a huge, baldheaded official clad in a blue shirt and badge, policeman's hat, a navy blue *lava lava* wrapped around his waist, and brown leather sandals. The waitresses stared sideways at Sally, Zoe and Russell; they all knew about the crash last week, as well as the inspection teams, news reporters and weeping families.

"Maybe this was a bad idea," said Zoe, of their volunteering to come down and help with the accident investigation. The FAA and the National Transportation Safety Board wanted to know why so many people died if they weren't killed by the impact, as the survivors testified. Every incoming flight had FAA check crews on it, and extra Pan Am personnel like Russell.

"Zoe, we have to know the truth, for Pualani's sake," said Sally. "We promised her family, remember?" She stirred her drink. "You know why I'm here. It should have been me," she said. "I should be dead and Pualani should be laughing with Walker. I will never have another day of rest until I know." Silently, she thought of the lives of 97 passengers and crew who had died that night, along with the public's confidence in Pan Am's safety procedures.

Zoe looked out at the water, milky in the late afternoon light, sipping her tonic water, and shaking her head. "You just can't ignore history and legends, and the old folks say there's a curse here. The old flight logs and reports say that Captain Ed Musik of the *China Clipper* hated this place; hated landing the Flying Boats in this teacup of a harbor. He died inbound into Pago Pago too, you know. Had an oil leak in one of the engines. When he went to dump fuel, the plane exploded."

Russell Cray gestured toward the harbor, "If my information is correct, the pilots don't think landing at the airport now is all that much safer than landing in the harbor during the Flying Boat days. They hate those two mountains, the steep glide slope, the short runway, the whole damned thing." He talked about the salt spray of the ocean at the end of the runway. "When there are bad squalls, not only do you have to worry about staying on course, but all the rain on the runway creates an optical illusion; makes you look higher than you are."

They sat numb, saddened and exhausted, oblivious to the scenery, the smell of the tuna cannery across the bay, and the ratty texture of the *fale*. The Rainmaker had seen better days.

Looking out over the harbor, Zoe thought of their arrival a few days before on the first flight into Pago after the crash, accompanying Pua's family and other bereaved passengers. She had sat on the forward jumpseat with Tom Ryan, a normally talkative, energetic New Yorker.

But this approach into Pago was different. Buffeted by the winds and their own fears, she and Ryan had clutched hands wordlessly as the aircraft descended, creaking and yawing, towards the blinking lights of the outer marker, the underbrush and jungle scarred by the still smoking hulk of the *Clipper Radiant*.

They had accompanied the family in the heavy rain to a nearby empty hangar, where the bodies of the victims had been retrieved. The remains were set in rows, organized alphabetically by surnames on rickety trestle tables in rough wooden boxes. They were covered with sheets and protected by a long plastic tarpaulin. Leis and candles had been set along the sad rows, placed there by tearful members of the nearby village. Family members of the Samoan victims had arrived in large crowds, clad in black shirts and *lava lava*, screaming their grief and claiming their loved ones' bodies to be lovingly wrapped in lengths of *tapa* cloth. The anonymity of death was broken by the small bodies of children, shapeless and tiny, alongside the corpses of their parents. The women keened, their eyes red with mourning and loss.

The operations manager had told Zoe that Pualani's body had been found in the forward galley of the wreckage, her hands fastened around the unbending handle of a warped door, blocking her exit. A dozen corpses of Samoan passengers, who had scraped their nails bloody on the unyielding doorframe, surrounded her body and lay on top of her, blocking any hope of escape. Zoe did not share that with Pua's parents, just the coroner's report that her face looked peaceful, as though she'd just gone to sleep. She lay now in a makeshift coffin, waiting with the other crewmembers' coffins to be loaded in the belly of the outbound flight. Sally and Zoe stood in a silent vigil with Pua's parents, her sister and Walker, sharing their pain, and respecting the mourning of devastated families of the other crew and passengers. They escorted Pua's family back towards the aircraft. The sad business of loading now complete, the Clipper made its take-off run and lifted off for Honolulu as the mists and rain swirled low again. They watched in a silent benediction to the tragedy, then trudged slowly back towards the crew bus,

During the past few days, Sally and Zoe and the other crewmembers had spent hours demonstrating evacuation exercises for the FAA and NTSB inspectors. They followed the training manual, running up and down the aisles of a 707 check plane, clocking exit times and kicking down middle seats to get to the window exits. They went through full-on drills, yanking window exits open and throwing them out onto the wings. They screamed instructions at the ground crew of frightened Samoan men and women who were standing in for passengers just like they had learned in training, the mantra burned in their brains, "Go! Go! Go! Jump into the slide! Jump! Jump and run away from the plane, away from the plane!" Then, through curtains of pouring rain, they'd race around to the steps and back up again into the airplane for another exercise.

Zoe sat quietly now, overlooking the harbor, examining her own fears, her own center. "Maybe it's not so bad," she said thoughtfully. "They are at peace now. They'll never get old and ugly and fat, and we will always remember them shining and happy." Sally looked at her strangely.

Russell said, "We already know that the investigation has found that almost all of the dead survived the crash itself, but for some reason the exit doors were blocked and the crewmembers were separated from their stations. We don't know yet, but it may have been structural damage forward and aft which buckled the door frames." They had all sat through the dreadful briefing earlier that day, where the entire investigation team had shown the graphic photos of the bodies; how they had piled up by the doorways, effectively forming human pyramids forward and aft. Only four survivors had made it out the window seats, opened by one of the survivors because the crewmembers were tangled in the gruesome blockades. Zoe kept thinking of the peaceful smile on Pualani's face.

The most awful conclusion they made was that the crash had killed very few—probably just the pilots. But all the remaining passengers perished quickly from cyanide gases caused by the burning plastic interior linings, seat cushions and modern finishings. It was a twentieth century firetrap, all technology and polish.

Zoe slammed a report down, rattling the table. "Nobody had to die here," she said with finality. "Let's be clear, we've been practicing for days so we know our training and emergency procedures would have worked. We know what happened: the passengers panicked and ran forward and aft, blocking the crew from getting to the window exits where they could have all been saved. It won't bring anybody back, but we do know why they all died."

She looked at her colleagues gathered around the table. "Panic killed them all. Just plain old human fight or flight instincts. Accidents like this make you wonder if we should be challenging so many statistical certainties. The odds aren't in our favor, you know. When our time is up, it's up and there is no argument. As for me, as long as I'm doing what I love and it's quick and painless, I'm not afraid. But let's not pretend for the cameras, either. This was a travesty, and the bastards will whitewash it."

They looked at each other, acknowledging Zoe's clear message, then moved off to an uneasy rest in a small Pacific island by an ancient sea, with new ghosts and good memories of their friends and companions, and the laughing, dancing daughter of the Pacific gone home.

The families gathered at Kawaihao Church in downtown Honolulu for a formal memorial service honoring all of the Honolulu based crewmembers. Walker Sheppard sat in full dress uniform beside the Kanawai family. Behind the rows of mourners, Sally stood with Lucien and Kaleo, Zoe stood behind Pua's family, next to Keoki. They listened with resignation to the beautiful singing of the Kawaihao Choir on the light morning breeze, the chirping of sparrows and the distant thrum of traffic. The air was fragrant with dozens of lei on each of six easels holding framed photographs of the deceased flight attendants. Rows of pews were packed with mourners, clad in Hawai'i's way in the colorful prints of long muumuus and bright shirts on the sad day, the sound of words and speeches of family and friends mingling with tears and muffled sobs.

Afterwards, they had gathered at a reception to honor the survivors: aging parents, siblings, cousins and friends. Because Pualani's family was from Hawai'i, they far outnumbered the relatives of those victims of the crash who had been from other places, but they wept together as one.

Zoe made her way through the receiving line behind Keoki, his eyes hidden behind dark glasses, his face composed, his thoughts unsaid. He approached Walker as the line of mourners filed past the families. He embraced him as a brother then abruptly turned away. Zoe looked after him, thinking of a harsh sunlit moment in a teak-mill yard long ago, when she first knew death. She went to him, taking his arm.

"Keoki," she said, "you know I'm not sugar-coating this, it's a complete tragedy. But Pualani would not want you to grieve so. She's right here with us now, reminding us that life will be joyful if we want it to be. What's your choice?"

He looked down at her, embraced her quickly and stroked her check. But he would not allow himself to be comforted, saying, "You of all people know, and since Tahiti, nothing is the same." He broke away from her, walking through the church's old cemetery, away from the crowd.

Zoe knew that her own heart was hard and angry at the waste of Pualani's life. And it's true, I will always watch Keoki walk away, she thought. And she mourned for Pualani and the sadness in her own heart, thinking again of the cold water and the drifting seaweed over the drum Hawea in another part of the Pacific, where there had been so much love.

A few months later, Walker opened the door of his commanding officer's office at Barbers Point.

"He said you could come right in," said the secretary, a look of tenderness on her face. The poor young man hadn't smiled since the crash.

"Good morning, sir," said Walker.

"At ease, Lt. Sheppard. Have a seat." Captain Blandford nodded toward a chair, "How are you?"

"Doing all right, sir. As well as can be expected," said Walker.

"Pualani's family is taking it pretty hard and I've been trying to spend time with them. It seems to help." Walker looked out the window at the flight line. "We all accept the danger inherent in flying. We know that most of the time when something goes wrong, it's usually catastrophic. But when it happens to someone in the civilian world, it's harder," he paused and swallowed hard, "especially since reports indicate that so many deaths could have been avoided."

Captain Blandford nodded, clapping a hand to Walker's shoulder. There was silence between them for a few moments before he picked up a paper on his desk and scanned it. "Walker, I've been assigned to the air wing command of the *USS Okinawa*. She's part of the Seventh Fleet, home ported out of Yokosuka, Japan. Looks like we're going to be doing some countermeasures for mining operations off of Haiphong, as well as some reconnaissance missions. Things could get interesting. I'd like for you to come with me, and it will mean a nice promotion for you. I've spoken with your father and he thinks it would be a good idea for you to have sea duty for a while. What do you say?"

Suddenly a breath of air wafted through the room, tinged with the smell of stephanotis, as if Pualani had just walked by. "When do we leave?" replied Walker, relief flooding his face.

CHAPTER THIRTEEN

CHOICES

AUGUST 21, 1974   THE NATIONAL MUSEUM, SINGAPORE

Zoe crouched in front of a display case in the newly renovated museum, once an important colonial building. The entire wall was covered with photographs and charts of World War II, depicting a fabulous history of treasure hunting and plunder entitled, "Yamashita Gold—the Tiger of Malaya, 1942-45". Maps featured storyboards of Burma, Malaya, Singapore and the Philippines, all conquered by the Japanese during the early days of World War II.

She remembered the tales of General Tomoyuki Yamashita's gold, millions of dollars of plundered treasure stolen by occupying Japanese forces, melted down into gold bullion and hidden. Some said it was sent to the Japanese Royal Family, or sunk in Japanese submarines, others that it was still booby-trapped in caves all over the Philippines; some claimed extortion by Ferdinand Marcos. There were whispers of the OSS and CIA involvement in the recovery, to finance Cold War operations all over the world. Zoe cringed, then, looking at her watch, headed away from the ancient intrigues. She remembered dimly, the old Karen warriors talking about the temple gold stolen by Japanese troops near her home in the Shan States, and unbidden, the memory of Sao Johnny's eyes.

Then and now, what was real and what was make-believe?

Sally sipped a Singapore Sling at the Long Bar, of the venerable Raffles Hotel just before noon, looking around the large room with its high ceiling, the shining expanse of the bar's polished wooden surface dominating the entire length of one wall. Ceiling fans twirled slowly overhead in the humid air while sheets of rain drummed on the corrugated iron awning covering the walkway outside through a luxuriant garden. The smell of fresh rain and old mold wafted in through the doorway, dark mildew stains spreading into shadowy blotches along the upper reaches of the walls and the elaborate crown moldings. The bar was deserted at this early hour, save one other patron at the far end.

"Hi, Sally. Hope you haven't been waiting long. I got caught up in an incredible exhibition at the Museum. And I have a truly amazing story to tell you," said Zoe, entering with her dripping umbrella, her shoes clicking across the marble floor as she deposited her book bag and the umbrella, ordering tea.

Sally said, "I'm all ears … go right ahead and amaze me! Pick up isn't till 8 p.m. tomorrow night, and we've got Guam to look forward to."

Zoe said, thoughtfully, "Well, I have to tell this slowly, and in installments. It may take a while."

She had proceeded to calmly recount her story in detail, while Sally sat listening, openmouthed.

Zoe spoke of a meeting, three days before, in a conservative Bangkok home where a friend had brought her into a select gathering of Burmese activists. There had been old school friends who were now Shan freedom fighters, Thai businessmen and foreign mercenaries, tangled up in the mix of activities taking place in the Golden Triangle—the complex business of arms acquisition, drugs and the sale of rubies and precious stones.

As Zoe related, the group had talked seriously of the struggle against General Ne Win, who'd been a great friend of her father's, and one of the original independence advocates before he'd turned to brutal socialist policies.

Suddenly, Zoe said, a man had leaned out of the shadows, looking at her, smiling tentatively. Oh, God, she had remembered—the eyes.

She shook her head, saying to Sally, "After all that time, so many miles, so many tears, there was Sao Johnny, in person, in the flesh." She said that they had moved away from the crowd of onlookers, and she had gone right into his arms as others watched, murmuring.

Zoe sat quietly for a minute, just remembering his voice. Sally held her hand, silent, just listening.

"You never wrote," she had said, when she and Johnny were

seated in a quiet corner.

He held her tightly. "What was there to say? You left. Now, amazingly, you are here. But I know your life will take you away again."

Zoe had traced his face; older, harder. His body was thin and wiry, almost emaciated. But his eyes blazed with the light of warriors. And now, softly, with the memory of long-lost love. The recollection brought tears to Zoe's eyes.

Zoe told Sally of their conversation and their urgent need to keep their connection, no matter how tenuous.

She had swallowed. "Well, whatever happens, we must at least know how to contact each other, just in case there is a chance that I can...can ever help you."

"Yes," he had smiled, kissing her in the Burmese way, an inhalation of breath on each cheek, "and I must know that you are safe, always."

Zoe had remembered her 6:00 a.m. pickup, but she and Johnny sipped hot, spicy lemon-grass tea and spoke of the hardships now going on in Burma.

Zoe reminded Sally that her parents had left the country, but she was still distanced from them. She and Johnny had spoken of friends, neighbors, families, and the huge changes that had taken place over the last decade.

Sally's heart ached for the suffering as she listened to Zoe recount the tale, tears in her eyes. She never cries, Sally thought. Never.

Then Zoe was silent again as she remembered. Holding her beside him, Sao Johnny had begun to whisper stories of border wars, of the Chinese Kuomintang's activities in the misty jungles of the Golden Triangle, of the regular attentions of foreign mercenaries, mostly American, and mostly CIA related. There were no laws or official press officers in these mountains, only what happened and who knew the truth. Zoe had listened to him quietly, knowing that he could never share these burdens with anyone. As the sky started to lighten, she had held Sao Johnny close, and then closer, remembering what had been.

Now, Zoe unfolded a piece of paper and showed it to Sally. It was a series of addresses and phone contacts, describing in detail how she could reach Sao Johnny, through mission stations on the Thai border...even locations in Laos and Vietnam.

Zoe wiped the tears away. "And we knew, holding each other, that this won't ever come again. It's like we know we won't see each other...not in this life, anyway, and it's okay." She smiled at Sally, whose own eyes brimmed.

Sally squeezed her hand. "Zoe, that is the saddest, saddest story I've ever heard. And I just don't want you to be unhappy ever again."

Zoe smiled, "Look at us blubbering; it's not even the booze talking."

Zoe finished the story with a brief account of what she'd seen in the Museum that morning, to verify all the talk of gold and jewels and treasure smuggled across borders. She looked out at the tangle of ferns and Traveler's Palms in the Raffles courtyard garden. "I don't know what history will say, Sally, but it's impossible for me to forget these ghosts, these friends, these believers. They are like *nats*, the Burmese spirits who all live their lives and try to do the right things, but come to a bad end. You pay to propitiate them so they *don't* come back," she sighed. "Let them go gently, I say, and I wish the endings to be happy."

Sally drained her glass, shaking her head in wonder. She stared thoughtfully at her friend. "I've known you for almost four years now, and I still can't get over your life. You just seem to accept it all, whatever comes."

Zoe smiled, toasting with her tea-cup. "Is there another choice?"

Sensing an opportunity for some socializing, the other bar patron eased down towards them, ordering a round of drinks. He introduced himself as a junior commercial attaché at the American Embassy in Singapore, after two years in-country in Vietnam. "You gotta be Pan Am stews, right? We don't see too many of you gals here these days. You've all been too busy up there in Vietnaaam doing the 'White Man's Burden' thing."

Zoe looked up, her eyes glinting. "Hmm, Kipling? You do know that he was kidding, right?" she smiled with her teeth only. "He wrote that business about the White Man's Burden to honor the United States' overthrow of the legitimate government of the Philippines in 1908. Kinda like the stuff we're still doing over there in Vietnaaam," she said, grinning and mimicking his pronunciation. "You know, Sally and I are part of history here, too. Real patriots. Pan Am was hauling soldiers out of Saigon at the rate of a thousand a day—live ones upstairs and coffins in the cargo hold. And I hear there's lots of other action that isn't printed in the newspapers." Zoe, her eyes frosty, leaned towards the alarmed man, pointing at the luxurious gardens. "See out there? Immutable Asia. It harbors snakes, and secrets, and pleasures. It will grow over you or around you in no time at all. And it never, ever surrenders." She smiled wickedly.

As the rains poured down, the startled young man stared at Zoe, his mouth hanging open. Recovering, he mumbled some excuses and made his escape.

Sally said, "You scared him to death."

Zoe nodded, thinking of Sao Johnny's arms around her, and his hard life. "Good. Maybe he will read some history. Sometimes it is necessary to just say what you think."

When they arrived home a few days later, they decided to have dinner at the Sea View Inn in Haleiwa. Television and newspapers headlined the resignation of President Richard Nixon, whose dark visage they both loved to hate. They breathed a sigh of relief that he was gone, memories of the Cambodian invasion and Kent State still clear in Sally's mind.

When Sally and Zoe walked into the restaurant, it was crowded with a mix of sugar cane workers, surfers, and other local residents. They found seats at the bar, and when their drinks arrived, Zoe lifted her tonic water and clinked Sally's glass. "You can only hide things for so long," she said. "Here's to Tricky Dick, whose lies finally caught up with him."

Sally made her way to the jukebox, slipping a coin into the slot and selecting the Harry Owens Orchestra's rendition of "Sweet

Leilani". Nothing happened. The records did not rotate, nor did any mechanical parts move. She drew back, puzzled.

"May I help you with that?" said a voice behind her. Turning, her eyes traveled upward to the face of a handsome, square-jawed young man. Oh my dear, sweet Lord, she thought, this is the most magnificent man I have ever seen and I am in trouble now.

He was tall and very suntanned, his sun-streaked brown hair cut short in a military style. The dim light in the bar hid his eyes but they looked hazel, set off by a dark green Aloha shirt patterned with outrigger canoes, covering the relaxed body of a professional athlete.

"I think it's jammed," he said.

Sally had not spoken; she merely nodded.

"Here, let me see if I can get your money back and we can try again another way." He leaned against the jukebox and gave it a hard, quick shove. There was a clunk, a bit of rattling, and her coin clattered down into the return box. Removing it, he inspected it in his palm. "Hmm…what are you doing putting a French franc in an American jukebox?"

Sally blinked her eyes at the coin in the man's hand, and finally cleared her throat. "I guess it's leftover from a Papeete trip, and it, uh, must have gotten mixed up with the change in my purse." Surely my face is purple, she thought, but I can't stop staring at him.

"Ah," he said, drawing back and regarding her with an easy smile. "Papeete. Then you must be with the airlines. What was the number again you wanted to play?"

Sally struggled to recover her voice. "K-K-K 14," she spluttered. He put in the dime and this time the records began to rotate, the sound of soft Hawai'ian music filling the air.

"I'm Sally Wilder," she said weakly, offering her hand in greeting. "Thanks for your help."

"Bill Spencer, and I hate to eat alone. Would you and your friend like to join me for dinner?" he asked, nodding at Zoe staring at them from the bar, her eyes cool.

Zoe regarded this little scene with concern. Sally had her head cocked upward at this man, a giddy little smile on her face. Clearly she was smitten. Figuring Sally might need rescuing in the event this guy oggnini

was an ax-murderer, married or just the standard drug-crazed surf rat, Zoe left her bar stool and sauntered over to them.

"Zoe Longfield," she said, extending her hand.

"Bill Spencer," replied Billy. "William Hannibal Spencer, in fact, but everybody calls me Billy."

Just then, a happy drunk shouted a greeting at their new escort. "Hey, Billy Righteous!! How you stay?" Billy smiled.

Sally blinked, remembering her trip around Waimea Bay, watching a golden man surf the giant waves, the rippling muscles, the black wetsuit glistening. "*You're* Billy Righteous? The guy who's done all the sea rescues and stuff?" she exclaimed.

Billy shrugged. "The sea rescues happened before I went to Vietnam the first time. We had enormous surf that winter and I had a few friends who were struggling, that's all. Anybody else would have done the same thing. So what brings you ladies to the Sea View tonight?"

"Actually, I can't speak for Sally, but I'm kind of celebrating the resignation of President Nixon," said Zoe, her voice edgy. "I suppose that might not go over so well with you."

Billy looked at her closely. "Well, I might not have agreed with everything he did," he said, choosing his words carefully, "but he was my Commander-in-Chief. I'm a Marine Corps helicopter pilot out at Kaneohe Bay, and now I'm saluting President Ford with enthusiasm." He grinned, snapping his right hand to attention.

Zoe looked at him coolly. "I have the highest regard for you folks in uniform, but I have a hard time with this duty-honor-country shtick from the civilian side of the government. And I really have a hard time with the fact that we're still propping up a government in South Vietnam. We never should have been there and it's time to be completely done with it."

Sally gave her best Southern belle drawl and said, "Well, we really can just let all that go for now, don't you think, Zoe?"

"That could change very shortly, Zoe," said Billy. "Congress may cut the funding now that Nixon is gone, and it'll be the end for South Vietnam."

"After all these years, not to mention losing over 50,000

American lives, hundreds of thousands of Vietnamese casualties, and billions of dollars, I'm not sure pouring more money into it makes any sense, does it?" wondered Zoe.

"You make a good point," said Billy. "But it wouldn't be the first time that our arrogance, combined with our idealism, has led us to make some bad decisions. We'll see what happens."

Zoe's face brightened a little. "You know, I respect you for saying that. I don't usually have much to say to military folks, and especially not to pilots, but you seem to have a level head." She patted Sally on the arm. "I'm not good company when I'm grouchy and tired. You two stay and enjoy dinner. I'm thinking this man can be trusted to get you home safely."

Billy grinned, and Sally hugged her good bye. "She's a real fireball, that one," said Sally, watching her go.

"That's an understatement," said Billy.

"But she cares about things, Billy, and she has passion for cultures, and history and archaeology, which I admire. She has stacks of history books beside her bed and reads stuff that I'd never touch in a million years."

"And what does she learn from you?" asked Billy.

"Oh, I don't know," replied Sally with a shrug. "I think she likes it because I'm so normal." Then she twinkled, "I taught her how to smoke a cigar once."

Billy laughed. "Somehow you don't strike me as the cigar type."

"Ah, don't bet on it, my friend," said Sally. "Appearances can be deceiving. My grandfather was a tobacco man in western Kentucky, and I learned the ropes from him. I'm one of the few women in the world who adores the smell of tobacco." After her initial flutters at the jukebox, Sally now felt comfortable. She and Billy ordered salads and seafood pasta, and enjoyed the meal and conversation. But soon she yawned, claiming Guam and Singapore fatigue.

"I'll take you home" said Billy, touching Sally's arm slightly. As they walked through the parking lot, a brief shimmer of rain passed over them. "In the Hawai'ian culture, a little shower like that is regarded as a blessing," he said, looking upwards. She felt a warm current, an electric shock where his finger had rested. She thought fleetingly of Dave…oh, God, another pilot. When they reached the front door of her house, they smiled into each other's eyes. "I'll call you," he whispered.

And she believed him.

The following week they arranged to meet at his home, an old Quonset hut on Ke Waena Road, for dinner and a bottle of wine. Walking inside through the carport, he switched on a lamp with an *abaca* shade from the Philippines, and lit a few candles around the living room. The soft, diffused light gently offset the insistent sound of the sea just outside. "It's a good life out here, and the ocean is, well, everything," said Billy, "except, of course, when it's angry."

"Yes, and then it pounds so hard the house shakes," added Sally. "It keeps me awake."

The small hut had a surf-shack charm to it. The living room gave way to a small kitchenette area, the sink strung with a skirt of blue trader cotton, next to a small stove and ancient squat refrigerator, humming loudly. Jalousie windows looked out onto a tiny yard, its grass and scraggly *naupaka* bushes giving way to the beach, the surfing break known around the world as the Banzai Pipeline. A clicking bamboo curtain separated the bedroom from the living room.

There was a large *hikie'e* in the living room, a Hawai'ian couch, which served the dual function of sofa and crash pad for visitors. Surfboards of various sizes, shapes and materials were strapped to the ceiling. On the walls hung maps of the Hawai'ian Islands and Pacific Basin, along with an assortment of old wooden canoe paddles.

"Ready for a glass of wine?" called Billy from the kitchenette.

"That would be lovely," replied Sally, taking in the room. There was no stereo or radio, but the shelves were piled with a startling number of books. She read down the list of titles: biographies of Churchill, Eisenhower, MacArthur, and various other World War II heroes, military strategists ancient and modern, even *The Seven Pillars of Wisdom*, by T.E. Lawrence. She stroked her hand down another shelf, this one of religious volumes: the *Bhagavad Gita,* the *Koran,* the

Ramayana, as well as the *King James Bible* and even Hermann Hesse.

"Your wine, mademoiselle," said Billy, coming to her side.

They drank in silence for a few moments, looking out at the deepening colors of night across the ocean. "Billy, I can't believe all these books," said Sally. "You and Zoe are a real pair. I don't know why I seem to surround myself with all these intellectual friends. You're either in training as a university lecturer, or you're the best-read helicopter pilot and surfer in the world! I can't decide which is better."

Billy laughed. "Yeah, it is a bit much, isn't it? Actually, my father taught me to love reading."

"And was your father in the Navy?" asked Sally.

"A mustang—from enlisted man up through the ranks to a wartime commission, then all the way up that flagpole to Admiral," said Billy. "In the early days, he educated himself by reading the classics aboard ship, hence my middle name of 'Hannibal'."

"As in Hannibal crossing the Alps?" Sally dimly remembered her high school Latin class taught by a defrocked Catholic priest.

"You are correct," said Billy, smiling down at her. "He was one of the great generals. He famously said, 'We will find a way or make one.' I must admit, though, my name is a bit of a mouthful, and it was difficult every time I went to a new school."

"So I assume you grew up moving around?"

"Yes, and we lived here for two tours," said Billy. "That's how I got interested in surfing. I was a teenager when we were at Pearl and I could drive up here and learn from the guys who really knew what they were doing. I also learned to fit in with and understand the local culture here, even though I'm *haole*."

"So what is it with this surfing stuff?" wondered Sally. "What makes people give up their lives for the waves and travel all over the world in search of them?"

"I think that at its most basic level, it's the feeling that you are part of a primeval force of nature," said Billy. He talked about how the power of the ocean fascinated him, the energy of motion that was inevitable, unstoppable. "It's the same as flying; when you're in the water, or in the air, you move with it and the life force is in you; it's like being rooted in the universe, for lack of a better way to say it. I'd hate to have to choose between them."

"I saw you two years ago when I first came to Hawai'i, riding the big waves at Waimea," said Sally, looking at the floor. "I love the water, too, but I prefer the safety of a tow rope behind a ski boat. But I do know all about roots. My family developed the putting down of roots into a holy sacrament, and sometimes you can have too much of a good thing. I think we were like a bunch of flowers that had been in the same pot for too long."

"And so that's why you're all the way out here," said Billy, moving to the kitchen where he unwrapped two large pieces of fresh mahi mahi.

"Yes, I guess so," said Sally, "that and just wanting to see more, do more, learn more about the world, music, art, all the things I love."

"I'll go light the grill. There stuff for a salad in there," Billy said, nodding at the refrigerator. Just as he passed by her, he brushed his arm with his forefinger, lingering just long enough for their eyes to meet. Once again, she felt a current sizzling between them.

After dinner, he poured some Amaretto into two glasses, and they settled onto the *hikie'e*. The house was silent, save the rustling of the palm fronds outside and the muffled boom of the ocean. The fresh breeze stole in through the jalousies in the kitchen, enveloping them with the smell of the sea and salt air. The candles flickered.

Sally looked about the room, clearly the residence of a bachelor. "Why isn't a guy like you married?"

"Oh, I've had a few close calls," said Billy, "but what I do is highly irregular, and sometimes dangerous. I've been reluctant to settle down until I find a person who will be strong enough to understand and accept the kind of life I lead. What about you? You must have them standing in line." He reached out and placed his hand in her hair and watching it filter through his fingers in the light, like strands of silk. "You're a world traveler, you flit from here to there, but your feet are firmly on the ground."

"I don't know if that's entirely the case."

"And I think you also have the heart of the girl next door," added Billy.

"That," responded Sally, "can get me into a great deal of

trouble."

"So, is there somebody?"

Sally remembered Dave McFarland and their Delhi trip together. "I had a 'near miss'—if you want to call it that—not long ago, but he was married. And I don't date married men; life is full of enough unattainable things as it is."

He drew her to him and she did not resist. Kissing her gently, he enfolded her in his arms. Then she drew back. He felt her reluctance, so they settled onto the *hikie'e*, propping themselves back against the large pillows. And they talked far into the night as people who know they are destined for one another do, unraveling the inevitable tale of their lives, every detail of which they knew would fit together, even before the words were spoken.

In the next weeks, Sally sweltered through trips to Tokyo and 10 days of monsoon rains in Manila and Guam, thinking constantly of Billy. She fantasized about the next stage of the romance, his arms, his lips, the future.

After she landed at Honolulu International from a Guam turn-around, she was surprised to find Billy waiting for her outside of Customs. He grabbed her bags and instead of turning onto the highway, headed for the Interisland Terminal where he hustled her, still in uniform, towards the gate where boarding was in process. They landed on Maui at Kahalui Airport and while Billy rented a car, Sally ducked into a ladies room where she changed into a tee shirt and shorts. Together, they drove the twisting and turning Hana Highway to the district of Kipahulu, with Billy handing her several newspaper articles about Charles Lindbergh's recent private internment right here in this remote Maui valley. Sally knew the legends about the "Lone Eagle", who happened to be a member of Pan Am's board of directors, his controversial public stands, his hidden years on Maui. A friend invited them to spend the weekend in a nearby guesthouse. When they turned into the winding drive, Sally was startled to see a sign painted white with Pan Am blue letters nailed to a tree:

If there be Paradise on earth,
It is this…it is this…it is this.

But of course, Sally thought, it's the Persian couplet from the inscription at the Red Fort in Delhi. She thought briefly of Dave McFarland; it seemed so long ago.

The caretaker was waiting for them in front of the house and offered to take them around. "I'll show you the main house first, just so you can get an idea of what it's like." They approached the simple, single-wall constructed house with large glass windows that looked out to the sea. Inside, the living area opened onto a gracious dining room that faced a sparkling waterfall arcing in a misty plume to a deep blue pool far below.

The rooms were decorated with the grand history and tastes of the owners, a retired Pan Am Senior Vice President, with a magnificent *kunjah* dagger bearing the royal seal of the Sultan of Oman framed in the entryway. There were photographs of Pan Am dignitaries, famous explorers, various foreign heads-of-state, athletes and glamorous movie stars.

They stepped out a side door onto a lanai with a breathtaking view of a deep ravine, just steps away. Sally stood back, giddy from the open space, the gentle breeze, the smell of ginger on the wind. Now they could see multiple waterfalls teeming down the cliffs opposite them, flowing from the high mountains to the pools far below, and thence to the sea. They walked leisurely down the long winding path to the guesthouse located in a garden down below, a toy house perched on a hillock by the stream. The door was open, and the simple rooms held a well-worn rattan couch, a small table and chairs. A large alcove contained a bed framed by windows open to the sea, with colorful curtains stirring as a puff of breeze passed through. A small bouquet of tuberoses and purple orchids stood in a vase on the little dining table next to a tray of fresh fruits, bottles of wine, iced beer and glasses. The caretaker smiled, "My wife has been decorating."

Sally's head swam from the fragrance of the blossoms, the beauty of the surroundings, the all-night flight and the events of the morning.

Billy and Sally stood in the center of the room, their hands clasped. Billy said, "I only know that this is Paradise, and I have never felt so much beauty, and laughter, and love, all in one place, all at one time. And I need to show you how I feel."

She met his lips in a long, intense kiss, matching his rhythm, feeling the longing rise in them both.

Then he picked her up and carried her to the bed, and surrounded by the fragrant blossoms and the murmur of the sea they made love as if they had always known one another's bodies and desires. They slept, and then loved again.

They did not emerge from the guesthouse until late afternoon, just as the eastern shadows brought on the evening light. They drove to nearby Palapala Ho'omau Congregational Church, which was situated a few hundred yards off the road on a muddy lane. They picked their way down the lane on foot, hand in hand, barefoot and laughing, the mud squishing between their toes, carrying their slippers. Sally looked up at Billy's face, then down at their hands clasped together.

The little white church stood unlocked in a glade, sheltered by its peeling roof and old-fashioned shutters. Inside, there were a few rows of wooden pews, frayed *lauhala* mats on the floor and above, a wrought-iron chandelier studded with candles. Carefully closing the door, they walked around to the little graveyard on the side, where generations of Hawai'ian families were buried side by side under engraved and worn stone markers. The Lindbergh grave stood apart, the earth freshly turned, mounds of withering leis on the low chain barriers, and the bronze marker set in concrete. Sally read the inscription: "It says 'wings of the morning.' Oh, Billy, it could be about you. It's about flying and the ocean. It's so beautiful."

He put his arm around her shoulder. "It's from one of the Psalms. The rest of the verse goes something like this: 'Even there shall thy hand lead me, and thy right hand shall hold me.'" He caressed her arm. "And you are my right hand."

Sally placed the bouquet from their dining table in the cottage on the grave, and they stood back in respect.

Billy pointed to a row of tiny tombstones below the Lindbergh grave and said, "Look Sally, I've heard of these. The owner of our guesthouse property raises the gibbons as pets for the Honolulu Zoo. The story goes that he said he preferred his apes to most people...what a character."

Sally looked askance. "But I thought Lindbergh didn't care much for evolutionary theory."

Billy smiled gently, "That's the whole point of poetic justice, eh?"

Back at the cottage, they had a simple dinner of grilled steaks, baked potatoes and a tossed salad. The moon was rising, its cold mysterious light filtering through the trees. They finished a bottle of red wine and Sally took a deep breath, simply putting aside her fatigue for another day, as Billy discussed the details of his tours in Vietnam.

"Will you ever have to go again?" Sally was not sure she wanted to hear his answer.

"Doubt it. There are only a few Marines left in-country; basically they're on Embassy guard duty after the drawdown two years ago. Now that Congress has cut the funding, who knows what will happen?"

"Why didn't you fly jets?" asked Sally. "I'm curious, because if you can take the big waves at Waimea, why not fly fighters? They're so daring."

"Helicopters provide support and rescue missions. And you're so close to the action in a helicopter, good or bad. It's important to see that, because it makes war very real. In a jet, you're dropping bombs according to a bunch of numbers. It's easy to forget who and what you're fighting for all the way up there."

"But don't you want to defend yourself?"

"Of course," said Billy. "That's the nature of Marines." He looked at Sally in the candlelight. "It can be easy to lose your moorings, when you live the life I do. That's why I like being with you," he said, "you can keep things in perspective for me."

"I don't know about that, Billy," said Sally. "I don't know what I can add to this. I'm so...so predictable, so everyday routine."

"My point exactly," he said, and then nodded toward the bed, his arms encircling her.

In the following months, Sally's heart and soul belonged to Billy, although she kept the house with Zoe. But she and Billy shared their lives in every other way. Lucien and his partner Kaleo drove out for weekends, cooking up French feasts in the tiny kitchenette and sleeping on the *hikie'e*. Zoe was preoccupied with Keoki, and the planning for the voyage of the long-distance canoe now under construction. They disappeared for days at a time. When Keoki was gone, Zoe flew extra trips or went out on local archaeological digs, turning up at odd hours with a strange assortment of scientists or site workers. Sally's world shrank; she bid only short turn-arounds, eager to stay with Billy in quiet hours and warm embraces.

One evening in late December, she grudgingly organized her things for a fast trip to Auckland and back. Everything had to be in order so she could be at Billy's for dinner, after which Zoe would take her to the airport for her 9:30 p.m. report. But when she arrived at the Quonset hut, she was startled to see his large duffle bag, fully packed. A box of books stood beside it, his uniform fatigue cap on top.

She kicked one corner of the bag. "What's this? You didn't tell me you were going anywhere."

The strands of the bamboo curtain clicked as he came out from the bedroom, dressed in his everyday combat battle dress fatigues. He stood close to her, his arms reaching to gently touch her shoulders. She saw the troubled look in his eyes as he began to speak.

"Sally, I have to leave tonight," he said, slowly, not wanting to deliver the bad news all at once. "They're sending me on special assignment."

"What? When did you find out?" She could barely get the words out.

"A few days ago."

"Why didn't you tell me?" Sally demanded, the pain of betrayal in her voice.

"I just...I can't tell you anything, sweetheart," he said simply.

"Oh shit, oh no," whimpered Sally, her hands clutched together.

"There's a MAC charter leaving from Hickam at about 10 o'clock. I need to be there by nine. I called Zoe while you were on the way over here so she could take us both to the airport."

Sally sank down on the *hikie'e* to ponder the situation. A swell had come in that afternoon and the waves hit the shoreline with a resounding boom. The casuarinas and the palm fronds rattled in the brisk trade winds, slapping against one another. Sounds just like I feel, she thought, slapped. "What's the charter's destination?" she asked dully.

"Andersen, then Clark," said Billy, referring to the air bases on Guam and in the northern Philippines. "And then Thailand. That's all I can tell you." He crouched down next to her, his hand stroking her hair, her face, her lips, and wiping away the tears that were flowing down her face.

They were silent, lost in thought and shock, then their eyes found each other's. "Sally," said Billy, "I know it's too soon, but I want you to think about a future with me while I'm gone. Think about it, please."

"Okay," Sally whispered, looking away to keep the tears in check.

He reached into his pocket and brought out a small box, handing it to her hesitantly. "I just picked this up today and didn't have time to wrap it, but I wanted you to remember my feelings."

Sally opened the box and pulled out a gold barrel bracelet in the Hawai'ian style, a legacy of the monarchy and the Victorian era, with etched flowers around the outside and the word *Kuuipo* painted in black enameled old-English script. "'Oh Billy, it means sweetheart. I'll be touching you every time I wear it." She threw her arms around him.

"Come," he said, taking her hand and guiding her through the bamboo curtains to the bedroom. "I need memories of you."

Outside, angry winter surf roiled toward the shoreline. It would be their last time for loving, and their embraces were urgent and hard, her tears and their sweat mingled, their bodies glowing, the bracelet shining around Sally's wrist. The candles glimmered on the table, the dinner untouched.

They dressed quickly and drove to Sally's house, where Zoe was waiting on the lanai. Sally ducked into the house to change into her uniform, her eyes red from weeping.

Zoe's eyes flashed as she waited outside with Billy. "I'm sorry you're leaving, Billy. I don't give a rat's ass what hero's game you're going on, I only know that my friend needs you and loves you probably more than you deserve. And you know that I know you don't have to go. I don't think you realize what you are leaving behind." She held his eyes, then left him on the lanai and emerged when Sally was ready, carrying her bags. In silence, they drove to Hickam Air Force Base, where Zoe dropped them off. She waited in the car, watching Sally and Billy walk inside together, sensing every ounce of pain they felt. She remembered Sao Johnny, thinking, but he made his choice, and it was not me.

When they stood in the departure lounge, Sally remembered the days when she had first arrived in the islands, when the lobby had been jammed with weeping families, distraught children frantically screaming over the impending departure of their fathers back to a war zone. Women had embraced their men, savoring the memories of their short respite, their time in the islands for R & R, their fingers clutching, desperate to hold on to them, just for a few moments more.

Tonight all was quiet, for this flight would not be taking anyone into harm's way. The Clipper would drop passengers off at Andersen and Clark air bases, swing down to the naval base at Subic Bay and Thailand. Uniformed men and a few civilians milled about, drinking coffee and chatting with one another. Billy's orders would take him elsewhere, she was sure.

Outside the departure lounge, the nose of the *Clipper Sea Warrior* pointed directly at the window, its interior cockpit lights on, the pilots busy with their pre-flight procedures. She stared at Billy, her voice choking. "I don't think it's hit me that you won't be here when I come home. Everything's happened so fast."

"Sally," said Billy slowly, "I need you to listen. We must have this conversation right now, even if we don't want to think about it." He hesitated for a moment then continued, "If something should happen to me and I don't come home, I want you to remember this. The

Hawai'ian expression *I Mua* means 'go forward.' I don't want you to forget me, or our wonderful time together, but you *will* have to move on. Just remember the good times. Can you understand that?"

And Billy lifted her up and held her close in his arms where she buried her face in his neck, inhaling the sweetness of him and tasting his goodness with her lips, her body limp, her heart pounding. Then he put her down and she managed a smile, wiping her eyes, patting her hair. "I don't want your last memory of me to be this sniveling creature." She hugged him close one last time, her eyes now clear and shining with all the love in her heart.

She broke their embrace and stepped back. As he turned to leave her and moved towards the tarmac, his eyes glinted with emotion. "Aloha, *kuuipo*," he said, holding onto her hand until their fingertips brushed in one last parting gesture. Moving to the window, she waved and blew kisses to him. She watched as Billy walked up the metal stairs and stepped into the aircraft with one last wave. And he was gone.

Sally joined Zoe outside the terminal, and went to stand with her as they watched the Pan Am 707 making its take-off run, its distinctive logo illuminated on the aircraft tail. The *Clipper Sea Warrior* rumbled down the runway to rotation speed, her nose gear lifting off the ground as she soared upward, engines screaming. The gear dutifully folded and the aircraft banked in a long turn that would take it in a westerly direction toward the islands of the North Hawai'ian Chain to Midway, and thence to Guam.

Zoe hugged her. "Fucking pilots. It had to be another goddamned fly-boy. It couldn't be an accountant or a lawyer who are allowed to have normal frailties." In spite of her sadness, Sally snuffled with unhappy laughter. Zoe looked at her grimly and gestured at the now vanishing Clipper. "Just remember this...all of it, Sally. These guys are not about love, they're about survival, and don't you forget it. You take care of yourself, not them. They make different choices."

Her words echoed in Sally's sad heart. Suddenly a wisp of rain shimmered over them, a liquid veil bringing with it the fragrance of the lands. "It's a blessing," she could hear Billy saying to her, "a Hawai'ian blessing."

The two women watched the blinking lights of the Clipper until they vanished in the darkness. Zoe hugged her again as they turned to leave. "Fucking pilots…fucking sailors…all the same." They laughed through their tears.

CHAPTER FOURTEEN

OPERATION BABYLIFT

APRIL 5, 1975   HONOLULU INTERNATIONAL AIRPORT
PAN AM FLIGHT 841OUTBOUND
HONOLULU-GUAM

Zoe and Lucien Martin were conducting their Pursers' crew briefing, and had just finished up the assignments for the long overnight flight to Guam when a uniformed captain appeared in the doorway.

"Excuse me for interrupting," he said, "do you mind if I have a word with your crew?"

"You must be…let me see, Captain Dave McFarland," said Zoe, glancing down at her paperwork. "Sorry, I didn't see you, Skipper. We're all ears." She smiled and put her briefing papers down.

"Thank you," he replied. Turning to the crew, he saw familiar faces from previous trips over the years. And there in the back row was Sally Wilder, suntanned and blonde, her eyes widening in surprise and recognition.

He swallowed, cleared his throat, nodded and smiled gravely as he introduced himself. "I'm Dave McFarland. Good to see some familiar faces tonight. I just checked into Pan Am Operations a few minutes ago and they told me our flight out to Guam is pretty routine: seven hours and 30 minutes at 40,000 feet. It may be a little rough up there, and some light headwinds along the way could cost us a few more minutes. We'll be going through some squalls on descent, not uncommon for Agaña at that hour of the day." He paused, shaking his head. "But I'm sure you know I'm not here for the weather report. I need to brief you on special circumstances which we've just been notified of that will affect the next flight segments from Guam to Manila and Saigon."

A collective groan arose around the room.

Dave allowed the litany of complaints to go on for a few

seconds, then he fixed a no-nonsense stare on the group and the conversation ceased. "I'm sure most of you have been reading the papers and are aware that the situation in South Vietnam has deteriorated." The crew sat quietly as he continued. "In light of the North Vietnamese advance towards Saigon, Pan Am has been contacted by several government and non-profit organizations to assist in the evacuation of a large number of civilians, including a substantial group of orphans from the Holt Orphan System, Catholic relief agencies and others. Our particular assignment in this effort is to fly out a charter planeload of infants and children from Tan Son Nhut airport as part of what has been labeled 'Operation Babylift.' A staff of escorts, doctors and nurses will be provided. This mission has been approved all the way up the civilian and governmental chains of command, all the way to the White House."

There were murmurs of surprise as Dave continued. "This assignment must be considered high risk. Although we've been advised that Tan Son Nut airport is still secure at this time, Lloyds of London has just cancelled the hull insurance for all aircraft flying into Vietnam as of today. As of now, you will be strictly volunteers for any mission into Saigon from this point forward. I need for you to understand that."

He looked down at his briefing papers and continued. "You've probably all seen the photos of World Airways' last flight out of Da Nang last week. That was no drill; this is a real, 'hot' war zone. As to our particular assignment, I'm sorry to have to tell you that an Air Force C5-A carrying a full load of orphans crashed after take-off in Saigon this afternoon, and we don't have confirmed survival statistics just yet. It's not yet clear whether the C-5's rear door blew out, or if it was brought down by enemy action. Our job is to bring out as many survivors of the C-5 crash as possible, as well as a large number of other minor children. I will advise Zoe and Lucien of further details as they become available, but you all need to make a decision immediately."

He paused to let his words sink in. "If there are any of you who do not want to volunteer, please raise your hands and the Pursers will advise Scheduling to call for replacements immediately. There is no negative connotation if you refuse this assignment." Dave looked around the room carefully, giving the crew time to think. The ticking wall clock sounded unnaturally loud in the small room's harsh silence.

Zoe surveyed the room, conferred with Lucien, and they nodded. "Captain," she said, "all crewmembers are staying with this flight."

"Good," he said. "Thank you and I'll see everybody on board," he said, turning from the doorway. He picked up his briefcases outside the office and proceeded back down the long hallway.

Sally followed quickly behind him. "Dave, it's good to see you. I'm so glad you're taking us out to Saigon. I feel safer just knowing that." She smiled warmly, and he returned her look; then she went back to her crew.

After the long, routine night flight from Honolulu through Guam and on to Manila, they landed in a rainy dawn, their approach bringing them in over Manila Bay. Throughout the flight, crewmembers had gathered quietly in galleys and on jumpseats to talk about the next phase of their assignment. The flight was less than half full, with passengers stretched out, sleeping in empty rows. Zoe whispered in the aft galley, "This feels like a stage set, waiting for the next act." Crewmembers nodded, disquieted by the potential hazards ahead.

On the crew bus into town, Dave leaned over Sally's seat to invite her to meet for a cocktail in the early evening. They met at the appointed hour, ordered and sat quietly, wordlessly, just stirring their drinks. He said, "You know, you seem older. Your features have become more...what is it? Womanly. So, what's happened?"

Her eyes widened. "Can you tell? I'm sorry I never got in touch, Dave."

"I must say I wanted you to."

"The last 18 months have been a rollercoaster. I lost my roommate Pualani on the Pago crash...she had traded the trip with me." Her eyes clouded at the memory, and she swallowed. "And we had that string of 707 crashes: Boston, Papeete, Bali...."

"Yes, that's made it rough on everybody. Some of the guys were friends of mine, and I know their families. If it's any consolation, a lot has changed through forced retirements, more training, updated equipment. It sure doesn't bring them back, but we all suffer together in these challenging times."

"That's sensible," said Sally. "But it seems like we've become some kind of target of opportunity. Remember our 707 that was bombed on the ground in Rome by the PLO just before the Pago crash? Another friend of mine lost her arm in that one. Between that and losing Pualani, and all the security checks and hijackings and bomb scares, I'm afraid to go to work some days."

Dave nodded pensively then changed the subject. "Tell me about him."

"Is it that transparent?"

"Crystal clear."

"He's a Marine helicopter pilot. We met in August of last year and then he was deployed in December on some special assignment that he couldn't tell me about. I'm pretty sure he's somewhere in South Vietnam, even though all the military personnel are supposed to be out except for the Embassy Marines. His letters never said much and now they've stopped coming. I'm...I'm worried and I'm scared."

He grinned, "Hey, if I can't have you, at least you've had the sense to pick a fellow airman, even if he is a jarhead. But don't be scared, Sally. You have to remember, there is always, *always*, that big sky up there." He shook his head thoughtfully. "And if it goes wrong, he is doing exactly what he wants and needs to do. I don't ever want to see you hurt, but understand those two things and you'll be all right."

Sally wiped away the tears, and squeezed his arm. Pleading fatigue, she headed to her room for room service and then uncertain, disturbed sleep.

"Alright, people, good morning and listen up." An Operations clerk hurried in with a clipboard full of briefing papers, as Zoe rapped the table in front of her in the dingy Manila Airport briefing room where they'd been waiting for two hours across from the noisy operations office.

She read from the telex. "Operations has advised that we have

SNAFU: the inbound aircraft into Manila has a major brake malfunction that will take hours to change, so we need to find a working airplane on this side of the Pacific Ocean to get us into Saigon with a few inbound passengers, then outbound with several hundred kids." The crew groaned.

Zoe waved it off. "Men plan, and God laughs. There's a perfectly fine aircraft sitting in Hong Kong right now, so the PanOPS gremlins have us deadheading commercially to Hong Kong, leaving in 30 minutes. We'll pick up the charter aircraft there and proceed into Saigon as the regular 841, then return to Manila as Operation Babylift. We are definitely 'off-off-schedule' and you know we're gonna roll with the punches." The crew laughed at the euphemism for the rolling delays that characterized their working lives.

She resumed. "Okay, gang. Follow me closely here, and you might want to take some notes. For right now, all we're going to assign is your crew stations on the aircraft out of Hong Kong." She proceeded down the list of mandatory door assignments on the aircraft for the 14 crewmembers. "We're deadheading from Manila to Hong Kong with about a dozen Saigon passengers, who are all VIPs—big wheels in the State Department and such," she said, glancing at the passenger manifest. "Then we take them into Saigon as a rerouted flight 841, where we turn-around, pick up the babies and escort team, and return with them to Manila, where this crew is done. Since we're already off-schedule by at least two hours and have to deadhead to Hong Kong before we even start our duty day, we are looking at extended duty time, and we don't even have an estimate. I'd be eyeballing at least 15 hours from now before you find a pillow, and we ain't even sure where." The flight attendants groaned in mock anguish, then settled back into attentive silence.

"This is in excess of our duty limits and I need to tell you that," said Zoe, grinning, "so if you want to bail like a lot of weenies would do in situations like this, now is the time. You can even call for crew-rest in Saigon if you want." The crew guffawed at such a ridiculous idea, calling for contractual layover time in a war zone. "But I'm not sure how your clock starts again when you're getting bombed by the North Vietnamese." Zoe grinned as she looked around. "Yup, war is hell, but somewhere out there the beer is still cold!"

Lucien nodded, "Now remember, no time for duty free shopping in Hong Kong. It's bad manners to take expensive booze into a war zone!" They all laughed as the energy in the room crackled; there were no quitters here.

Zoe shuffled her papers. "I'm not sure if I'm seeing this right, but here's the story just off an AP newswire. A man named Bob McGregor heard about the C-5A crash and called Pan Am out of southern California, where he put a second mortgage on his house for 50 grand to charter a flight to pick up these kids. The South Vietnamese government originally objected, but now they've lifted the sanctions and given the Babylift flight permission to operate. By the way, like Captain McFarland said, this has gone all the way up the food chain to President Ford. The Pan Am brass are doing everything they can to have a full-court press on arrival back in San Francisco, including a Presidential greeting on board the aircraft. Are you with me so far?"

The crew nodded solemnly, accustomed to bizarre shifts in movement and work rules, but sensed this was history in the making. She looked at the computer printout with the estimated passenger count out of Saigon that stated simply: "Excess Limits." She decided to wait until they got to Hong Kong to survey the next steps.

"So Lucien and I'll save the gory details on the flight plan out of Hong Kong until we get there." Zoe looked up towards the hallway. "I see Captain McFarland waiting in the wings here, and would like him to say a few words."

She smiled broadly at the crew as Dave entered the room. "But first, Lucien and I have to say, with the Captain present, that we have never been prouder to serve with such a superb group of professionals. Give yourselves a round of applause. We'll talk in Hong Kong." The crewmembers cheered, as much for the accolades as for the excitement of being in this place, in this time, viewing the razor's edge.

Dave McFarland surveyed the room, making eye contact with every crewmember. "In the event that there isn't a lot of time for a formal briefing on the ground in Hong Kong," he said, clearing his throat of a slight catch, "I wanted to advise you again that we are entering a shooting war zone. We will more than likely be given a flight plan that calls for avoidance maneuvers on approach into Saigon, and takeoff from there. It'll be a steep corkscrew, so stay seated."

"We won't know how this ends," continued Dave, "but we are here at the beginning, and we'll see it through together. As Zoe said, I'm proud and honored to work with you. I must tell you that this is the first time in United States history that civilians are shutting down a war zone. In accordance with the Paris Peace Accords, there are fewer than 35 U.S. Marines in Vietnam, so we're going into harm's way without armed support. Nevertheless, we'll do our duty, and the drinks are on me at the InterContinental back here in Manila—whenever we return tonight!"

Sally met his eyes across the room as the entire crew stood, and the applause resounded. Zoe stood too, her eyes gleaming, thinking of the firelight and other jungle wars.

After landing at Kai Tak on this steamy morning, the Pan Am crewmembers walked quickly from their Philippine Airlines arrival gate to the Pan Am end of the airport. Zoe moved double-time, her wheeled totebag humming along the metal floor behind her. The crew spread out in a crocodile formation across the terminal floor, an airline fantasy of in-your-face attitude; the string of beautiful young women in high heels and blue uniforms, their scarves fashionably knotted, their faces set with self-confidence and machisma. This *was* fun. It was fast, dangerous, unpredictable and there were no rules. Zoe thought briefly of the lives of gamblers, treasure-hunters, big-wave surfers and adventurers—adrenaline junkies all who came to love the rush. I should not be enjoying this so much, she realized.

Zoe and Lucien turned to motion the team on board. "Let's meet in the back galley to confirm our assignments and see what's next." Within minutes, all 14 of them were assembled on either side of the rear galley counter. Zoe slapped the assignment sheet up on the clipboard. "Here you are, in case you've forgotten your door assignment; everything else is up for discussion. And Sally, we'll put all nine of our VIP passengers upstairs. You can take care of both the cockpit and passengers from that galley, if that's okay. Looks like they are giving you 14 pre-set trays and First Class meals up there." Sally nodded.

Zoe paused and opened her Flight Service Handbook. "So we're en route to Saigon for two hours and 35 minutes, and we'll be able to use the time to prep the cabin for a standard city evacuation mission from a war zone. To make a long story short, it basically says there are NO rules." The crew murmured uncertainly. "The manifest right now says we will be authorized to carry "Excess Limits" passenger load. That could be 300, or it could be 700, depending on how carefully we pack 'em in. Are we agreed that the major objective is to take out as many kids as possible?" Heads nodded in affirmation. Lucien said, "We need to hear you say it: what is the mission?"

The response came back loud and clear. "Get all the kids out!"

Zoe nodded. "That's what I thought. We just wanted to be sure we're all on the same wavelength. Take just a few minutes to read the rest of the section, because it does go into the Rules of War for the Geneva Convention, the treatment of civilians and crewmember status. I know we can't do anything about it now, but does everyone have their Geneva Convention Card?" There were nods all around. "Please take a moment to put it with your passport before you do anything else." Documents shuffled, as Zoe checked her own card, which read "2nd Lieutenant, USAir Force". Just like the ones the POWs carry, she thought.

Lucien read further from his papers. "For service and supplies out of Saigon, the whole upper deck is going to be reserved for a number of really sick kids with meningitis, along with their doctors. That means limited contact with crewmembers up there, as it's a highly infectious disease. Don't worry, it won't penetrate the cockpit door!" He paused, and said mischievously, "Hmm, looks like the First Class cabin is going from the Press Corps to the Plague." Everyone laughed loudly, the adrenaline of the adventure kicking in. Now they'd heard everything.

Zoe continued, "There are 250 bassinets and about 500 pillows and blankets stored in the First Class section, so we'll be unpacking those. Looks like there's no estimated passenger count still—just 'Exceeds Limits'—but we know we got a whole bunch of children and infants, 36 Holt Volunteer escorts, and seven medical professionals. The way I read it, that's about 50 adults to around 500 kids, so the odds are, well, survivable." Again, the galley area erupted in laughter. "The crew meals for both legs will be in the forward economy galley, so eat when you can. Given that this isn't exactly a standard boarding procedure, does anyone have a suggestion for the cabin logistics?"

Sally volunteered, "We should have a human chain of adults: crew and Holt folks down the right aisle for the babies, and move the older kids down the left aisle. Then the adults can settle them into each row starting from the rear. You know, baby in bassinet, bassinet down the line, bassinet under seat, and an older kid in each row."

Zoe and Lucien grabbed the concept. "Done. Great idea, Sally," said Lucien.

Zoe peered at the catering forms. "Uh-oh, here's a problem. Mr. McGregor, who mortgaged his house for this charter, has also requested that the children be welcomed aboard their first arrival on an American aircraft with an American meal of hamburgers and milkshakes. Oh, my God, that'll be the showstopper. Folks, I'm going to find the Catering Manager."

Zoe turned the briefing over to Lucien, and headed purposefully towards First Class, where an older Chinese gentleman was engaged in rapid-fire conversation between ground staff and a walkie-talkie radio. "Mr. Tak Lee! I need your help, please!"

Zoe sat, dejected, on the armrest next to Mr. Lee. "You know Mr. Lee, sometimes American peoples have good hearts and no brains," she said. "If 400, 500 Vietnam babies eat your good hamburgers and milkshakes today, this airplane's gonna be a big mess. Can we do something easy?"

Mr. Lee nodded rapidly, his eyes twinkling as he calculated the offload and resale feasibilities of 400 hamburgers and milkshakes, spoilage, and the time needed to supply new provisions. "Oh, easy, Miss. We take out hamburger-milkshake, bring *jook* and tea."

Jook was a savoury, nourishing broth made from a soup of stewed chicken-bones mixed with spices and soft rice. It was New

Year's food, monk food, refugee food. It symbolized new beginnings, and they shook hands on their happy conspiracy. Zoe whispered, "Now, Mr. Lee, this is our secret, okay? Don't tell New York!"

Mr. Lee laughed, nodding gleefully, his gold tooth shining. Within minutes, a dozen workers offloaded the hamburgers and a single truck pulled up to deliver dozens of aluminum pans filled with rice, jugs of chicken broth and tea and hundreds of plastic bowls. Galley attendants shook their heads at the spare offerings, and plotted the use of teapots and plastic scoopers to get the meal to the children. The crew prepared the cabin for departure, while Sally greeted her few passengers upstairs with cool drinks and a smile. Captain Dave McFarland shook hands with each of them, then withdrew to the cockpit.

The Operations manager maneuvered the heavy door shut. Zoe loved the ritual of the door closing; there was always a brief moment of silence afterwards, when the aircraft unofficially became the turf of the flight crew.

This was all definitely off-schedule and out of the box, and the aircraft hummed with excitement as they secured their positions for take-off. Sally remembered the excitement of the "Laundry Line" landing, and she smiled to herself as the rooftops and fluttering laundry-lines of Kowloon swept by on the apartments below.

Across the aisle, Zoe reflected on the work ahead, closing her eyes and resting her head for a minute on the crew headrest at the Purser's station next to the left front door.

Suddenly, she thought, when I get out of this mess, I'm going to have a baby with Keoki. The thought came unbidden out of nowhere, and she shook her head in shock at the permanent and alarming consequences of such an action. How completely stupid! But...but it could be fun. She grinned at her priorities: see Sao Johnny in Bangkok, rescue kids and clean up vomit in Saigon, get the Yamashita Gold in Manila, start a baby in Hawai'i. Yeah, sure. Makes all the sense in the world. But just about *anything* would make sense on a day like this.

Lucien made his way through the aircraft lowering all the window blinds so that the cabin glowed in a soft, reflective light. The flight had reached its cruising altitude, and in the First Class and Clipper Class sections, crewmembers hauled out hundreds of pillows and bassinets, then re-stacked them in front rows. Large boxes of disposable diapers were positioned in every closet and in strategic overhead bins, while all blankets were deposited on seats throughout the aircraft. One enterprising crewmember had grabbed an entire case of hand-towels, which were quickly distributed to apron pockets, crew seats, bathrooms and galleys for easy access. Once they were finished, the crew rested, curling up in First Class or business class seats, instantly asleep in the darkened, quiet aircraft.

On the upper deck, Sally had greeted the Washington passengers with a chilled glass of orange juice. "I'm so sorry, but we're not provisioned with a full bar for this flight. Kind of slim pickings today."

One of the younger men smiled, his short crew cut and direct gaze a contradiction to his casual jacket, his blue eyes tired and his face worn. "I'd say the pickings today are pretty heroic, Miss Wilder," he said, reading her uniform name tag, "and I thank you all for what you are doing today for America. This is the one bright moment we've had in months of watching this show-down."

Sally moved efficiently through the upstairs lounge, offering soft drinks and soothing comments for the three senior correspondents who were working on a deadline, assuaging their worries about access to working telex connections in Saigon.

She completed another cockpit check, surveying the clear air and blue seas far below them. "See the clouds over there?" said the First Officer, "that's Vietnam. We should make landfall in about 45 minutes, and that's about the time we'll start feeling like mortar magnets."

Sally was startled, while the men chortled appreciatively. "They wouldn't fire at an unarmed refugee evacuation flight would they?" she asked hesitantly.

The Flight Engineer added, "You know, it's really hard to say what we're going to see down there. It could be simple, and it could also be a real royal pain." They talked about press reports on the C-5A orphan casualties.

"It's nasty for sure," continued the engineer, "the local papers were saying that America was stealing Vietnamese children, and the papers supposedly don't even know about this Operation Babylift yet. So we should be prepared for just about any reaction, and get in and out of Dodge as fast as we can."

Sally contemplated the ironies, that the diplomats considered the crew heroes; that one man cared enough to mortgage his life savings and house to save Vietnamese kids; and that Vietnamese and Hong Kong newspapers could harangue Americans for stealing children. That's just the way of the world, she thought. But in the next moment, she felt proud of her country; that after this terrible, divisive, painful conflict, the American people moved swiftly to take care of the war's youngest victims. That was heart.

Dave McFarland signaled with his eyes for her to leave the cockpit. A few minutes later he joined her and said, "Let's walk. I need to talk to you." They made their way back through the darkened front cabin, past the deserted galleys and sleeping crew, to the empty aft section of the airplane, where they were completely alone. He motioned her into the last row of seats. He held her shoulders and gazed intently into her eyes. "Sally, if we never see each other again, I want you to know that...that I love you. It does not matter that we're not together, only that we've had a few hours of our lives to connect, and they'll last."

She found herself melting into his arms and raising her lips to kiss him, long, hard and passionately. She thought of Billy, of all she loved. But Dave returned her ardor with an equal fervor, holding her tight, touching her face as though to imprint the memory. They embraced again, and then broke apart. He looked at her, then rose and walked briskly up the aisle and out of sight. Sally sat confused, overwhelmed by the tension of the last few months, missing Billy, and feeling an immediate stab of guilt at the spark still present with Dave. One man in harm's way somewhere in Southeast Asia, the other unattainable, she sniffled.

Zoe's eyes snapped open when she heard the timbre of the engines change to start the prescribed fast, steep descent into Saigon. She raised the window shade to see a hazy cloud cover and the indistinct outline of the familiar southern coast of South Vietnam in the distance. Even from this altitude, she could see dark clouds signaling the smoke of heavy artillery. She sighed and went up to the cockpit, saying "Any special wisdom from PanOPS?"

Dave turned his head to her, "No specific word yet, but we'll need to talk to the station manager. After we offload this bunch, we're planning to reposition ourselves for an immediate take-off on the runway and use hardstands for boarding from the aft door." Zoe nodded.

"And Zoe," said Dave, "Just remind the crew to get seated at the top of descent, right? Remember we're planning to come in steep and hot. Same thing on take-off, okay?"

"Yes Captain," said Zoe, leaving the cockpit. Thousands of pounds of metal, fuel, equipment, *jook* and 17 hearty souls descended in a long spiral down to the steaming grey tarmac of Tan Son Nhut airport in Saigon, in a green country still known as South Vietnam.

After the aircraft taxied to a stop, Zoe peered out the porthole as the Station Manager Al Topping came bounding up the metal stairs. He cracked the door seal from the outside before the hydraulic system took over and swung it outward, letting in a rush of hot, steamy Saigon air. Al's high-energy personality carried him into the aircraft. A tall, handsome bear of a man with a grand smile and a big hug, his island heritage was evident in his light eyes and honey-colored skin.

"Hey girl, saw your name on the arrival telex and figured, yessir, she's gotta be right there in the middle of this stuff!" He clapped her on the back and leaned closer to whisper, "We don't know how long this will take. Everything was cleared, and now we've been told we have to have all the kids inspected again in the military section on the other side of the airport."

Zoe shrugged and motioned her head towards the cockpit. "I think the guys upstairs want to talk with you about placing the hardstand at the aft doors in case we have to high tail it out of here in a hurry."

He nodded, "Good plan, we'll reposition right away." He spoke into the crackling walkie-talkie, squeezed her arm and waved to several other crewmembers as he rushed up the narrow circular stairs towards the cockpit.

Right behind Al came several Saigon airport passenger service agents, who reached for the passenger briefcase and transmittal of the crew log, followed by several blank-faced uniformed Vietnamese officials who proceeded slowly down the aisles.

The passenger agents ushered the diplomats and the members of the press corps out to the waiting bus. A handsome young man with a short haircut and steely blue eyes followed behind, smiling as he handed Zoe his card. "Miss Longfield, my name is Bob Wagner, and I'll be happy to help in any way I can whenever you need me. This phone number here," he said, indicating a number underlined on the card that carried a discreet logo and the words, Air America, "will reach me anytime. And by the way, like I said to Miss Wilder upstairs, you folks are heroes." He snapped a salute and nodded goodbye.

Well, thought Zoe, he sure looks like he knows his way around, but heroes?

In the back galley, the Saigon ground staff stood with Senior Agent George Trinh and several crewmembers, and looked up as Zoe entered. She said, " I know there are lots of things to do first, but can you give us an idea of how many kids are here?"

Trinh brightened, "Yes. It looks like we've got about 400 here now and probably another 200 trying to get out from town. First we will load the meningitis cases because they have to be in isolation. Don't go into the terminal. People are crowding and starting to panic."

After what seemed like an eternity, in the hot, steamy cabin, a Pan Am Passenger Service car arrived at the foot of the stairs. A few of the flight attendants had disobeyed Trinh's advisory and gone into the airport terminal, returning with harrowing stories of hundreds of frantic people held behind the barbed wire barricades. A grey-robed Catholic nun started up the steps, and Zoe hurried to meet her.

"Good afternoon," said the nun, "I am Sister Therese from St. Paul's Convent and we are here to help you with the sick babies. Can you show me where they will be placed?"

"Yes, sister," said Zoe, "let Lucien show you." They went upstairs to meet Sally, and review the medical equipment logistics. Zoe noted that Sally had been sitting with Dave McFarland, and wondered briefly if that was on again; foolishness, she thought.

Back in the main cabin, she made an announcement. "Ladies and gentlemen, Operation Babylift boarding is about to commence, just as we discussed, and we plan to get out of here as fast as possible before we all melt!" Cheers echoed throughout the aircraft. Within moments, mechanics appeared, jockeying the heavy aircraft doors to close them, as the hardstands were moved to the aft doors. A caravan of buses could be seen leaving the Vietnamese Air Force compound across the runway.

As soon as the buses braked at the bottom of the stairs, crewmembers and Saigon ground staff positioned on the tarmac and throughout the aircraft cabin went into action along with the Holt workers. They ran the bigger children up the stairs, and passed the smaller children and babies, two at a time up the hardstands. Babies went into waiting bassinets if they were small enough, and the bassinets were passed down the line hand-over-hand to the back of the aircraft with the older children assisting in each row, just as Sally had suggested.

Dave had come halfway down the stairs to take a quick look at the spectacle, just in time to see Sally rushing up the metal stairs with an infant under each arm. He caught her glance briefly and she smiled, unaccountably happy with this small, warm moment.

Within 30 minutes the plane was loaded, and Zoe called the cockpit, reporting that the boarding process was complete.

Al Topping radioed the Pan Am Operations Center, and stood sweating and laughing at the front door. "This one," he shook his head at Zoe, "this one we'll remember for the rest of our lives. Now you stay safe, hear? And for God's sake come back and pick us up!"

Zoe hugged the big man, "You got it, Al."

He waved and slammed down the front hardstand after closing the door. Zoe could hear the stairs being quickly wheeled away from the aircraft, as the figures on the ramp waved goodbye.

At first the heat was no worse than usual. But as the minutes dragged by and the plane remained idle at the blocks, the temperature and the humidity rose in the aircraft, acting as an automatic trigger to hundreds of uncomfortable, hot, scared, hungry, thirsty and crying children. As the temperature increased, the din in the cabin rose to an appalling level. Children escaped from their bassinets or seats and crawled or toddled through the cabins, crying for help, in fright, discomfort and thirst. Crewmembers and Holt workers grabbed babies and small toddlers, while others frantically made trays of tiny cups of water from the water fountains and tried to quiet the screaming children. And along with the heat and the noise came another abomination: the smell of vomit and loosened bowels, a chain reaction of smell, heat and noise of lunatic proportions.

Zoe stood in the middle of the economy cabin with her colleagues around her, surrounded by hundreds of screaming children. "Listen!" she said, laughing hugely, absorbing the sounds and smells, "Go on! Celebrate life!" She clapped and waved, and the children and volunteers cheered. Then mercifully, they felt the aircraft move slowly forward, its cool-air vents opening, as fresh air began to sweep over the hot, steaming miasma, calming the fright and the squirming, squealing, crying mass.

"Flight attendants prepare for departure," Dave's voice announced reassuringly from the cockpit. "Ladies and gentlemen, Operation Babylift is underway!" As he pushed the throttles forward, the engines roared in response.

As Zoe ran for her seat, a little figure in a pink jumpsuit slid head over heels down the aisle towards her. She reached out and grabbed the screaming, flailing infant and tucked it into her lap as she strapped on her safety harness. As the aircraft hit rotation and moved away from the earth, the little squirming bundle stopped, and regarded the window next to her as the green fields, red roofs and whitewashed walls of her homeland flashed by. The child seemed to absorb the intensity of the moment, an indelible memory of change. Zoe's throat caught and, unmaternal as she had been to that moment, she rocked the tiny child with its wide eyes and enigmatic expression. She cuddled the child close and surveyed the sudden quiet throughout the aircraft as it corkscrewed rapidly upwards, heading away from the light and heat of the late afternoon sun.

Sally sat through the take-off roll, looking down the long aisles through one cabin after another that appeared to be almost empty of passengers, an adult head poking up here and there. Even though every inch of available space was crammed with infants, toddlers, children, volunteers and equipment, the aircraft seemed empty. Higher and higher the Clipper climbed, turning out towards the coast, golden sunlight streaming in through the windows and bathing the children in its glow, children who now belonged to the world. Below lay the endless green rice paddies of the Mekong Delta region, their watery surfaces shimmering pink and coral in the afternoon light, revolving slowly as the plane ascended.

Suddenly, a little boy of five or six sitting across from her began to cry. He was clutching a Magic Slate, his hair slicked back and a bandage on his arm. Sally brought him to her jumpseat, holding him close to her and rocking him. The child buried his face in her neck, clinging to her. Soon, he was sleeping, and she strapped him gently into his seat with his Magic Slate and a pillow.

Upstairs, she marveled at the transformation of the upscale dining cabin into a makeshift hospital, where tiny babies lay in respirators watched over by doctors and nurses in scrub suits and masks, the oxygen tents covering each tiny crib strapped into the first class seats. Cargo tie-down straps held the oxygen tanks and other life-support equipment.

When they reached cruising altitude, Sally picked up a tray of water and tea and walked down the aisle. Almost all the crewmembers and volunteers were carrying small children, or had strapped babies to their backs, and were proceeding about their work as if this were an everyday occurrence.

After dropping off a garbage bag with another load of cups and soiled clothes, she returned to check on the little boy. He was awake, and gazed at her solemnly, his eyes gentle but his face expressionless. She smiled and proffered a candy. He tentatively raised it to his lips and tasted, a big smile appearing slowly on his face. Sally was captivated, and motioned him to show her the picture on the slate, a child's drawing of an airplane and a stick figure. She motioned to the figure and then to the boy. One of the Holt volunteers passed by and said, "So sad; he and his brother were on the C-5, but his brother was killed."

Sally said, "Come on, come with me!" and brought him forward into the galley. She found a container for him to stand on, and put him to work dishing out ice cubes, his serious face concentrating on the task.

With a full tray of water and a miniature version for the little boy, Sally walked down the aisles offering the children water while the child copied her movements. The older children laughed and gabbled at her helper while the volunteers smiled to see him moving around the cabin. His name, she found, was Nguyen, and he stuck to Sally for the remainder of the flight, even visiting the cockpit with her to give the pilots water and juice, and copying everything she did from cleaning to washing faces. She nodded approvingly, "You're going to be a doctor when you grow up!" she laughed. Nguyen smiled back, saying nothing, but his face open and expressive as she sat him back in his seat and headed forward.

On initial descent into Manila, Zoe surveyed the cabin, now quiet but busy. Throughout the flight, crewmembers and Holt volunteers had scrubbed and changed, hauled huge trash bags down aisles to secure soiled diapers and clothes, mixed *jook*, poured trays of tea and water, and watched over exhausted children, sleeping deeply as they traveled out of harm's way.

We never had a chance in Vietnam, thought Zoe. We never took the time to learn.

She went upstairs once more during the long descent and placed her final signatures on the ship's documents, pausing to talk to the quiet nun. "Sister, what will happen to these children? Is this a good thing we're doing?"

The nun's eyes flashed. "You ask a big question. For now, you are doing what you must. These children are going to have a good chance. It won't be a Vietnamese life, but it will be a good life. Some will be happy, and some will never understand, and hopefully someday many of them can come home and rebuild their country. For me, I only wish others could consider more wisely before they make war in another country in the first place. You know, there is an old Cham legend. We say that the peasant rises from the maw of the sleeping buffalo, and that he will fight forever to save his lands, and will never surrender. That has happened again, just as it did to the Chinese, and the Burmese and the French. We could have told you as much. But you were all too proud to ask what we wanted for our country."

She patted Zoe's hand. "You are all doing your best, and God sees this. We are so grateful for your kindness. I love my country, and we will work again to rebuild as God sees fit."

Zoe bowed in respect of this unwavering faith in the nun's God, her country, and her knowledge of fickle human nature, remembering a night train and another nun, many years before.

In the sunset hour, the Clipper descended quietly and settled down next to Manila Bay. The children and volunteers clapped and applauded, and officials came aboard to ensure that no one left the aircraft during the transit except the crew, due to the quarantine situation. Sally went to Nguyen to say goodbye. The little boy smiled solemnly at her and proffered his slate. Gone from the frame were the aircraft and the lost brother. Instead, he had painstakingly drawn a stick figure of himself carrying a tray in one hand, and a smiling female figure holding his other hand. Sally cried, "Oh, Nguyen, I'll never forget you!" He smiled again, putting his little arms tightly around her neck and resting his head briefly on her shoulder.

Publicity had preceded their arrival and hundreds of well-wishers strained at the gate, a crowd of photographers, Pan Am officials, Embassy and support staff. Zoe and her crew stood bedraggled, their hair slick with sweat, their clothes stained with vomit, jook and unknown grime. They followed Captain McFarland off the jetway, moving to the right of the crowd, guided by excited ground staff.

"I'm not really interested in a media frenzy, folks, but it is up to you," said Zoe. The exhausted crew surveyed the scene, the crisply uniformed outbound crew and dignitaries bathed in bright lights and surrounded by reporter and camera crews.

Sally laughed, "No, these guys are not going to put me in their movies. I'm saving myself for the Hollywood version with James Earl

Jones playing Al Topping!" They laughed and turned towards the arrival exit, and to the promise of hot showers and Dave's cold beers at the hotel.

Hours later, adrenalin spent and cheerfully drunk, the crew stumbled back into their hotel rooms to sleep. But Sally Wilder was not sleeping tonight, not after everything that had happened. Though exhausted from the events of the day, and though Billy's memory nudged her, she moved down the hall and scratched lightly on a door, hoping no one would answer.

But it swung open as though its occupant had been standing there, waiting, and Dave swept her into his arms.

CHAPTER FIFTEEN

LAST FLIGHT OUT
APRIL 26, 1975   TAN SON NHUT AIRPORT
CLIPPER UNITY
OUTBOUND SAIGON

Zoe sweated, the wet heat streaming down her back and staining her uniform. Drops beaded on her upper lip and trickled down her arms, her whole body slippery. She sat on the jumpseat in the forward cabin of the 747, the heat steaming off the 12 crewmembers, all of whom bore the discomfort in stoic silence, waiting, waiting for the passengers. Through the porthole, she could see a small portion of the runway's edge that gave way to green jungle, a small empty hut, several plastic containers on the ground, and a sense of abandonment.

She thought of how different the mood was from Operation Babylift barely two weeks ago, with its mantra of manic hope, the noise and the smells. The atmosphere was close and tired, the sour smell of fear and fatigue everywhere. Now suddenly, here it was. The end. There were no headlines, no signposts or heroics. It was just…over. They'd only discovered this upon landing in Saigon a few hours before, when Al Topping trudged heavily up the stairs, his face subdued, his eyes dark, "It's over, Zoe, this is it, this will be the last flight out of Saigon."

She'd nodded, her heart twisting. "Oh Jesus, Al. Just let us know what you need. You know we'll try to help in any way we can." He nodded, pressing her hand, and rattled up the stairs to the cockpit.

Zoe had volunteered for this trip late last night in Manila, flying as a stewardess rather than a Purser. PanOPS was desperately trying to pull together a crew, not knowing it was the end. They didn't care where she worked or in what position, so long as they had a warm body.

Closing her eyes, she leaned her head back on the headrest and thought of the events of the last weeks. After Babylift, she and Sally had been temporarily based on Guam, where they had been flying shuttles in and out of the war zone—Manila, Saigon, Hong Kong, Taiwan— anywhere the refugee charters or evacuation missions were headed. Life settled into a bizarre pattern of lunatic normalcy. Each day at 10:00 a.m., all volunteer crewmembers would roll downstairs to the Hotel Okura's bar to drink coffee and play what they called "Saigon Roulette".

Those assigned would run for their uniforms, still warm from the dry cleaning machines which never took out all the spots or smells, and crew buses would leave the hotel by 11 a.m. in order to get in and out of Saigon before curfew. The rest took refuge in typical down line pursuits of sex, sun and swimming. In recent days, the crews had been volunteering to serve at the new "Tent Cities" sheltering the refugees.

There were dozens of sorry and heroic war stories emerging from these evacuation flights. On one occasion, Zoe returned to Guam enraged; she and her crew had waited for six hours in the Saigon heat on a stripped-down 707 for passengers to board their USAID charter. Finally, four Embassy cars arrived and disgorged 12 obviously intoxicated individuals who stumbled up the hardstand, laughing uproariously. A large man weaved in front of Zoe. "Stewardess, bring on the champagne!"

Zoe, regarding the man's condition, spoke in frosty tones with a toothy smile. "Sir, I regret that we are operating today under war zone city evacuation regulations. Accordingly, we are unable to offer our standard service." That's a ten-dollar sentence for fuck you, buddy, she thought.

The man, blundering towards a seat in First Class, issued a parting shot over his shoulder. "Pan Am—it figures."

Zoe watched him collapse in his seat, along with his fellow passengers, then glanced back at the economy section. It was empty. The aircraft contained not one single Vietnamese passenger. Here are these government jerks in front while hundreds of seats in the back go out empty, she fumed. Frustrated with such bureaucratic foolishness, she turned in cold fury to speak to the Pan Am agent, George Trinh. "Mr. Trinh, do you have 176 refugees you'd like to bring aboard right now?"

The man brightened. "Yes, yes…uh, we don't have official authorization, but we have a large group of…of military dependent spouses and sponsored individuals with … ah, military connections."

Zoe nodded and strode to the cockpit. "Captain, request permission to board sponsored evacuees with authorization to land at Andersen."

Wearily, the Captain turned back to look at her. "Would we go to jail for this?" he asked.

"Only if they catch us in Saigon," Zoe responded.

The Captain, one of the last of the "Old Pelicans" who wasn't afraid of going against procedures, considered the matter for a moment. "Well, if they aren't manifested, we're good to go," he pronounced.

Zoe closed the cockpit door triumphantly and returned to Trinh. "The Skipper says maximum load, no manifest, and no service available. You just make damn sure Andersen will take 'em."

Trinh's eyes lit up. "No problem! Give me 20 minutes." He started for the stairs then paused. "Ah, by the way, just so you know, Zoe, these are mostly Tu Doh Street bargirls and their half-American children who have no status in Vietnam. If they don't leave with their children, it will be very bad for both." He grinned. "It's a different kind of Babylift!"

Zoe had exploded with laughter. Drunk USAID workers up front and military camp followers behind. "You're darned right, Mr. Trinh. We'll get 'em out of this place." Within minutes, Trinh had silently loaded the economy section of the aircraft from the rear hardstand. While the USAID contingent passed out in the First Class section, the bar girls and their families settled in. They were all survivors, hard-edged and glittery, beautiful and absolutely fierce in their determination to make a new life—it did not much matter where. The flight proceeded to Guam, where ground agents discreetly disembarked the two groups into their separate worlds.

The aircrews' frustration at the wasted aspect of the evacuation charters finally boiled over one night in Hong Kong when Zoe joined an unofficial group of crews and press people at a bar in Wanchai.

"This brings a whole new meaning to Re-Settlement of

Military Families," laughed a highly respected anchorman after hearing Zoe's story about the Tu Doh Street girls.

"We don't give a shit who is paying for the ride," said one angry pilot. "The planes are there, we are there, and we are taking out flight after flight with practically nobody on board. There are so many lives that could be saved."

A *New York Times* reporter quickly wrote an inflammatory article, its sources protected, which recounted their high-risk status as volunteers into the war zone to take out refugees, only to be met with bureaucratic red tape forbidding non-Americans on board. The paper's next edition featured the story and within hours, the Guam PanOPS Center had a burning telex from the Hong Kong-based Regional Vice President underscoring the need for crewmembers to clear all press communications with management. Zoe groaned. "Okay, another stroke of genius by the rear-echelon gang." But the article had the desired result. The operations tempo picked up and they were flying full loads every day now under the Exceed Limits rules.

In hotel lobbies and airport departure lounges, Zoe occasionally saw banks of lights and television cameras focused in on smooth-talking senior executives and diplomats who were supposedly the "faces" of the war zone. But the irony was that it was the newsmen and the crews who knew the real story of what was happening.

One serious young diplomat engaged them in discussion, trying to convince them of the "systematic reductions in force" that were underway, and that everything was being handled according to plan. Zoe pounced. "Bullshit, my friend. There's no plan. We got whupped. It's done. We'll all do our jobs as best we can, and maybe next time we'll have some sensible up-front dialogue and not let the politicians run the show." The young man went quiet, then proceeded to get seriously drunk.

Yesterday, she'd had a sense of urgency during the short transit on the ground in Saigon and made a special trip into the terminal, wending her way through the desperate crowds. Families were perched on chairs, crouching on floors, rolled in sleeping blankets, hushing babies, feeding elderly parents. She made her way towards the Pan Am counter, where the agent nodded to her enquiry and pointed her to the next counter. No signage advertised the services, just four American men sat, talking quietly with one another.

This was the Air America section, which was well-known but not discussed.

She stepped up to the counter. "Anybody here know a crazy Marine Corps helicopter pilot named Bill Spencer?" she asked, attempting a smile.

A laconic reply came back, "And what would I say to him if I did?"

Zoe gulped, having come this far. "Just tell him that Sally loves him, and we're all waiting for him to come home."

The young crew-cut Army officer's blue eyes sparkled. "Hey, I remember you. And I remember Sally, too, from the Babylift." He paused as he looked long and hard at Zoe. "Anything else?"

Zoe gulped. "Yes, well, there's someone who could help." She handed over a sheet of paper with names, addresses and telephone numbers. "I know this man, Sao Johnny. He knows how to get things done. He could help Billy, and he could help you guys."

He regarded her with surprise. "Yes, we know these names real well. You've got some interesting friends," he said, intrigued. "We'll get the messages out, and thank you for stopping by. Far as we know, Billy's doing great."

Bingo, thought Zoe. "Thanks," she said, reaching out, unaccountably moved, to shake his hand, warm and strong. "Now you keep safe too, and come home quickly," she said quietly, her eyes moist, knowing there could be no more messages for Sao Johnny. Then, on impulse, she said, "Tell...tell Sao Johnny you saw this." She reached under her collar and pulled out the silver shrivasa coin. He nodded, unblinking. They smiled into each other's eyes, as she moved back into the throngs of refugees.

As they corkscrewed out of Saigon, the Captain had pointed out the artillery smoke off Nha Trang as evidence of NVA progress. Every single one of us knows it's the end, Zoe thought. We are not finished, but we are done. The faster we swallow hard and leave, the better for all. Ah, *dokha, dokha*...the sadness of trouble.

Zoe started, back now to reality from her musings about the last two weeks, looking out again at the stifling cabin and its quiet occupants. She walked upstairs to the cockpit to check departure status with the pilots, who were shaking their heads. The Captain said, "You won't believe this. Al Topping has adopted every single South Vietnamese Pan Am employee and their family members in order to get departure permission for them."

The First Officer had been monitoring the ground operations radio. Suddenly, he barked with laughter, exclaiming, "Holy shit!" He pointed off to the active runway where a departing aircraft was beginning its take-off roll. "See that Bal Air flight with blue and white markings and a Swiss flag? The PanOPS frequency says it's carrying $1.1 billion in gold bullion along with former President Nguyen Van Thieu on his way to Taipei and then to the U.S. for, uh, retirement." They watched silently as the aircraft lifted away from the tarmac, the waterways of South Vietnam glistening in the morning sun, highlighting burnished gold and man's greed.

Al came back in the cockpit, saying, "Okay, folks. The passengers of Pan Am's last flight out of Saigon are on their way." The crew sprang into action, manning their assigned stations, while Zoe watched the buses drive slowly out to their aircraft.

The *Clipper Unity*, Zoe noted. What irony. What day was it? Hell, it was April 25th in Honolulu, and April 26th here in Saigon, she thought. Maybe. What time? She'd forgotten to keep track of the dates, the hours, some signposts of reality; it all blended together with the harsh days that had gone before, all leading up to this final flight. Now, it was too late—though the flight logs would help detail out the research for some historian some day.

Moving quickly, dozens of quiet men, women and children with one suitcase apiece filed forward, stacking their bags neatly below on the trolleys, mounting the steps, bowing with folded arms to the uniformed passenger agents at the door, their spotless white silk *ao-dai* uniforms fluttering in the breeze. The passengers proceeded into the cabin where crewmembers seated as many as possible into each row of seats. Soon, every seat was filled and still, they waited in complete silence. Zoe could feel the heartbreak and broken spirits around her, and wished she could somehow erase some measure of all the pain.

On the tarmac, the sun glared off metal surfaces and reflected heat from the rusted debris and oozing tar beneath the rickety hardstand. Several uniformed South Vietnamese officials clustered around Topping and his Senior Operations Agent, their images shimmering in waves of heat bouncing off the white paint of the taxiway markings that led to the runway corridor, a shining path that hung breathless and humid. They had been in tense discussion for some time, the Vietnamese official motioning the Operations Agent away from the plane towards a waiting bus. Al stood hunched toward the officials, pleading his case with large, open-armed gestures.

Zoe strained to see farther towards the departure terminal, where a small transport vehicle was headed towards the aircraft. She looked out the window again, as a Vietnamese woman, an elderly couple, and several children rushed up the stairs. Walking forward up the starboard aisle, she caught a glimpse of Al as he mounted the last steps, entered the aircraft and squeezed these last passengers into already occupied seats or floor spaces. His face was distraught as he shook hands with the Operations Agent at the door, gently prying loose the man's weeping wife and escorting her into the cabin, where she collapsed into the arms of relatives, moaning softly. Al took a long look, hugged the man, and gently closed the aircraft door while the forward Purser grabbed for the announcement phone with fake, hearty car-salesman bonhomie.

"Ladies and gentlemen, we're on our way out of here!" he said, as the operations agent rapped the "all secure" sign from outside in the window of the door, his face tense, his eyes riveted on them, his smile sad in farewell to his family, colleagues and friends.

Al murmured to Zoe that the agent had elected to stay behind, and watched him heading down the hardstand with the government officials to an uncertain future. As he turned toward the winding stairs leading to the lounge, he squeezed Zoe's arm and hugged her quickly, pain in his voice. "I just needed more time," he said, tears in his eyes, frustration in every gesture.

She returned his touch. "You did everything you could, Al. Everything. I'd say you've covered all bases."

He shook his head, "I couldn't get him to leave. That was his family that just came aboard. I couldn't help him. I should have done more." Then he was gone, up the stairs, his job done but never finished.

As the *Clipper Unity* moved immediately into take-off position, the flight attendants quickly went through the standard safety demonstration. It was almost macabre, given that the entire silent cabin—seats, aisles and galley spaces—was crammed with people and their pitifully small personal effects, breaking every rule of passenger and baggage restraint requirements. Zoe thought of the absurdity of the situation, this attempt at order in a chaotic political endgame, where an entire nation would change in hours or short days.

After what seemed like an eternity on the taxiway, the aircraft paused before commencing its take-off roll, faster...faster. Zoe felt a chill run up and down her spine as the sweat cooled and hardened on her skin, the cool air clammy and smelling of mourning. Her eyes were glued to the window, as were those of every passenger, as the green spaces and red roofs of their homeland went racing by. Almost immediately upon rotation, the captain banked hard to the right, heading away from Saigon and out towards the South China Sea. The air-vents were working double-time to cool the cabin, the creak of metal and the vibration of the hydraulics as the engines drowned out any other sound. The landing gear thumped into place. The silence on board was eerie, enveloping. There were no shouts, applause, or sighs of relief; just the soft, sorrowful sounds of weeping for a country lost, the pent-up fears from weeks of anxiety, months of agonizing decision-making of whether to go or stay, and the terrible choices of which family members to bring and whom to leave behind—all as a nation broke and its citizens bent to the burden of loss and shame, the ultimate toll of war to victor and vanquished alike.

As the Clipper veered steeply out over the ocean, a flotilla of ships of the U.S. Navy's Seventh Fleet stood by, preparing to commence an entirely new phase, a rescue and evacuation mission from Vung Tao and other coastal villages. In these last dire days, the war zone was now drawing near the coast.

Zoe looked out over the sea and ships, thinking of Sally and Billy, of Keoki, of Sao Johnny and all lovers separated by conflict. She thought also of the many friends they had all known who were among the dead and wounded. There were the Vietnamese troops and civilians, too, victims of the ten long years of a war that never should have happened, and the French conflict before that. She sighed wearily.

Over the intercom, the Captain's voice boomed, "Ladies and Gentlemen, friends and family from Pan Am Saigon, welcome to freedom!"

The silence that greeted his announcement was palpable. There was no celebration, only relief that the end had finally come, and come so swiftly. Zoe thought of Captain Dave McFarland's comment during their Babylift briefing a few scant weeks before, that this was the first time in U.S history that a skimpy volunteer civilian labor force was marshaled to dismantle a war zone. In spite of the huge naval display on the waters far below, it was over. It had been coming for weeks and months and years, but it was finally, irrevocably done.

During the silent flight to Clark Air Force Base, Zoe sat listening to Al in the upstairs cabin, as he recounted the last days and hours. He spoke of the adoption of all 463 of their passengers in order to sponsor them out of the country; the encouragement of the embassy, the support of Pan Am's corporate leaders, the balking of the South Vietnamese authorities. He shook his head at the terrible obligations of having to choose the numbers and limits of each Pan Am family member; the harsh reality of leaving loved ones behind, the securing of Pan Am's property and assets. She marveled at the strange humor of people calling to book space out of Saigon next week or a month later, other enquiries for tourists wanting to visit South Vietnam, apparently oblivious of the conditions of the war zone and the daily reminders of all that is life in Asia.

His saddest recollections were stories of his personal staff and mementoes of years and friends and family...all gone. He spoke without rancor or passion; it was just another day at work. What would happen next? He'd see; there was discussion about a special operations job in New York, maybe a vacation to visit friends and family. But his first priority was just to take his 463 new family members home to America and make them welcome in a new place, a new life, with a new identity he could not even begin to describe.

Too soon, Zoe hugged him one last time, knowing that a

chapter was closing and hoping that his good deeds would be recognized. The Clark terminal was full of cameras and lights as members of the press descended on *Clipper Unity* this late spring evening before transiting to Manila on its way to San Francisco, the very cities which Captain Ed Musik's *China Clipper* had linked on a November morning 40 years before. Zoe and the rest of the crew stood gravely in front of the cameras, then quickly moved out of the glare of the lights towards the shadows of the street and the crew bus, heading for rest.

Who will mourn with us, she wondered. Other nations perhaps? The generals and the politicians who unleashed this horror? The cobra stirred within her.

Sally woke up in her room at the Okura Hotel on Guam right at 9 a.m., rose from the bed and turned off the rumbling air conditioning, then opened the blackout curtains and blinked in the bright light of the morning. The Saigon Roulette crews will be meeting in an hour, she realized. If she didn't get a trip, she could cadge a ride to the refugee camp with one of the hotel employees or Pan Am personnel. Rooting through her suitcase for some shorts and a tee shirt, she headed for the shower. She decided this was going to be a good day, and she looked forward to dinner with Diz Langford, who was here on special assignment with his unit to help organize the Tent Cities.

Downstairs, the group in the lobby was gathered in unusual silence around a radio, the Pan Am operations representative Art Seagrave standing to one side, as they all listened gravely to the news. The announcer's voice was somber as he recounted the departure of the "last Pan Am flight out of Saigon yesterday afternoon." He reported a passenger load of almost 500 Pan Am employees and family members, now heading for San Francisco. He said, "This appears to be very close to the end." The crewmembers groaned.

One of the pilots stood, clearing his throat. "Ladies and gentlemen, colleagues, friends, well, I guess it is over. That was the last flight out of Saigon. It's been a great effort, and I'm proud to know you all. I'm pretty sure Art here will be relieved that he doesn't have to pick up the beer tab any more." A round of applause followed. "And I'm sure he'll have some words about our various departures, but since we don't get to be 'Mortar Magnets' again, hey, see ya'll down-line." The group cheered, hugging each other, shaking hands, wiping tears, and clustered around the assignment sheets.

Sally felt numb. After all this time and effort, it ended with...nothing; just a reporter's recounting. Tick-tock; the clock moved on. She couldn't speak, just noted her next assignment as "TBA." She hugged Art, accepting a ride to the camps in 30 minutes.

She sighed. It was over. The realities of Babylift and the refugee charters were finished, even that tenuous link to Billy. No Billy, no Dave. She needed to deal with the emotional letdown of going back to her regular life.

Sally retreated to her room, looking out over the ocean swells. She wondered if she had been unrealistic about her love for Billy. Flying had a way of yanking one in and out of relationships when they were at their most exciting, all bright and shiny, always keeping the emotion high, with no chance to tarnish and settle or stabilize. It was a life of permanent loose ends, and she could not face the terrible possibility of losing anyone, anymore. She longed for certainty, for continuity. Dammit, she thought, Pie was right. In one of her letters, she remarked that he should be back here taking care of me, not the other way around. Instantly, she dismissed the thought as disloyal. She loved Billy, didn't she?

For the last several days, she'd latched on to Diz Langford, who'd been assigned to handle the logistics of the huge refugee population. He had proudly taken Sally on a tour of Camp Freedom, which was located near Anderson Air Force Base, and had organized a dinner with her that evening. She had immediately volunteered to help, joining dozens of military wives, crewmembers, community volunteers and staff members to help cope with the growing population of refugees.

Just working the food-line, teaching kids, or cradling babies and the simple act of handing out blankets settled her for a while—that is, until the next wave of anxiety hit. The Red Cross, Catholic Relief efforts and other volunteer groups were hard at work at these camps, a number of which had sprung up around the island and were growing larger every day.

The dirt roads went around in a large circle, the residential tents on the outlying part with the dining facilities in the center, separating the different communities of ethnic groups, bachelors and a large contingent of Tu Doh Street bargirls. The latter group had set up shop practically overnight and instantly swung into operation. Both charter and military aircraft screamed overhead bringing in hundreds more each day, as Pan Am and other commercial carriers flew refugees to their new life in the United States and other nations. Confusion reigned as one truck after another rumbled through the gates with supplies and more refugees, threading their way through a gauntlet of tents and new coral roads and shelters.

The air was filled with dust. The odor of diesel fumes and lime from the latrine toilets mingled with the cooking smells from the mobile kitchens. Every now and then, gusts of wind would blow it all out to sea, only to have the pungent mantle reconstitute itself and settle over the camp again in a matter of minutes. Sally knew that one of the biggest problems for the refugees was unfamiliarity with American food; most longed for rice and fish, and did not eat the hot dogs or hamburgers with mustard and ketchup that had been provided. They missed the ingredients and flavors of their native cuisine. Complaints were legion: no fish sauce and chilis, no rice or noodles.

When Art dropped Sally at Camp Freedom, she learned that today's assignment, thankfully, was taking inventory in the dry-stores storage area, giving her a chance to be alone. In mid-afternoon, remembering her date with Diz to Joe and Flo's famous Mexican restaurant, she hitched a ride back to the Okura, waving and smiling at the camp children that followed the jeep, calling for candy. She showered and met him out front, promptly at six.

"Hey, Sally," said Diz, leaning over for a hug, seeing that her normal sparkle had been replaced by a somber quality.

"Diz, it looks like it's over," she said flatly. "The news reported that the last flight left Saigon yesterday afternoon." He hugged her again as she settled into the truck beside him.

They headed around Tumon Bay past the Happy Landing, the funny little beer shack with a corrugated roof beloved by the crews. The jukebox had an amazing screen attached that showed naughty videos as the songs played. Turning onto Hospital Road, they reached the arterial highway that led south in the direction of Apra Harbor. The parking lot of Joe and Flo's was packed. The restaurant's windows were fogged and it was meat locker cold inside.

"A Margarita for the lady," said Diz when a sweet middle-aged Filipina approached, "and I'll have a San Miguel, please. Thanks, Flo." Then he turned to Sally, his face serious. "I heard it was a wild week in Saigon. Guys on *cyclos* were looting the commissary and carrying out monster TV's and refrigerators on the handlebars. People were swarming on the roads, trying to get out to Tan Son Nhut, stuff like that. There were just a few more military evacuation flights yesterday afternoon after Pan Am's last flight out. But once the runway was bombed early this morning, they had to go to the helicopters. Guys spent the whole day tearing around the city or picking people off the tops of buildings and getting them out to the ships."

"Makes you wonder why the politicians in Washington didn't see that coming and get the evacuation started sooner," said Diz. "It certainly would have been a lot more efficient and a whole lot less dangerous."

"Diz, I need to ask you something," said Sally. "What do you know about Air America? I've been hearing things about a spook airline that has been active since the drawdown."

"Well, I'm not the one to ask. I'm not sure of the details, but I've heard rumors that in the old days they were flying out dope from Laos, or Cambodia, Thailand, Vietnam and other places. From what I understand, most of the time the pilots didn't know—or care—what they were carrying and they certainly didn't ask questions. They apparently made a lot of money doing it."

"It just helps when I can learn something—anything. I don't even know if that's where Billy is." said Sally.

"Welcome to the world of the military spouse," mused Diz. "They're buzzing around up there in the sky and you people don't know shit on the ground." In spite of herself, Sally laughed at the image.

After dinner they drove back to the Okura in leisurely fashion through the humid tropical night. "Hey, isn't that Zoe?" said Diz, as he pulled up at the entrance.

Sally glanced toward the glass doors and there stood Zoe, her uniform rumpled. "Hey sister! When did you get in?" Sally called. Diz hugged them hello and goodbye, and returned to his car.

Zoe turned to Sally and said flatly, "We took the last flight out yesterday with all the Pan Am Saigon people, I slept over in Manila and got a jump-seat here. I'm kind of messed up about all of it right now. Let's go find me a shower."

They headed up to her room, where Zoe turned to face Sally, and said purposefully, "Sally, I was able to get to the Air America counter in the Saigon terminal, and speak to the guy who was on our Babylift flight into Saigon. He gave a pretty clear signal that Billy's there. I just spoke as though I assumed he was flying for them. I told them to tell Billy you loved him and to come home soon."

"What did he say?" Sally asked, her eyes pleading.

"He said that he'd tell him, and as far as he knew, Billy was all right."

"Oh God, thank God!" Sally's eyes sparkled. "That means he's okay."

"Well, at least it means you know where he's been, and he was fine as of a few days ago, and he's probably busy. The sea evacuation is apparently underway off of Vung Tao, and it is huge."

Zoe ran a hot shower while Sally digested the information, emerging in her Keio Plaza *yukata*. She rummaged in her totebag for three cans of aircraft tonic water, muttering about the lack of limes.

She continued. "According to the news, there have been three rocket attacks on the city in the last two days, and two more at Tan Son Nhut. They say that General Duong Van Minh—you know—that guy they call Big Minh—got appointed President yesterday, and then they started playing 'White Christmas' on the radio. That was supposed to be the secret signal for all American personnel to evacuate. Of course everybody in town knew about it and all the stations started playing it at all hours, which only added to the confusion. But apparently it was for real this time."

Sally poured herself a strong gin. It was all so weird. "Diz said that Tan Son Nhut was bombed early this morning, and they had to get the remaining people out by helicopter, probably operated by Air America." She shook her head sadly. "It's all way too little, and way, way too late, isn't it? And you've always known it would be this way, haven't you, Zoe?"

Zoe patted her arm. "Let's just pray that everybody who needs to get out does."

A week crawled by, as they flew more intense refugee evacuations from Manila to Guam. It's still not over, Sally realized. These were the first of the "Boat People" who had escaped with nothing, and were missing family members and travel papers. When Sally and Zoe returned to the hotel from double shuttle that brought more than 700 people from Manila into Orete Point and Camp Freedom, Sally said, "Look, Zoe, isn't that Walker Sheppard out in front of the hotel?"

Walker looked uncomfortable, standing in the porte cochere in his navy uniform. He hugged her tightly. Sally looked again at Zoe, then to Walker, searching his face intently. "I don't think I like this," she said slowly.

"Sally," said Zoe, grabbing Walker's arm. "Let's go upstairs so we can talk." They made their way through the lobby to the elevators.

When they reached her room, Sally turned to them, her face ashen. "He's gone, isn't he?"

"We don't know anything specific," said Walker. "Sally, you know first hand how crazy things have been during these last weeks."

Sally glared. "Look, we know he's been flying for Air America, right?"

Walker looked down at her pale face. "Yes. But Billy's been listed as MIA—that's Missing In Action. We don't know all of the details. We'd heard that Pan Am had a big operation with the refugee charters going here on Guam, so I got special permission from my CO to get a hop over here. I'd heard that you all were on Babylift, so I figured you'd be in the middle of this, too. We go way back, Sally, and I wanted to tell you myself. I'll never forget what you did for me when Pua...."

Zoe mixed stiff drinks for Sally and Walker, and sat beside them.

Walker took a large gulp from his glass. Reaching into his pocket, he handed Sally a Teletype report on grainy paper, its typeface capitals smeared. Slowly, she read:

"Volunteer air evacs were conducted by Air America personnel and equipment under dangerous circumstances after all commercial and military action had been terminated. The heroism of these individual airmen has been significant."

By the last sentence, her voice had dissolved into a whisper as she began to sob.

Zoe said softly, "Don't take it all on now, Sal."

Sally turned, her eyes glaring. "'Don't take it all on now, Sal'," she snapped, her voice rising. "And don't give me all that crap about hope and no-news-is-good-news. Hell, he was fine just a few days ago. You said so yourself. Now this. Why? That's all I want to know. Why Billy? Why any of our guys? So many dead, so many missing, and no answers anywhere." She sobbed in great gasps as Walker held her.

Zoe said, "It's okay. You need to be mad as hell and let it all out, whichever way you can. And as harsh as it sounds, this was Billy's choice. He never saw any limits anywhere. Whatever it was, he found a way to do it."

Walker sat Sally back down on the bed, pocketed the Teletype report and said quietly, "Sally, we've begun the process to notify Billy's parents. We can't say anything to anyone about this until his family receives the news, okay? And I want you to be realistic. Yes, it's a possibility that Billy could still be alive. But we no longer have any diplomatic relations with this country. South Vietnam is gone. It will be almost impossible to get him out, even if he has survived. I won't kid you; it's about as bad as it can get."

Sally looked at them. "I am so scared and I'm so fucking tired of being scared. I'm just not brave like you. I'm so angry about all of this, for me and for us, and everything we've tried to do. I just don't know anything any more, except how much I hate what has happened. I just don't understand."

Zoe nodded. "Sally, this situation was never ours to understand. It's what these guys do, and unfortunately, it's their choice all the way. And tomorrow it'll be time for us to go home."

Sally remembered Dave McFarland's words when they were in Manila during Babylift. Raising her glass, she said, "Well, dammit, here's to Billy. He loved that big sky up there, and he wanted more than anything to be out in it. He was doing what he needed to do. God bless you, Billy, wherever you are." Then she sank back down while Walker and Zoe tiptoed out, closing her eyes, feeling the pain of loss and loneliness. And the anger that Billy had chosen that bloody sky over her. Who'll take care of me? She thought again of Zoe's angry words: "You take care of you."

The next day, they headed quietly for Hawai'i. The American War in Asia was over. And for so many POWs and MIAs and their families, the long twilight continued.

CHAPTER SIXTEEN

THE DARK WAR
APRIL 29, 1976   KYOTO, JAPAN

Zoe was insistent. "We've got a three-day layover in Tokyo, and we *have* to go see the cherry-blossoms at this incredible Japanese inn in Kyoto." Sally demurred, feeling more like hibernating. But Zoe persisted. They travelled by train and bus to the 400 year-old *ryokan*, famous all over Japan for its beautiful gardens and hot springs.

Zoe actually had presented an "official" letter to the management, which she called her "*Ryokan* Visa." Written for them by one of their Japanese stewardess friends, it stated that the bearers were knowledgeable in *ryokan* protocol and would not embarrass the house. The manageress, who carefully surveyed the young *gaijin* women standing before her, accepted them—albeit with some reluctance. Sally and Zoe bowed deeply as the establishment's tradition dictated, then smiled as they doffed their street shoes and coats at the ancient wooden door and proceeded to their room. They shuffled carefully in their *yukata* into the baths, carrying their bath slippers to the entrance of the *ofuro*. Dutifully bowing, they accepted a napkin-sized towel, stool, bowl and soap in exchange for the safety of their *yukata*. They sat, scrubbing their nakedness near the steaming communal tub, dipping water to rinse and sliding pink and scrubbed into the enveloping steam.

"Just bow," said Zoe. "They've just seen everything they ever wondered about the *gaijin*, so just bow and smile."

Sally looked impassively at the group of women floating naked in the big steaming pool, then gave them a big Southern grin and bow before climbing in.

The women tittered. One woman, emboldened at the sight of the two foreigners, said, "You *gaijin*, very lucky—big," motioning to her own beautifully formed small breasts. "Husband like very much, no?"

Sally shook her head, "Oh, sorry no husband."

Then a cultured voice rang out in a British accent, "I say, how did you get in? This is the most conservative inn in Japan!"

Zoe acknowledged the beautiful Japanese woman who had spoken and joked, "I have a Ryokan visa because I was able to pass the *gaijin* bath-slipper test!"

The room broke up in laughter. Soon, between combined translations and mime, the *ofuro* was a laughing group of women sharing similar stories. Yuriko, the woman who spoke such beautiful English, joined them for their *kai-seki* dinner. The room's shoji screens had been parted to reveal a large window that looked out onto a rushing stream and late snow-laden forest with its bursting pink cherry trees.

"It's like they've composed a painting," Sally said, marveling at how no attention to detail had been spared in the arrangement of the winter garden outside and the breathtaking contrast of the early cherry blossoms. She and Zoe sat warmed and comforted by their table-quilt of thick cotton and silk, hiding a small heater. Happily, Sally and Yuriko consumed copious amounts of warmed sake in tiny raku bowls, Zoe toasting them with ancient *pu-erh* jasmine tea, while they slowly ate a delectable fourteen-course meal of bite-size, exquisitely presented dishes. "I feel like I'm floating," said Sally.

"Ah, but you are," smiled Yuriko. "Here, you are in the center of what is known in Japan as the Floating World."

Outside the snow fell silently, deeply, turning the world an ethereal white in the light of a moon they could barely see. Everything was nuance and suggestion, style and shadow, a hint of so much more to come. After their meal, the three women lay together on their sleeping mats while a blind male masseuse kneaded their muscles to comfort and relax. His last act was to wrap them in their sleeping quilts and withdraw, the shoji screen sliding smoothly shut.

Sally thought, I've even forgotten to be sad today. She regarded the almost frozen stream in front of their window; they were in another world. A small fox emerged from the brush a few feet away to drink from the steam, and caught the reflection of her startled movement. For a second, fox and human stood transfixed, then as quickly as it had come, the animal melted away. Sally nestled in, safe and warm in a storming world. At first she breathed peacefully, listening to the sleeping sounds of the two women next to her.

Then her thoughts drifted, remembering the beautiful flowers at Billy's memorial service on the beach last summer. She caressed the talisman bracelet on her arm, Billy's parting gift. It was one year ago that he had been declared MIA, even longer since she had felt his arms around her, the light of his spirit lifting her own.

The circumstances of his disappearance were still unknown. She knew nothing. She knew less than nothing—not if, not how, not where he might have died (if he was dead), or if he was living still. It was that special purgatory called Missing In Action, a crowded place full of wives or lovers, family members, a few MIA coordinators, many caring clerics, lots of media. But the MIA himself? He was just… gone.

A few months after Billy's disappearance, Admiral and Mrs. Spencer had come to Hawai'i to collect his personal effects and join Sally for a sunset commemoration service on the beach behind his house on Ke Waena Road. Since there were no ashes or remains to honor, much less any definite word of his status, Billy's friends created their own tribute to his life. They planted a line of surfboards in the sand decked with leis of purple orchids, orange *ilima* and delicately scented *pikake*. Around the upper part of Billy's board, Sally entwined a lei of woodsy, fragrant *maile* leaves, a lei of honor. Admiral Spencer saluted Billy's lei-covered surfboard, then together with his wife, stepped back in silence to honor their son.

People crowded the beach to remember him. The Color Guard from the Kaneohe Bay Marine Corps Air Station performed military honors, trooping the Colors to position with smooth precision in spite of the sandy footing. Sally stood with Zoe and their Pan Am friends, clad in light summer attire, shoeless in the sand, joining with suntanned surfers, heavily muscled Hawaiians, military and civilian friends, standing together in silence as the flag was folded and presented to Billy's mother.

In rich voices, Moke Cabral and Keoki Kanawai had sung the old Hawai'ian Congregational Hymn, "*Ho'onani ka Makua mau*", "How Great Thou Art", and friends spoke words of comfort and aloha. After the service, with the sun slipping away behind a veil of pink and gold, Moke, Keoki and the other surfers dived into the water and symbolically swam the missing ashes out into the sea.

Sally swallowed, remembering her mother's cold reaction to this tragedy. While Billy's parents had come to Hawai'i and embraced Sally as part of their family to share their grief, Sugar Pie refused to attend. Pie wrote that she was sympathetic to Billy's death or disappearance, but wasn't this just a romance, and a brief one at that? It wasn't as if they were married or even engaged, and wasn't Sally being just a bit overly dramatic? Sally wondered if Pie didn't enjoy a tiny bit of satisfaction from her heartbreak. She sensed that her mother wanted her to suffer, that somehow it was her turn.

And now, in this place that was so different and so far away, her heart cried out, not only for Billy, but the losses of her brother, her grandparents, her father and Pualani, and for her own emotional hibernation. She sat up, staring out into the night, watching the snow fall softly and the cherry blossoms gleam.

The following morning, Zoe had reached across to her on the train. "Billy is gone. He either cannot come back, or will not come back. But you only hurt yourself more by dreaming of things you can't change. Stop it. It's time to move on and think of other things." Her voice was serious and sharp.

The next leg of their trip was to Guam, transiting to Manila. As they were completing the breakfast service in First Class, a young man who had been asleep the entire flight awoke as Sally walked by passing out hot towels.

"Is it too late for breakfast?" he asked.

"We're about ready to start down, but I think I can bring something," said Sally. "Eggs Benedict ok?"

"Great" the man said appreciatively, wiping the towel over his face. Sally went back to the galley, pulled out a tray and on it placed a folded napkin with an orchid. On a china plate, she carefully ladled warm Hollandaise sauce over two parboiled eggs on toast with ham, adding hot, flaky croissants, and an orange twist.

"The eggs are a little overcooked because they've been in the oven for a while. Hope you don't mind," said Sally. "Would you like coffee or tea?"

"Coffee, please. Black," he said. Sally looked at him carefully. He was a rare sight on a commercial Pan Am flight in the Pacific, much less in First Class: he was young, attractive, medium in height, with sun-streaked hair worn just shy of shoulder length. No wedding ring. Mid 30s, she guessed. She went to get the coffee pot.

"So what's a guy like you doing all the way out here?" she asked.

"I'm with a movie production that's being filmed in the Philippines," he said, eating his breakfast with gusto.

"Oh! You're an actor?" Sally was intrigued. This sounded glamorous.

"No, I'm part of the crew," he replied. "I'm a helicopter pilot; I'm doing some stunts."

Sally thought, oh, not again. "Oh really? What's the movie?"

"It's a film about Vietnam," he said. "The director is Michael Fitzgerald."

Sally's eyes widened. "Yes, I've heard of him. Are you sure we're ready for a movie about Vietnam?"

"I don't know," the man said quietly, fiddling with the orchid Sally had placed on his tray. "I guess we'll find out."

Growing more interested by the minute, Sally said, "I'm Sally Wilder, and you are?"

"Ben Harris," said the man. "I'm crashing tonight at a cast-member's apartment in Makati. We head up-country to the set tomorrow. Where do you folks stay?"

"We're at the InterContinental. It's in Makati as well," said Sally.

"Well, if that's the case," Ben said, "maybe I could swing by for a beer tonight?"

Sally nodded. "That would be great."

"About six okay?" asked Ben.

Zoe passed her on her way up to the cockpit. "What's that all about?"

Sally grinned. "A date, tonight, and he's a stunt pilot for a movie company."

Zoe groaned. "Will you never, *ever* learn? Well, two out of three is better than nothing."

That night, Sally greeted Ben in the lobby and showed him to the Boulevardier Lounge. A waiter appeared, and they ordered two San Miguel beers. "So tell me more about the movie."

"It's called *The Dark War.* The scenes they're shooting right now are being filmed outside a little village a few hundred miles north of here. A young captain has been given a top-secret mission that takes him to the jungles of Cambodia. I've been flying stunts in a battle sequence, but I had to go back to L.A. on other business." Ben took a long drink of his beer. "They're using some far out opera music— spooky stuff called 'The Ride of the Valkyries'."

Sally started to take a sip of her beer and queried, "'The Ride of the Valkyries'? That's a great choice. It's from a Wagnerian opera. The warrior goddess Valkyries flew on winged horses throughout the world, picking up fallen heroes from the battlefield."

"Just like the helicopters in Vietnam," said Ben, putting down his glass slowly. "So this is more than just scary music."

"Exactly. Ben, were you in Vietnam?" Sally asked.

"Yeah." His tone was flat, without emotion.

"Which outfit were you with?" she asked, her fingers nervously fiddling with Billy's bracelet.

"The 101st Airborne."

"The Screaming Eagles," she nodded. "I was born and raised in Latham, Kentucky. Ft. Campbell was right outside my doorstep."

"Well, well, a Latham girl," said Ben smiling. They clinked their glasses. But slowly, his smile vanished. "And not only that, but a Latham girl with a beautiful bracelet, and probably a sad romantic problem to go with it," he said. "May I?" He examined the design of the bangle carefully. "Who is he?"

Sally looked down at her wrist, her eyes softening. "His name is—or was Bill Spencer—a Marine, Kaneohe Bay. He left on special assignment toward the end of the war last year and went down during the fall of Saigon," said Sally. "He was listed as MIA a year ago yesterday, and now he's presumed dead. That's all I know. We weren't married, but we might as well have been."

"I'm sorry," said Ben. "Vietnam was one complicated piece of shit, and MIA status is the worst, because you just don't know."

Sally nodded. "Where was your unit? I think I remember that the 101st spent a lot of time in the north, up near the DMZ. Khe Sanh and all that."

"We were in a bad-assed place called the A Shau Valley," said Ben.

"I'm glad you're, uh, here," said Sally, recalling the heavy casualties taken by the 101st there, and her friends from Latham who'd been injured.

"I don't know if I'm glad to be here or not, quite frankly. There were so many...." he said, his voice quieting.

He changed his tone. "Sally, maybe you could come up to the set with us tomorrow and take a look at the filming."

"Well, I'm here for five days," she replied. "It might be interesting."

"The director has a plane that flies up to the village of Balingian a couple of times a day from Manila. I've been staying in a house that has a spare bedroom. One of the guys is in L.A. and won't be back until the weekend, so you can stay in his room. You can catch a hop back whenever you need to."

"I don't know, Ben," said Sally. "I don't want you to get the wrong idea. I'm not ready to get involved."

Ben reached for her hand, holding it in both of his while he measured his words. "I know. Neither am I. But maybe the best way to honor your man is to understand what Vietnam was really like for him. It might be good for you. For both of us."

Sally took a deep breath. "All right. What time do we leave?"

Sally left the hotel with Zoe's frosty gaze at her back. Zoe hadn't minced words; she thought this was a very bad plan and said so. But Sally was not deterred, and soon she and Ben stood on the tarmac at

Manila International Airport in the area set aside for private planes. She was dressed casually, her totebag packed with clothes and essentials at her feet. A mustard-colored twin propeller aircraft taxied towards them.

When they were seated, Ben handed her a thick bound document. "The script," he said, "thought you'd like to take a look at it. Then he reached in his pocket and pulled out a plastic covered badge that read: THE DARK WAR: VISITOR.

Clearing the Manila metropolitan area after take-off, she saw terraced rice paddies bordering the hillsides in neat concentric half-circles. Luxurious green mountains cradled valleys with toy villages nestled in them. Dirt roads snaked in and out of these valleys, which was bound to make driving up to Balingian a lengthy and somewhat dangerous endeavor. Sally opened the script and began to read. The flight was short; they landed in a large field just outside the town, but she had read enough to know that this movie was based on an old Joseph Conrad book about a voyage up a river to find a rogue colonel. More than that, the script was a journey into the American heart and experience in Vietnam. It was about a loss of control, not only on the part of commanders, but the average American soldier who fought in the sweltering jungles, often under the influence of hallucinogenic drugs. It was, as the script said, about the cycles of love and loss. She thought this could be a deeply disturbing personal journey for everyone involved, including herself. She bundled the script into her bag as they disembarked onto a grassy airfield.

A jeepney was waiting to take them into town, dropping Sally and Ben off by a small house with a white wrought-iron gate. A sign hanging on the gate read: DARK WAR: House #6. By the door, a clipboard held call sheets with dates and wake-up times for the various people staying at the house. Ben was lucky to be billeted here; there weren't too many places in the village with running water and electricity, and many of the crew bunked four to five in a room at the town's small hotel. Conditions were Spartan, but that added an element of adventure. The first floor contained a large living and dining area, a master bedroom, a kitchen and a small maid's room. They took their things up the broad stairs to the bedrooms on the second level.

Ben carefully walked her to a room at one end of the breezeway. "Meet you downstairs in a few minutes and we'll go on over to the set," he said, disappearing into his own room down the hall.

Sally surveyed the bedroom. It was painted white and simply furnished. The double bed was draped with an embroidered white cotton bedspread. A teak chest stood against one wall, a palm leaf running the length of its top. Freshly picked white plumeria blossoms and a nautilus shell had been carefully arranged on the palm leaf. Louvered windows allowed a gentle cross breeze to bring in the fragrance of the mock orange hedges nestled along the edges of the driveway below.

After slathering on suntan lotion in the bathroom, Sally looked at her face in the mirror. While it impressed her to think that she would be visiting a movie set for the first time and watching a famous director and well-known actors at work, she could not lose sight of the fact that they were attempting to recreate the war in Vietnam, officially over just a year earlier, with all the losses that miserable ending had entailed. Worst of all for Sally, the war had taken Billy from her. Was she ready to confront that? She pinned on her badge, pulled on her hat and sunglasses, grabbed the script, and headed downstairs.

Ben led her down the narrow lane to an area near the school. A crowd of people milled around in the blazing heat of midday, loading equipment onto a truck. A helicopter, as well as several motorcycles, stood waiting to transport people out to the set, which was a couple of miles outside town near the mouth of the river. The pilot was waiting for the two of them to board. Sally turned from the helicopter and looked at Ben, fear in her eyes. She had never flown in a chopper before, and she didn't know if this would be the right moment for a maiden voyage. They looked so fragile, these small flying machines. This was a little too close to Billy, and she wasn't yet ready for it. Sensing her hesitation, Ben moved toward one of the nearby motorcycles.

"Why don't we take one of these and drive out there on the beach?" he said, patting the seat. Sally marveled at the various modes of transportation available, but shrugged it off; this was a movie set after all, wasn't it? She jumped on, placing the script in front of her chest, and clasped her arms around Ben's waist. Off they went over a series of small sand dunes followed by little Filipino boys running as fast as they could. The dunes quickly gave way to a broad flat beach, with the surf breaking at three to four feet. The breeze puffed the waves into the perfect shape for riding, either by board or bodysurfing. As they sped down the beach, the wind roared in Sally's ears and swept the white sand into wispy little arcs.

The set was a beehive of activity. It consisted of a village, the center of which was a courtyard that contained a small building, a school, at one end. Other buildings surrounded the courtyard, some partially burned as part of the set. Clotheslines strung between palm trees were laden with costumes: the *ao dai* worn by Vietnamese women and black pajamas worn by the Viet Cong, the green uniforms worn by NVA regulars. Small trailers painted in camouflage served as retreats for the lead actors between takes. Helicopters flew overhead as the director called out instructions through a megaphone to people on the ground.

The afternoon shooting revolved around an attack sequence, where helicopters strafed the village with lots of smoke effects and fake fires. Sally noticed several folding canvas chairs behind the cameras; in true movie fashion, they bore the names of the stars, the director and producers. She found a shady spot under a palm tree and opened the script, pausing every now and then as filming began. The story called for the choppers to be hit by ground fire, large fireballs billowing out of their bellies, rotating in circles as if they were going to crash. Take after take was filmed. Although the explosions weren't real or the noise loud, Sally began to feel like she herself was in a combat zone, hiding behind some tropical foliage, observing up close a war in which she didn't fight, but in which she had participated. The true nature of armed conflict was not even a part of her imagination: the noise, the filth, the confusion, the fear, the fight-or-flight reaction, the intensity of the individual drive for survival. She felt herself go faint for a minute, and leaned her head back against the palm tree, its fronds slapping together in the breeze far above her face.

Sally watched the shooting patiently all day, joining Ben to eat their meals with the cast and crew in the village's school cafeteria. A movie screen had been erected in the school's play yard for evening entertainment, but instead they chose to walk the streets of the town and observe village life. The rainy season had not yet begun, and the narrow streets were dusty. Dimly lit shops sold candies, soap, tobacco, magazines and other necessities.

After their stroll through town, Sally and Ben returned to House #6. Various members of the crew had dropped by and were already well into their evening revelries, swigging San Miguels and sipping vodka, dancing to a rhythmic guitar. On another table, some were rolling joints and arranging lines of cocaine.

"It's Buddha time!" a voice chanted.

Sally was tempted by what lay before her. The heat and the images that she had seen in two days on the set had upset her; a line or two of coke might pull her out of the doldrums, she thought. But she backed away, choosing a strong vodka and limejuice when Ben asked her if she wanted a drink.

He disappeared into the kitchen, returning with a beer for himself and vodka with several squeezes of *kalamansi* limes for Sally. They sat on the floor with their backs against the wall. At first, the group's conversation centered on the day's shooting, on the gossip of the industry, on some of the crazy moments of the day.

Sally found herself speaking to a group of make-up and wardrobe people. "I never knew anything about flying until I started working for Pan Am. And this old-time Navy pilot told us the definition of flight propulsion, when we were right out of training school: he said, 'It's just suck, squeeze, bang and blow.'" The movie group howled with laughter at the crude but simple explanation of jet flight—science made simple.

Soon they drifted into talk of the war so recently ended, which they were re-creating on film. A few people were vets, but most had not fought in Vietnam. But they had all had been touched by it, by having a close brush with the draft, or knowing someone who had served, been wounded, killed—and how it hit the families.

"When I was in college," said one man from southern California, "our whole mentality was focused on how to get out of the draft. Everybody was constantly sharing ideas about what doctors to contact, how to get into the Reserves. We actually found ourselves going to class and studying so we could stay 2-S," referring to the classification used for student deferments. "We were so busy figuring out how to stay out of Vietnam that we didn't have time to think about the guys who were going, much less the ones who were already there…so this war shit is pretty freaky for me."

Sally asked Ben for another drink. She drank quickly, the *kalamansi* juice masking the strength of the alcohol. She leaned her head back against the wall, her body relaxing, her mind wandering, listening to the stories.

"Shit, I remember the night they had that televised lottery," said another man. "It was in December, 1969. Remember that, where they drew the days of the year? I was in the lobby of my dorm at school my senior year. When my birthday drew a really high number and I knew I was going to be in the clear, I got up, walked back to my room, lit a joint and poured a drink. Put on Led Zeppelin and listened to 'Stairway to Heaven' over and over again until the sun came up." The rest of the room laughed, some of it tinged by the effects of drugs and alcohol.

The stories continued, most of them about burning draft cards, friends who had left for Canada, or tales of attending various anti-war rallies around the nation. Sally listened carefully, digesting it all, anger rising within her. They were treating the subject so lightly, the stuff of casual conversation at a cocktail party. Suddenly she stood up and shook her head, fogged by alcohol. Except for Ben and one or two others who were vets, none of them had summoned their courage and served. She glared at them. "You folks should be ashamed of yourselves. You are working on a movie that's supposed to tell the real story of Vietnam, and most of you don't know anything because you weren't there. And the worst of it is that you don't give a shit, you think it is a joke, you just don't care. The truth is that *none* of us did enough to stop the killing. You let other people serve in your places and then spat on them when they came home."

She swung around the room, gesturing wildly as she spoke, her words becoming disjointed. "And now that it's over, what about the ones left behind…the children, the wives, the lovers?" she cried. Her voice rose and she began sobbing. "You just don't know what it feels like to be in a real war zone, to watch people lose everything. You don't know what it means to…to lose somebody you love in combat…the anger and desperation and hatred you feel…." She was growing overwhelmed and confused. "What happens now? Why doesn't anybody ever talk about that!" she screamed.

The room was silent.

Ben rose and came to Sally's side. "Sally, don't. We do care, we all have our place in this thing, and we're doing what we can. What happens now is that the story has to be told through this movie so we can start to heal. We're trying to do this for you and all our buddies who didn't make it back. We'll do it right. It's our debt of honor." He paused, framing her face in his hands. "It's my debt of honor," he said.

A lighting technician came over and joined them. "We all lost something in this war, even if it wasn't a friend or a family member; we lost faith in our country. Now we all have to hang together to tell the tale and honor both the dead and those who served, and most of all, try to make damned sure it doesn't happen again." he said. Embracing her, he looked at Ben and those around the room, pausing when his gaze connected with the hollow eyes of those few who had served in active combat.

Spent, Sally sat down next to Ben, quiet now, her anger receding. The tiny Filipina maid who had been peering out from the kitchen came to her with a glass of mineral water in hand. Sally drank deep, swallowing her sorrow and anger. It was all so futile, she thought, reaching for the mirror and the lines of cocaine.

By her last day in Balingian, Sally felt she was actually *in* Vietnam. She had been sailing high on cocaine, her nerves jangling and her thoughts disjointed. She could see and feel every part of the experience of the war zone. Hour by hour, she was aware of Billy coming closer to her. The day's filming schedule called for exploding a helicopter in the central square of the village. The helicopter itself had been constructed of plywood, and the stunt man, who was to leap out in flames, wore a heavy protective asbestos suit. When the appointed hour arrived, Sally squeezed behind the little school building along with Ben and the other onlookers.

The director called for quiet over the megaphone. The palm fronds slapped against each other overhead like the beating of helicopter blades, and the sultry afternoon heat bore down. Then at the director's command, giant balls of black smoke and fire belched forth and the helicopter burst into flames. The stunt man rolled out as planned.

But something else happened inside Sally's head; the conflagration was thunderous, as if the sun itself had exploded and split the sky in two. The cocaine left in her system crushed her. She stopped breathing, her knees buckling as she collapsed, her conscious mind spinning out of control. Slowly she felt her face turning toward the blinding sunlight, as if she were being pulled upwards by some unknown force. She heard the Valkyrie goddess, Brünnhilde, singing her battle cry, as visions of helicopters in flames whirled before her eyes. She felt the music in her mind now, a gigantic, thundering Wagnerian orchestra, echoing Brünnhilde's cry. Suddenly, Billy was there by her side, reaching out to steady her, his voice lost in the thunderous music. Then, they were in the helicopter together, smoke enveloping them, twisting round and round in free fall. Flames of red and yellow and orange swept before her, rising toward the heavens and engulfing them. Blindly, she reached for Billy and then she was flying, alone, skimming atop foaming, churning waves, as blue-green waters washed over the earth. And at last, an incredibly tender feeling of love plunged her weary mind into jagged darkness. Somewhere, there were voices....

At first she smelled the scent of mock orange carried by puff of breeze. Opening her eyes, she saw the nautilus shell on the little chest in her room, the plumeria blossoms pink now instead of white. Ben sat by her side.

"What happened?" she asked weakly.

"You've been on a long trip for the last hour, right through all the action. After the explosion on the set, you just passed out colder than a stone," said Ben. " Then you came to for a bit, then you were so groggy that I carried you to one of the helicopters, and we got you back here. If you hadn't woken up pretty quickly, we were going to radio for the plane to come and evacuate you to Manila."

She put her hands on her head, struggling to remember what had taken place. "When the explosion happened, I just went somewhere else in my mind...I can't explain it." Then suddenly, she looked at Ben and gripped his arm. "But I saw Billy! I saw him. I was *with* him. He was wounded and covered in blood and his chopper...." She stopped as she felt the dryness in her throat. "There was fire and music. Ben, I swear, it was the music of the Valkyries. It was the end of the world. Everything was burning and water was flooding everywhere...."

"Quite an accomplishment to dream in stereophonic sound and living color," said Ben, smiling. "You must have a terrific imagination."

Sally looked at him. "Ben, I think Billy was badly wounded when his helicopter was shot down." Her voice dwindled to a whisper. "I know it now."

Ben gathered her in his arms and held her as she cried. He cradled her close, his warmth comforting her. "It's just pain, Sally," he said quietly, "just pain." His words had a calming effect. He stroked her hair, inhaling her fragrance, knowing what not to say.

"I don't know what the hell is going on inside me right now, Ben. I feel so out of control."

"Sally, you've had a load of grief and dope in you, and it needs to come out."

And she cried from the depths of her heart, as much for herself as for the memories of Billy, Dave and her uphill journey to find peace and safety. After a time, she began to calm, and seeing that she had finally pulled herself together, Ben got up, went to the chest and picked up a capsule from an ashtray. "There aren't any doctors here, Sally, but this might enable you to relax and help you sleep. Under the circumstances, it's the best I could do."

"What is it?" she asked.

"It's a Quaalude. Maybe we both need one. And a lot of people take them after doing coke. It settles them down." He handed her a bottle of water and she swigged down the capsule.

"You aren't going to leave me, are you, Ben?" asked Sally, nodding toward the downstairs where the nightly party was swinging into high gear.

"No, I'm going to lie here right beside you until you go to sleep, all right?"

"I'd like that."

They lay quietly on the bed together, listening to the frogs and the swishing of the breeze outside, the mumble of conversation in the living room below punctuated with occasional laughter. Sally closed her eyes for a while. As she began to feel the drug take effect, she also felt passion, long dormant, rising within her. Getting up from the bed, she lit the candle on the little chest and turned out the light. She could feel Ben's eyes on her, questioning, as she slowly turned back to him. He was stretched out languidly, suntanned and lean. Slipping off her shorts and tee shirt, she went to him in the candlelight and he took her in his arms. And when he turned her over on her back to kiss her body, she surrendered.

Early the next morning, Sally bade farewell to Ben. They said nothing about their time together, but gave one another a long, knowing, forgiving embrace. She boarded a jeepney and they headed for the airfield just outside of town. As the yellow plane lifted off, she could see the set below with the crew scurrying about, making preparations for the day's shooting. Pressing her nose to the window, she watched the little school building and its courtyard grow smaller and smaller.

She breathed out, letting go. She knew then that while nothing would ever bring Billy back again, the overwhelming feeling of love she had experienced in her dream was his parting gift to her, and that realization brought closure, healing and acceptance. And after years of wondering who would take care of her, Sally finally understood that she had been asking the wrong question. She needed to find confidence in caring for others, without expectations.

Again, Zoe's words came back to her, "You take care of you."

The arch of a rainbow stretched through the clouds in the light rain. She thought of Dave's words, that Billy was doing what he needed to do. She felt the bracelet on her wrist. *I Mua*, Billy had told her, "Go forward."

CHAPTER SEVENTEEN

RUBAIYAT
NOVEMBER 17, 1978 DJAKARTA, INDONESIA

Zoe threw her bags on the hotel room floor and undressed, almost in the same motion. She faced her image in the shadowy mirror and put on an alarming, toothy airline grin. "I–like–people–and–I–love–to–travel," she pantomimed, turning the taps in the tub, throwing her uniform into a laundry bag, sidestepping naked at the door to toss the bag into the hallway. She was happy to be alone, as she stepped into the humid, eucalyptus-tinged smell of the bath foam and hot water.

For ten days since she'd left Honolulu, she had flown non-stop charter operations in and out of Djakarta and Manila, Dacca, Islamabad, Karachi and Teheran. All were pick-up and drop-off stops on the way to Riyadh, Saudi Arabia, and the holy city of Mekkah down the coast of the desert peninsula for the annual Hajj, the pilgrimage required as the "5th Pillar of Islam" for all good Muslims at least once in their lifetime. She thought of the week with Keoki in Moloka'i before she'd left for this desert, the hard work on an ancient heiau, the warmth of the campfire, and his embrace. Somehow, she felt incomplete, strange.

The operations were chaotic; hot desert days or cold dark nights, crowded aircraft filled with serious, bearded men in white robes. Almost all wore a small white knitted cap under turbans or shawls. Their few accompanying women also wore the white robes, and were covered from head to toe for the journey. They smelled of rosewater and exhaustion. Announcements were done by tour-group managers, who seemed as bewildered as the pilgrims as to the exact logistics of their journey. Crewmembers were simply dog-tired, and it wasn't fun.

Toweling herself off, Zoe stepped into an old pair of faded red silk Chinese lounging pants and a soft cotton shirt, just right for the massage to follow. The hotel's blind masseur came with his quiet, gentle female attendant with a bright flower in her hair. He was a handsome man in his 40s, with steel hands that worked away at every tension knot and sore muscle. Zoe had often wondered if he was really blind, but he seemed so—his calm face and unblinking eyes regarding the middle distance in the manner of those who cannot see, his total concentration on the work of his hands, no two movements the same, completely sure of his work. His knees pressed up against the back of her upper thighs as he worked rhythmically, walking his elbows or knees up and down her sore muscles, his body above hers, a faint scent of sandalwood as his clothing rustled against her, the feeling sensual, knowing, intimate, sometimes even erotic, but never overtly sexual. She sighed and thought about other things.

In the comfortable gloom of this Djakarta evening, she listened to the muezzin in a nearby mosque. The tinny sound of the amplification overcame the roar of the traffic in this huge crowded city of 18 million people—the largest capital in Asia. Nothing worked. The roads were narrow or flooded, the sewers were blocked or running open, the telephone system was sporadic, and working electricity involved the thumping of back-up generators. But the people were calm, peaceful, eternally smiling, and absolutely exquisite, with their doe eyes, tiny hands and feet. Their supple bodies were clad in beautiful patterns of batik sarongs, a single flower in a checkered headband on the forehead accenting side-ways flashing glances. Zoe sighed as she thought of the glorious foods of Indonesia. As the masseur gently tapped the back of her knee, she rolled over, picturing a plate of fresh, peeled fruits with a chilled fresh yogurt. She felt unaccountably sluggish, nestling her head into the pillow, and slept.

When she woke, it was dawn. She felt dizzy and disconnected, a recurring fatigue. She reached for the phone, ordering coffee and return of her laundry, then hauled back the blackout blinds and sheer drapes, shoved open the heavy glass verandah door, and emerged into a misty grey dawn.

She stood braced against the balustrade and stretched, her arms forming an arc over her head as she tried to balance herself and steady her breathing.

The city lay below, wreathed in exhaust fumes, the distant discordance of honking horns and clashing delivery wagons. As the sun rose, the amplified sounds of the muezzin's calls began again, almost in unison, for the morning call to prayer, the echoes creating a wave of sound from dozens and dozens of mosques.

Two hours later, she was strapped into the forward jumpseat, observing the crowded aft passenger cabin past the First Class section. It was filled with another group of the faithful, now heading for Karachi, Teheran, Riyadh and thence to Mekkah. She and her crew would stay overnight, in Teheran, and then to Jeddah where they would pick up a returning load of passengers.

She gazed briefly at the passenger in the window seat opposite her, and then looked again. He is simply beautiful, she decided. He looks just like the head of a Persian bas-relief or a Greek coin, his face in pensive profile as he gazed out the window, his wavy hair picking up glints from the reflected sunlight. Suddenly his gaze shifted directly to her, and she did not look away from his eyes. They were deep blue, almost violet. They both smiled, caught in the act of curiosity…what ship, where from, where bound? She acknowledged him without judgment, and his eyes returned the compliment.

She released her seat belt and stood, smiling in salute, then headed across the cabin, feeling his eyes follow her. How nice to be old enough not to panic when a man catches your eye, she thought, reading the passenger manifest to determine his identity. Seat 5A— Cyrus Constantine Pahlavian, Iranian Embassy, Djakarta, and a string of coded VIP messages after his name; destination: Teheran.

She spent most of the flight in the Economy cabin, completing the paperwork during the Karachi transit in the upstairs lounge. As she signed off on the logs, she looked up to see her Iranian seatmate ascending the circular staircase, taking the swivel chair opposite her.

"I'm glad you are still here; I was afraid that you'd left us in Karachi," he said leaning forward. "Look, I don't want to be presumptuous, but in case you don't have any plans in Teheran, I wonder if you could consider having dinner with me tonight. Your station manager in Djakarta was most kind to put me on this Hajj charter as the quickest way to Teheran, and the very least I can do is invite you for a decent meal in my home town after your long, hard day. My name is Cyrus Pahlavian, and my intentions are honorable." He bowed slightly, with a slight smile.

Zoe pondered, her face serious. She looked again into his deep violet eyes and beautiful face, thinking how different they were from Keoki's dark eyes. "Mr. Pahlavian, I'm delighted to accept your offer of hospitality. And I will also say that you are possibly the handsomest man I have ever seen, and quite difficult to resist. I hope you are more than just a beautiful face." He smiled at her words, bowing slightly as she moved to the staircase.

As they commenced their descent into Teheran, she returned to her jumpseat. Pahlavian beckoned her to join him for a moment in the adjacent seat.

"I have a favor to ask you," he said. "I have nothing to hide. I have only my small valise here, but I wish to avoid questions. It is somewhat unusual for diplomatic corps members to travel on religious charters." He seemed vaguely uncomfortable. "If I could depart through the economy section, and if by chance I were wearing a Hajji robe, would it be noticed?"

Zoe looked at him in appraisal. More here than meets the eye, she thought. "No, I doubt there would be questions from the passenger agents. But I can assure you I will have lots of questions later."

He nodded. "Good, I will transform myself for our arrival, and I will explain fully when I see you at the lobby bar of the InterContinental Hotel 8 p.m., if that is convenient?"

Zoe smiled, enjoying their conspiracy. "That's fine, but I think that Hajjis don't frequent the bar at the InterContinental, so I will look for your other persona?" He laughed and moved away to the rest rooms, emerging in a few moments in a full white robe and headgear. As he slipped through the curtains carrying his valise, he flashed her a look. "Until eight o'clock, then!"

Zoe wrapped herself in her thick wool crew coat and an extra pashmina shawl for the ride to the hotel. It was located in a sophisticated downtown area of Teheran, which sprawled for miles along the foothills of the Elbruz Mountains, now dusted with snow almost to the edge of the city. All along the road into town, heavily armed soldiers patrolled watchtowers and barrier gates. On the walls, spray-painted signs, posters and placards called for the ouster of the Shah in rude cartoons. Many more women on the streets were now wrapped in full-length *chadors*, black-turbaned clerics and white-capped men talked in groups, armed guards patrolled and tanks stood at many intersections. The crew exclaimed at the changes in just a few short months.

Hiding out in the hotel, she read several papers and took a long leisurely shower. She paid careful attention to her appearance for the evening, even as her mind engaged in a debate. She thought of Keoki, far across the Pacific, and of Sao Johnny, hidden in jungles. Why am I always attracted to beautiful, unsuitable men—and now this gorgeous mystery hunk—just because he looks like something off a coin from a Persian Emperor? She settled her shawl around her shoulders and smoothed her dark brown silk dress, checking the mirror's image for approval. Her eyes smiled in answer: because they are so good to touch; that's all—nothing more.

Pahlavian stood as she approached and nodded approvingly, his dark slacks and sweater a contrast to his earlier Hajj attire. "So, we have changed into butterflies." They sipped sweet tea quickly, the warm fragrance steaming in the air. He said, "My car is just outside," and they slipped through a side door into the cold. A waiter bowed, then moved towards a house telephone, his eyes watchful, as the car moved away.

The streets looked cold and deserted, but he drew up to a large warmly lit establishment where they were soon seated on large cushions atop silk carpets at a low table. Warm brass lanterns lit the area softly; plants lined both walls, and archways to the restaurant were covered with ornate blue tiles. Soft music played: flutes, percussion, a woman's smoky voice weaving more mystery. He said, "This is the University district, where I grew up, and I've known this restaurant for most of my life."

As they ate a delicious country meal of lamb and vegetables, he recounted his childhood in Teheran, overseas travel and education, and his life in the diplomatic corps, as well as his alienation as a Christian in the increasingly fundamentalist society. Zoe related stories of her life in post–World War II Asia and her career with Pan Am.

He spoke of the politics of modern life in Iran, starting with the widespread resentment of the Shah's excesses, the secret police, the corruption, the influence of the CIA. There was growing anger and calls for reform, most notably by conservative clerics. Pahlavian was worried that these clerics would use the abuses to their advantage, and sweep Iran back to the Middle Ages.

He said, "I wish to return, to settle here in my homeland, to live a good and honest life, to raise a family and do the right things here at home. But right now I feel exiled, and there are so many changes happening."

At that moment, their host slipped in and whispered something to Pahlavian, who glanced quickly at the door as two men in dark shirts and glasses entered and took a look around the room. He murmured, "Quickly, Zoe, lie down on the pillows next to me." She complied, and he held her closely as they sank further into the shadows. Her heart beat against his warmth.

Slowly, the visitors left after surveying the room, their menace barely veiled.

Zoe said, "What on earth?"

Pahlavian helped her to sit, holding her arm and looking deep in her eyes. "Savak. The Shah's secret police. This is how we live now."

She looked at him, puzzled, "You need to tell me more."

He talked in muted tones, about the new military government and the exiled cleric known as the Ayatollah Khomeini, a man almost unknown in America.

"These changes are huge," said Pahlavian. "Just two months ago, on Black Friday, hundreds of thousands of demonstrators marched to overturn progressive programs for education, and women's rights and constitutional laws that have been in place since the 1930s. Iran will disappear."

The restaurant owner and his wife joined them for dessert, accompanied by a young University professor, who Pahlavian introduced as a leader of many protests. "I do not look for a war," said the professor. "Government leaders are regular confidantes of the CIA; they say there is no problem, that it will blow over, and they have even written a report two months ago for the President of the United States. They do not understand at all what they are facing; this is a total revolution by the people against the cruelty and corruption of the Shah and his regime."

The hour was late. After saying their goodbyes, Zoe and Pahlavian slipped out a side door and into his car for the journey back to the hotel. He sat for a moment, holding her hand. "In another time, I would say sweet words to you and we could think of pleasant things. But this is not that time, and I do regret it." He glanced at her, turned her palm up and caressed her hand, kissing it lightly.

Zoe looked at him. "You haven't told me why you came here in disguise, or why those men were looking for you." When he didn't answer, she asked, "Is it wise for me to think of seeing you again?"

He nodded. "Yes, yes, we must meet. I will return to Djakarta in a week or so. But know this: Iran will not be safe, and there will very soon be massive demonstrations that are only just beginning, to force the change we need. I must do my part, and then I must be available to others."

They drove in silence, her hand tucked in his, their thoughts unspoken. He knows, she thought, he knows what he has to do. Like Keoki and Sao Johnny, they are driven. And I know I must do my part, but I don't know what. She sat in miserable silence.

He stopped the car briefly, down the road from the hotel. "You must know this. I will do nothing dishonorable, or that would hurt people, or that would in any way harm you." Wordlessly, his arm encircled her. She nestled her head briefly into the soft fabric of his jacket, feeling his warmth, his strength.

He drove the short distance to the side door of the hotel, and she hurried from the cold into the lobby. Two men in dark shirts and glasses sat watching the main lobby door. She moved further back and slipped into the nearest elevator. I'd make a really shitty spy, she mused, as the door closed.

After a few hours of restless sleep, Zoe was back in uniform on the crew bus, only half listening to excited chatter about heavy security checks at the hotel the previous evening. Then, with growing alarm, she realized that the search had been focused on identifying every crewmember in the hotel, everyone except herself, because she had been out. She listened to bits of conversations: "…the two Iranians wanted to know about a First Class…there was an American with them, he seemed to be in charge…they asked if we knew any local Iranians, and who…." Discussions whirled around her, and she mentally prepared herself for, for what? What could happen?

As soon as their bus arrived at the terminal, she grabbed the Captain's arm. "Skipper, I wasn't in the hotel until late last night, so someone might come looking for me on a curfew violation or something. What do you suggest I say?"

The Captain nodded, understanding her question. "Zoe, I know you can handle anything. I suggest you listen to any questions, and say as little as possible. Did anything bad happen to you?"

"No, sir. Nothing happened. Nothing at all."

"Good. Keep it simple. And we won't leave without you." He squeezed her arm in reassurance. Zoe took a deep breath as they proceeded towards the Pan Am counters and offices beyond.

She did not have long to wait. The Passenger Service Manager, a middle-aged Iranian man, approached her at the door of the briefing office, his face serious. He whispered, "Some people want to talk to you about a passenger on yesterday's flight. Be careful, I think they are CIA."

Zoe nodded. "Did you have any dealings with the passenger?" she asked carefully.

He nodded, hesitantly. "Not directly, but I do know him. He is a distant cousin of my wife's, of very good family." His eyes spoke volumes.

"Thanks for the heads-up. I certainly don't know anything at all, other than that he has exquisite manners." She smiled carefully, as they reached the Station Manager's office, and he knocked sharply before opening the door.

Seated across the room were two men with flat eyes and closed faces, who rose as they entered. They were both tall, one slender and one heavily built. The Station Manager was finishing a phone call,

"Yes, thanks. I will explain the circumstances to the crew; the Purser is with me now."

He smiled hastily and said, "Miss Longfield...uh, Zoe. This is...uh, these are gentlemen from the U.S. Embassy who wanted to meet you." The men did not introduce themselves or shake hands, so Zoe smiled briefly and seated herself at a chair fronting the Station Manager's desk.

"Good morning, gentlemen" she said. "Is there anything I can help you with?"

The slender one nodded his head sharply. "We're looking for information on a passenger from the Hajj charter that arrived early yesterday evening, and we understand you might have spent some time with him."

They were still standing. Zoe was half-turned to address them. "I'm not sure how much I can help you," she smiled. "We had a full flight of Hajj pilgrims from Djakarta to Karachi, then almost the same load into Teheran." She smiled brightly, still turned at an angle to speak directly to them.

The slender man said, "No, we're more interested in your dinner date. Didn't you pick him up on the flight?"

Zoe cringed inwardly at the inference. "Actually, one of the passengers seated in First Class invited me for dinner. But I really can't tell you much about him, other than what was on the passenger manifest. His name is Cyril, no, Cyrus Pahlavian, I think, and he is with the Iranian Embassy in Djakarta right now, I believe." She waved her hands vaguely.

"Look, hon, we know you spent a long evening with him, so there has to be more." The heavily built man spoke up.

Zoe replied coolly, "I really don't know what you want to know. And if you are from the American Embassy, I assume you're here to help me as an American citizen. You could start by introducing yourselves, and telling me what this is about." With sweaty palms, she turned her chair around to face them, placing it firmly and nodding in apology to the Station Manager as she did so.

The larger man said, "Miss Longfield, I'm Max Johnson and my colleague here is Ira Smith. We will be most grateful for any information on this man. He's on the United States watch-lists for suspected terrorist activity in connection with the upheavals here in Teheran. He arrived on your flight and you had dinner with him. What did you talk about?"

Zoe stared, genuinely taken aback. "Terrorist activity? It would be hard to imagine. We talked about where he grew up, how his family was connected with the University for a long time. I told him I'm an amateur archaeologist so I'm very interested in the cultural sites here in Iran, and that's pretty much what we talked about." She smiled ruefully, shaking her head, a charming and relaxed professional—on the surface, at least.

The slender one said, "And you are sure he didn't mention any activity here in Teheran?"

"No," said Zoe, "only that he's concerned about current unrest and will be going back to Djakarta, and that he wants what is best for the Iranian people."

"We just have one more question. Did he leave the airplane yesterday in a disguise of some kind?"

Her brow wrinkled, "Gosh, I don't know. I was dealing with so many passengers I can't say I saw him leave. Departures and arrivals can be pretty frantic, sometimes."

Zoe's brain was spinning, her stomach in knots. It took all her poise to smile brightly and say, "Well, if there isn't anything else, I'm sure our Station Manager wants us to make that nine o'clock departure."

The men nodded, conferring briefly with each other, and the slender one offered his hand, "Thanks for coming in. We know this is all pretty confusing stuff for you, and we sure didn't want to alarm you. But the way things are in Eye-ran these days we have to keep an eye on any potential troublemakers. You understand, right?" Zoe nodded, the grateful ingénue.

"Now if you hear from him again, we'd be grateful to know what you find out. We want you to be safe." He handed her an engraved business card with the logo of the State Department.

Zoe nodded, "Well, you're kind to think of it that way. I sure don't know how to reach him, but I'll let you know if he contacts me.

Thanks for your concern." She flashed a professional stewardess smile and a practiced "'Bye, now!" as she moved out of the room.

In the few short steps to the Briefing Office, she ticked off what they possibly knew: Pahlavian's arrival in Hajj attire, their meeting at the side-lobby, their quick departure, possibly her late return back to the side-lobby. She was chilled at the thought of who else could be watching all of them all the time, and his comments about Savak police. One thing was certainly true; she had no idea how to reach him even if she wanted to. But did she want to? And, what, in fact, did she know about him and his motives? She exhaled, tired of the climate of fear and mistrust, the bogeymen said to lurk in every dark corner.

She opened the door to the Briefing Office, where the junior Purser was conducting assignments, and gave another bright stewardess smile. "Just some more questions on our Hajj passengers yesterday. Carry on!"

Later, on board the aircraft, the Passenger Service Manager was handing her the Flight Logs and Purser Briefcase, when he whispered, "Thank you, that was very brave. I can assure you that our friend is a good and honest man, and has only the best interests of the people of Iran at heart."

Zoe smiled briefly, "He's lucky. He knows what he has to do, and good luck to you all."

Dozens of white-clad passengers moved about the cabin, conferring with senior Hajj leaders and clerics on the protocols to be followed on arrival. She completed her Purser Log early, filling in the boxes for the 19th of November, 1978, the crew names, identification numbers, bases, the flight legs of Teheran to Jeddah and back.

The flight was quiet, the silent passengers in their white *imram* robes. Half an hour before their designated arrival time, the Captain's voice came over the public address system. "Ladies and gentlemen, we are 30 minutes out of Jeddah, and we have been advised that there are some unanticipated events in the cities of Mekkah and Medinah which will affect your onwards travel. Please remain seated on arrival so that the passenger service team can advise you of the plans at that time. We'll do our best to assist your safe transit."

The Captain's words were translated by one of the

representatives, whereupon a howl of anguish rose throughout the aircraft, and several of the most senior Hajjis headed for the front of the aircraft, their eyes wide, shouting. The charter representative scurried down the aisle to speak with them, the volume rising, hands gesturing, other seated passengers rising to enter the discussion. Zoe said, "There is nothing to be done until we can speak to the authorities on the ground. Now, please sit!"

The blank, grey slate and sand of the lands around Jeddah's airport came up quickly, and soon they were parked outside a half-built modern airport in desert surroundings. Cargo trams encircled the airplane, driven by men in white caftans with fluttering red and white *abiyehs*, the headwear of the Saudi people. Inside the terminal, chaos reigned in 10 different languages, as their passengers joined a throng of hundreds of others, all angrily demanding answers from the Hajj authorities.

The maintenance supervisor directed the crew towards the operations office.

"We are not entirely sure what is going on in Mekkah," he said. "Apparently there was an accident, and now we must load many injured on your aircraft back to Teheran. There are several ambulances, buses and other types of transport headed our way, but we really don't have a handle on the kind of injuries, or the level of medical support they have received." The crew nodded, taking in the information.

A tall, immaculately groomed Arab in traditional dress entered the room. "I am here from the Ministry of Religious Affairs," he said. "We have received word of some serious complications in Mekkah today. During the crush of emotion and religious ecstasy, several hundred pilgrims pushed forward on a recently erected concrete ramp, which collapsed on top of the stream of other people ascending the staircase below. Pilgrims were crushed and trampled, trapped under falling concrete blocks, or pushed out of the arena towards the next step, the sacrificial killing grounds. Unfortunately, many were killed and injured."

He sighed. "These are ancient customs," he said slowly. "Last year, it was more than 200 dead in a fire in the tents. The year before, it was 340 trampled in a ritual. We are changing the site, but it is not now enough, and we can only do our best."

Zoe said to the crew, "We need to make a decision here. Do we stay to help these passengers, or do we get out of town as fast as possible?"

One crewmember raised her hand. "I heard all about the mess in Vietnam, and I'm not interested in heroics." One by one, the crew nodded agreement. They'd take the victims out, but no extra measures, no evacuation rules.

Zoe sighed inwardly, remembering Saigon and the excitement and exhilaration of those weeks, the camaraderie and the feeling of getting something done right, beyond the call of duty. This just does not feel good, she thought, wondering if Pahlavian would appear again, and where.

Two passenger agents appeared at the door. "The buses are here from Mekkah, with many injured. We will be sending a team of doctors and nurses with you to Teheran, so you will have medical assistance on the way." He handed over a large box of United Nations medical supplies: bandages, surgical tape, various types of disinfectant and antibiotic creams. Oh great, thought Zoe, now it is Florence Nightingale time.

She alerted the crew to stand by for boarding, just as the first passengers arrived, moaning in pain and fear, supported by teams of Hajj assistants. Within moments, the aircraft was filling with a stream of filthy, bloodied men and women, their ritual clothing soaked with blood, dirt, their faces contorted in pain or anger.

Zoe and the crew moved quickly to fill the aircraft, and to give the injured a sense of immediate assistance. All through the cabin, harsh weeping changed to low moans as men and women sat back, their eyes closed, some in tears, but comforted. Slowly, a sense of calm returned to the cabin as medical personnel assisted the injured. The crewmembers mostly maintained a distance, providing water but no physical support. Zoe thought, how sad it is that we've changed so much, in so short a time.

Within moments they were airborne, and the silence lengthened in the afternoon shadows over the desert until they touched down in Teheran in the early evening, and medical crews swarmed aboard to take over.

The trip to the hotel was quiet, and mercifully fast. Traffic seemed to have disappeared. A few pedestrians scurried for doorways and buses.

She could smell the danger, like an ozone breeze. Something was happening.

As their crew bus drew up beside the entrance to the hotel it was blocked by a dark Mercedes limousine. Zoe descended to the street, just as a mature, distinguished man clad in an immaculate cashmere coat emerged from the back compartment of the Mercedes in front of her. The crew bus driver standing beside her breathed, "It is Mehdi Bazargan. He is Islamic Reform Movement, a good man."

As she stood watching, waiting for her crew bag, a tall wavy-haired man in a dark suit emerged from the opposite side of the car, and proceeded, without a glance in her direction, towards the hotel entrance. He passed immediately in front of her as she stepped forward, and then she quickly moved back. It was Pahlavian. She could almost hear him, willing her to silence. She watched him go, thinking that she was unlikely to ever see him again, unlikely to have her questions answered.

She awoke early the next morning, November 20th, the telephone ringing incessantly. "We leave in one hour, and that's an order," barked the Captain. "Turn on the TV and you'll see why."

The television news showed thousands of students carrying banners for the Islamic Reform Movement, calling for a return to the 1907 Constitution, for the ouster of the Shah, for democratic governance. She absorbed it all as she showered and packed, heading for the crew bus, leaving a country behind, leaving Pahlavian.

The station manager nodded, "Yes, Bazargan is taking charge, and I believe our friend is at his side. But we don't know if it is already too late." He signed.

Perhaps there is hope, Zoe thought.

Three days later, the telephone rang in her Djakarta hotel room.

"Zoe, may I meet you this evening?" His voice was instantly recognizable. Her heart jumped.

"I know you'll tell me what you can. But that was quite an

entrance you made at the hotel the other day, and I'm not at all sure it's good for me to see you." She was thoughtful, not judging him, but protective of her own peace.

"Zoe, this is the worst time I can imagine to ask for patience, but I must see you, and I must ask for your forgiveness and understanding now. I am in this hotel, in the rooms adjoining the President's Suite. Please, I know this is unusual, but I ask you to see me."

She could hear the urgency in his voice, and responded, weakly. "Yes, I'll be there."

She knocked tentatively on the side door to the Presidential Suite. The door swung quietly open and he stood in silhouette. In the early evening light from the verandah, breezes ruffled soft silk curtains, and a small gamelan wind-chime sounded sweetly. No words were spoken, none needed, as she went into his arms.

Hours passed as they clung to each other, first breathless. Then again, slowly and languorously, their bodies exploring, shifting, moving to a timeless music, their eyes and mouths open as they touched and felt for hidden places, his hardness, her softness, the wonder of wordless emotion. So good to touch, she thought.

Sometime after dark, the wind shifted and they wrapped themselves in the hotel's batik sarongs to sit in the moonlight with a plate of fruits, delicate coconut-flavored sweetmeats, sips from a bottle of brandy. He murmured kisses with the brandy, toasting her breasts, her neck, feeding her small sips of the sweet, hot liquid fire, as she shook her head, no-no-no, and he turned to her again and she drowned in his eyes while the heat rose and she thrust, and thrust and cried with joy.

And afterwards, they spoke. He had committed to his cause, to his country. The student revolutions of the week were increasingly crowded, thousands marching each day. In all the years of revolutions, said the newscasters, there had never been these numbers. Almost one per cent of the entire population of Iran was on the move, demonstrating their hatred for the Shah, their demand for change.

There was no going back on his word. He had resigned his commission in the diplomatic corps, and was now attached to the UN emergency committee that was meeting in Djakarta. He would be leaving in days for Teheran, disgraced as a traitor to the Shah. His colleagues visited with him privately, congratulating him for his courage, making their own overtures towards a freedom for themselves and their families, towards the change that was coming. There was no guarantee of anything. There was the possibility within a few weeks or months of a new coalition government headed by Bazargan. There were rumors of his meetings with representatives of the Ayatollah Khomeini. There was only now, this moment. In coming weeks or months, there would be time for more, but not now. She felt a strange quiet, a calm center, a warmth, as she sank back towards his smooth chest, her head nestled to his neck, breathing in the moonlight, the night breeze. This is all there is, she thought. I am never allowed to want more than this.

She left him, sleeping, with a kiss, an hour before dawn.

Later, dressed in her uniform, her stewardess smile in place, she boarded the crew bus and looked up towards the dark windows and the verandah, caressing him again in her mind, already gone, the moment passed, fleeting, impermanent. The gears ground harshly as she tightened her overcoat and the pashmina shawl covering her face, breathing in jasmine, breathing out dreams.

At the airport, the passenger service manager nodded to two familiar men standing away from the counter crowds who were here again, to see her before the flight check-in.

Zoe smiled brightly. Well, it's Tweedledumb and Tweedledumber, she said to herself, advancing towards Agents Smith and Johnson. I really know nothing. There is nothing I can tell them that will help them, or me, or Pahlavian and his difficult course.

"Gentlemen, it is a pleasure to see you again. Are you joining us to Hawai'i?"

Smith turned to her, his voice steely. "No, Miss Longfield, we are not. We understand you may have seen your friend Pahlavian this week, and we'd like to know more about his friends in Eye-ran. What are his plans?"

Zoe smiled, "You know, gentlemen, I just wish I could help you, but I haven't got the vaguest idea of what you are talking about.

Why, I've spent the last day just so ill, I never left my bed." She looked at each of them in turn. "Well, if there's nothing else, I'll be off to my briefing. Now you just have a really good day now!" She leaned towards them with the intense smile on her lips and none in her eyes. Fuck you and your Shah, boys. Nothing I know matters to you at all.

Honolulu and the North Shore were restoratives after the Hajj. Sally welcomed her home joyously, with stories about a new man, Jack Wright. They'd all met him years before, and he'd reappeared while Sally was jogging near Lucien and Kaleo's house at the foot of Diamond Head. It was a whirlwind romance, and Sally was full of dreams and plans for the future.

Zoe felt disconnected, unaccountably dizzy in the mornings, bloated and uncomfortable. She paddled every day with Moke's racing canoe group, and they talked about the imminent arrival of the voyaging canoe with Keoki and his crew of watermen.

Together, she and Sally scoured reports in the papers on the days of December 10th and 11th, as over 10 million people flooded the streets of Teheran, demanding an end to the Shah's regime, the installation of the puppet regime of Dr. Shapour Bakhtiar as a sop to the opposition elements, and, sadly, the last flight of Pan Am #104 out of Teheran on December 13, 1978.

Sally looked pensive. "You know, we're getting good at this last-out stuff."

And a few weeks later, there was Keoki, full of stories of the blue-water sailors and their fine adventures, and ambitious new plans for the North West Hawai'ian Islands and Moku Manamana, 2300 miles into the Pacific. But somehow, their embraces were stilted, incomplete. They needed to talk, but there were no words. It was not the same.

Finally, Keoki broke the silence.

"Zoe, I don't know how to say this, so I'm just going to say it. I've been offered a three-year research opportunity at the new excavations at Manamana at the end of the Northwest Hawai'ian

Island chain. I need to do this for so many reasons, especially as a Polynesian. This is like the chance my father had on Howland Island, and it is essential for me to go. It's not that I don't love you. I just don't love you enough to stop the journey."

She stared at him, willing herself to breathe slowly, breathe in, breathe out. Say nothing, she thought, lest she break up and throw rocks at him, and bits of driftwood and sand, and beat on his head and chest and cry out her awful anger, at having tricked him—and herself—and lied to him through not telling him first that her love, too, had just melted away. What do either Pahlavian or Keoki—these incredibly gorgeous men—really mean to me? She swallowed the manic laughter that threatened to erupt, kept her face pensive, almost grave, as she thought of things to say, and nodded in serious understanding.

"Keoki, that is a whole lot to absorb all at once. I'm going to have to think about what I feel now." He nodded, and she walked slowly away from him in the early evening light, her *pareau* fluttering in the evening breeze. Now I'm the one who is walking away, she thought.

Her entire body was tingling with relief, a shedding of worry, a release from lies and deceit. You son of a bitch, she thought. You selfish, gorgeous, asshole of the universe—and probably Pahlavian fits in here too—you two fucking assholes of the universe, you two man-things. I don't need either of you!

As she turned the corner of the beach and out of Keoki's sight, she paused.

Oh shit! I know why I've been feeling so weird. I'm pregnant! I'm 32 years old. I said I wanted a baby. I still have not figured out what I'm going to do when I grow up. I don't have a husband or a prospect of one to help support me, And, because of my own idiocy, I don't know which one of these two incredibly stupid, beautiful men is the father of my child." She looked back at the sea and started laughing uncontrollably, hugging herself and jumping up and down. She ran towards Sally, who was standing in the sunset.

CHAPTER EIGHTEEN

CHANGES
JULY 30, 1079   HONOLULU, HAWAI'I

Sally and Zoe stood facing the old-fashioned pier glass in the downstairs bedroom of Jack Wright's family home on Tantalus ridge. They could hear the slamming of car doors, clashing of crockery from the caterer's tent, the Hawai'ian trio warming up voices and instruments on the lawn under the spreading monkey-pod tree. It was the perfect day for a wedding. While Zoe fussed over their clothes, Sally smiled at her reflection, thinking back on how she had rediscovered Jack, and his proposal just a few short months ago. They had laughed at the notion of wedding protocols, but here they were, minutes away.

"Come on, Sally, you'd better get into your dress. It's time." She lifted the formal white lace *mu'umu'u* up from the bed and Sally slipped it over her head. Zoe ran the zipper up the back then turned her around and looked her up and down. "Perfect. Now the flowers." Carefully she placed the *maile* leis that had been intertwined with tiny *pikake* blossoms and pink rosebuds around Sally's neck, then the *lei po'o* of pink rosebuds around her head.

"You'd better not have that baby tonight and screw up my wedding," Sally joked, poking a finger at the swollen belly straining through the fabric of Zoe's pink floral *mu'umu'u*.

"You worry too much," replied Zoe. "But I want to thank you for not tracking down Keoki. This baby will be just fine, and it'll have the best aunties and uncles in the world. Besides, I've got my hula all ready to perform during the reception. You're just a nervous bride." Awkwardly, Zoe backed away from the dressing table and sat on the bed. She picked up a pair of pumps that were lying beside her, eyeing them carefully. After making a half-hearted attempt to put them on her feet, she tossed them in the corner. "To hell with these. I'm going barefoot."

Sally giggled. "Nothing about this whole affair has been traditional. Why stop now?"

Sugar Pie had despaired at the cultural clashes. She had arrived from Kentucky with Stanton Gardner two weeks before the wedding to supervise preparations with Jack's mother. While Pie was delighted with the fact that Sally had asked Stanton to give her away, she was shocked that two of the attendants would be Lucien Martin and his partner, Kaleo; that the wedding would take place outside in the lower garden of Jack's house and not at St. Andrew's Cathedral; that Sally would wear a formal Hawai'ian *mu'umu'u* with flowers intertwined with what looked to her like weeds; and that the bridal couple would be barefoot.

"How can a man *really* be a bridesmaid?" she asked forlornly when Sally told her.

"Mother, it's simple," Sally shrugged. "They're bridesmen, that's all."

Then when Zoe appeared for the rehearsal in her advanced stage of pregnancy, Pie groaned and turned away, her face the color of wallpaper glue. But ultimately she took it all in stride, embracing the gracious setting of Jack's home and his family hospitality. Sally would be fine, she knew. She was Old South, this was Old Hawai'i. Some things just weren't so different.

They were interrupted by a knock on the door and Stanton Gardner's voice.

"I've just taken Sugar Pie down the aisle," he said. "Are you ready, Sally?"

Sally smiled "I'm ready," she said, taking his arm as they walked through the living room out into the garden.

"Wait, wait!" Zoe called, grabbing her bouquet. "You can't get married without your maid of honor."

As they stood poised at the top of the path to the lower garden, Sally looked out to see the group of friends and family clustered below the spreading banyan tree. Standing on the left were Lucien and Kaleo, Sally's "bridesmen". Jack's law partner Moke Cabral stood on the groom's side, along with Walker Sheppard, who had flown in from San Diego to stand as best man. And there was Jack, in a white shirt and pants with a wide scarlet sash, a double *maile lei* encircling his neck, looking up at her, his blue eyes smiling.

Hearing the music, Zoe gave Sally a gentle hug and a long look, "This is it, Sally, and you will be so happy. It's all been a wonderful journey." Sally squeezed her hand, then she turned to Stanton and took his arm.

"Your father would be proud, Sally," Stanton said, escorting her down the gentle slope.

Jack stood beside the minister, his eyes steady on her. Walker, handsome in his dress whites, was close by. Zoe was at her side as Sally exchanged the timeless vows with Jack, gripping his hand tightly. The trees rained a gentle shower of blossoms in the light breeze.

After the ceremony, the guests were served Stanton's Old Fashioned cocktails, a big batch of which had been made with his special Kentucky bourbon. The guests moved through the buffet line to the spacious tent, laughing and chatting. The bridal party entered to the sound of strumming guitars and applause, the perfume of *maile* and tuberose carried on the breeze.

Walker Sheppard led the salute, and stepped up to a microphone, clearing his throat. "I've been asked to comment on these splendid proceedings," he said, "but to tell you the truth, we've been trying to get these two to this stage for quite a while, whether they knew it or not."

Walker continued. "As most of you know, we've all known each other for a long time, loved some great people, and lost some of the best of our colleagues and friends, including Billy Righteous, and…and Pualani." He paused. "Wherever they are, they're probably looking at us right this minute, happy that we're here together celebrating these moments. I cannot think of a happier beginning for Jack and Sally, who finally found each other beside the Amelia Earhart Lookout at Diamond Head, of all places. And if anybody played Cupid, let's be sure to acknowledge Lucien and Kaleo here…." He clapped to encourage the audience, as Lucien and Kaleo rose and bowed, "…who plotted for months, just so they could organize this wedding, and force all of us into formal Hawai'ian attire. Ladies and gentlemen, be upstanding. I give you Mr. and Mrs. Jack Wright." The audience cheered.

The band launched into a sassy rendition of "The Keyhole Hula", a naughty dance about betrayal and infidelity witnessed through the keyhole of a door. Zoe danced the song with zest, in spite of her bulk, the guests laughing at the boisterous female lament. Then everyone gathered in a circle for the Bride's Hula.

The lead singer began to sing in warm, rich tones about love for one's sweetheart. Sally let the song move her as she swayed gracefully, just as Pualani had taught her. She finished up to wild applause and an embrace from her new husband.

Then Zoe grabbed her, a strange look on her face. "I think...I think I may mess up your wedding after all," she said. In one hand she clutched a large fold of fabric from her dress. There was a large damp area. "The contractions are steady. They aren't painful, but they aren't going away."

"Oh my God, Zoe!" Sally screamed with delight, pulling at Jack's arm to tell him the news.

Jack signaled the guests for attention. "I'm sorry but we're going to have to move part of the reception downtown. Zoe's baby has decided to be born, and my bride is her labor coach!" There were cries and cheers of celebration, then he continued, "but I want everybody— you musicians included—to continue the party, and we'll report in." Moke has instructions on how to play the Baby Birthday Football Pool, so get your money out!" With whoops of delight, the group lined the driveway as the bride and groom bundled Zoe into the car, and they sped away with a clattering of bouncing cans and shoes.

Sugar Pie looked at Stanton with disbelief bordering on hysteria. "Come along, Pie," said Stanton gently, "let me take you back to the Royal Hawai'ian. You've had enough for one night."

While the party continued, Zoe was wheeled into the delivery room at Kaiser Hospital, overlooking the blue Pacific, attempting to tell the little Jamaican nurse that she didn't want the customary prep, and the nurse grinned, "Honey, you don't have any time to speak of. Just let us get to work."

Sally, still in her wedding dress, stood by Zoe's side, giving her encouragement and coaching her breathing. Finally, in between contractions, the nurse helped her to remove the lace and linen muumuu, now stained by sweat, and helped her into hospital fatigues.

Zoe huffed and groaned, sometimes grabbing Sally as they counted through the contractions.

"Where the hell is that doctor?" yelled Sally, while the nurse shook her head and said, "Honey, dat baby need to come out, so just push, NOW!"

Zoe gulped down a huge breath of air and howled, feeling the pushing and tearing that seemed to go on forever. "Oh my God, oh, shit, ohhhhhhhhhh!" She grabbed for Sally's hand and together, they pushed and pushed, feeling the baby coming faster than Zoe expected. Right after 9:00 p.m., a baby girl was born, just in time to welcome the doctor.

Zoe laughed joyously, her face luminous with sweat, as she and Sally embraced. Out in the hallway, a few dedicated wedding guests cheered, and trooped into the delivery room with champagne and a "Birth Day" cake for the baby.

"Her name is Hawea," Zoe said, hoarse from the yelling in childbirth. "She is named for the ancient drum of the Pacific, and she is a special gift."

This baby would surely be a voice for something very significant one day Sally decided, holding the tiny creature in her arms. She, too, felt a sense of happiness that was quite extraordinary, as if being here at Hawea's birth would connect her to the child always.

Zoe hugged her baby close, tired from the day's events. As she sank into sleep, she stroked Hawea's cheek, and the baby turned to her, opening a pair of bright eyes. They were intense, almost violet. Zoe looked at her daughter's eyes again, not believing, her heart racing, hiding the shock. Babies' eyes change color, don't they? They could be grey-blue, like mine. It doesn't mean...it *can't* mean anything definite—yet. She laughed at the possibilities then turned on her side, embracing her daughter, and slept.

Sally remained at Zoe's side for a while, then made her way down to the waiting room where her new husband lay stretched out on a sofa on the open-air lobby. He slept peacefully, still clad in his crumpled white shirt and red sash, his *maile* lei draped over a nearby pedestal. Sinking to the floor, she rested her head on his arm and fell instantly asleep in her birthing fatigues, her wedding *mu'umu'u* next to her, her bridal leis draped on the pedestal with Jack's, wilted but still fragrant. Before dawn, they rose and slipped to the car, riding through deserted streets up to the Tantalus house, where they jumped into the shower overlooking the garden, throwing crumpled clothes and fragrant leis to the floor, exultant, the streams of hot, cleansing water arousing them, the soap slipping on his back, her breasts, their breath quickening, their hearts pounding as they made love for the first time as man and wife, in the rosy sunlight of the dawn.

I love this man, she thought. He's not Billy, whom she'd loved so much, but it didn't matter. There would always be memories, things she would hold in her heart alone. Jack sensed her feelings and returned her embrace, an almost harsh hug signifying his love, but something more. Perhaps there were secrets that he, too, held in his heart. But Sally did not mind; he's had to make peace with what was. And I'm peaceful with what will come. Any other secrets will have to wait for another day.

Six months later, on a January morning in 1980, Sally sat between Lucien and Zoe as she watched their union representatives, brothers Kenny and Dicky Alonso organize their papers for a special session of the Air Transport Workers Union, Local 737. Beside them, Hawea snoozed peacefully in the arms of her formidable Tongan nanny Malia. Mechanics, port stewards, pantry women and cooks, ramp supervisors and flight attendants crowded into a room that was much too small for the overflow crowd, which ranged down the hallways and out the front door in the industrial waterfront district of Honolulu.

As the temperature began to rise, Sally, who was by now visibly pregnant, cooled herself in the waterfront breeze that wafted in through the open door. Even though she was on maternity leave and not flying the line, she made a special effort to attend the meeting. All

Pan Am employees and their families were closely knit, and all were keenly interested in the increasingly bizarre decisions made by the company's executives in recent years.

It was unfathomable, the prospect of Pan Am in decline. The Clippers were as much a part of the fabric of American life as the flag and apple pie. Pan Am had been the world's pre-eminent airline for as long as anyone could remember. When natural disasters and political demonstrations occurred in foreign countries, people were often in front of the Pan Am ticket office rather than the American Embassy. Experienced travelers everywhere knew that the best way to get out of a *coup d'etat*, a flood zone, an earthquake, a minor legal difficulty or a visa problem was to call the Pan Am station manager. The managers could get things done in a fraction of the time that government channels took.

But strange things were happening. Zoe had tracked earlier news reports that the Shah of Iran would buy a 30% interest in Pan Am to back up Iran Air. But now the Shah had fled, and the Ayatollah Khomeini had made a triumphant return to Iran for his appointment as Supreme Ruler of the Islamic Republic. Doors to the west audibly slammed shut. Fundamentalism descended, obliterating the legendary hospitality, arts and history of the Persian Empire. Then the world was rudely awakened to a terrorist act of worldwide magnitude: a group of Iranian students, demonstrators, fundamentalists and paramilitary gunmen had overrun the American Embassy in Teheran, captured 66 staff members and visitors, and announced an international hostage crisis. Within days, the Islamic Republic's first Prime Minister, Mehdi Bazargan, had resigned. The Iranian hostage crisis was front-and-center stage for American foreign policy, and was featured in every newspaper. Khomeini stood for every kind of evil in the minds of many Americans, and every day the airwaves were filled with chaotic arguments equating all "Arabs" with all sins against Jesus, and confusing Muslim and Coptic Christian Iranians in the same general condemnation. And here in this hot, smoky Union Hall, the discussion was equally heated but for different reasons.

"Why hasn't the government given us the right to international air-mail contracts?" Zoe asked. "All the international carriers are carrying U.S. mail, which we started in 1935. There is no logic to this concept that Pan Am has to be America's *flagship* carrier, which seems to mean we have to fly strictly international routes, but can't carry U.S. mail!"

Sally added, "And why do they charge a Qantas 747 landing in Los Angeles a $350 pittance in landing fees, when a Pan Am 747 pays $5000 when it lands in Sydney? The playing field just doesn't seem level."

Kenny Alonso replied. "Sister, there are a lot of things going on at the top of that Pan Am building on Park Avenue that we don't agree with. The union thinks Pan Am management figured that just because they started the airline industry, they would always own the market. As the market becomes more and more deregulated, all the airlines are going to have to do things very differently. We aren't the accountants or the marketing folks; we're just the workers. But we know bullshit when we see it."

In years past, the Civil Aeronautics Board had controlled the route structures of the airlines, along with setting fares and schedules. The major carriers were comfortable with this system because it ensured a reasonable rate of return. But the now defunct CAB was notoriously unresponsive to rapid changes in the market, taking months, even years to render decisions on requests made by the airlines. Zoe had helped organize a statewide demonstration, and worked with the Washington lobbyists and powerful union interests to get the message to Congress. Pan Am employees were voters, and the unions were a strong political force. Hawaii's Senator Dan Inouye was the lone Senator speaking against the Deregulation Act. But President Carter's appointee to the CAB, Alfred Khan argued forcefully against the union petitions for the Fair Competitive Practices Act, snapping, "Pan Am can go to hell."

And if government officials weren't being supportive, the press was downright brutal. Pan Am's past arrogance was legendary, they said. One writer sneered at the number of vice presidents, and jeered at the $100,000 salaries paid to pilot "bus-drivers".

Even the *Wall Street Journal* piled on, saying, "They were autocratic 25 years ago and they're still autocratic today."

Kenny cleared his throat and stepped to the microphone. Vice-Chairman Doug Correa stood at his side. "This morning, January 7, 1980," said Kenny, "Pan Am chairman William Seawell announced that Pan Am will buy National Airlines for $374 million dollars." He had barely finished the sentence when the room erupted in roars of disbelief.

Sally turned to Zoe in shock. "National? Who the hell are they?" she gasped.

Zoe's face was dark. "It's a two-bit airline that specializes in flying from Tallahassee to Pensacola. A north-south airline! Pan Am's a five-ocean carrier; we need east-west routes."

The mechanics bombarded the union officials with questions about maintenance of the different types of aircraft. And National's route structure was designed for runs up and down the eastern seaboard; Pan Am needed connecting flights in a much larger east-west direction to link up with their enormously profitable Asia-Pacific routes to the Atlantic, Africa and South America. The whole thing seemed too impractical to comprehend.

There were other critical problems of immediate concern, especially merging the seniority lists of the various craft and class unions, and cross-training on both properties. The flight attendants worried about seniority, wondering how the National flight crews would be folded into their organization. Losing seniority would mean losing one's choice in bidding for flight schedules and base preferences. And what about uniforms and service training? Did these people have any idea of what Pan Am's First Class service was like? Could they really make the transition from flying between small cities in Florida and the big leagues of international travel? What about pay scales? National didn't pay as much as Pan Am.

And then there was the biggest worry of all. Who was in charge? How sound was the business decision to buy a second-tier carrier? They knew all about the bidding war between Pan Am and Frank Lorenzo of Texas International and Frank Borman of Eastern Airlines, and they could scarcely believe that Pan Am would pursue such folly. Together with an inflated purchase price and the mushrooming costs of blending the two companies into one another, how much was this deal going to cost to execute? And all this was before anyone factored in an economy that was sliding into recession.

Sally realized the situation was dire. But at least she had Jack and his struggling law practice. But what would happen to Zoe and Hawea if something bad happened? Malia had taken Hawea out for a walk on the waterfront, and they just returned with big smiles.

Doug quieted the audience long enough to explain some of the details of the merger. "President Seawell has said that no one is going to lose their job."

"Are you kidding?" Zoe scoffed. "You can't tell me there won't be duplication in administrative and operations functions, not to mention stations down line. They'll have to let *somebody* go to make the whole thing financially viable. It better goddamned well not be Pan Am people."

Sally sat quietly as Doug went on to discuss other union business, picturing the image of Pan Am's next generation of supersonic aircraft, built for glamour and sophistication, now struggling for survival. It was just...just un-American, she thought.

Squirming in her seat, Zoe fumed at this decision. She didn't like Seawell, the latest CEO of Pan Am. A former Air Force general, his cold, calculating face reminded her of the faceless appointees who had conducted the Vietnam War. Images of the CIA and its activities in Miami, Central America, Southeast Asia and Iran clouded her mind. And then in the next moment, a very ominous thought occurred to her: just like the Vietnam War, who the hell is running this insane asylum? Who gives these people the okay to do what they do? She felt they were entering an orchestrated, downward spiral that would be long, bloody and painful.

Still, their lives were joyful and they celebrated special moments. Zoe threw a huge beach party to celebrate Hawea's first birthday, and the recent arrival of her goddaughter, Sally and Jack's baby, named Zoe Pualani Wright. Outside Zoe's old shack on the North Shore, guitars sounded, ice chinked over beer cans in large, battered coolers, maracas clattered, the scent of teriyaki barbecue filled the air. Friends from the neighborhood, Pan Am and family members greeted each other. Voices were raised in sweet Hawai'ian harmony by Moke Cabral, Jack Wright and his surfing partners, and Walker Sheppard came to visit on leave between Naval shore and sea assignments.

Zoe had gone on a mission early that morning to find Keoki, back from the Northwest Hawai'ian Islands, determined to get him to the birthday party that afternoon. They'd had several exchanges of correspondence, and he'd even suggested using his last name for the birth certificate; but he'd never taken the time to visit.

Her attempt at a reunion had not gone well. He'd returned two weeks earlier with a group from the expedition aboard the supply boat for Manamana. Zoe had called him repeatedly and left messages, and finally this morning she had gone down to the pier, only to find that he was over on the Polynesian Voyaging Society's *Hokule'a,* "talking stories" with his blue-water sailing brothers.

She walked hesitantly out on the pier, self-conscious and uncomfortable. Maybe I should have just brought Hawea with me to shame him into holding her, she thought. She recognized most of the crew, and waved in greeting. All returned her wave except for one beautiful young Polynesian woman, sitting next to Keoki, whose back was turned. They were deep in conversation, her hand on his arm.

Zoe called out, "Hey, sailor, new in town?" The body language from the young woman told her everything she needed to know. The other men nodded hello somewhat sheepishly, while Keoki turned to greet her.

"Hey, Zoe, sorry, it's been crazy busy since we got in. Good you found me." He nodded at the men, pointedly ignoring the girl, and jumped ashore to take her arm and move away, towards the activities at the bustling pier.

It was so bizarre that Zoe burst out laughing. "Oh, Keoki, there's no need to hide your girlfriend, and you don't have to pretend with me! I can see what's going on, and she's beautiful, and very Polynesian just like you wanted."

She turned to face him, her face serious. "It's okay that you were gone for the whole time while Hawea was born. I didn't ask or expect that you would be signing up for Father of the Year. And it's okay that your sailing buddies come first. It's even okay that you apparently have not been lonely." Her voice choked a little, "But hey, you do know that there's an absolutely incredible one-year-old girl named Hawea Kanawai, right?"

She smiled, ignoring his grim expression. "Keoki, really, really. It is all okay. I would be lying if I said it didn't hurt, because it does. This is hard for me, but the most important thing is, while you're here, that you come and see Hawea. Come and hold her. You can't imagine how incredible she is, and today's her first birthday party up at the North Shore."

Keoki, his eyes cloudy, hung his head. "Yeah, this has been a weird deal all the way around. Of course I want to see Hawea, and of course I think it's wonderful that you named her after the drum we found. You're an amazing woman. You've carried this all by yourself all these months, and I'm a total, irresponsible asshole."

She faced him, "No, there are no bad guys here. It just worked out this way, and it just needs for you to spend time with Hawea, for her sake. You gave her your name, now it's important for you to give her time whenever you can. Come to the luau this afternoon. It's all the usual suspects, and they've all known you long enough to love you, no matter what. And that includes me." She smiled, her eyes brimming. "Just come."

He reached for her. "God, you are really something. I'll be there; I wouldn't miss it for anything."

He turned back towards the voyaging canoe, then stopped. "And you are still the most beautiful woman I've ever known."

She smiled as she turned to walk away, feeling his eyes on her and thinking, finally I am the one walking away instead of watching him leave. It really is okay, she thought, surprised that it was true.

As she drove away, she surveyed the waterfront, the racing crews practicing in the limpid water. She sighed. Right or wrong, it's my decision for Hawea to have a Pacific life. She should not grow up a displaced person as I have. At least this way she has roots, and family, and a place she can always look to that is hers.

That afternoon at the beach, the feeling was soft…*nahe nahe*, the Hawaiians called it. Keoki appeared just in time to join the impromptu band with his worn guitar, and spent time walking on the beach alone with Hawea, who took to him just like one of her friendly uncles. His eyes were gentle, and he said softly, "You know, Zoe, this is something I never imagined. How beautiful she is." They smiled into each other's eyes.

As night fell and the last guests left the beach, the well-known KCCN radio announcer, Honolulu Skylark, gave details of the news of the day. Her voice was clear across the airwaves. "...And at top of the news on this July 27, 1980, in Cairo, Egypt, the government has announced the death of former Iranian Shah Mohammed Reza Pahlavi of complications from cancer...."

Walker nodded. "Well, another one's gone. He tried his best to support America's interests in Iran."

Zoe turned. "Walker, are you serious?" Her eyes darkened as she thought of the sea of *chadors*, shouting voices, graffiti on walls and banners, the passion of the Hajj, the anger in the streets of Teheran.

"Why, of course," said Walker, his expression grave. "The new regime is anarchist and utterly committed to taking the country back to the Stone Age. No education, no women's rights, no free trade, no civil rights, nothing. They're bent on replacing a sophisticated, modern democracy with an 11th century theocracy run by a bunch of guys in black-and-white bathrobes."

"I'm sorry, Walker, but I see it very differently. The Shah's regime was run by some very special interests helped by the CIA," said Zoe. "And we've seen this all before. Like Vietnam, maybe? Or how about Nicaragua? Or Afghanistan? Or Iraq? Or Venezuela?"

She shook her head. "It should not be about doing things our way, the American agenda. Maybe it's about having enough respect for the emerging nations to leave them alone to make their own decisions. Maybe it's not about our version of freedom, maybe it's about letting traditional societies find their own way. But we always seem to take the shorts cuts, and in the end, it's about controlling the oil, right?" She glared, "Walker, I know it's not the military interests that run this stuff."

Walker remained silent, regarding her with a blank expression.

Sally stepped forward, reaching a hand to her friend. "Zoe," she said gently, "maybe our country's leaders seem out of touch, but they do have more information than we do to make decisions for overseas policy. I think it's just above our pay-grade."

Zoe whirled. "That's the whole problem. It *is* our business. It is the business of the everyday person to get passionately involved and ask questions and demand accountability."

She shook her head. "We seem to elect people who get involved in other nations' business, without any real understanding of the issues of history. We're blowing it again all over the Middle East, just like Vietnam. We swore we wouldn't let it happen, but it's crystal clear that we're allowing the bureaucrats to run the whole show, and they don't care about ideology or doing the right thing. It's all about power and control."

Sally said, "Zoe, it isn't like that; we elect people we trust."

Zoe turned. "You are absolutely right. We elect people we trust, but they can't do anything without the huge immoveable bureaucracy, all the alphabet soups of government agencies, the little grey men in dark suits who write the plans that dictate the nation's direction. We—all of us—we are the irresponsible ones, stuck in some Yankee Doodle Dandy dream that our government servants—not elected, dammit—will do the right thing, and serve this country honorably. You seem to think other countries are beholden to us as their saviors, but we know differently from our trips, from our local friends. But hey, we ignore the warning signs and their anger, and just go shopping in the *souks*."

Sally stood her ground. "I don't know, Zoe. These are huge, multi-faceted international issues that have complex consequences, and we can't know how to deal in those circles."

Zoe laughed, a hollow sound. "Sally, stop being so goddamned naïve. That is such paternalistic bullshit. You said the right word—it's about trust, and I don't trust these manipulative bastards as far as I can throw them."

She shook her head. "You know, we are losing something really valuable here; Pan Am has been independent icon of America around the world, and people came to us as insiders because they could rely on us."

She turned to Sally. "Remember Saigon? And the evacuations

in Central America and Africa and Teheran? People counted on us…the old Blue Meatball…because we got it done, and we got it done right the first time with no excuses about whose ass got burned. But now the Pan Am brass have made so many enemies in Washington that it's getting dangerous, and the CIA's got its own airline—they think they don't need us anymore."

She sighed. "It is total crap to say we don't know what has been happening to our airline through the political establishment. These nameless people in powerful agencies have intentionally gutted this incredibly complex international company because they can't control it." She looked directly at the small circle around her.

Zoe said, "I think I've just seen too much in my time. Now it's all about doing the right deal as dictated by a small bunch of faceless guys in Langley, the Department of Transportation, and a whole lot of other government bureaucrats who have the ears of Presidents and Congressmen and business cartels, and who are the real architects of this not-so-great global society we seem to be heading towards. I'm afraid for all of us, because we have allowed it to happen … we have lost control."

She looked at Walker. "Walker, the irony is that the guys in uniform are truly the last honorable servants of our society. It's the civilians that run the show, but it's all hidden and we don't even know their names. How incredible it would be if we could break through the code and the political shadow play and decipher the bullshit. But something tells me that someday soon, something awful will happen that will affect all of us, because we didn't pay attention to the political deals that were being made, and the power of the oil interests."

She drew herself up, and nodded to them all. "You know, I certainly did not intend to turn this family gathering into a fish-or-cut-bait session, but here it is, so I'm dealing with it. Sally and Jack, I love you and everything you have done for me, and I love all of our friends, but I cannot watch this anymore. I've decided to accept a scholarship at the Society of Oriental and Asian Studies in London. It's the best chance I'll ever have to work on the historical record, to tell the truth as I see it. And I can support Hawea and me by flying out of Pan Am's base there."

Sally stood slack-jawed, astounded and angry that Zoe had made such a huge decision without her knowledge. "Zoe, this is ridiculous. You just can't do this," she said sharply.

Zoe said, "I don't have a choice. I do respect and love this nation. But I don't have any use for the power-and-control freaks who are burrowing deep into our government, and who will in a few short years start to run the show. What they do is dishonorable, to us, and most of all, to those of you in uniform. I hope you'll keep watching." Walker nodded gravely.

Zoe nodded to Sally and Jack. "I think it's best if Keoki and I take Hawea for a sail now." She scooped up Hawea, now stirring from a nap on the warm sands with Malia, and Keoki joined them, while Sally pleaded with Jack and Walker to go after her. Frustrated, Sally started to walk down the beach, but Jack held her arm, counseling silence.

Later that night, Zoe and Keoki sailed down a moonlit passage, while Hawea lay sleeping at her breast. On the ocean, they headed out towards the deep water, the winds keening in the sheets, the cleats rattling, stars gleaming down, almost big enough to touch. Wordlessly they embraced, perhaps for the last time. It did not matter that he had other dreams, other women, other islands in his mind. It did not matter than she had just bluntly severed her place in this familiar world, and was now floating free, stateless, flying, displaced again. They embraced and held on to the brief sparks of the old fire. Hawea stirred between them.

On a blustery morning a few months later, Lucien and Kaleo reluctantly took Zoe and Hawea to the airport. Malia wept openly as they embraced, before boarding the flight to Los Angeles and on to London.

Lucien shook his head, "This is not right. Sally needs to see you to say goodbye."

Zoe said gravely, "No, Lucien. There's nothing to worry about. I simply have things I have to do now, and the rest does not matter. Hawea will always have her Auntie Sally, Zoe Pualani will always know her godmother, and you two will always be the glue. Keoki's back in the Northwest Hawai'ian Islands where he needs to be. And Hawea and I have places to discover and lots to learn, and we'll be back from time to time. As long as Pan Am's around, I'll be able to stay close."

On January 20, 1981, Ronald Reagan was sworn in as the 40th President of the United States. That same day, Ayatollah Khomeini announced the release of the 66 hostages following 444 days of captivity. A new world order had arrived. Zoe, her long-term leave of absence approved, sat hunched in the warm breakfast room of her University study, Hawea sleeping at her side, surrounded by a new world of books and history and learning. For a moment, she thought of the warmth of the Pacific, the whoosh of the deep blue seas, the rhythm of Keoki steering the canoe, and the moonlit passages of faraway islands. And then, unbidden, the violet eyes of a man smiling at her, locked with her in passion at dawn, the call of a muezzin floating on the wind.

CHAPTER NINETEEN

TE DEUM LAUDAMUS
DECEMBER 21, 1988   OUTBOUND LONDON/NEW YORK
PAN AM FLIGHT 103

Zoe heaved her crew-bag over the aircraft's wet doorsill, the rain seeping around the jetway's transom on this rainy evening. Hawea's nanny had been late arriving at the flat, so she'd rushed to the airport in a hurry. As she passed through the doorway, she noticed a small chip in the molding of the emergency slide.

"Damn, *Morning Light,* here you are again!" She smiled ruefully at the maintenance chief, who turned the pages of the ship's maintenance log for the engineer's signature as he headed out on his pre-flight check. Making a bet with herself, she checked the history of cabin maintenance items going back several weeks. Sure enough, N739PA's aft toilet banks had been inoperable on at least 15 log entries, and all had been written off. One acknowledgement out of Amsterdam responded to the entry "Toilet 4-3 broken," with a terse, "Still broken, but trying." She laughed and showed the maintenance chief.

"Yes, miss, sometimes it's a bit tough to get all these moving parts moving in the proper order." He noted that the aircraft had just come in from San Francisco some four hours earlier, and they had not been able to schedule several major cabin items due to a worker shortage and the weather.

She responded, "You know, Chief, this *Clipper Morning Light* is almost older than I am! I remember her from that tiny chip on the slide cover at the L-1 door on my training flight in 1970, and the damned toilet was broken then!"

He laughed, "G'wan, then. Yer not that old! Besides, she was *Morning Light* for a long bit, and then the big brains changed her name to protect the innocent. Now they've called her *Maid of the Seas.*"

Look, they've even repainted the name on the nosecone." And sure enough, they had.

Zoe said, "I surely did not know that, but thanks for the history lesson. I feel younger already." He saluted and sauntered off the airplane while she turned to her duties, thinking of the day's events and watching the parade on the ramp below. Maintenance workers in blue uniforms swarmed over the exterior of the aircraft, refueling from massive fuel points set into the cement apron and conferring over maintenance items. Ramp workers drove out the long buggies of baggage containers, which had sat in the rain all day, unsupervised, set up by some anonymous daily planning docket. She looked casually out as the ramp workers maneuvered the first silver baggage container tagged AVE4041 up the belt. Engines roared from the takeoff runway, aluminum baggage cans rattled, and voices crackled loudly on two-way radios, their words indistinct. Permeating all of this familiar mayhem was the heavy, sweet-thick smell of jet fuel and machine oil and the constant scream of accelerating engines.

Zoe looked out at the rain falling steadily, softly, creating a grey ground fog on the tarmac and a ghostly pall over the other aircraft in the middle taxiway as they glided past towards the active runway, their colors muted in the mist. In the First Class galley before her, two port stewards conferred with the flight attendant on duty, covering the inventory of meals, equipment, supplies and special orders that had been loaded and labeled in each galley compartment. They laughed companionably, and the younger of the two men, a handsome man of Mediterranean complexion, flirted amiably with the attractive German flight attendant. Zoe smiled, catching the eye of the older steward and rolling her eyes, causing him to laugh out loud and nudge his colleague. She laughed, shaking her head and heading down the left aisle to the economy section galley.

Several of the crewmembers were gathered there, discussing the latest in the depressing news about Pan Am's seemingly endless financial woes while they went about the business of preparing for another load of passengers. They were a collegial, cosmopolitan group. Zoe had met or flown with most of them in one place or another. She had shared the December 24th birthday of the French woman some years ago in Beirut at a wild all-night party. She heard the accents of Germany, England, Ireland, Spain and the Scandinavian countries. Crewmembers recounted stories of paying several hundred dollars to commute from Berlin to London on a Pan Am subsidiary, and then working back from London to Frankfurt later that day. It was a crazy world, and every dollar was measured twice.

Most of Pan Am's business and First Class customers were repeat flyers with literally millions of air-miles in their Pan Am Mileage accounts which they never used, and in-flight services which they rarely were awake to enjoy, other than extra leg-room and silence.

This afternoon as she got off the express bus from London, Zoe had seen one of them, a senior vice-president of an international defense supplier, at the First Class check-in counter and made a detour to greet him. James Horsey harrumphed as usual. "Spumoni yesterday, Zoe, Spumoni out of Frankfurt."

She regarded him gravely and replied, "Mr. Horsey, the German caterers have it rough; they have to appease the chocolate and vanilla crowd as well as us strawberry fans. We'll try not to let it happen again, sir." She patted his arm and smiled.

He grimaced in place of an answer, and looked at her appraisingly. "Have I ever mentioned that you need to get away from these third-rate sons of bitches?"

Zoe laughed, "Yes, sir, I do believe you've mentioned that on a few occasions."

This time he regarded her seriously, "Well, you just make sure you're protected against the storms. They'll take us all down, and I tell 'em that regularly in Washington."

Zoe glanced down at his ticket jacket. "You aren't travelling to New York this evening with me?"

"No, I'm afraid I've got to get to Washington for an early meeting. But if you are coming back to London on Tuesday, I'll see you then."

Zoe smiled affectionately at him, knowing his reputation as a curmudgeon. He was a lonely, hard-working driven businessman and philosophical idealist who cared deeply for his country and his work, and she enjoyed his brittle humor and wisdom. "It's a date then," she said, patting his shoulder again.

Jim Horsey looked at her carefully and spoke softly. "Watch everything and everyone, Zoe. These are challenging times, especially since the *USS Vincennes* incident this last July, and it pays to be very careful. Take extra care of yourself." She nodded, discomfited, as she walked away towards the secure elevators leading to the cargo ramps and crew briefing areas in the world's busiest airport, her nerve-endings tingling with a faint whisper of apprehension. When does the luck run out?

As soon as she had signed in at the Briefing Desk, she looked around for her briefing room assignment and fellow crewmembers. She was flying only when absolutely necessary to keep her emergency qualification and Purser status current. She'd completed all her doctoral dissertation requirements, and expected to be moving on to her new career in research archaeology with the prestigious School of Oriental and African Studies. She'd tell Jim Horsey on Tuesday, knowing he'd be pleased.

Today, she was travelling as a supernumerary Purser, check-riding probationary flight attendants, and was scheduled to do several check-rides on the way back to London in two days. There were 13 working crew altogether, almost all based in London. The cockpit crew was from New York, and all were tired from the ongoing anonymity of the new scheduling policies, in which practically everyone was a stranger. The cabin crew were somewhat alienated by the new locked doors and cockpit-exclusive rules. Everything appeared to be more-or-less on time for a 6 p.m. departure, with the cooperation of the weather.

The load was forecast at 257, with a few deadheading crew and Christmas vacation non-revenue passengers hitching a ride stateside for the holidays ahead. There was the usual mix of Europeans, Americans, students, diplomats, military and civilian families, single soldiers, businessmen and professionals. As was typical these days, the load was heavy in First Class and Clipper Class, and fairly light in the three economy sections, where savvy travelers could snag several adjacent seats in a row for a good night's sleep. She had volunteered to work in the First Class section where there was an extra jumpseat, and the load certainly warranted the extra hand. The briefing was soon over, and the crew dispersed for duty-free shopping, set to reconvene at the boarding gate at 5:50 p.m.

The passenger service agents announced a brief delay in boarding due to extra security checks, and she thought again with qualms of Mr. Horsey's warning earlier that evening. What was the use, she thought, of planning for one more in an endless series of disasters that committed terrorists could get around, if they had a mind to do so?

She thought of the dozens of security breaches over the years, the flurry of security actions following them, the sophomoric silliness in First Class cabins as senior business executives tried to identify the Sky Marshall. And the Marshalls themselves were none too stable; usually they were paramilitary men with a history in Vietnam or law enforcement, often trigger-happy and slightly paranoid, intimidated by the cosmopolitan internationalism of the airline industry, and always lonely. These Justice Department and Treasury employees were often trained to guard politicians and presidents, but they did not deal well with the constant variables in the airline industry, where no day and no flight was like any other.

Zoe felt sorry for them, and often took a few moments to sit with them and go over the passenger manifest. One Marshall, who wore heavy Navajo jewelry and a serious crew cut, had been very helpful in helping to decode information on passenger manifests; how to group people, who matched, who didn't, the tiny movements that could signal trouble. He had a tattoo on his wrist underneath his watchband, in which she could decipher the letters "V-i-e-t ..." and surmised the rest. Hello, brother, she had thought, suddenly remembering that they'd had a cup of coffee in Istanbul, and he instantly tried to hit on her.

Recently, there had been dozens of delays due to bomb scares. She and her fellow crewmembers had often been "volunteered" for early boarding duties to go through every seat searching for allegedly thin bags of fake plastique or C-4. Who knew? The "practice plastique" looked like Hawea's silly putty. They'd had alert codes— Bravo Whiskey Charlie and Code Red—and numerical series that were supposed to disarm the bomber, based on PSYOPS profiles. All were courtesy of some consultant's grandiose plan. Rumors abounded, and there was a growing climate and culture of fear. The USS Vincennes incident was a horrible mistake that had happened on July 3, just six months ago when the ship had misidentified an Iran Air airbus flight from Bandar Abbas to Dubai as an F-14 Tomcat, and had unwittingly shot 290 people out of the sky, including more than 60 children.

This was the stuff of late-night galley conversations and the few crew parties that still took place. Pilots and conservative crewmembers argued for more security. Zoe vehemently argued against it. "The only thing that works is random checking. We should do it the Israeli way—a handsome Sabra with a huge smile and an Uzi submachine gun." The crews laughed at the idea.

"Soon," she said, "the entire industry will be gridlocked in fear, but we'll never feel safe enough because the fear is in us, not in the bombers. They know how to manipulate our fear, and we enable them. We're handing over our freedoms whenever we submit to racial profiling, to ritual searches and an endless stream of edicts to be afraid of everything." She knew that fellow crewmembers passed looks and shook their heads, relegating her to the status of an eccentric, but they were uneasy, too. And everywhere, there were rumors and gossip about more incidents of anti-Americanism and passive-aggressive behavior, of smiles and non-cooperation.

This evening, with time on her hands after boarding the aircraft and checking the emergency equipment at her station, she took a few minutes in the jumpseat to gather her thoughts. She closed her eyes for an instant, picturing the events of that afternoon. And she had letters to write, she reminded herself.

As a Christmas treat, she had taken Hawea to St. Martin-In-The-Fields to introduce her to one of their oldest traditions: the opportunity for children to make their very own brass rubbing from dozens of etched plaques and carved headstones. Hawea had chosen a damsel in a wimple and elaborate coned headdress, her gown flowing, her hand lifted in greeting.

Zoe recalled the light filtering down from a stained-glass window onto the serious face of her daughter, her riot of soft tightly curly hair, her violet-grey eyes focused on the work of rubbing a silver crayon against a dark parchment taped to the plaque.

She listened to the men's choir perform the "Te Deum", a Latin hymn of thanksgiving, their sonorous voices echoing in the cloisters. When she thought of what she had to be thankful for, she fingered the tiny silver Pyu coin, with its image of the shrivatsa, the endless knot, still on its worn chain around her neck. On impulse, she unfastened it and put it around Hawea's neck, to match the silver sheen on the rubbing. Hawea's eyes regarded her seriously, "Thanks mummy. I always think of you when I see the shell shining." And she spun it, smiling.

She returned to the moment, to look through the preliminary passenger manifest, listed by name and seat number. Businessmen and senior professionals in the First Class and Upper Lounge, many with VIP codes next to their names: DALPO—do all possible, or EXCOR—extend courtesies. A number of diplomats, techies and university professors in Business Class were often distinguished by their titles. She thought of the impossibly handsome man she'd known briefly, seated opposite her jumpseat, his slow smile of recognition, their brief and white-hot affair. Pahlavian had reappeared in her life just days before with pleasant surprises, and they'd agreed to have dinner when she returned, after Christmas. Nowadays, most surprises have to do with who might blow us up.

She noted two stars in the Clipper Class section: Gannon, 14-J and McKee, 15-F, who appeared to be travelling under diplomatic status but with military recognition. Another Swedish diplomat named Carlsson was seated nearby in 17-H. She frowned slightly and noted the anomaly.

In the economy sections, the demographics loosened up and passengers were spread out, leaving empty rows in the middle of the aircraft. The list showed lots of single travelers—professionals or sales executives, military officers and enlisted, some with family members seated next to them. There would be many students travelling alone for the holidays. She noted the name of a young student, Khalid Jaafar in 53-K, almost the last row, as the only "profile" candidate on the plane. Stop being stupid, she told herself. There were several young couples.

Some special needs coded: diabetic meal, vegetarian, hamburgers, seats together. No birthdays or wedding cakes today. These codes were clustered around seven families travelling with elderly parents or teenagers, some younger children. Baby meals and bassinets were noted for six infants and toddlers travelling with their families. On a flight like this, it would be easy to move passengers around, ensuring an empty seat next to a young military sergeant travelling with her infant child in seat 32-K.

Waiting for the boarding announcement, she took a few moments to observe the actions of the young flight attendant she was check-riding, noting her calm assurance and professional demeanor with approval. She thought of her training check-ride so many years ago with Sally—sweet Sally so far away in Hawai'i, so happy and settled. She was sorry that their friendship had gone on hold.

She suddenly remembered the letter she needed to finish, and pulled out a Christmas card and envelope, ready to mail when the passenger service agent closed the door. The envelope was already addressed to Mr. and Mrs. Jack Wright, and she wrote quickly.

Sally, Jack and Zoe P,

Happy holidays, and we hope to see you soon. I'm sorry for letting all this time go by, because our friendship is more important than anything.

You probably know I've seen Keoki from time to time. He is in New York and I'll see him tomorrow, almost for Christmas. Most important…remember my story of Sao Johnny? I had a letter from old friends in Thailand who knew him. He had been working closely with the Air America folks on the border after the war, and apparently had information on Billy. Don't know how recent but I'm following up. I thought you'd want to know.

There's something else. This is really for Jack and my legal files. An Iranian man named Cyrus Pahlavian may contact him with some interesting DNA information on Hawea. I can't give you all the details right now, but will try to fill you in. You know, in life, there are always surprises.

Stay safe,

Zoe

She put a stamp on the letter and stuck it in the headrest of the jumpseat to remind herself to hand it to the passenger service agent.

Zoe noticed that another Army family, the Williams family from

Crown Point, New York, were traveling with a two infants, one barely two months old, the other less than a year, seated in two seats, 46JK, with their parents, according to the rules. Now I know we can do better than that, she thought, circling the names and looking for an empty row instead of squashing the family into the practically the narrowest spot on the aircraft. She kept on at her detective game. It wasn't rocket science; after a while, you could read details of people's lives long before you saw them passing through the aisles, or sitting in front of you.

The old-timers and the Sky Marshalls had taught her to read the manifests, something crews rarely had time to do these days, but it gave an airline an advantage to find someone a birthday cake and have the crew sing, to deliver a bottle of champagne for an anniversary or to an obviously enamored honeymoon couple, or even to folks who had just met. At least tonight, just a few days before Christmas, she thought it might be a great gesture to offer a bottle of champagne to the oldest passenger, seated in 26-F, Ibolya Robertine Gabor, a 79-year-old Hungarian who had ordered a wheelchair on arrival in New York.

Military personnel were noted on the manifest for any special duties and emergency assistance, primarily because of their training. Some Pursers at holiday times offered on-the-spot upgrades, or asked other passengers to step aside to allow the young soldiers to leave the aircraft first, a form of honor reserved only to the Purser's discretion, and not found in any regulation book.

She took her assigned position as the passenger-boarding phase was announced, greeting passengers cheerfully and recognizing names or seat numbers she had noted.

The Purser signaled the imminent departure by announcing that the doors had been closed, and she realized that her letter to Sally was stuck on the jumpseat. Oh well, she thought, retrieving it and sticking it in her purse. I'll mail it in New York tomorrow.

She moved the Williams family and blocked the seats for Lawanda Thomas and her tiny son Jonathan. There were very few requests: water here, a pillow there, junior pilot or Purser wings to children under 12.

The aircraft hummed along its taxiway, finally turning into the active runway and revving for takeoff position. She noted her watch at 6:56 p.m., the clouds still scudding by with intermittent rain and a fitful sunset, as the huge aircraft started its ponderous take-off roll. She pressed her head back, completely relaxed, always anticipating this special moment when rotation took away the thudding roar and the thousands of pounds of aircraft became airborne, every time a miracle of flight.

The mechanical systems took over, growling hydraulics, hissing air and pressure equalizers, unknown thuds and clangs in galleys and below-decks as items shifted. She drifted again, thinking again of the magnificent chanting reverberating off the vaulted ceiling of St. Martin's, stroking Hawea's soft springy hair and the curve of her cheek. She thought of the phone call from Keoki that evening as she was leaving for the airport. He'd be in New York tomorrow, meeting with major sponsors for the Polynesian Voyaging Society and doing a presentation at the Explorers' Club. They were talking occasionally, a tenuous relationship picked up again after so many years, but she simply did not think about where it might lead.

She thought about her discussions with Pahlavian in recent weeks. He had married, had no children. His wife had returned to Iran. He was hopeful of immigrating to the United States, and wondered if she could help. They had walked with Hawea in the park, and she'd seen his recognition of the child's eyes, so similar to his own. Life had taken her to so many places, and she felt there were miles to go. She had smiled at them both, but said nothing.

She thought of the Christmas dinner she had always planned, but not this year: roast goose and fruit stuffing, new potatoes, fresh peas, mince pies, a flamed Christmas pudding. It was always a splurge for her but she did it every year, even in Hawai'i, and had invited close friends or her fellow students in recent years in London, as well as Hawea's classmates and friends. She remembered rounding up the frozen Christmas puddings steamed in July and re-soaking them with more brandy. "Those things are lethal weapons, Zoe," Sally would admonish. "Nobody eats that stuff, it is just nut-and-fruit-soaked booze!"

Zoe left her seat, smiling at the memory, heading for the galley and the coffee-maker controls, while the galley attendant labored over folding starched napkins into elaborate designs for the cart presentations. As the bitter-nutty smell of fresh coffee filled the galley, Zoe folded a napkin over the center console, and then stood along the main Purser station at the left side of the aircraft. The Clipper had banked out over the English countryside, and 20 minutes into the flight was now proceeding out towards the Atlantic Ocean, crossing over the coast of Scotland barely visible far below. They were only a few minutes late, and a long, peaceful night lay ahead.

Suddenly, Zoe's eyes snapped open. She had no reason to feel concern; there was no signal, no violent movement. She just felt cold, then colder, and her heart pounded with a fear of something coming, coming fast, coming soon. She looked around, apprehensive that this was some sort of heart attack, that she should alert someone. She thought of the legends of Asia and the Polynesians who could sense disaster. She thought of her childhood nightmares of the cobra in its lair, poised to strike, its eyes glinting.

At a distance, she watched the Chief Purser in his dinner jacket walking down the aisle distributing immigration cards. Hanging onto the jumpseat frame, she managed to keep her composure and gazed for a moment at the winking wing-lights outside, feeling the smooth acceleration of the engines, breathing deeply, waiting for the panic to pass.

And then the world exploded around her where she stood, braced momentarily at her workstation, and she felt her breath sucked out as the huge aircraft was pulverized by massive explosions beneath her feet, and the world disappeared into the cold, freezing air and howling winds of a nightmare and the cobra's roar.

She dreamed of the darkness of a Hawai'ian night long ago, floating down a moonless windward passage at sea between night-dark islands, clasped in Keoki's arms, held safe by a tandem harness and his strong hard, warm body, both of them straining to gusty tradewinds and the clatter of the sails on a dark starlit night, the glint of phosphorescent sea creatures in the embracing waters, the thick, acrid smell of his rubber wet suit, the smell of the air of the sea and sky. And she knew her time had come.

She thought of Hawea's warmth, her nine year-old beauty, her laughing eyes and beautiful soul reflected in the transcendent afternoon light at St. Martin's. She thought of Keoki—oh, so close—smelling of the fragrance of salt and the clean sea. And she let life go of life as death approached.

Te Deum, laudamus, she breathed.

She was not afraid. She felt the comforting presence of other spirits that were long gone: Pualani's smile, Po Sein and Khin Khin Su from so long ago, her guardians throughout this transient life, and the blessings of a generous God. The earth hurtled up towards her and she breathed out, a long sigh of relief with no sob to catch her at the end. She composed herself as she heard Keoki's voice in her mind, gently instructing her, "Arch your back. Arch your back. Trust me and you'll be safe…don't freeze or tense up…be relaxed and open your mouth…extend your limbs like a crab…hang on." It was the ultimate act of almost sexual surrender as she inhaled, fighting for her position in the skies, willing herself to face the stars and greet the light with her back arched and the wind screaming past her. Her mind was clear, a glorious, ineffable light shone brightly as she recalled the tones of the hymn, *"sanctus, sanctus"*, the cold not biting anymore, no anger any more, no fear of pain or death, her heart and mind filled with all the loves and laughter of the years.

She closed her eyes and willed herself to fly into infinity.

On the other side of the world, on the island of Oahu, the morning broke through a curtain of wind and rain. Sally awoke suddenly from a deep sleep, startled by a sudden gust of wind coursing though the tall Norfolk pines that surrounded their home. She rose quietly, careful not to awaken Jack. She slipped on a heavy terry cloth robe and a pair of slippers, then walked out of the bedroom past her sleeping daughter Zoe's room and made her way down the steps, running her hand lightly on the wrought iron banister. As she passed through the living room, she caught a glint of silver in the corner, the tinsel of their Christmas tree. Once out in the yard, she gazed toward the dark ridge of the Waianae Mountains, searching for answers. The lights of Kalihi and Pearl City shimmered below. A lone aircraft lifted off from Honolulu International and turned away from the island, soundless, its lights flashing.

Then came another gust of wind, this one more urgent. Sally had lived in the islands long enough to know that the ancient Hawaiians paid attention to these signs. She did not know what this wind was trying to tell her, but it made her uncomfortable. Shivering, she went back inside and crawled under the pile of quilts beside Jack and went back to sleep, secure in his warmth.

Later that morning, Jack had taken Zoe Pualani down the hill to a birthday party. Sally was in the kitchen baking Christmas cookies when the telephone rang. She hesitated before she picked up the receiver, remembering the cold gusts of wind in the early morning.

"Sally, this is Jennifer Edgerton calling from London. I'm a Pan Am supervisor here at the London base. I'm here at Zoe's house with Hawea and the housekeeper." Her voice sounded muffled, deadened.

Sally's spirits sank. "Is everything all right?"

"Sally," Jennifer said, "Pan Am's just had a crash. A 747 went down over a place called Lockerbie village up in Scotland. Flight 103 from London headed to New York. I'm sorry to tell you that Zoe was on board with 247 passengers and crew."

Sally's shoulders slumped and she sat down at the kitchen table. This is the end, she thought.

"Sally, Zoe and all the others on board may be gone. You might want to turn on the television and find out what the status is; the BBC reporters say that one minute the pilots were talking to Prestwick getting their overwater clearances, the next they were off the radar screen. No hint of a problem, no May Day, no nothing. They...they think it was a bomb." Jennifer's voice dissolved into a hoarse whisper.

Sally groaned.

Jennifer continued. "There is absolutely nothing to be done now, and you know that Hawea is safe with us. I've just volunteered to go to Lockerbie and work with the recovery teams, and I'll report as I can. Watch the news, hug your family, and pray for all of us."

The phone went silent. Sally nodded, as she headed for the

television room.

Half an hour later, Jack returned. He heard Sally screaming before he had even reached the house. He found her standing in the television room, sobbing, fists knotted, shrieking at the top of her lungs, "You bastards…you goddamn bastards…you killed them all! You killed Zoe!" When he reached her, she collapsed in his arms, still screaming and sobbing.

"Sweetheart, what on earth?" He could hear the words "Lockerbie" and "Pan Am 103 crash" spoken in somber tones by the television announcer.

"Zoe's flight crashed," Sally sobbed. "It had just taken off from London, and…and she's gone." Jack helped her sit down on the *pune'e*. Then the enormity of the tragedy became clear to him as the announcer parroted words: "…no survivors, 31,000 feet, unable to commence rescue activities, fatalities on the ground, suspected terrorist bomb…."

"God in heaven," he said slowly, "Zoe's gone? Oh, Jesus."

Then Sally broke completely. Her brilliant, driven, friend had been blown out of the sky by terrorists.

Their worst fears were confirmed later that night when, as daylight broke in far-away Scotland, the networks were broadcasting an unforgettable image that sent chills around the world: a severed section of the nosecone of the Pan Am jet, lying on its side on the ground, its edges in shards, the clear legend on the side panel that read: *Maid of the Seas.* There were additional images of an enormous smoking crater in the town in a section known as Sherwood Crescent, that had taken the lives of 11 people from three families and neighbors, plus reports of wreckage scattered over an 80-mile area.

For hours they had hardly moved from the television room. A phone call came in from Keoki in New York, having heard the news on every television station. He was angry and bitter in his grief, but relieved to know that Hawea was safe in London. She and Jack discussed the next steps. Another call came from Clarice James, who was now a newly minted attorney with the National Transportation Safety Board, and promised to keep them current on the progress of the investigation. Sally and Clarice cried together, remembering those days of innocence so long ago when they were trainees in Miami.

"Jack," said Sally, the fog clearing momentarily as she put aside her grief to think of Zoe's daughter Hawea. "If it's okay with you and Keoki, Hawea must come live with us. It's the best thing for her, and we'll make sure that Keoki's comfortable with the arrangements."

When Sally and Jack brought Keoki home on his return from New York, he was weighed down with sadness. He did not have to be convinced; he was grateful for Jack and Sally's offer of shelter for Hawea. He sighed. "I'll do everything I can to be her father when this voyaging is done. She'll be so lucky to have you love her. It's the Hawai'ian *hanai* family way," he said, speaking of the informal adoption system that had existed in the islands for centuries. He hugged them long and hard. Lucien and Kaleo, as Hawea's godparents, were included in all the family discussions and spent long hours comforting Sally with their presence, their incessant banter, and cooking skills.

It wasn't long before it was determined that the *Maid of the Seas* had been brought down by a plastic explosive called Semtex that had been placed inside a radio, then packed in a bag that was eventually loaded inside a forward cargo compartment in the aircraft hold. The disaster was no longer being investigated as an accident; this was now was an act of terrorism, of mass murder. Zoe and the other passengers on board had been murdered in cold blood. Clarice called to let them know that formal charges were pending.

Sally learned more of the dreadful details from Jennifer and other Pan Am sources during their telephone conversations concerning Hawea's move to Hawai'i. She thought of the London-based employees, who felt under siege from media and security interests, and dunning lawyers looking for cases, and the endless rumors of conspiracy and underworld implications from many sources.

The television news went into endless detail, describing the macabre remains scattered across the countryside and the contents of hundreds of suitcases—Christmas presents were found still wrapped, along with children's toys, a tray of hors d'oeuvres, clothes, shoes.

They had discussed the worst subject of all with Jennifer and the investigation chief. Indistinguishable human remains were identified through DNA or dental records to the extent practical. No trace of Zoe's body was found, only a soiled, blue jacket with her name-badge affixed, and a near empty purse with her name on the label. The purse contained a waterlogged letter, only a few words decipherable. But the envelope was addressed to Sally, and the investigator promised to send it on to Jack as Zoe's legal counsel.

As the investigation progressed, Jennifer and Clarice confirmed inside information. "The most ominous thing we've heard from the investigators was that the terrorists had intended to blow the aircraft out of the sky over the ocean so no traces of evidence would be found. They feel it will happen again."

Late one day, Jennifer cried on the phone, "You know, Sally, this is the end. It will take a while but this is it. We see it every day on every aircraft with all the crewmembers—the fear in people's eyes, their reluctance to talk to us. That is the very worst of it." Her steady, assured voice broke. "One simply cannot do more to reassure them."

The rumors of a Lockerbie conspiracy continued, now focusing on Libya. There were other suspects, but almost everywhere, allegations included the name of a senior Libyan official and intelligence expert Mohmed Al-Megrahi and his links to Moammar Gaddafi, Libya's leader. There was international condemnation, wrangling, but no legal action.

Jack sighed, conferring with Clarice. "It'll be years. Years before there's a formulated theory of what happened. Years to determine who is responsible and how to prosecute, just…years." He shrugged helplessly, talking often to Keoki about the legal implications for the terrorist act, but also to reassure him about Hawea, and offering him a home with them in between his ocean voyages.

"I'm grateful, and I'll come as often as the budget allows," Keoki said. In the meantime, you've a big job on your hands. Hawea's every bit as feisty as her mother was. And, you know, remember that last discussion you had on the beach? Zoe was right. There's no way around it. Those bastards saw all this coming, and did nothing."

In late January, Sally stood solemnly in front of the Gate 31 jetway area at Honolulu International Airport with Keoki beside her. Jennifer had called the previous night after putting Hawea on the London/Los Angeles flight, reporting that she was excited about her trip to Hawai'i, away from the sadness and the cold of London. Jennifer said, "She's quite remarkable. She knows her mother is gone and that she died in the Lockerbie tragedy, but she's quite calm and realistic about traveling, and not afraid at all. We've got supernumerary crew who will transit her from London to Los Angeles, and another escort on to Honolulu tomorrow; of course she insists she doesn't need it. I wish more adults had her fortitude." They rang off, with promises to check in as soon as Hawea had reached her new home.

The 747 nosed up to the Gate area, and Sally watched as passengers emerged. Then a uniformed flight crewmember appeared, holding hands with a slender young girl with olive skin, who broke away from the flight attendant escort and ran into Keoki's arms, burying her head in his chest.

"It's all right, sweetie, it's all right," said Sally. "You're here with us now, and your Daddy. She put her hands on the child's shoulders and enfolded her in her arms. Then something caught her eye; around Hawea's neck was the ancient Pyu necklace that Zoe had always worn. Hawea stroked it and said solemnly, "Mummy gave it to me right before she left, at the old church. She always said it was her memory, so it's my memory now."

Keoki crouched next to her, holding her close. "Hawea, you have your mother's strong heart, which you have to share with us all. We all need that courage. *E komo mai, kuuipo,* welcome home."

CHAPTER TWENTY

AULD LANG SYNE
APRIL 24, 2005   OUTBOUND–LAX/DULLES AIRPORT

Sally dozed lightly aboard the all-night flight from Honolulu through Los Angeles, now bound for Washington D.C, in the early morning light. Two flight attendants appeared at the front row of the cabin with a clanking service cart, struggling to position it in the aisle correctly.

She sat up, thinking of the adventure that lay ahead of her. It had been 30 years since Operation Babylift and the Fall of Saigon; now she would have an opportunity to see, touch and remember so many people and places from so long ago…a lifetime, she thought. And Pan Am had disappeared from the skies almost 15 years ago. Good God, she thought, that makes me practically a relic. She looked at her grown daughters sleeping in their seats. They had reached the age that she and Zoe Longfield had been, when so much chaos had changed their lives. And now these young women were setting their own course in very different ways.

She greeted the stiff-faced flight attendants as the cart reached her, and asked for a cup of coffee, which was provided without a smile or comment in a half-full plastic cup, tepid and tasteless. She sighed, recalling other airborne breakfasts in days gone by: aromatic, piping hot Jamaican Blue Mountain coffee, eggs-to-order, spicy baked tomatoes with parmesan, filet mignon cooked pink, "banger" sausages and hot, flaky pastries. Her mouth watered at the memories.

Sally looked at her adopted daughter Hawea sleeping against the window, the tiny silver Pyu coin she always wore glinting at her neck. She possessed the tall, statuesque build and golden skin that reflected her mixed blood, her hair wound into tight springy curls framing intriguing smoky violet-blue eyes. She was so like Zoe, so feisty and smart—sometimes more than we could handle—Sally noted, remembering difficult teenage negotiations over the years. She and Jack were proud that Hawea was working on her PhD in Archaeology, and crewing with her father Keoki aboard the Polynesian Voyaging Society's ocean-going canoe, the *Hokule'a*, as he lectured and explored archeological sites throughout the Pacific. Where had the time gone?

Her gaze moved to her own daughter, Zoe Pualani, who was so close to her sister they completed each other's sentences. Zoe's blonde hair tumbled to her shoulders and she had her father's extraordinary eyes: startling blue and always smiling. She, too, was a spirited young woman who directed her energies towards remembering everything that happened in her life. Sometimes the intensity of all the detail almost caused her to short circuit, but she had graduated with honors in Journalism and English, and just returned from two years in the Peace Corps working in Indonesia. Her field reports and letters home had provided an outlet for all that descriptive energy, and now she was looking for the perfect reporting job.

Sally reached out to smooth their blankets. She did not have the heart to wake them and envied their ability to sleep so soundly.

Her thoughts turned to Jack. Wonderful, funny, witty, solid-as-a-rock Jack. A formal, serious lawyer by day and a stand-up comic by night, he talked Hawai'ian pidgin to her and the girls, calling them funny names, making up incredible stories and adventures. All these years he had been as steady as the Norfolk pines near their house, loving her and their girls. He had seen them off at the airport in Honolulu yesterday, providing leis and bags of junk food for the girls.

She felt the thump of the airplane's slight reduction in speed, as the Boeing 767 tilted forward to begin its initial descent into Dulles Airport. Crewmembers went through the aisles to clear the cabin. The captain and co-pilot made safety announcements, warning that absolutely no movement was permitted in the cabin for the last half hour of the flight. Sally noted that both voices were female, and smiled at the memory of Zoe Longfield, so contemptuous of these types of precautions. But how she would love to have seen women running the cockpit. She would not have liked the post 9-11 world though, with the gauntlet of security checkpoints, and dozens of new rules run by the bureaucrats she had railed against, so long ago.

The two young women next to her finally stirred, stretched, blinked and came wide-awake almost at once. "Good morning, Mom. Are we almost there?" said Zoe, looking out the window at the plane's descent path and the shadowy fields below. Hawea, more serious and methodical, busied herself organizing the books she was reading into her carry-on bag and shoved it under her seat.

"Jeez, Hawea, how you gonna have time to do things here in Washington if you're going to be reading all those books?" said Zoe. "We have some fun stuff to do, right?"

They bantered back and forth as the aircraft flared, hesitated for a brief second, then landed in a squeal of airbrakes and rumble of hydraulics.

Moving quickly through the crowded arrival hall and the baggage area, they retrieved their bags and found a Washington Flyer about to depart for the city.

"The Willard, please," Sally requested. The traffic was light on this fine spring morning, with a riot of daffodils and crocuses in the median strips. Pulling up in front of the hotel, they moved into the old-world elegance of the lobby, the original home of the professional "lobbyists" that crowded the city. The reception area featured huge bouquets of dried flowers, luxurious carpets and rococo ceilings, gleaming chandeliers and the famous Willard clock.

"Good morning, Mrs. Wright, and welcome to the Willard" said the young receptionist at the check-in counter, handing her keys and a large manila envelope addressed to *"Sally Wilder Wright, Crewmember, Pan Am Saigon Reunion."*

"What is it, Mom?" asked Hawea, peering over her shoulder at the envelope.

Sally was thrilled to see her name noted as crewmember for a Pan Am event, but remained nonchalant. "Probably just details of the event. Let's go see our room so I can check the program." They rounded up a porter and proceeded to the 12th floor, the girls squealing with delight when they walked in the door of the Jenny Lind suite to an elegant sitting room with adjoining bedrooms, overlooking the White House lawn and Pennsylvania Avenue.

The suite was named in honor of the Swedish opera singer who gave a series of concerts in America in the 1850s and broke hearts throughout her tour. There was a pale yellow bedroom with twin beds and attached bath for Hawea and Zoe. Sally's room was decorated in luxurious cream brocade, with a massive wrought-iron four-poster bedstead, and a not-so-old-fashioned Jacuzzi overlooking the Washington Monument through a huge portal window. "This will do *quite* nicely," she said to the porter, as he moved about the room, explaining the amenities, turning on lights, opening armoires, tapping on the wet-bar and television consoles.

Hawea and Zoe grabbed the room service menu. "Okay, Mom. It's time for food and more food—an enormous breakfast and coffee and lots and lots of strawberry jam." Sally marveled at their elegant surroundings as the girls called in their order. "We could just stay here for a week, couldn't we?" they pleaded.

After breakfast they showered, then collapsed into sleep. Sally slept fitfully, dreaming of shadows and old images. In mid-afternoon, she dragged them out of bed saying, "Get dressed girls. We have a special place to go."

Climbing into a taxi, Sally said to the driver, "The Vietnam Memorial, please." While the driver carefully picked his way through snarls of traffic, Sally had a moment of panic about what lay ahead, involving her not-so-maternal history and the events surrounding the Fall of Saigon so long ago.

The taxi pulled over to the curb, and the three women made their way across the Mall, passing the Lincoln and Jefferson Memorials to the pathway of the Vietnam Memorial, known simply as The Wall. They walked carefully and deliberately, carrying flower leis, *kukuna o kala, hala* and fragrant plumeria, grave flowers all and appropriate for memorials—especially for this holy ground.

For the Vietnam Memorial is like no other monument on earth. All visitors come to it as pilgrims. Some call it Gethsemane because of its surrounding garden of rolling green commons dotted with carefully tended beds of flowers. Others call it The Scar, viewing it as a gash of dark stone, a cruel incision that mars a setting reminiscent of the bucolic serenity of Gettysburg. The memorial, designed by a young female architect, answered both the nation's grief and its need to remember and touch the inexplicable. Its simple, stark lines linked the past with many futures: fathers and sons; mothers and children; teachers and students; friends and lovers; war and peace. There are no casual visitors to The Wall, Sally thought, and the experience is different for each and every person.

As soon as they saw the panels set even with the earth's surface in stark, descending rows, they clasped hands, starting the journey together. They moved slowly down the gardenlike ellipse, as if into an outdoor crypt filled with sunshine and new-mown grass. The downhill slope and the long line of panels began to enfold them into the sadness, outrage and courage of this history called Vietnam. They walked downhill together, uneasy, uncomfortable when they suddenly saw their whole images reflected in the polished granite covered with inscriptions of names…and names…and more names. The names were not listed in easy alphabetical order, but in the hardest memory of their lives: the order of the moment and the day and the month and the year in which they fell.

"They died so young," said Zoe Pualani. "Everything was before them." They reached out hesitantly, touching the cold panels, reflecting on the names spreading out endlessly before them, 58,000 and counting.

"You're meant to touch the names," said Sally, tracing them carefully. "When you touch them, you touch their lives and their passing and all they meant; still mirrored in us, here on the other side." She looked at their reflections, always haunted by how The Wall kept creating new participants. Hawea and Zoe reached hesitantly, following Sally's guide.

Sally bowed her head. "This is ours…our legacy."

The voices of The Wall seemed to whisper, "Yes, we shared all of this together."

They touched the names, the last substance of lives recorded on cold stone. They saw the floral offerings, the candles, the cheerful ribbon on a fluttering card, the cans of beer, the rubbings, the letters— all tributes of mourning families, friends, aging lovers. Members of the Vietnam Veterans of America stood constant watch nearby in peaceful contemplation, remembering those honored here, as well as those who came to touch the memories, so many overwhelmed with grief.

And the voices of The Wall echoed back, "There, there, we loved you then and now. We are at peace. We did it for you and our buddies and our nation."

Sally whispered to the girls, "Just remember, The Wall doesn't judge. It doesn't preach. It just remembers." Together, they walked to Sally's own benediction site, reaching out to touch the panel in reverence and salutation.

"I'm here, Billy," Sally said to herself, "I'm here."

At the bottom of the slope, on the last panel at 1W, the last line of 124, were the memories of her generation's last days of war in April of 1975. They stood at the apex, the center, the first panel of 1959 to their left, the last panel of 1975 to their right, all reflected in the cool and forgiving stone. Silently, Sally arranged the strands of perfumed blossoms on the ground below.

And there they were, the names of the last few Marines killed in the Vietnam conflict: Lance Corporal Darwin Lee Judge of Marshalltown, Iowa, 19 years old and in Vietnam less than two weeks, and Corporal Charles McMahon of Woburn, Massachusetts, killed April 29, 1975. On the same panel a few entries later, the name of 1st Lieutenant Michael J. Shea was inscribed along with Captain William C. Nystul.

Then Sally bent to honor the memory of William Hannibal Spencer, and all the pain she could not express. She could hear his voice, "There now, sweet Sally, *I Mua*, no tears."

The memories of the events of those days were as fresh for Sally as the flowers she had placed beneath this last panel. She recalled again the pain mourning, of death without closure, a longing for explanations of events unknown and never properly accounted for. Only the memories came, unbidden, at all the wrong times. She could feel Zoe and Hawea's eyes on her.

She took their arms, saying, "We'll talk later." They walked slowly and silently back up towards the Mall with troubled expressions, the lingering questions not framed. Above them in the late afternoon sky, the contrails of a fast moving jet aircraft described a pattern, reminders of the white and silver aircraft with the blue logos that had once circumnavigated the globe.

All fleeting, Sally thought, but part of the adventures of a lifetime. They returned to the Willard, happy to enjoy an early dinner in the romantic dining room, and Sally retired early, leaving the girls to explore Georgetown clubs.

The Pan Am reunion the next day was joyful and chaotic, much like the evacuation itself 30 years before. The Smithsonian had prepared a special exhibit called "The New Americans" featuring the refugee sagas from Vietnam, Cambodia and Laos. Prominent displays featured stories of Operation Babylift evacuees, ground staff, crewmembers, and grim photographs of the Last Flight Out, and then the Fall of Saigon days later.

Hawea's eyes widened at the entryway, which featured a life-size photograph of her mother—a laughing, vibrant Zoe Longfield holding a chubby infant in her arms, seated with three pilots in the cockpit of the Babylift flight. She sighed, "It's unbelievable. She had this huge life force, didn't she? My mother, happy and laughing, in the middle of the war zone!" The photo was the centerpiece of the exhibition, drawing people's attention to the happiness in so many photographs. Reporters, video photographers and news cameras crowded the aisles.

The room was filled with former Pan Am personnel from Saigon: flight service, cockpit crew and family members. Moving through the crowd were young Vietnamese people in their 30s, strong and handsome former C-5A survivors, Holt orphans, refugees, all thoroughly American and comfortably Vietnamese. Many were already friends from the various refugee and birth-parent associations, and they enthusiastically greeted the former crewmembers and pilots in their midst, identified by large colorful name badges as "Babylift Crew". Sally caught sight of old friends, laughing and hugging her way through the crowd, reminiscing about "Saigon Roulette" all those years before. And there, in the midst of the crew was Lucien, arriving on the spur of the moment as the special guest of the Saigon staff. Sally and the girls embraced him with glee.

Former Station Manager Al Topping, somewhat older and greyer, rose to speak about Pan Am's role in the evacuation during

Saigon's last days. After so many historic "Firsts", he said, he had felt the pain of so many of the airline's "Last Flights" in the later years. He had also officiated at the last flight of Pan Am on December 4, 1991, when the Miami tower brought in the *Clipper Goodwill* from Barbados in a long, low, honorary fly-by pass over the terminal at Dinner Key on its final approach to Miami International Airport. Sally remembered her trip there with Zoe and Pua during training, gazing together at the giant mural that was being restored, their whole lives ahead of them.

Al described the outpouring of emotion by Miami citizens, former employees, passengers, and thousands of well-wishers, at this very last flight arrival. Sally recalled her own last flight: the last Pan Am Pacific flight from Tokyo to Honolulu with Lucien on February 11, 1986, when the Pacific routes were sold to United Airlines. They had been watching when the entire Pan Am maintenance staff filed out onto the tarmac and executed a deep bow, a show of respect and farewell, as the Clipper was pushed back from the gate for the last time. She'd left the airline then, but was never far from old friends and fellow airline veterans. She clutched Lucien's hand as they remembered together.

"It was a day America thought it would never, ever see," said Al of the *Clipper Goodwill's* landing in Miami. "It was the end of an era. For many of us, it was the last, long heartbreak."

The room went entirely silent for a moment. Then Topping returned to the subject of the day: the young veterans of Pan Am's Operation Babylift, the "New Americans" of this exhibition. He introduced the featured speaker, Dr. Michael Peterson, a Vietnamese orphan, and a leader in the linkage between the orphans' history and their American upbringing.

The handsome young man stood. "Good evening, ladies and gentlemen. I am Dr. Mike Peterson. I'm a trauma surgeon at Massachusetts General Hospital in Boston, and I do work for the Red Cross and other NGO relief agencies in various parts of the world whenever they need my help. Thirty years ago, I was one of the orphans on Pan Am's Operation Babylift on April 8th. I was six years old, and my name was Nguyen—at least that's how old they thought

I was—but I do remember quite a few details. What I don't remember was where I came from or who my family was. My parents had both died in the conflict and I had been in an orphanage for several years, and my brother was killed on the C5-A crash. I have scars on my back, but I don't know where they came from. All I can tell you is that when I got on that plane, you all changed my life."

Sally reached for the girls, her eyes brimming. She thought, he's the right age, certainly he could be my Nguyen, the boy with the magic slate and huge smile.

He cleared his throat. "In many ways, it's been a long, hard journey, and it's not over. Many of us fight depression and a feeling of cultural displacement. Many of us have suffered from racism and family dysfunction. But because of Operation Babylift and all the Vietnamese, Laotian and Cambodian immigrants, America has a whole contingent of new citizens who appreciate the opportunity that has been given them. I'd like to think that we, the newest Americans, can help to create a lasting bridge between Asia and America." The audience cheered, and Al Topping returned to the podium.

He said, "As you can imagine, this is an emotional day for me. I need to introduce two very special people, who found each other just today. Madame Bernadette Vuong, who now lives in Paris, wrote a ticket jacket on April 8, 1975 for a little girl who had lost everything and was going abroad to start a new life. Thirty years later, that little girl brought her ticket jacket back today." He waved a blue-and-white Pan Am envelope in the air, "and our amazing Saigon ground personnel recognized Madame Vuong's handwriting. I'd like to present them to you all as Pan Am winners!"

The two emerged on stage, holding hands, as the audience stood to applaud them both. Madame Vuong took the microphone. "Ladies and gentlemen, tonight will be full of many adventures and finding each other, because we all share so much. But one man made it all possible, the man who adopted all of us—all 370 of us—on the Last Flight Out of Saigon. May I present, our "Papa", our father, our brother, our friend, Al Topping." The audience stood to thunderous applause.

On the stage, a young guitarist sat, while Al announced the

finale. "Ladies and gentlemen, we'd like all the Pan Am crewmembers and ground staff of Operation Babylift and the Last Flight Out to join us on the stage. We have a special presentation from Babylift's own Jared Rehberg here." The young guitarist smiled and stroked the strings, as the Pan Am veterans took the stage.

A single spotlight fell on Jared, who strummed the introductory chords of his song. "This is a tribute to all of you. Those of us on Operation Babylift didn't know where we were going back then and we still don't know where it all will lead. But you were just angels, all of you." And he sang softly,

And she says
I'm scared for you,
And I love you.
You're the flesh of my flesh,
The bone of my bone,
You're my home, my own.
And there are angels standing by,
Tonight,
It's gonna be all right. [2]

The Pan Am veterans hugged and kissed, not wanting the evening to end. They were all part of a special family. Sally hugged Bernadette Vuong and George Trinh, Jared and Dr. Peterson, and the dozens of others who had been part of the amazing experience so long ago, now reconnected again. Looking around the room, she realized that all these dozens and hundreds of fresh young men and women…they could all be her Nguyen, and so she hugged them closer.

After dinner and so many happy farewells, Sally pulled herself away and they headed for the taxi stand with Lucien and the girls. He hugged them good-bye and left to go to a friend's flat, promising to visit the Tantalus house soon. Back at the Willard, they trooped up to the Circle Bar, where Hawea and Zoe turned to Sally and demanded, "All right, mother, no more fairy stories. We want you to tell us about what really happened in those days."

"Well, we had an awful lot of fun, you know," said Sally, her eyes twinkling.

"How much of this is going to be repeatable?" joked Hawea.

Sally took a deep breath, and began. "April of 1975 was the end of a lot of illusions," she said, "but in order to understand what happened then, you have to go back farther. Your generation needs to learn what it was like to grow up as part of the Baby Boomers after World War II. We were a raucous and undisciplined generation, and we tore into that incredible airline lifestyle, and everything else that came our way. We came from everywhere and we weren't going back. But in the end, we were always looking for our roots."

She talked about their experiences, about her envy at the sophistication of the European flight attendants and her shock at some of their activities, about Zoe's irrepressible antics, about the naughty and sometimes dangerous things they did. Many of the tales had been bedtime stories for the girls, but here they were learning together as adults. Sally talked about how deeply the country had been divided over the war. She held nothing back, describing her relationship with Dave, later with Billy and the unresolved pain of his disappearance, as well as the horrible uncertainties of Billy's memorial, her own doubts, the surreal adventures of being on the movie set of the Vietnam saga, even the drugs, and finally her salvation: meeting their father, Jack.

She tried to describe Zoe, her wanderlust, her star-crossed love for Keoki, her eccentricity and independence, and above all, her refusal to accept controls or rules that were imposed by political expediencies. She described their last huge argument, Zoe's departure with Hawea for London, her cold anger and ability to reject those who disappointed her. At the end, she shrugged, "Frankly, I don't think any of us truly understood her. She was a free spirit, displaced of her own volition, and she'd accept no limits. She'd let you get close, but always, there was the line, and she controlled who crossed it. Sometimes I think I never really knew her at all." The young women's faces were intent and serious as they heard their genealogy.

Zoe and Hawea hugged Sally. "Thanks, Mom. You've lived some incredible adventures."

The next night, Sally had planned to visit Walker Sheppard and his wife. She was going alone, the girls having decided to attend a performance of *1776* at the Ford Theater. As she walked through the lobby on the way to get a taxi, she was astounded to see Jack Wright— her Jack—coming through the front entrance. She gaped in surprise and approached him quickly, but he didn't even bat an eyelid.

"So are we taking the Navy staff car out to Walker's or having a drink here first?" he smiled.

Sally laughed, "Well, well. I should have known you couldn't pass this up!" They sauntered towards the bar, the piano player breaking into an upbeat melody.

Later, at Walker's quarters, they worked through several cocktails and dinner courses. Walker's career had prospered, attested by the four-star flag that flew above the imposing mansion. His assignments included Naval Intelligence, which would be his last posting before retirement.

After dinner, an attentive orderly cleared the dishes from the table while Walker's wife ushered them into the book-lined study.

Sally sat quietly with Walker and Jack, staring at a warm fire.

"Brandy?" asked Walker.

"Sure," replied Jack. "Sally?"

"Just a little," said Sally, made unaccountably nervous by the formality in the room.

Walker poured the drinks then went to his desk where he fingered a manila folder, turning it over in his hands before he spoke. Underneath the folder was a slender envelope, and beneath that a large metal box.

"Sally, it's no surprise that Jack's here, you know. Some information came into Camp Smith in Honolulu a few days ago, and when I became aware of it, I called Jack immediately. He said he'd just put you on the plane for Washington, and I suggested that he might want to grab the next flight over to join you. The Pacific Command has confirmed that they have retrieved the remains of Captain William Hannibal Spencer from a site adjacent to the Thai/Cambodian border."

Sally gasped, hearing Billy's voice from The Wall.

Walker waited for this bit of news to sink in, then continued gently. Jack held his wife's hands in his as she struggled with the emotions of so many years past.

"There are a number of personal effects, including a letter to you which is unopened. It is sealed in oilskin, so it is probably still legible." Walker handed the letter to Sally.

Weakly, she took a long gulp of brandy before taking the package from him. The envelope had a slick surface. She rubbed her fingers over it, looking at the familiar handwriting with her name on it. Breathlessly, she opened it, afraid that it might tear or crumble after all these years. She read quickly:

April 29, 1975
Saigon
Dear Sally,

I am writing to you because I believe Saigon will fall to the Communists soon, and things might get messy. Last night, Tan Son Nhut was bombed and the explosions shook the apartment building where I'm staying, which is about a mile from the airfield.

Sally, if you are reading this, then something has happened to me. This letter will get to you sooner or later, I hope, but I want you to know the truth. I have spent the last months on loan from the Marines to the CIA's Air America, and I'm not sure how long this assignment will last.

My next mission is very dangerous. I will be attempting to pick up some important intelligence personnel near the Cambodian border who have been in hiding. You probably won't be surprised, but the man I'm meeting is named Sao Johnny. He's a friend of Zoe's, and apparently, she sent word that I needed his help. I don't know how you women do these things, but Zoe made the contacts in Saigon.

I haven't got much time, but I just wanted you to know how grateful I am for our sweet time together. I want you to understand that I am doing what I wanted to do.

It's now 4 o'clock in the morning, and they've started bombing Tan Son Nhut again. The AA pilots are all up on the roof watching the show, with leftover liquor from the vacant apartments of the Embassy folks. We're waiting until it gets light so the choppers that survived can come pick us up right here on the roof. Yes, we are crazy.

Remember what I told you at Hickam before I left? I Mua. Move forward. Both you and the country will have to do that. I have loved you, Sally. Never doubt that.

Me kea aloha pumehana,
With my great love and affection,
Billy

Walker said, "When I got the news from Camp Smith about Billy's remains being identified, I located his file, which provides some additional details." He pulled a report from the file. "Sally, before you read this, I want you to understand that it is technically still classified information."

"I understand." Sally nodded slowly, taking the report from Walker's hands.

On April 29, 1975, I was standing on top of the apartment building near Tan Son Nhut where we had been watching the bombing since four o'clock that morning. Captain Spencer and I had received the orders for our mission the day before. We were to pick up a group of intelligence assets in the jungle close to the Cambodian border. We were supposed to leave before dawn, however the bombing of Tan Son Nhut precluded that until after first light when we left in two choppers flown by myself, and Captain Spencer.

The next few lines were blacked out. Sally read on.

When we arrived at the border clearing, we set the choppers down and a number of the intended passengers boarded. We began taking enemy gunfire and mortars, and Captain Spencer's helicopter was strafed by bullets and burst into flames. Bleeding from wounds to his left leg and shrapnel wounds in the face and neck area, Captain Spencer still managed to haul six wounded passengers over to my chopper. He was weakened by the smoke, numerous injuries and loss of blood. He knew

*I was already overloaded, so he instructed me to leave him behind with
a Shan Army guerilla fighter called Sao Johnny.*

*The last I saw of them, they were moving back into the jungle to
take cover. I was able to stay below radar and mortar fire through the
advancing enemy units and landed at Tan Son Nhut, where I refueled.
Then I headed out toward Vung Tao to the Fleet, landing on the*
Okinawa.

The report was signed at the bottom in a familiar script. Sally
sucked in her breath, startled. The signature read *"Jack Wright, Captain,
USMC."*

She glanced up at her husband, seeing the look of pain on his
face. She had recognized it on that first morning of their marriage, and
again over the years, but she had never questioned him because so
many vets never wanted to talk about their wartime experiences. Sally
looked up at Jack intently, "So all these years, you knew. Goddamit, you
knew, and you never told me." He gazed at her silently.

"Sally, that last day when Jack flew his last mission, he landed on
the *Okinawa* where he told me that Billy was probably MIA," said
Walker. "I did some checking and verified it. We checked the Pan Am
crew lists on Guam, and knew that you or Zoe might be there so I
could tell you personally. It was the least I could do…." His voice
trailed off, remembering that blustery January dawn in Honolulu
when Sally had seen to it that the news of Pualani's death reached him
as soon as possible.

Sally sat quietly absorbing the information, then burst out.
"Damn you all. None of you—Walker, Jack, Billy—none of you were
even 30 years old then. You were playing goddamn games. My God,
after your years in the Marine Corps, why Air America? Wasn't a tour
in Vietnam enough? Did you people need your fix that badly?"

Jack said, "You remember what we were like when we were
young. It was the razor's edge. But thanks to you and the children, I've
been able to put it behind me and go on with a normal life." He
paused. "Billy was a good man—the best—and I grew to love him like
a brother."

Walker cleared his throat. "There is more, Sally. You and I have been through some tough times in the past together, and we've always given it to each other straight." He handed her a second report. "I'm not going to whitewash this. It comes from our commission to recover the remains of our MIA soldiers in Vietnam."

Sally looked at the yellowed manuscript files, stamped top and bottom with classified emblems and signature blocks. She clutched her brandy and drained the glass, the liquid soothing and healing. She started to read:

> *The remains of Captain Spencer were exhumed together with the attached artifacts in a recently dug shallow grave by Catholic Relief workers just short of the Thai border on January 12, 2004. Soil analysis at the site confirmed this to be a reburial, original internment site and date unknown.*
>
> *Observation of the remains indicates extreme malnourishment for a prolonged period; a weakened condition, with broken ribs and a broken arm, evidence of typhoid, chronic malaria and other earlier injuries. The last known information about him was received in 1979 through Shan National Army contacts, as he had evidently been imprisoned and tortured by the Khmer Rouge following an earlier rescue attempt in 1975 and again in 1976. Details of that action and all other activity are available through the appropriate command authorities as Pacific Command. MIA support personnel familiar with the case indicate that Spencer's survival efforts seem extraordinary. The best estimate of his date of death is approximately the late 1970s, much earlier than the unknown date of burial and exhumation in 2004. The case will remain open for further investigation, but official notification is appropriate.*

Sally sat quietly, motionless almost, as the waves of shock rolled over her. She thought of the dates…the late 1970s…he might still have been alive when she and Jack reconnected, when they were married. Her mind was filled with questions. But most of all, Sally finally understood Zoe's anger and rejection of everything this war had meant, and her admonishment that these men chose the war instead of their women. So Billy was a war junkie, she thought bitterly, remembering the years of torment and loneliness.

She sighed and pressed Jack's hand tightly, thinking that since Billy had made his choice, she was glad she got to make hers. "All that matters now is that we know the truth, that Billy's been found and that we can all be at peace." She gazed into her husband's intense blue eyes. In the end Billy was a selfish bastard, she said to herself, and I am so lucky I got another chance at a life with a good man, with no more shadows.

"Sally, are you okay?" Her husband's eyes searched her face.

She took a deep breath. "I feel as though a 40-pound load has lifted from my shoulders. I never realized just how much tension I've been carrying around for so long, and how it must have affected our lives in so many ways."

Walker cleared his throat. "Well, there is one more thing. This box here was discovered with Billy's remains. We have reason to believe that there is a connection between Billy's lengthy incarceration, his eventual rescue, and the recent discovery of his remains. Out there in the Golden Triangle, there are only a very few people who can negotiate all the borders. It's the guy mentioned in Billy's letter— we've known about him for years, but have never been able to pin him down—Sao Johnny. He's probably in his late 50s now, but he's literally a legend as a leader and a fighting man, and we're pretty sure he's still alive. We know that he helped Billy in 1975, rescued him at least once, possibly in 1976, and kept an eye on him while he was incarcerated until he finally succumbed—it could have been as late as 1979. It's no surprise that the relief workers found all of these things in Billy's grave; the site was pointed out to them pretty clearly by the Shans, who both protected the graves and kept a close watch on the recovery efforts."

Walker handed Sally a metal chest, which she opened. Inside, a simple dark unpolished wooden box sat, approximately eight inches square. She eased open a rusting lock, pulled back the lid—and gasped. The firelight lit up a treasure chest of gold and silver coins, huge glittering rubies, gold chains and a massive gold snake bracelet, coiled to strike. She picked up a single coin, emblazoned with the Pyu shrivatsa symbol—the endless knot and the conch shell—that Zoe had always worn. She shut the box quickly, astounded.

Walker nodded, "Yes, we thought so too. This came with it." She looked at a faded black and white photograph of smiling young Zoe Longfield with the simple message: "To Sao Johnny…With all my love, September 1963." The photograph was sealed in plastic, with the date clearly stamped on the border. On the back was a message, printed simply:

> *Tell Zoe this came from the Shwenyaung pagoda. I wish I could have done more for your kind friend. He fought well.*

There was no signature or date on the message. Oh God, Sally thought, it doesn't end here. Neither Zoe nor Billy nor Sao Johnny had ever counted the cost of what they did. Only that it needed to be done, all the way to the end, wherever it led, without expectations.

Straightening in her chair, she said, "Walker, you'd better pour some more brandy because I have a toast. It may not be a very traditional toast, but I want you all to join me in saluting the memory of William Hannibal Spencer and Zoe Longfield, who both died doing just exactly what they wanted to do, and who can now rest peacefully. Roll Tide, Billy and Zoe! *I Mua!*" And they toasted them, smiling at the good memories of amazing friends in long-ago days.

Walker said, "I have one final toast. I'd like to toast Pan American World Airways. The contributions you all made to our nation, and to the world of aviation, are incalculable. Whatever Pan Am did, the other airlines followed, and the rest is history."

Soon the late hour demanded they begin the journey back to the hotel. In the Admiral's car, Jack held her close. "There is one other matter that I didn't need to share with Walker," he said, "unless you want to." He opened a plastic-sealed container framing the remnants of an envelope and a faded letter in what could have been Zoe's writing. She blanched, thinking, no more, not tonight.

She could barely make out the dates and words, except for the date: December 21, 1988. She said, "Oh, Jack. This is the letter Jennifer Edgerton mentioned…this was Zoe's letter from the Lockerbie flight."

Jack said, "Yes, it was sent to me as Zoe's counsel of record. I've hesitated because there has been no more specific information until recently."

In the water-stained letter, Sally could barely make out dates, names, places. She could read the names "Billy" and "____ Johnny", and in another paragraph, "A man named ____ Pah___ will contact Jack …" but nothing more. There was a disjointed sentence about seeing them soon. She sighed. It was all so long ago, and so sad.

Jack said, "A month ago, a former Iranian diplomat named Cyrus Pahlavian contacted me. He is looking for refugee status to the United States, and he named Zoe Longfield as a reference. He also provided DNA samples to attest to his having fathered a child with Zoe. Apparently Zoe must have allowed him to test Hawea's DNA in London in 1988, which is when she wrote this letter that we can barely decipher."

Jack folded the letter carefully. "Sally, this man Phalavian could be her father, not Keoki."

Sally clutched the small wooden box, thinking of her crazy friend, and unaccountably, of what Sugar Pie would think of all of this.

She said, "You know, I've been raised and educated to handle pretty bizarre situations in my time, and I'm going to make some decisions right now, no matter how it falls. We've always told the girls everything. Hawea gets to know about Sao Johnny and obviously, about this…this treasure that was meant for her mother. It's her birthright and then some."

Then Sally's back stiffened. "Jack, I will tell Hawea, but I want to wait until the right time to talk to her about the possibility that this other man could be her real father. But as far as I'm concerned, neither Keoki nor Pahla-what's-his-name deserve the right to claim her. You have been her father in every way since she came to us."

Jack smiled contentedly, holding her close and said, "Tomorrow, I'm taking my girls home. All my girls…all the way home."

Notes:

2 Music and Lyrics by Jared Rehberg. Used by permission.

EPILOGUE

ABOARD M.V. COURAGE   PAPE'ETE HARBOR, TAHITI

The sun crept above the equatorial horizon, casting a creamy glow on the waters in Papeete Harbor and the outline of Mo'orea rising beyond the reef. The ship's horn sounded as the engine began to churn the water, and slowly the old motor vessel began to slide away from the dock. As they left the harbor, Sally and Jack Wright re-read the lead article in the newspaper they had brought with them:

July 3, Special Contribution to The Pacific Advertiser
By Zoe Pualani Wright
A University of Hawai'i Marine Archaeology team today reported cautious optimism in the search to find the remains of an alleged ancient Tahitian war-drum that was lost in July, 1976, aboard a Pan Am jet Clipper bound for Honolulu. The aircraft crashed after an unknown engine malfunction after its late-night take-off, and sank immediately off the reef in approximately 1,500 feet of water. Seventy-six passengers and 14 crewmembers were killed in the accident. No previous recovery attempts had been made in almost 40 years due to the precarious underwater position of the wreckage.

Dr. Hawea Kanawai, who posed the Deep-Water Recovery Theory in her doctoral dissertation, heads the University of Hawai'i's team from the College of Marine Archaeology. The Kanawai Trust and a National Science Foundation grant have funded the project. She has radioed information that the wreckage has been found on a steep underwater shelf, and that initial radar images have located a large storage container in what remains of the forward hold of the Pan Am 707 aircraft, which broke apart on impact, and has been scattered in the intervening years

Dr. Kanawai said that her recently deceased father Keoki Kanawai, a founding member of the Polynesian Voyaging Society, proposed the original project. Together with her mother, deceased Pan Am Purser and archaeologist Zoe Longfield, he participated in the 1970s with a Bishop Museum field excavation team in Huahine, which originally recovered the artifact. He was killed last year in a marine accident on Manamana Island in the Northwest Hawai'ian Line Islands.

Dr. Kanawai and her father were also well known for their work on Howland Island and Nikumaroro Atoll, where pioneer aviator Amelia Earhart and her navigator, Fred Noonan, disappeared after leaving New Guinea for Howland on July 2, 1937. Evidence of aircraft wreckage, which has yet to be authenticated as Earhart's plane, was found by divers in the waters between Howland and Jarvis Atoll, near the atoll of Nikumaroro, where bone and metal fragments have also been found. The team worked off of Howland for six months to validate an original theory on navigation.

Dr. Kanawai noted that Fred Noonan had been a navigator for the historic Pan American World Airways, serving on the famous epic voyage of the China Clipper from San Francisco to Manila on Nov. 22, 1935. He and Earhart departed from New Guinea for Howland on their ill-fated quest for Earhart to become the first woman to fly around the world.

Dr. Kanawai is the granddaughter of George Puunui Kanawai, one of the original Panalaa'u settlers of Howland, Jarvis and Baker Atolls in the mid-1930s. The Panalaa'u Boys, as they came to be known, were 1935 graduates of the Kamehameha Schools, and were charged with the secret mission of colonizing the atolls and claiming them for the United States. Because of their courageous efforts, the development of Pacific aviation could proceed apace. The three atolls provided invaluable coordinate information to passing aircraft, a capability of crucial importance when the United States entered the Second World War. The islands also served as radio contacts and checkpoints for Pan Am's Clippers on their long night voyages throughout the pre-war Pacific region, serving together with the Coast Guard cutter USS Itasca as Ocean Station Charlie.

Dr. Kanawai and her team of marine archaeologists, Bishop Museum historians and Polynesian Voyaging Society mariners will examine the artifact once it is recovered and stabilized, and will provide an update on progress. They are confident of a successful conclusion for *the voyage of this ancient artifact, which may be the drum Hawea, for whom Dr. Kanawai is named.*

Sally nestled against Jack's shoulder as they looked toward the cluster of marine vessels anchored just off the reef, in the deep waters between Tahiti and Mo'orea, thinking of their daughter Zoe's newspaper story, and Hawea's adventure in the waters right ahead of them.

"It is so totally different from life in the 60s and 70s—me trying so hard to belong, to fit in, Zoe trying even harder to stay a displaced person," remarked Sally, shaking her head. "These two don't seem to worry about it one bit; they belong to the whole world. And just like Zoe, they aren't afraid of anything."

Jack said, "You're right, and hell, I don't think anything short of locking them in a jail cell would have kept them from everything they've done or want to do. They're...they're just..." He looked at his wife, and she joined him in finishing the sentence, "*flying.*"

Their laughter echoed over the calm seas.

Sally smiled, "And somewhere, Zoe Longfield is laughing, and telling the stories."

CPSIA information can be obtained at www.ICGtesting.com
Printed in the USA
LVOW13s0706280314

379344LV00003B/6/P